Details about Roger Taylor can be found on Website,
www.hawklan.demon.co.uk. Roger Taylor has also
written the four Chronicles of Hawklan (*The Call of
the Sword*, *The Fall of Fyorlund*, *The Waking of
Orthlund* and *Into Narsindal*) and the epic fantasies
Dream Finder, *Farnor*, *Valderen*, *Whistler*, *Ibryen* and
Arash-Felloren, also available from Headline Feature.

'A classic effort which deserves to sell well' *Bookshelf*

'A delightful fantasy . . . easy to read, with a strong
plot' *Norwich Evening News*

'Easy story-teller's style . . . rip-roaring climax' *Chorley
Guardian*

Caddoran

Roger Taylor

HEADLINE
FEATURE

First published in 1998
by HEADLINE BOOK PUBLISHING

First published in paperback in 1998
by HEADLINE BOOK PUBLISHING

A HEADLINE FEATURE paperback

10 9 8 7 6 5 4 3 2 1

ISBN 0 7472 5898 8

Typeset by CBS, Felixstowe, Suffolk

Printed and bound in Great Britain by
Mackays of Chatham plc, Chatham, Kent

HEADLINE BOOK PUBLISHING
A division of Hodder Headline PLC
338 Euston Road
London NW1 3BH

For my wife and children.

Chapter 1

Mist folded around the five figures on the beach, reducing their world to a grey, shifting dome, and deadening everything around them. Even if they had not been afraid of discovery, it would have made them lower their voices.

Hyrald massaged his left arm with his right hand, to stave off the chilly dampness that was threatening to make him shiver. His sister moved to his side and voiced the inevitable question.

'Where are we?'

Hyrald would have liked to reply, 'Just another damned lake. We'll find shelter for the night and move around it in the morning,' but every sense told him otherwise.

'It's the sea, Adren,' he said flatly.

Standing only a few paces away, Thyrn, slight and restless, and his uncle, Nordath, both turned to him as they caught the reply. The third man, Rhavvan, taller and heavier than the others, presumably also heard but made no response. He continued staring intently into the mist.

'What?' Thyrn demanded querulously.

'The sea,' Hyrald confirmed, more relaxed now that the word had been spoken, though he glanced uneasily at Rhavvan, who had moved further away and now stood vague and insubstantial at the shadowy limit of his vision.

Thyrn looked around into the greyness as if for an ally. 'The sea! It can't be. The sea's to the east, not north. Are you sure?

How do you know? Gods, we'll be trapped if we can't move on . . .'

'Sniff the air.' Hyrald cut across the outburst almost viciously. He was in no mood to debate the obvious and Thyrn's nervous disposition had to be firmly handled if it was not to run out of control. 'That's salt. I remember it well enough now. Be quiet.' He raised a hand to emphasize the order.

Thyrn blew out a steaming breath into the mist and stamped a foot irritably. Water welled up around his boot. Hyrald caught his eye and he fell still.

Into the ensuing silence came the sound that Hyrald was listening for. A soft, distant lapping. He motioned the group forward and soon they were standing at the water's edge. It glistened oily in the dull light, and was quite still save for an occasional slow welling like the sleeping breath of a great animal. A thin foam-specked rim slithered slightly towards them, then retreated.

'This is the sea?' Thyrn whispered, curious now, as well as frightened. 'I always thought it would be noisy – violent – great waves crashing in. Like in the old tales – and pictures.' He waved his arms in imitation, then crouched down and tentatively dipped a finger into the water. Hyrald watched him – Thyrn could bring an almost uncanny intensity to the most trivial of actions – and it was rarely possible to predict what he would do next. He sniffed his damp finger then, without hesitation, sucked it noisily. His face wrinkled in distaste and he spat drily and wiped his hand across his mouth.

'I just told you it was salt,' Hyrald said. Almost in spite of himself, and as had proved the case before, he felt his irritation turning into a mixture of compassion and amusement at Thyrn's naïve curiosity. 'It's the sea all right. I've only seen it once, and that briefly and a long time ago – before Adren here was born – but that smell's unmistakable. Takes me right back.' He pulled a wry face as he pushed the old memories away.

They were too much of a burden now, too full of different times. 'I suppose it's quiet because there's no wind, or—'

'*Move!*'

The voice was soft, but commanding. It was Rhavvan's. He was abruptly among them, urging them forwards, his arms spread as if to gather them all together. There was the same purposefulness in his moving as previously there had been in his motionless watching. It allowed no pause. Thyrn staggered to his feet fearfully, but made no sound. Hyrald and Adren took his arms to steady him, but he needed little support and was almost immediately half walking, half trotting ahead of them, his uncle following close behind him.

Hyrald looked significantly at Rhavvan serving as rearguard. He was answered with a brief hand mime that told him, 'Riders,' and fingers held up which said, 'Two, maybe three.'

Hyrald nodded and drew his sword nervously. Both circumstances and his personal inclination led him towards evasion in preference to confrontation, but with no idea where they were or where they were going, the latter was very probable. Noting her brother's action, Adren drew her sword also. They strode on in silence, Rhavvan occasionally inclining his head to catch any sounds behind them. Hyrald took solace from the fact that though they were lost, so too were their pursuers, and the mist hid everyone alike. Then the soft padding of his feet intruded to dispel this faint comfort and he looked down – mist would not hide the footprints they were leaving.

Even as the realization impinged on him, Rhavvan grimaced and hissed out, 'Stand, they're on us!'

Nordath moved in front of Thyrn protectively, his sword uneasily extended. Thyrn crouched low behind him. In front of them in turn, Hyrald and Adren stood either side of Rhavvan. Both kept a good distance away from him however, noting that he was hefting his long staff in preference to his sword, and to be hit accidentally by that was only marginally less damaging than being hit on purpose!

Then Rhavvan was crouching low and signalling them to do the same.

Struggling to control his breathing, Hyrald screwed up his eyes and peered into the shifting greyness. More thoughts that he did not want leaked into his mind. What was he doing here? What madness was abroad that would make Vashnar proclaim the Death Cry against them, turning him, his sister and Rhavvan from hunters into hunted? He tightened his grip on the sword and gritted his teeth to dispel the questions; there were no answers to be had here – they were only a hindrance. He must focus completely on what was happening.

Within a heartbeat of this resolve, a shapeless movement in the mist ahead of him formed itself into a rider.

Perhaps they're not after us. Perhaps they're fishermen or something. Not everyone in the country's searching for us – surely? It was an unexpected and unsettling thought, and it made Hyrald falter as he braced himself. Then it and all doubts were gone, for as the rider drew nearer he saw the drawn sword. And he recognized the uniform of the Arvenshelm Wardens.

This was no foolish villager looking for easy money. Vashnar was sending his own men the length of the country against them! And they had drawn swords without challenge.

The implications almost unmanned Hyrald. He began to tremble violently, and his mind was filled with visions of throwing down his own sword and begging for mercy, or alternatively, dashing off into the mist and abandoning everything.

Rhavvan's voice cut through his fear. 'Yours, Hyrald! Left side!'

At the same time he became aware of Rhavvan surging upwards, his long staff lunging towards the rider's head. The Death Cry was the Death Cry – no choices – and as though drawn after him, like an inadequate shadow, Hyrald too was on his feet and swinging a wild double-handed blow at the figure now above him, sword raised. The rider gave a brief cry of alarm and instinctively straightened up to avoid Rhavvan's staff, but the speed of his horse and that of Rhavvan's attack gave him little chance; Hyrald knew that the man's neck had been broken even as the flat of his own sword struck him across the chest. The impact knocked Hyrald backwards and he tripped, nearly losing the sword. The falling corpse fell clear of him but he rolled over several times nevertheless, desperate to be away from it.

As he staggered to his feet he was aware of violent action to his left as Adren and Rhavvan encountered a second rider, but before he could move to help them a third rider was emerging from the mist. He saw that it was another Warden but half in stark panic and half in a sudden, raging anger, he somehow jumped aside from the galloping horse and blindly thrust out his sword.

This time, he did lose it, though he was dragged some way before it was torn from him. As he tumbled on to all fours, he saw the rider sliding gracefully out of his saddle. Hyrald hesitated for a moment then stood up, reaching for a long knife in his belt. But the rider dropped on to his knees and slowly fell forwards. His fall was halted momentarily as the sword, embedded in his chest, struck the sand, then he tumbled on to his side.

A noise behind Hyrald made him turn sharply, his knife extended in front of him and swinging from side to side in a dangerous arc.

'Easy.'

It was Rhavvan, crouching low, and edging towards him sideways, his staff extended and sweeping like Hyrald's knife. Adren, some way from them and hazy in the mist, was crouching similarly. Nordath and Thyrn seemed not to have moved.

How long had that taken? Hyrald thought, irrelevantly. Scarcely seconds, he presumed – and almost certainly two men were dead – suddenly cold now beyond anything this mist could bring. But time in combat was not measured thus. The moments just gone when he had seen Thyrn taste the seawater and pushed aside his own unwanted childhood memories were now the dim past.

'Are you all right?'

Rhavvan had to ask the question twice before Hyrald heard it. 'Yes, yes,' he nodded eventually. He was shivering.

For another strange passage of time, the five remained silent and still, partly uncertain what to do, partly watching and listening for any further attack. Then a groan rose into the damp air, drawing them all back to the present. It was the rider that Rhavvan and Adren had dealt with. Rhavvan slowly straightened and walked over to him.

'I can't hear anyone else,' he said. 'And they'd be on us by now if there were others nearby. Get their horses, Adren. Nordath, see what they've got in the way of supplies.' He glanced at Hyrald and then at the third fallen rider. 'You go and get your sword back.' An unsteadiness in his voice marred the briskness he was affecting.

Knife poised and teeth bared uneasily, Hyrald lifted the cloak which had draped itself over the fallen rider's head. He was relieved to see a heavily bearded and lined face. He was far from certain how he would have responded, had he found himself looking into a face he knew, or that of some fresh-faced young recruit. Gingerly, he felt about the man's throat for a pulse, though he knew he would find nothing. There was a stillness about the body that he recognized well enough.

More distressing was the retrieval of his sword. It had jammed between the man's ribs, and freeing it involved a deal of brute force, causing the corpse to twitch disturbingly and to emit strange noises. When he finally succeeded in wrenching it

6

free, he pushed it three times into the soft sand to clean it, then skimmed it noisily through the silent sea.

'Wardens,' he said needlessly as he joined Rhavvan, kneeling by the second downed rider. 'Vashnar's.' Rhavvan nodded but held up a hand for silence.

'How many more of you are there?' he asked the rider.

Hyrald knelt beside him. This time the victim *was* a young man, his face distorted by pain and fear, but again Hyrald was relieved not to recognize him. Not that it gave him much consolation. Stranger or no, he was still a Warden, and they were all a long way from Arvenshelm. His earlier questions about what Vashnar was doing returned in full force.

'How many more of you are there?' Rhavvan was asking again.

'You've killed me,' the rider said through clenched teeth. 'I'm dying.'

'I don't think so,' Rhavvan said. 'You've been lucky. Especially drawing on us without a challenge. Your two companions are dead but all you've got, as far as I can tell, is a broken shoulder.'

Fear returned to the rider's face, then he made a lunge towards a knife in his belt. The attempt ended in his crying out in pain and collapsing back.

'I did tell you you'd broken your shoulder,' Rhavvan said, shaking his head. 'but then I suppose if you'd been the kind of person to listen to advice, you'd never have ended up in the Wardens, would you?'

With a deft movement he produced his own knife and brandished it significantly in the man's face. Then, none too gently, he heaved him into a sitting position, cut a length from his surcoat, bound the injured arm across his chest, and dragged him to his feet. It was swiftly done, but it was a noisy procedure which made Hyrald and the others wince openly and left the young man gasping with pain and leaning heavily on Rhavvan.

7

'Listen to me,' the big man said forcefully.

He had to say it twice more before the rider looked at him, eyes ill-focused.

'How many are in your company? Where are they?'

The rider's face became sullen.

Rhavvan gave up. 'All right. We can't help you further. Go back along your tracks. You'll find help eventually.'

'We can't leave him,' Nordath objected. 'He can hardly stand, let alone walk.'

'What the hell else *can* we do with him?' Rhavvan retorted.

Nordath stammered. 'I . . . I don't know, but we haven't seen even a farmhouse for two days and if there were only these three, he'll die of exposure . . . or starvation, or something.'

'So might we all, before we're through,' Rhavvan snapped. He pressed the palm of his hand against his forehead and voiced the question that kept returning to Hyrald. 'What in the name of all that's sane is happening?' He flicked a thumb towards Thyrn. 'We start off chasing this errant Caddoran. "A discreet matter," Vashnar tells us – Warden to Warden. No Cry to be called – no public fuss. Then, no sooner do we find him than the *Death* Cry's proclaimed against us. I didn't even know it was still legal. And against *all* of us! It's madness. What are we doing wandering about in a part of the country where no one lives, no idea where we are, where we're going . . .'

'We're going north, Rhavvan.' It was Thyrn, anxious and earnest. 'There are other countries up there, and a great city – so big that—'

Rhavvan turned to him angrily, making him flinch and step backwards. The big man pointed upwards. 'There's a moon up there, boy, but it doesn't mean we can get to it. City or no city, it may have escaped your notice but we've just run into the sea where we didn't expect to find it. And now we've got Wardens – Wardens, no less – our own people, at our backs.'

Hyrald laid a quietening hand on his arm.

Rhavvan paused, then growling to himself and shaking off the hand, he turned away from Thyrn. 'I know, I know,' he said to Hyrald. 'Not his fault. No one's fault – except Vashnar's. But . . .'

'Come on,' Hyrald said. 'Let's move. We haven't the time for debate. We've got to keep moving. We'll have to head west along the coast and see where we come to. At least anyone following will be as lost as we are.' He looked at the young Warden still leaning on Rhavvan. 'You've got a choice. Stay here, or come with us. If we come across a village we'll leave you there.'

The Warden, holding his bound arm stiffly and swaying slightly, returned his gaze. 'Can I have my horse?' he asked.

Hyrald extended his arm to stop Rhavvan's advance. 'You're lucky to be alive, lad. Just take this message back to the others. We don't know what's going on. Whatever Thyrn's done, it probably needs no more than disciplining by the Caddoran Congress, and the rest of us have done nothing. Vashnar had no right to proclaim even the Cry against us, let alone the Death Cry – we're here at his asking.' He leaned forward. 'We've had no Hearing – nothing.'

'I don't know anything about that,' the Warden said, shifting uncomfortably.

'Well, you do now.'

The young man met his gaze awkwardly. Hyrald looked at him intently, then at the bodies of the two other men lying nearby. It was not difficult to see what had happened once the Death Cry had been proclaimed. 'Barrack room talk, eh? Told you it would be easy money, did they? Or put you in well with Vashnar?' There was no reply. 'Well, you're a lifetime wiser than you were a few minutes ago. As are your friends. Ask more questions in future.' He glanced at his companions. 'We'll give you a couple of days' food and water – that's the best we can do. Head back the way you came – you won't enjoy it but

9

you should make it. And anyone you meet on the way, tell them what I've said. The more people who've heard about it, the safer you'll be when you get back to Arvenshelm – whatever's going on there.' An unexpected thought came to him. 'And tell them too, that as things are, we've no choice but to treat anyone who tries to stop us as mortal enemies, but one day, somehow, we'll be back for a Hearing – for justice. Do you understand?'

A soft cry from Thyrn and a gasp from Rhavvan made the Warden start before he could reply. Rhavvan stepped forward, his staff poised defensively as a strange swaying shape emerged uneasily from the mist.

Chapter 2

Krim glowered bleary-eyed at the grimy window through which the spring sunlight was filtering into the murky hall. His hand clutched fitfully at a shabby remnant of what had once been an ornately embroidered curtain but withdrew at the first hint of a snowfall of ancient dust. The curtain, swaying up to the gloomy ceiling, was attached to a mechanism that had ceased to function shortly after Krim had arrived to take up his late father's duties many years ago. It was one of several things that had been a constant source of strain between Krim and Ector – the Moot Palace's Most Noble Artisan – a man of similar vintage and disposition whose charge it was to maintain the fabric of the rambling cluster of buildings that constituted the Moot Palace.

Krim curled his lip and turned away from the window to look to the protection of his own charges from the blanching touch of the sun. Tall, thin, and alarmingly straight, he moved like a large and very stiff insect. So much so that even those who knew him, caught unawares, would tend to flinch in anticipation of the creaking of joints that might reasonably be expected from such a gait. But Krim moved silently. Indeed, but for the occasional hacking cough – not dissimilar to that of a gagging dog, though explosively short and very loud – everything about Krim was silent. It was a necessary part of his office.

For Krim was the Venerable and Honoured Cushion Bearer

to the Striker of the Moot, the oldest and most dignified of the clutch of ancient offices that served the will and the needs of Arvenstaat's Great Moot and which, tradition had it, were essential to its continuance. His formal title was actually Venerable and Honoured Cushion Bearer and Assassin to the Striker of the Moot, though the word Assassin, being a reminder of the distant bloody origins of the Moot, had long since been dropped from routine usage. Indeed, in this more enlightened age, moves were afoot to have all reference to it removed even from the written records of the Moot.

Krim's attitude to such proposals, however softly worded, could best be described as venomous. The Moot *was* tradition. That was the very foundation of his life and work, as it had been for his father before him and *his* father, and all his forebears back through many generations. Change was anathema. To change was to destroy. The Moot was the pulsing heart of Arvenstaat and to deviate from its ancient ways was thus to threaten the stability of the entire state and all its peoples. Indeed, such troubles as Arvenstaat now suffered from, and insofar as he understood any of them, could all, in Krim's estimation, be directly attributed to the embracing of needless change. With dark silence Krim quietly smothered all fledgling hints of ingenuity and originality whenever he could. His very presence at the councils of the Moot Officers dulled the bright eye and crushed the eager green shoot.

But while such matters underscored his life, it was a more pressing call that now occupied him. Moving only his head, he scanned the objects of his responsibility, seeking out those that were being touched by, or in the probable path of, the intrusive sunlight. Not that, to an outside observer, a great deal of sunlight survived passage through the fly-blown window. What might have been direct and brilliant outside was diffuse and hesitant inside. But to Krim's eyes – eyes that rarely ventured beyond the Moot Palace, and had not been outside its gloomy

12

courtyards in decades – the light glared and, in glaring, menaced his domain – the Striker's cushions. The Moot's cushions. *His* cushions. Cushions designed for and used by all the Strikers that had ever been, each housed in its individual alcove in shelves which towered in serried ranks around the circular tiered floor and rose up the curved and irregularly recessed walls from floor to ceiling. Access to these upper shelves was gained from balconies which, in their turn, were linked by an intricate arrangement of ramping walkways and stairways – straight stairways, spiralled stairways and strangely dog-legged stairways, all with uneven steps twisted by age and use and neglect. The whole formed a rambling vertical and horizontal maze. The parts swayed unsteadily when trodden upon and often creaked for no apparent reason.

The cushions were laid out meticulously in accordance with the dictates of Akharim the Great – the first Cushion Bearer and Founding Striker. The original Assassin, it was he who had dispatched the last Dictator, Koron Marab, and he whom Krim had been discreetly named after, in an uncharacteristic spasm of boldness by his father. However, as Krim had foreseen many years before, this session of the Moot was proving particularly trying, for the strict ordering of the cushions brought those that were now in current use directly into the path of light from the offending window. It left him with a profound dilemma. The cushions belonged where they belonged, as decreed by Akharim. They could not, for example, arbitrarily be moved to those empty and more shaded alcoves intended for the cushions of Strikers yet to come. Even to think of such a thing disturbed Krim deeply. It was not for Moot Officers – or anyone – to question Akharim's wisdom. Yet to leave the cushions where they were was to see their ornate and colourful embroidery washed and drained by the sunlight with all that that meant to the tenor of the conduct of the Moot's debates.

Krim, however, knew the history of his office and that it had been peopled from time to time by men of resolution and determination in the face of such difficulties. Secretly, he fancied himself one such and, donning this heroic garb, he had finally *acted* – an almost unheard-of occurrence in a Moot Officer. With great trepidation and in great secrecy, he had acquired materials and after edging and embroidering them – with an undeniable skill – he had carefully draped them over the assaulted cushions. But the daring had taken its toll and left him ever nervous of discovery – constantly alert to the sound of approaching feet. His spindly frame shuddered throughout its entire length at the thought of some wretched Moot Page barging in on him inopportunely, seeing his subterfuge and recklessly proclaiming it through the corridors of the Palace.

With this in mind he had prepared a written report to the Striker *and* the Under Striker, expressing his deep regrets at what he had been obliged to do, and pleading the desperate exigencies of the time and the continued negligence of the Palace's Most Noble Artisan who 'has been told repeatedly, both verbally and in writing, of the nature and urgency of the problem, and who has consistently declined to effect the necessary repairs'. Accompanying this immaculately written report was a carefully annotated and cross-referenced list of all his pleas to Ector. When not actually tending to his charges, Krim spent much of his time weighing this report and making subtle changes here and there, to ensure that all the nuances of his distress and justification would be properly appreciated.

Occasionally, in his less troubled moments, Krim wove other fantasies – fantasies as elaborate as his embroidery. One of these had him being honoured by the Moot for his devotion to duty and culminated in his impromptu covers becoming part of the Moot's revered traditions, their use perhaps even being enshrined in an addendum to Akharim's Treatise.

Today, however, was not such a moment. Today the Striker himself was coming to the Cushion Hall. And coming at Krim's own request, after he noticed that the cushion beneath the Striker's feet had become worn and flattened. Krim was twitching. He had left his guilty coverlets on the cushions as long as he dared, but the Striker would be here at any moment and he had no choice but to remove them now, leaving the precious fabrics exposed to the ruthless glare of the sun.

His mouth stiffened into a thin line as he steeled himself to this grim task. It occurred to him in a desperate moment that perhaps he might raise the matter with the Striker directly, but the very thought chilled him. The Striker had no authority to intervene arbitrarily in such matters. He too, was bound by the Moot's ancient traditions and the Treatise. He would have to judge the Striker's mood and act accordingly.

A familiar tapping reached him through the muffled air of the hall. Arms and legs flapping he made his way down a stepped aisle and up a narrow stair to the scene of his treachery where, with practised speed, he deftly removed the covers and thrust them into the Bag of his Office which hung by his side.

Scarcely had he finished than three solemn knocks announced the Striker.

Nervously, Krim straightened his Bag of Office, barked out a loud cough, then stretched himself to his full height and moved to open the door.

Striker Bowlott rolled in. A loud rap on the floor with his long cane and an airy gesture sent the two Moot Pages who attended him scuttling forward to lay out their burden of cushions by the Fitting Chair. A further tap dismissed them to wait outside.

Small and stout, Bowlott was typical of the line of Moot Strikers. Pompous and self-opinionated, he fondly mistook his considerable low cunning, and nit-picking knowledge of the Moot's arcane procedures, for wisdom.

15

'Venerable and Honoured Cushion Bearer,' he said, acknowledging Krim's low and disconcertingly unsteady bow with a mannered nod.

'Striker Bowlott,' replied Krim. 'My apologies for disturbing your busy day with such a matter, but your comfort is the comfort of the Moot and the ease of the State.'

It was a traditional greeting which the Striker acknowledged this time with a limp-handed gesture.

Krim's lanky arm stretched out, motioning him to the Fitting Chair. This was an exact replica of the Throne of Marab, the ancient chair which stood in the Moot Hall and which had accommodated successive Strikers since its original owner's demise. Undecorated by so much as even a chamfer or a rounded edge, it was stoutly built and profoundly uncomfortable. Ostensibly this was because Marab was a battle-hardened warrior unaffected by such niceties, but the reality was that he hardly ever sat on it. In his time, the assembly which was to become the Moot was a token representation of the people which Marab, nothing if not shrewd and perceptive, had invented so that he would have plenty of scapegoats ready to blame whenever anything went wrong. On the rare occasions when he actually summoned the assembly, he would drape an arm over the back of the chair and, with his other hand on his sword hilt, tell the people's representatives what was needed of them. Then he would leave. Once, when he had actually sat in it, Akharim, young, ambitious, and looking to ingratiate himself, had obsequiously offered him his own cushion; Marab had sneered and caustically blessed him with the title of Venerable and Honoured Cushion Bearer. In so doing, and untypically, he completely underestimated both Akharim's dark and vengeful nature, and his almost inhuman patience. As did several other members of the assembly who chose subsequently to make Akharim the butt of their humour because of this humiliation.

16

After Marab's death – an event much appreciated by the people – Akharim had retained the throne and most of the power that went with it, while ostentatiously rejecting the actual title of Dictator. Subsequently he had taken delight in enshrining the post of Cushion Bearer in his elaborate and obsessive Treatise on the Procedures for the Proper Ordering of the Moot.

Striker Bowlott heaved himself into the chair and Krim immediately began the ritual of positioning and adjusting the cushions which the Pages had brought. During this, Bowlott let out a noisy sigh. Krim noted the sound. It was good. The Striker was in a confiding mood. He must stay alert, ready to seize any opportunity that might present itself to bring his problem to the Striker's notice. Like most of the Moot Senators, Bowlott's dominant concern was with his own dignity or, more correctly, with the appearance of dignity, and thus almost his entire life was spent hiding behind a screen of empty words and gestures. Unaware that he was exactly the same, it was one of Krim's secret conceits that he could see through such, to the real man lurking within, and thereby manipulate him. As a result he despised most of the Moot Senators, and Striker Bowlott in particular, as vain self-seekers and unworthy of the offices that they held. In this, he was at one with most of the population of Arvenstaat, even those who bothered to participate in the four-yearly Acclamations – fewer and fewer with each session of the Moot and now only about one out of every three eligible electors.

However, illogical though it was that the people should willingly accept such folly in high places, the Moot Senators *did* exercise power over the land, albeit not as much as they imagined, and the Striker, in his privileged position as an ostensibly independent arbiter, exercised power over the Senators. And Krim in his turn, saw himself as exercising influence, if not power, over the Striker. Not that he involved himself in the squabbling of the innumerable and shifting factions that comprised the Moot. Like Striker Bowlott, he understood that while the Senators indulged in this, they would be less likely to turn their attention to anything else. Krim used his perceived power exclusively to enhance the esteem in which the office of Cushion Bearer should be held and, by the same token, to undermine the positions of his fellow officers, particularly the Most Noble Artisan.

As was his habit, he stood back and cast a professional eye over the seated Striker. Bowlott's mean little eyes were as peevish as ever and his down-turned mouth had a particularly self-pitying look. While in genuine awe of the office, Krim really couldn't stand the man. Perhaps it was because he was already agitated by concern about the destruction of his cushions by the intruding sunlight, but Krim felt something else stirring within him. His gaze drifted away from the sour spectacle in the chair to a cushion that lay on a shelf beneath the chair. This was a special cushion, the Blue Cushion. As with all the other cushions, one such was made for each new Striker. It was fashioned after the one with which Akharim had smothered Marab and was used ceremonially to menace each new Striker on his selection by the Shout of the Moot.

Assassin!

The increasingly unspoken portion of his title came to Krim so unexpectedly and with such force that it made him start. He disguised the movement by returning to his inspection of the Striker with a vague wave of his hands. However, this did not prevent a small flood of other thoughts bubbling out in the wake of the word.

What an odious little wretch Bowlott was. What a pity the title of Assassin was purely formal. Right now, he could just . . .

To his horror, Krim found his fingers curling as if to grip the edges of an imaginary Blue Cushion. Other resources rallied to rescue him from this bizarre interior onslaught and two violent high-pitched coughs shook him free.

They shook Striker Bowlott too. His eyes became almost round and he winced conspicuously at having someone else's affliction so thoughtlessly imposed on his own deep and profound concerns. He sighed again.

Krim, unsteady, but now well away from the edge of the abyss which had so abruptly opened at his feet, clasped his hands and cocked his long thin head on one side to denote that he was in reality deep in concentration.

'Ah, I see the problem,' he said, the sound of his own voice further helping him back to normality. 'I suspected as much when I saw you in the Hall.'

He knelt down and began to move the padded footstool which ensured that the Striker would not suffer the indignity of having his legs swinging freely. Though furniture rather than a cushion, and thus technically falling within the remit of the Moot's Most Noble Assistant Artisan (Furniture), this stool had been deemed to be the responsibility of the Venerable and Honoured Cushion Bearer by a ruling of the twenty-third Striker, now enshrined in the Addendum to the Treatise.

'I did not feel particularly uncomfortable,' Bowlott said, venturing a little sternness to offset the fact that he quite enjoyed Krim's fussy ministrations.

Krim became knowing. He straightened up so that, though still kneeling, he was almost face to face with the seated Striker. 'It is because the conscientiousness of Strikers can lead to such neglect of their personal needs, that my office exists. It is my duty – my honour – to anticipate such matters. Should you actually feel uncomfortable, then I would indeed have failed.'

Bowlott nodded understandingly. Krim tapped the footstool, then drawing out a brass measuring rod from his Bag of Office, he lowered his face so that one cheek almost touched the floor. In this position, he began crawling around the footstool, placing the measuring rod at strategic points and mouthing measurements to himself. With his long limbs protruding, he looked like a great spider.

'The burdens of office manifest themselves in many ways,' he said. 'In this instance, the repeated need for you to stand to gain order in the Hall has reduced the height of the stool, causing subtle signs of strain in your seated posture.' He pursed his lips and nodded to himself as though approving this diagnosis, though his true assessment was that the damage was due to the fat little oaf paddling his feet in tantrums as he shrieked to make himself heard. Krim had seen it coming for weeks and it was concern for his workmanship rather than the Striker's comfort that had prompted him to act.

'I'll have the stool re-upholstered before the next meeting. Now, if I may . . .'

There followed a routine, but thorough check of all the cushions that supported the Striker. This was the pampering that Bowlott enjoyed.

Krim clucked and hummed to himself as he continued his inspection, gently moving the Striker's head from side to side, and positioning his hands and arms.

'Good, good, good,' he concluded eventually.

He stepped back to admire his work, then, satisfied, and noting the Striker's relaxed, if not drowsy condition, he saw the opening he had been waiting for.

'But it occurs to me that there's much to be said for such examinations being made regularly. Say perhaps, every twenty meetings, so that these little faults can be noted and corrected before they manifest themselves.'

Making the inspections a regular event in the calendar of the Moot would bring them within the purview of one of the several Outer Moot Sub-committees dealing with the activities of the Most Noble Artisan and his various assistants, and was, of course, like most matters involving change, out of the question. Krim knew this well enough, but he had made the

20

suggestion purely so that he could drag the Most Noble Artisan into the ensuing conversation and thence discreetly complain about his neglected curtains and the depredations that would be wrought on his charges by the sun if they were not repaired. There were other, more formal ways of doing this but they were time-consuming, spectacularly ineffective even by Moot standards, and liable to bring him into direct conflict with the Most Noble Artisan, all of which enabled him to justify his disregard of them on the grounds of the desperate seriousness of what was going to happen. His action also chimed with another of the more raffish images of himself that he entertained from time to time. This portrayed him as the last great protector of the Moot, striking boldly with an unspecified, but revolutionary action of some kind which would rescue the Moot from an encroaching but equally unspecified danger and bring it back to its time-honoured way of acting in strict accordance with the Treatise.

Not that he was allowing himself such indulgence at the moment. Indeed, he began to feel uneasy about his impetuosity almost as soon as he had spoken. He braced himself for a reproachful diatribe on the subject.

But the remark seemingly went ignored.

'Fretful times, Krim. Fretful times.'

Krim blinked. Bowlott had called him by name – he must be in a particularly relaxed mood today. This *was* the moment. He was searching for a suitable response when Bowlott continued. 'This affair of Vashnar proclaiming the Death Cry against Hyrald and the others is causing great problems. The corridors are ringing with it. It's going to interfere with the business of the Moot if it continues.'

In spite of himself, Krim gaped. For a moment even his concerns about the sunlight vanished. He had not expected *this*! Striker Bowlott concerning himself with matters outside Moot business.

Though not a gossip – indeed, he was a sink of silence – Krim listened a great deal and little that happened in the Moot Palace passed him by. He had heard about what Vashnar had done but paid no great heed to it. As a matter outside the Moot it was of little import. Besides, the Wardens were an odd lot – one of the more regrettable legacies of the Moot's long history. As a body they were perhaps tolerable enough, but as individuals most of them were quite beyond the pale, showing – even revelling in – a complete disregard for the intricacies of the traditions and procedures of the Moot.

And now their antics had brought this about! The Striker driven to discussing them with an Officer of the Moot. Yet, he could not forbear a frisson of excitement as the image of himself as saviour of the Moot stirred contentedly deep within him – the Striker raising this matter with him!

Self-interest quickly reasserted itself. Starting from so unusual a topic, it should not be too difficult to direct the conversation back to Moot matters and thus his duties as Venerable and Honoured Cushion Bearer. Then it would be a simple matter to introduce the name of the Most Noble Artisan at some point . . .

He must be bold.

'I'm unfamiliar with the details of the affair, Striker Bowlott. I tend not to listen to Corridor gossip. I have quite pressing problems here in the Cushion Repository.' He turned and indicated the offending window. 'The curtains, you see . . .'

'Your discretion is well-known, Krim, and you're not alone in being unfamiliar with the details.' Bowlott tapped his hand on the arm of the chair agitatedly. 'Everyone's talking about it, but *no one* seems to know what's actually happened.'

This was not what Krim had had in mind. His hand hovered in the general direction of the window for a moment, before he realized that he was going to have to pursue the Striker's choice of topic until a better opportunity could be found to bring him back to matters of real moment.

'Surely the Death Cry is not a Moot matter,' he offered, laying heavy emphasis on the word *Moot* in an attempt to imply that the Striker should not be concerning himself with it.

'All things are matters for the Moot, when the Moot so determines,' Bowlott rebutted sternly, furrowing his brow so that his tiny eyes almost vanished.

Krim, crushed by this proclamation, bowed.

'And the Moot may yet so determine if this affair continues to be a distracting subject of debate and gossip amongst its members.' The eyes reappeared and Bowlott pressed back hard against the cushion that supported his head and shoulders. Recovering himself, Krim unfolded to his full height and nimbly made minor adjustments to the cushion.

Bowlott's face relaxed 'Technically, you are correct. The Cry is one of the ancient and fundamental rights of the people, the protection of which is the Moot's fundamental duty. However, there are times when to protect such a right, it becomes necessary to circumscribe . . . or even curtail it . . .'

Bowlott's voice faded away as he made this last pronouncement. Krim was genuinely disturbed. He found himself gaping again. Although he had been too long ensconced in the Moot Palace even to envisage clearly what might happen, he remembered enough from his younger days to know that the Cry was a right particularly cherished by the public, and that to interfere with it would be to bring about open defiance of the Moot's authority. And it was a basic, if unspoken, tenet of both Senators and the Moot's officers alike that attracting the people's attention to the activities of the Moot was a bad thing.

There was an uncomfortable silence. Even thinking about the people beyond the Moot unsettled Krim. Now he found himself assailed by the thought that faced with Bowlott's remark, he should actually *do* something! But what? His mind began to spiral towards panic. Then he heard himself speaking.

'I haven't your deep understanding of such matters, Striker Bowlott. The Treatise. The Addenda. Ancient rights. But perhaps if . . .' He hesitated. 'If you were to . . . speak to Commander Vashnar . . . perhaps ask him why he proclaimed the Death Cry against Hyrald and the others . . . why . . .'

His voice faded as Bowlott turned to him, eyes glinting enigmatically out of the depths. Then, abruptly, he was out of the chair and pacing to and fro.

The Fitting Chair stood at the centre of a small circular arena, the lowest point of the Cushion Repository and a focus for the rows of tiered shelves. After traversing this a couple of times, Bowlott, hands clenched behind his back and head bowed, turned into one of the aisles that led up from it. After an unsteady start, Krim strode after him, swaying stiffly, long hands nervously fiddling with the brass measuring rod. What had prompted him to speak as he had? Such recklessness. Was he to be rebuked? Was perhaps the Striker going to make an impromptu inspection of his domain, in search of something that might be wanting, to sharpen further his rebuke? Krim's hands began to shake. The sun glinted malevolently off the brass rod sending shards of mocking light into the dingiest reaches of the Repository.

The Striker stopped as he reached the top of the steps and turned to look over the arena as though he were facing the fully assembled Moot. Krim, some way below, stared up at him apprehensively.

Looking over Krim's head at his invisible audience, Bowlott proclaimed: 'Your skills are a great comfort to us, Venerable and Honoured Cushion Bearer.'

Us, Krim noted ecstatically. Not a rebuke, but a formal Striker's commendation. A great honour, both to him and his office. He glowed under it, forgetting his recent concerns and quite forgetting his real opinion of the Striker.

Bowlott continued: 'After long and taxing consideration of the relevant precedents, I have determined what must be done to resolve this matter. I shall speak to Commander Vashnar. I shall *ask* him why he has done what he has done.'

Krim bowed, flushed with delight. Such wisdom, he thought.

Chapter 3

' It's a sea monster.' Thyrn was wide-eyed as he stared at the approaching shape. Hyrald shot him a silencing glance, though there was as much doubt in his eyes as anger, and he half drew his sword as he moved to stand by Rhavvan. One of the horses whinnied. Adren reached up to calm it.

As if in response, the shape stopped its advance and stood swaying slightly.

'Who are you? What's been happening here?'

An unsteady voice, a man's, reached them through the mist.

Rhavvan frowned. 'Who're you?' he echoed back, following it with a more uncertain, '*What* are you?'

The shape wavered, then replied, 'I'm a shoreman.'

And, abruptly, with two cautious paces forward, it was a man. What had made his mist-shrouded form seem strange was a long object he was carrying on his back. His loose-fitting calf-length boots and hooded long coat were patently working clothes of some kind, and they glistened dully as if wet. The coat was unfastened and Hyrald noted immediately that he was unarmed, apart from what was obviously a working knife in a rough string-bound sheath shoved into his belt. The object on his back exaggerated his movements, which in turn demonstrated that he was torn between staying and fleeing. He was also edging sideways slightly, as if he were trying to move around and past them. Whatever else he might be, Hyrald decided, he was no immediate threat. He released his sword

27

and Rhavvan, reaching the same conclusion, lowered his staff.

'Who are you?' the newcomer repeated, clearly afraid. 'What are you doing here?' Then he saw the bodies of the dead Wardens. He stepped back with a cry, half stumbling as he did so.

Rhavvan moved forward quickly and caught his arm.

'What are *you* doing here?'

'I . . . I told you . . . I'm a shoreman. Let me go. Don't hurt me. I've nothing worth having on me. Hardly any fish even, today.' Then, more urgently, 'I must get off the shore.' He tried to shake free of Rhavvan's grip, but was apparently no match for the big man. He made no attempt to draw his knife with his free hand.

Hyrald intervened. 'Don't be afraid. We mean you no harm.' He nodded to Rhavvan, who reluctantly eased his grip on the man. Hyrald met his frightened but unexpectedly searching gaze. 'Don't be afraid,' he repeated earnestly, willing calmness into the man. He pointed to the two bodies. 'I can explain what's happened here. There's been . . . an accident. We're not going to hurt you. We just want—'

A raucous cry from above made all of them start. It was followed by the sound of a wave gently breaking.

With unexpected force the man tore his arm free from Rhavvan. His face was desperate now and it was obvious he was going to flee no matter what the cost. Yet, as Hyrald held his gaze, he hesitated. Hyrald held out a hand to stop Rhavvan seizing him again. The man pointed past the group, into the mist. His mouth worked silently for a moment before he managed to say, 'For mercy's sake, man, the tide's turning. Get off the shore.'

Somewhere, another wave broke, louder this time. The nearby water's edge suddenly retreated then surged forward with unexpected force, splashing over Hyrald's boots, tugging at him impatiently. The shoreman began running, deftly evading a lunge from Rhavvan despite his cumbersome burden.

A cold breeze brushed Hyrald's face and the man's fear swept over him. 'We're lost. Help us,' he shouted after the retreating form. 'Please.'

The shoreman stopped and turned, then gestured to them.

'Get on your horses – follow me, quickly.' And he was running again.

His urgency infected the others, and without any debate, Rhavvan mounted, dragging the injured and protesting Warden unceremoniously across his saddle, while Hyrald and Nordath took the other two horses with Adren and Thyrn. Another wave lapped around the horses' hooves. Then they were galloping after the fleeing shoreman. It took them longer to catch him than Hyrald had anticipated – he was running very quickly, despite his burden.

As they rode, it came to Hyrald briefly that he might perhaps be dreaming, following this silent figure through the cold greyness that constantly unfocused his eyes. He could hear nothing above the dull sound of hooves on the soft sand and the disordered clatter of tackle, though somewhere he sensed a growing sound trying to be heard. The runner's urgency pervaded everything, drawing the three riders after him, like an army, unmanned and turned into a rout by a single sudden deserter.

Then they were moving alongside a wide foaming stream running between sharp, fresh-cut banks in the sand – it too, seemed to be fleeing. Once again Hyrald felt disorientated as the stream was moving faster than they were, giving the impression when he looked down at it that he was not moving, or even moving backwards. He shook his head to rid himself of the disconcerting image.

The shoreman, running along the edge of the stream was looking at it intently, though occasionally he glanced backwards at the riders. He reached a decision and shouted something.

Hyrald caught the words, 'Risk it,' and 'Follow me,' then with bewildering speed, the shoreman had swung his burden from his back, dropped it into the water and stepped into it – it was a narrow boat. He snatched up a paddle hung on the side and gesticulated urgently with it to the riders, before plunging it into the racing water. 'Quickly,' he kept shouting.

Hyrald hesitated for a moment, but Rhavvan dashed past him, echoing the shoreman's cry. Nordath and Hyrald spurred forwards after him.

Though the stream was not very wide, it was deeper than Hyrald had expected and he could feel the fear in his horse as the water dragged at its legs. Then, as the water deepened further, everything was confusion and near-panic, with spray and curses filling the air as the horses struggled to stay upright against the power of the stream and the riders struggled to stay mounted.

When they were halfway across, a sudden surge in the stream made Nordath's horse lose its footing. It recovered, but as it did, Thyrn lost his grip on Nordath and, with a cry, tumbled into the water. Hyrald watched horrified as, arms thrashing, Thyrn floated for a moment then disappeared beneath the water. The sight of his upturned, terrified face, and the knowledge of his own helplessness, brought the futility and insanity of the past few weeks crashing down on Hyrald. A frantic roar of rage and frustration formed in his throat as the current relentlessly carried Thyrn away.

'Keep going!'

It was the shoreman. His voice barely penetrated the din of the splashing horses and the turmoil filling Hyrald's mind, but a blow from his paddle and his urgent gesturing did. Adren shook her brother and shouted the same message directly into his ear. 'Get us out or we'll be joining him!'

As Hyrald returned to his own struggle, he could see the shoreman, his paddle working desperately, now one side of his boat, now the other, pursuing Thyrn, his boat twisting and turning as he manoeuvred it through the increasingly turbulent stream while he peered into the depths in search of the young man.

Hyrald could see no sign of Thyrn, but the shoreman suddenly spun his boat about and plunged an arm into the water. The boat tilted perilously and for a long moment everything seemed to be motionless and balanced. Then the boat turned and abruptly righted itself and Thyrn was being lifted out of the water. He was flailing his arms frantically, causing the boat to rock violently. Hyrald was about to call out to him to be still when the shoreman gave him a powerful slap across the face, and somehow managed to drag him half across the boat where he pinioned him with a none too gentle boot.

Hyrald's horse was the last to reach the far side of the stream. When it arrived, Rhavvan and Nordath had already ridden downstream to meet the shoreman and his passenger. Thyrn spilled out on to the sand, coughing and retching, as the boat was driven into the bank at speed. The shoreman vaulted out of it and dragged it from the water. Rhavvan hoisted Thyrn to his feet with the intention of examining him, but the shoreman urgently signalled him to keep moving. By way of emphasis, he himself began running again, slinging the boat across his back as he ran and scarcely breaking stride. Rhavvan hastily thrust Thyrn up behind Nordath with the injunction, 'Hang on!' and remounted.

With the riders trotting beside him, the shoreman maintained the same headlong pace for some while until the sand became dry and loose and dotted with occasional clumps of hard green grass.

Finally he stopped and dropped to his knees, breathing heavily. Rhavvan dismounted and lifted the injured Warden down, a little more gently than he had handled him before. The man was unconscious.

'He's only passed out,' Rhavvan said, laying him down. 'Probably the best thing he could have done in the circumstances.'

Hyrald cast a glance at Thyrn, slithering down from Nordath's horse. The young man, wringing wet and still coughing, was a dismal sight, but seemingly unhurt so, his own knees shaking, he crouched down unsteadily by the panting shoreman. 'Thank you,' he said, resting a hand on his shoulder. 'We'd no idea where we were, or the danger we were in. It seems to me you risked your own life to save us – especially Thyrn here.'

'We were nearly too late,' the man replied breathlessly. He was patting his boat as if he wanted to embrace it. 'But I couldn't leave you, could I? Whoever you are. Not to the sea.' He shivered then looked at Hyrald intently. 'What possessed you to go out that far?'

'We need to light a fire,' Nordath interrupted before Hyrald could reply. He indicated Thyrn, hugging himself. 'He's sodden. The last thing we need now is him down with a fever.'

Hyrald looked around. 'I doubt there's any wood lying about here. See if there's anything in the Wardens' packs.'

'They *were* Wardens then, those men – those bodies we left. I thought I recognized the uniforms.' The shoreman looked at the unconscious figure by Rhavvan. 'He's one too. What are Wardens doing up here? Who are you people? What's going on?'

'There's a tent – and food, but no wood,' Nordath called out.

'This lot won't burn,' Rhavvan said, tugging at a clump of the tough grass.

'Where can we find firewood around here?' Hyrald asked the shoreman, ignoring his questions. 'We've got to get Thyrn dry and warm. I'll answer your questions then.'

The shoreman peered into the mist. Orientating himself.

'That way,' he said eventually, standing up and pointing. With a final pat he swung the boat on to his back. 'I've got a shelter you can use. It's not much, but there's wood there, and some food and water. It's not far.'

As they followed him, leading the horses, the mist began to yellow and then to clear, revealing a blue sky and a late afternoon sun. It was a welcome sight and the warmth it brought began to ease the mood of the group. Hyrald looked back, but though he could hear the distant clamour of the sea, he could see only sand dunes and the dull grey haziness of the mist. Rhavvan scrambled to the top of the highest nearby dune and peered around.

'I can't see anyone,' he reported when he came down. The shoreman watched him warily.

'There were only three of us.' It was the young Warden.

'Back with us, eh?' Rhavvan said, almost heartily. 'Slept through all the fun.'

The Warden grimaced in pain as he dropped down from the horse. Rhavvan caught him. 'You may as well ride,' he said.

The Warden scowled at him and shook his hand free. 'Wherever you're taking me I'd rather walk.'

'We're not taking you anywhere,' Hyrald said. 'You're free to go anytime you want to.' He pointed to the shoreman. 'But that man just saved all our lives and now he's offering us shelter. It's up to you whether you accept it or not but, if you're leaving, the least you can do is thank him.'

The Warden looked at him, bewildered, but did not reject Rhavvan's supporting hand as the group set off again. They continued in silence as the dunes gradually merged into undulating countryside. Swathes of purple and white flowers splashed the short turf, and birdsong filled the air. More and more trees and bushes began to appear and it was in a dip at the edge of a small copse that they came to the shoreman's shelter. It was a ramshackle collection of stones, weathered timbers and branches, and plaited grasses. As they approached it, a large dog emerged from the trees. Hackles raised, teeth bared and growling ominously it looked at each of the newcomers in turn as it moved towards them. Its slow, deliberate gait was more menacing than any demented charge.

'Stay here,' the shoreman said to the others needlessly. He went forward and, squatting down by the dog, spoke to it softly. None of the watchers could hear what he said, but the dog walked a little way from the shelter and lay down. It did not close its eyes however, but kept them fixed on the new arrivals.

'Fine dog,' Adren said nervously.

The shoreman grunted. He seemed a little more at ease now. 'Don't go near him, and don't make any sudden movements,' he said tersely as he disappeared into the shelter. A moment later he emerged with an armful of wood which he took to a small, stone-lined pit. Within minutes a fire was blazing and Thyrn was enthusiastically drying himself and his clothes while the others sat and examined the contents of the Wardens' packs.

With the unspoken consent of the others, Rhavvan offered the food to the shoreman, but he took only a loaf which he promptly proceeded to cut up and hand around.

'I've plenty of food,' he said. 'And I'm not lost. Your need seems to be greater than mine.'

His earlier questions were implicit in the statement and Hyrald introduced himself and the others. The Warden eventually called himself Oudrence.

'My name's Endryk,' the shoreman said.

Rhavvan frowned slightly. 'That's not an Arvens name.'

Endryk looked at him, but said nothing.

'Well, wherever you hail from, it's our good fortune you were here today and we're all indebted to you,' Hyrald said, breaking the awkward silence. He indicated the food again. 'Are you sure there's nothing here that you want?'

'I've everything I need,' Endryk replied. 'Except an explanation of what you're all doing here and what possessed you to go so far out on the shore. It's a dangerous place for even those who know it well.' He looked around the seated circle and quickly glanced at his watchful dog. Then he looked directly at Hyrald. 'I heard you shouting and fighting, before you try to tell me there was an accident out there again. The only reason I came near you was because I'd no choice. That's the only way off the shore.'

Hyrald gave a guilty shrug. 'I'm sorry. I was just trying to reassure you once I knew you weren't another attacker. We were lost. We needed your help – more than we realized, as it turned out.'

'Tell him everything,' Nordath said. 'He's entitled to know. He could have left us, and without him we'd all be dead now.' He motioned towards Oudrence. 'And he *needs* to know if he's going back. We've got to start getting our side of this business widely known somehow.'

Hyrald nodded. He stared into the fire for a moment, wondering where to begin.

'It's difficult,' he said. 'We've nothing to hide, but we really don't know what's happened. Or rather, we don't know *why* it's happened.'

He plunged in. 'The fact is, the Death Cry's been proclaimed against all of us. We're trying to get out of the country – to go north until we can find some way of having it annulled. Oudrence here came with two other Wardens to find us, but . . .' He grimaced. 'We killed them when they attacked us.'

Endryk looked at Oudrence, pale and stiff. 'Why didn't you kill him, as well?'

It was an unexpectedly cold question. 'We're not murderers,' Hyrald replied angrily. 'We were attacked, we defended ourselves, we survived. Two died, he didn't. None of it was of our seeking and what we did – what we've done since all this

35

started – we'll defend before any tribunal.'

Endryk's face was unreadable. Increasingly, Hyrald noted, he was becoming less and less the frightened man they had encountered on the shore. His response was blunt.

'You can't have the Death Cry proclaimed against you and not know what it's about, still less have the Wardens coming all the way up here to find you. I doubt there's anyone in Arvenshelm who even knows this place exists.'

'That's true enough,' Rhavvan replied. 'The only maps we could find of this region are vague to say the least. But what Hyrald's just told you is true. We were sent to find Thyrn by his employer – Commander Vashnar – our own senior officer. Nothing urgent or particularly unusual – not even the Cry. Just find him and quietly bring him back. Then we've no sooner found him than we're *all* being hunted. And the Death Cry isn't something to stand and debate about, is it?'

'But you're telling me about it.'

Rhavvan shrugged. 'As Nordath said, you're entitled to know. We've done nothing wrong and we've got to start saying that sooner or later.'

Endryk looked at Thyrn. 'He doesn't look particularly dangerous to me. What did you do, young man, to upset your employer so badly?'

Thyrn stared at him blankly.

'It was a Caddoran matter,' Nordath answered for him protectively.

Interest flickered briefly in Endryk's eyes. 'Caddoran, eh? Heirs to the ancient battle messengers and the great storytellers.' His face darkened. 'Reduced to runners for merchants and the Wardens.'

Nordath's eyes narrowed at the barely disguised sarcasm in his voice. 'Thyrn's is a rare gift these days,' he protested. 'And being a Caddoran is a respected and useful profession.'

'I apologize,' Endryk said, without hesitation. 'I meant no

36

reproach to the lad. You must forgive me, I'm not used to company.'

He turned to Oudrence. 'Is all this true, Warden?'

The sudden question made Oudrence start and then flinch as the movement hurt him. 'I don't know. There is a Death Cry for them, but I don't know why. The two I was with said it would put us in well with Commander Vashnar if we found them and brought them back. It seemed like a good idea at the time – the way they explained it.' He looked round at the others. 'I didn't know they were going to attack you like that – not draw on fellow Wardens.'

'What in mercy's name did you think they were going to do?' Rhavvan snapped angrily. 'Three of you against five? Take us all the way back to Arvenshelm in chains?'

'I told you, I don't know,' Oudrence shouted. 'I didn't even know what the Death Cry really meant.' He was suddenly very young and defensive. 'I only finished my basic training a few weeks ago. I just did as I was told, followed the others.'

'They brought him along to do the work, Rhavvan, that's all,' Hyrald said dismissively. 'We've done it to new recruits ourselves before now – and had it done to us when we first started.'

'What . . . what'll happen to their bodies?' The question burst out Oudrence.

'From this part of the shore they'll be washed out to sea,' Endryk replied gently. 'They'll be long gone already. The tide's very powerful. A few minutes more and we'd all have been lost – horses included.'

The group fell silent. Oudrence put his head in his free hand.

'What's the matter with your arm?' Endryk asked.

'His shoulder's broken,' Rhavvan replied as Oudrence opened his mouth. 'I just bound it up to keep it still.'

'I know a little about healing,' Endryk said. 'May I look at it?'

37

Oudrence looked at Rhavvan who shrugged.

Endryk's examination was markedly more gentle than Rhavvan's had been, and Oudrence relaxed noticeably as his injured shoulder was carefully tested and manipulated. Seemingly satisfied, Endryk announced, 'You're lucky, it's not broken, just dislocated. Hang on.' Before Oudrence could respond, Endryk wound his arms about him in an elaborate embrace and then jerked him violently. There was a cracking sound that made all the watchers start and then cringe, and such colour as there was in Oudrence's cheeks drained away instantly as his mouth opened to draw in a loud breath of disbelief and horror.

'There, that's better,' Endryk said briskly, releasing him and slipping Oudrence's arm back into Rhavvan's impromptu sling. 'It's going to hurt like hell for a while, but at least it's back in place. Rest it as much as you can – keep it relaxed.'

Oudrence, staring wide-eyed into the fire, let out the breath he had taken in, in a series of short, distressed gasps.

'Anyone else got any problems?' Endryk asked, sitting down and looking expectantly round the circle. A series of vigorous head shakes greeted this inquiry.

'Will he be fit to move on – on his own?' Hyrald asked, a little hoarsely.

Endryk nodded. 'The nearest village is a long day's walk away, but it's not difficult. He won't enjoy it, but he should be all right if he takes it easy. He can rest here tonight – you all can, if you want. I'll show him the way tomorrow.'

'We seem to be growing more and more in your debt,' Hyrald said.

'You've lived too long in Arvenshelm,' Endryk said. 'What else could I have done? Left you? Walked on?'

'Even so . . .'

'Nothing you've told me makes any sense,' Endryk interrupted. 'But that's the way it is with the Moot and its

38

officers and everything around it.' He tapped his head. 'Devoid of logic and reason. Full of self-deception, vanity, corruption.' His tone was bitter. 'That someone's proclaimed the Death Cry – with or without so-called just cause – shows that clearly enough. It's barbarous – a relic of times long gone!' He ended abruptly with a gesture of disgust. 'Just offering you a hand when you were in danger, helping the lad with his injury – incurs no debt. How could I have done less?'

'I didn't mean to offend,' Hyrald replied, taken aback by this sudden passion.

'You didn't, you didn't,' Endryk said hastily. 'I didn't realize I still felt so strongly about such matters. You must forgive me. As I said, I'm not used to company.'

'Where are you from?' Rhavvan asked.

'Or questions,' Endryk added forcefully. Rhavvan raised an apologetic hand and sat back. 'If you want to carry on north, I'll show *you* the way as well, though it's at least four days west, inland past the estuary, before there's a river narrow enough to cross. And it's no easy crossing.'

'Have you ever been north?' Adren asked. Rhavvan looked at Endryk in anticipation of another rebuke, but none came, just a slight nod.

'What kind of place is it?' Thyrn burst in, wide-eyed. 'There's a great city there, isn't there? Bigger even than a dozen Arvenshelms. And a land where everyone rides horses . . .'

'There are towns and cities, and people,' Endryk replied quietly. 'And people are the same everywhere.'

'Can you tell us anything about these places? Would we be safe there?' Hyrald asked.

'From the Death Cry, yes. But you'd be safe from that here. No one in the village, or in any of the villages within a week's walk, gives a damn about anything that happens in Arvenshelm.' He chuckled to himself. It was a warming sound. 'In fact, most of them probably have no idea where Arvenshelm is. Still less what the Moot and Wardens are. It might be that your journey's ended.'

Hyrald shook his head. 'They found us once, they'll find us again. If we stayed, we might only bring trouble to you.' He let out a noisy breath. 'We have to leave Arvenstaat. Settle into new lives somewhere until we can find out what's happened – have the Death Cry set aside.'

'How are you going to do that from exile?'

Hyrald made a helpless gesture. 'I don't know. I haven't thought about it. None of us have. We—'

'Think about it now,' Endryk said bluntly. 'While you can. There *are* other lands to the north, and you could survive there, even live well. But maybe not, too. And this land is yours. Don't be too anxious to be rid of it. Its roots will go deeper than you know.'

'We've no choice.'

'There are always choices.'

Hyrald shrugged to end the discussion. He was finding the course of the conversation oddly disturbing. The sun had set and though the sky was still clear, it had become quite dark in the dip.

'My choice now then is to rest,' he said, stretching. 'We'll accept your offer to stay here tonight, with thanks. This is the first time we've stopped running since all this started. Perhaps you're right. Perhaps we need to pause and think for a while. And we'll certainly need to put today behind us before we can do that.'

Hyrald woke the next day with bright daylight shining in his face. It was obviously long past dawn. Although he was uncomfortable, he felt refreshed. He had envisaged a disturbed and difficult night, cramped as they all were in the shelter and following on the day's desperate events, but he had gone to sleep as soon as he had lain down. The light was coming through the doorway of the shelter which had been left open and it

40

enabled him to disentangle himself gently from Nordath's legs. Stiffly he levered himself upright and went outside.

Endryk was talking to the horses, tethered to a nearby tree. Rhavvan was crouched over the fire prodding something in a pan. 'Very useful, those supplies our colleagues brought.'

Hyrald frowned at the remark. 'First shade of the day,' he said. Rhavvan looked up at him questioningly.

'I was just feeling glad to be awake after a good night's sleep, and you remind me we killed two of our own yesterday.' He raised a hand to forestall Rhavvan's protest. 'I know. They asked for it. They drew on us. We couldn't have done anything else. But that doesn't make it any easier.'

Rhavvan returned to his cooking. 'It does for me,' he said. 'A damned sight easier. For crying out, Hyrald, would *you* have gone tearing all the way up here on such an errand? They came in blades swinging and they got what they deserved. I've taken my stick to a few in my time, but I can count on one hand the number I've drawn against – and none of them without damned good justification. Here, sit and eat, it'll clear your mind – you must've got sand in it. It's got everywhere else!'

Gradually the others emerged from the shelter. Reproach was offered to Hyrald for managing to sleep through Oudrence's tossing and turning as he had striven unsuccessfully to find a comfortable position, but Hyrald could tell that the events of the previous day and the night's sleep had somehow renewed the group's determination.

Despite some initial wariness, not to say downright alarm, on the part of the young Warden, Endryk examined Oudrence's shoulder again and pronounced it sound.

When they had finished eating – a bizarre mixture of dried meats that the Wardens had carried, and fresh fish that Endryk had provided – Hyrald turned to Oudrence.

'Time for you to go now, if you're going,' he said. He looked at Endryk for confirmation. 'It's going to be a fine day. You

41

should make good progress. You'll be all right once you reach the village, I'm sure. You might even be able to borrow a horse.' He bent close and looked directly into Oudrence's eyes. 'You can tell anyone you meet what's happened here, and everything we've said. When you get back to Arvenshelm – you are from Commander Vashnar's own district, aren't you?'

'Yes.'

'Well, tell Vashnar – tell everyone – the truth. Don't lie about anything. And tell him we're going north, but that we'll be back, and looking for justice when we come. Do you understand?'

Oudrence nodded.

Hyrald answered an unasked question. 'And don't blame yourself for what happened to your companions. They were experienced men, they knew what they were doing and the risks they ran. They misled you and you were lucky not to get killed along with them.' He turned to Endryk. 'You can show him the way?'

'I'll have to take him part of the way.'

'How long will you be?'

'A few hours.'

Hyrald thought for a moment. 'Take one of the horses,' he said. 'We'll be ready to leave when you get back. I want to make as much progress as possible today.'

Thyrn rubbed his hands excitedly. Endryk and Oudrence had been gone some time.

'West along the coast for about four days, he said. Then across the river and we'll be there – safe.'

Hyrald thought for a moment then shook his head. 'No,' he said. 'I've been thinking. We can't go on like this. We should go west along the coast, but only until we reach the Karpas Mountains. Then south. Back to Arvenshelm.'

Chapter 4

Apart from two doors, recessed so deeply into the walls that they looked like darkened cave entrances, Bowlott's office was bounded, floor to ceiling, by shelves. Crooked and bowed by their long service to the Moot, they loomed ominously over the room. Peering over their tilting edges were books and documents of all shapes and sizes: weighty tomes, slender volumes, wax-sealed scrolls, stacks of papers bound with faded ribbons, leaflets, pamphlets, mysterious well-worn boxes, and more than a few wrapped objects not readily identifiable.

Bearing the Moot's crest and covered with a variety of ponderous and old-fashioned scripts, age-browned labels marked past attempts to bring order to this domain, but, curled and brittle, this slender shield line had been long overwhelmed, leaving confusion to hold the field unchallenged. Unchallenged that is, except for a dusty gauze of ancient cobwebs which brought a certain unity to the tumbled documents on the upper shelves and which was moving steadily downwards like a frayed grey curtain. It petered out at those levels where the spiders, paper-loving insects and small wildlife were diligently continuing their self-appointed task of mummifying the accumulated wisdom of the Moot.

Further down, small stretches of order hinted at a lingering rearguard action as occasional ranks of stiff leather spines and gold embossing stood out boldly. These however merely served as a metaphor for the constant defeat of the Moot's present by its lumbering past.

The floor complemented the descending greyness. Ragged stacks reached up the walls, like wind-carved buttresses, from an uneven landscape of boxes and books which fell away to a central plain of musty carpeted floor. Rising from this, like a massif, was Bowlott's desk, seemingly the inspiration and model for the whole room, with its own miniature central plain surrounded by overspilling disorder. Had Krim ever seen this room, he would have been consumed with envy, for it had no windows. No daylight intruded its blanching fingers into Bowlott's lair. Such light as there was came from lanterns mounted on four austerely straight pedestals. They heightened the darkness above.

Striker Bowlott sat frowning at his desk. He was always ambivalent about visiting Krim. Though he could not have admitted it to himself, one reason for this unease was that the Venerable Cushion Bearer was extremely good at his job. Further, he was very reliable. Indeed, the man was *efficient*. This unsettled Bowlott at a level far below his conscious awareness. Efficiency was a word not merely rarely heard in the Moot, but actually shied away from. It had powerful and disturbing undertones of workmanlike vulgarity, of *doing* things, of practical achievement, and, as such, suggested matters far beneath the dignity and the lofty principles which inspired this revered seat of government. Nevertheless, Krim *was* efficient. His cushions transformed the Throne of Marab from a jagged torture seat into the vertical equivalent of a luxurious, supportive and well-sprung bed whose only disadvantage was that it was sometimes difficult to stay awake when sat in it. And, when on Throne Duty himself, rather than his crumpled and even older junior assistant, the alacrity with which Krim could adjust and change cushions to maintain the Striker's comfort as he shifted and turned through 'long and taxing'

44

meetings was legendary amongst those who took an interest in such matters.

Then, of course, and even worse, like all the Moot Officers, there was an air of continuity about Krim that irked Bowlott. It was deeply unjust that the likes of Krim and Ector, mere craftsmen after all, should be allowed to remain here in perpetuity when such as he, a lawyer, no less, an undisputed master of the ways of the Moot, and a natural leader, chosen by the chosen of the people, were there like temporary servants, their tenure at the fickle whim of those same people. Bowlott had little sense of circular reasoning. His ten years in the office and the very high likelihood of another ten did nothing to allay this insecurity and he twitched nervously whenever he thought about it. He really should do something about having the position of Striker made permanent. In fact, this whole business of Acclamations needed to be looked at carefully. The governing of Arvenstaat, a matter which, to Bowlott – and most Senators – meant, above all, a knowledge of the deep intricacies of the Moot and its procedures, was not something that should properly be left to the arbitrary choices of the ignorant and untutored masses.

These were old and familiar thoughts and Bowlott made no effort to pursue them. He was always like this after he had visited Krim – relaxed by the man's ministrations and made tense by the obsessive, gangling presence. That was another thing about Krim – he was too tall. And too straight. Bowlott could never decide what it was about Krim that he liked the least.

'Long streak of cold water,' he muttered to himself into the dusty silence. The prejudice voiced, his little eyes flicked peevishly from side to side as if half-expecting the shade of the Venerable Cushion Bearer to appear out of the gloom, wild-eyed and vengeful now, and purposefully bearing the Blue Cushion.

45

Almost in panic, Bowlott thrust the vision away and snatched up a pen. Its point buckled as he thrust it into the paper, making an image like a squashed spider. He threw it away irritably. It struck a box and fell on to an uneven heap of papers before dropping on the floor. A few sheets of paper avalanched silently off the heap, gently covering the broken pen for ever.

This sudden flurry of activity dispatched the lingering after-image of Krim and brought Bowlott to the matter which had been increasingly making itself felt over the past few weeks and which he had, for some unknown reason, raised with Krim.

'Vashnar, Vashnar, Vashnar,' he mouthed silently, as if forming the man's name might somehow produce an explanation for what he had done.

The governing of Arvenstaat was an ill-defined affair. In so far as he had bothered with such constitutional matters, Akharim, in his Treatise on the Procedures for the Proper Ordering of the Moot, had been wilfully evasive. After all, like many a usurper before him, he had only written the Treatise to give some spurious credence to his own seizure of power. It was sufficient for him that his charges consisted of followers and leaders. The followers, the masses, on the whole were best left undisturbed. There was little point in seeking their opinion about anything, least of all who should rule them. Not only were they not interested but, as his own example served to show, there were always incipient leaders amongst them. It was best that such random forces were not encouraged. As for the leaders, he further divided these into those who talked their way to power and those who fought their way. It was thus his task to ensure that the existing talkers and the fighters be kept aware of their common interest in maintaining him in power. The Treatise, in many ways an unexpectedly elegant and convincing piece of work, occupied the talkers, while persuading most of the fighters to form a guard to enforce his will. These last he further controlled by encouraging mutual suspicion and by the occasional use of silent knives.

In the end, the combination of Akharim's shrewd judgement and those silent knives proved extremely effective, and it was the talkers who prevailed as nominal rulers while the guards enjoyed the actual power, equilibrium being maintained by their unspoken agreement that the masses should remain undisturbed. Thus the Moot and the Wardens began their long journey through Arvenstaat's history. And thus it was that Bowlott and the Moot Senators believed that their people could only be governed by written words – by laws. Only laws could make right the failings of the foolish and the wicked, and once a law was passed, nothing else was needed. And laws, in their turn, could be made only by the Moot, with its fund of ancient wisdom.

As with much that happened in the Moot, Bowlott's vision had little contact with reality. The accountability of the Wardens, for example, consisted of a yearly formalized report from Vashnar, some solemn but token questioning on trivial procedural points by one of the Moot's many sub-committees followed by a fulsome vote of thanks from the Moot assembled. As for the interminable new laws that the Moot passed, the Wardens and the local Watches, which served in lieu of the Wardens in the smaller towns and villages, generally ignored them, confining themselves to their long-established role of ensuring that the wilder elements of society were kept quiet, one way or another, so that the bulk of the people could get on with their lives in peace. On the whole, this had become an agreeable arrangement and it worked well enough while nothing particularly untoward happened. Lately, however, untoward things *had* been happening, and this lethargic stability was beginning to waver ominously.

News had come from the coast that the Morlider islands had been seen again. Until some sixteen years ago, these floating islands had returned every year or so for generations and, while powerful tides protected Arvenstaat from the worst excesses of their vicious inhabitants, coastal villages had been regularly raided. Then, coinciding with rumours of a terrible war in lands to the north, the visits had mysteriously stopped. Their equally mysterious return now was causing great unease.

More tangibly, trade with Nesdiryn, over the mountains to the west, declining ever since the ousting of the Count by its strange new rulers, had eventually come to a complete halt. As a result, traders had been seeking out their Senators and asking for help. And too, alarming stories had come from there recently: a great army was being gathered with the intention of making a war of expansion against Nesdiryn's neighbours; the Count had ousted his rivals in a fearful battle in the mountains; the Count had been defeated and killed by them; and many variations upon these themes, but all involving the threat of armed violence.

And now this business with Vashnar and the Death Cry.

Bowlott picked up another pen and began decorating the image of the squashed spider. The Cry was a routine device used by the Wardens and the Watches for dealing with thieves and other wrongdoers. True, it stirred people out of their routines and was thus a little risky, but there was sufficient momentum in the ordinary lives of most of them to ensure that nothing got out of hand. The Death Cry, however, was another matter. That *had* caused a stir. All the more so for its involving another Warden. Again, it had provoked people into pestering their Senators about it. Though he had skilfully avoided showing any response when he heard about it, it had come as a shock to Bowlott to realize that the Death Cry could still be invoked, and that, like the Cry, it was officially outside the remit of the Moot.

He shook his head as the spider slowly turned into a rather grotesque blossom.

'I shall speak to Commander Vashnar. I shall ask him why

he has done what he has done.' The words he had uttered to a rapt Krim – Bowlott was always sensitive to the mood of his audience – returned to him. Barbed thorns sprang out of the blossom. Rather an impetuous declaration, that, for all it fell only into Krim's ear. Probably brought on by the man's comforting attention. He should have been more careful. Still, it seemed that it was all that was left. It was some time before Vashnar was to report to the Moot and, in any event, this was unequivocally *not* a matter to be dealt with in such a public way. He drew an elaborate border around the blossom then screwed up the paper and threw it on the floor.

For a little while, he leaned back and stared up at the grey, ill-shaped and shadowy ceiling. The sight comforted him. Nothing had disturbed those uppermost volumes in generations. All was well. All was preserved. The wisdom of the Moot lay coiled and ready to spring to the defence of the land should dire times come to pass.

He took up another piece of paper and began writing. When he had finished he removed a plug from a funnel-ended tube fastened to one arm of his chair, and coughed into it. The sound passed along the tube to emerge in an adjacent room as a tetchy grunt. Two Moot Pages looked up irritably from a board game they were playing.

'Oink, oink,' one of them said quickly, laughing and pointing at the other. 'Piggy's calling. Your turn.'

The ritual having been observed, his companion scowled and stabbed the board with his finger as he stood up. 'I can remember where all those pieces are,' he said significantly, a declaration which was received with raised hands and an expression of profound innocence.

'Will it be six copies, Striker Bowlott?' the Page asked uncertainly as he examined the paper.

Bowlott frowned and shook his head. 'Six copies is for official memoranda to members of the Outer Moot, Page, or, during recess, for informal notifications to the Moot Hall Attendants. You should know this by now.' He reached out and tapped the paper. 'This is a special docket of interview, Striker to Officer – very confidential. *Four* copies and one on vellum for the Registrar. And don't forget to bring the finished copy back to me for my personal seal. See to it quickly now. This is an urgent matter.'

The page pulled an unhappy face for the benefit of his companion as he emerged through the cave entrance from Bowlott's office. Being a Moot Page was an esteemed position in certain sections of Arvenshelm society, particularly that occupied by the clerks and copyists who dealt with the Moot's extensive output of words. It was not particularly well paid, but it was secure for life, presented little intellectual challenge and, almost inevitably, led its holders on to become Attendants or Official Scribes – part of the self-perpetuating bureaucracy that had accreted around the Moot, as it does about all governments. Fond parents would glow when one of their children was accepted for such a post and, if not careful, could become a grievously unctuous burden to their friends and neighbours. Generally, a Page's life was a relaxed affair and, mimicking the Moot itself, it had long-established and unofficial procedures of its own to ensure that this remained so. Nevertheless, from time to time, there were problems.

'What's the matter?' asked the companion, guiltily repositioning a piece on the board on seeing his friend's distress. He anticipated with a grimace. 'Not a twenty copy?'

The Page shook his head. 'Striker to Officer – four and a V.' He held out the paper. 'But it's to Commander Vashnar. Over in the Warden's Section.' This provoked a further grimace – a genuine one. Uncomfortably, a request was made. 'Will you come with me?' There was a brief pause while friendship and peer loyalty were tested, then a reluctant, 'Yes,' followed by another brief silence which ended in a livelier, 'What is it?'

Bowlott's message was simple to the point of sparseness. *Attend on me at close of Moot today. By Order, Bowlott, Striker to the Moot.* At the top it bore the instruction, *To Commander Vashnar, in person.*

It was greeted with a long indrawn whistle. 'Vashnar, in person. And here!' The reader was wide-eyed. He pointed to the tube from which Bowlott's cough had emerged a few moments earlier and his voice fell to a whisper. 'We'll *have* to listen to *that.*' He became thoughtful. 'And we'd better do all the copies as well.' The first Page stared at him in surprise, only to be met with a knowing pout from his more experienced companion. 'You never know,' he declared, bureaucrat-to-be. 'Vashnar could check up on us.'

There were two reasons why the Page had asked his friend to accompany him. One was that, being relatively new to the job, he was far from certain of the way to the Warden's Section through the Moot Palace's convoluted corridors and closed courtyards. The other was that, though rarely visited, the Warden's Section was a place universally feared by Pages. Civilian officers of the Moot, of all ranks, were generally despised by the Wardens but while adults might expect some surliness or outright sneers, Pages could usually look to more physical humiliation.

However, in this instance, Bowlott's personal seal and Vashnar's name had the effect of a talisman and, though flushed and flustered with the haste and anxiety of their journey, the two Pages reached Vashnar unmolested.

The room from which Vashnar conducted most of his day-to-day work was starkly different from Bowlott's dusty office. Amongst other things, it was light, with a large window occupying almost the whole of one wall. It was also bare of any form of ornamentation and there was not a vestige of disorder. A plain but well-made and highly polished wooden table served as a desk, and pens, inks and various writing tablets were laid out on it with meticulous precision. A carved crystal ink-stand stood at the heart of the display. The pale grey walls bore only maps of Arvenshelm and Arvenstaat, while a set of shelves stood to attention in one corner, displaying two rows of neatly arranged books. Dominant amongst these was one written by Vashnar's paternal grandfather on the history and duties of the Wardens. Akharim had left no Treatise for the guidance of the Wardens. His thoughts on that had come down as an oral tradition which had necessarily shifted and changed as convenience had dictated over the years. Vashnar's grandfather had set down this tradition together with an extensive analysis and commentary. It was a weighty and stern work, generally known as The Commentaries. It was prefaced by the maxim *Above all things, there shall be order.* Vashnar's thoughts were very much those of his grandfather.

Vashnar stood up as the two Pages were shown in. Taller than most men, and heavily built, he had a stillness about him that could be mistaken for ponderousness. In fact this was because he moved economically, using the minimum of effort in all things. This same economy made him both powerful and fast in his reactions when need arose, as many a wrongdoer could testify to as the young Vashnar had progressed through the ranks of the Wardens. Though it had been a long time since the position of leader of the Wardens had been open to challenge by physical combat, a residue of that thinking still allied itself keenly with Vashnar's own grasp of the realities of power.

Both Pages looked up at him. His presence filled the room for them as he looked slowly from one to the other. Their already flushed faces reddened further under this scrutiny, until a surreptitious elbow in the ribs jolted the official bearer of the message back to his duties.

'From Striker Bowlott . . . Commander . . . sir,' came a dry-throated announcement.

Vashnar extended a large hand and took the shaking paper.

The Pages noted no response as he read it, though those who knew Vashnar well would have detected a momentary narrowing of his cold black-irised eyes. And those who knew him well *would* have detected it, for no one grew to know Vashnar well without being sensitive to such minutiae.

He moved to the window, noticeably darkening the room. The two Pages risked an unhappy glance at one another as he turned his back to them and stared out at the view. Making people feel guilty was something that Vashnar did without even thinking about it.

After a distressingly long pause and without relinquishing his vigil, he spoke. 'Tell Striker Bowlott that I shall attend on him as . . .' He looked down at the paper again. 'As ordered.'

'Sir.'

Vashnar remained by the window for some time. When he turned, it needed no subtle perception to read the surprise and irritation that flickered across his face at finding the two Pages still there.

A second trembling paper was held out to him. 'Would you sign this, please, Commander.'

'To show we've delivered the message, sir.'

Vashnar stared at the shaking duo. 'What was the reply I just gave you?' he said. 'Speak it, now.'

He had to repeat this instruction before the two Pages stammered out variations of, 'You'll attend on Striker Bowlott as ordered . . . sir.'

Vashnar gave a curt nod then slowly extended a forefinger towards the door. 'My aide signs . . . papers. See that you deliver my reply quickly and accurately.'

When the two Pages had scurried out, Vashnar took The Commentaries from the bookshelf and laid it carefully on the desk as he sat down. He did not open it, but laid his hand on it as though he were about to take an oath. He often sat thus when he was angry or unsettled. It brought the supporting shade of his grandfather to him, carrying him past that of his weak and despised father. It was one of his few regrets that he had never met the old man, though this did not stop him from forming a clear impression of him.

And, although no sign of it showed other than his hand on The Commentaries, he was both angry and unsettled now. Angry at Bowlott's thoughtless and pompous, By Order, and unsettled by his being driven to the point of seeking an interview with him. It did not help that he knew it was his own fault that this had come about.

He drummed a brief tattoo on The Commentaries. He did not need to read his grandfather's comments on the Death Cry. He knew that his actions had been in accordance with established tradition and that no reference to the Moot was needed, but . . .

But what had possessed him to do it? What demon had reached into him and persuaded him to this deed which might undo the years of steady progress he had been making in consolidating power to himself? He ran his thumb gently over the inside of the ring that graced the second finger of his right hand. The ring was his only needless decoration and touching it was his only nervous mannerism. Both were very discreet.

With no other outward sign of the turmoil within, he cursed Thyrn. It was not a new curse. Indeed, it was one that was almost constantly in his mind. And, as it was apt to do, it spiralled out into a curse against all the Caddoran. Damned freaks. Why couldn't some other way be found to . . . ?

Here the anger turned on itself. Vashnar was not given to railing against what could not be altered and it angered him further that he could not restrain himself from doing just that. The Caddoran had been an integral part of Arvenstaat's culture since before the state had existed as such, their origins rolling back into the ancient tribal times and thence into myth where they played elaborate roles of confidants, go-betweens and manipulators to the peculiar gods of the old Arvenwern. Even now, though notionally they were only message carriers, they were in fact much more. Routinely, any Caddoran could memorize a spoken message almost instantaneously and retain it for as long as the sender required. Masters of the art, however, could carry subtleties of intonation, gesture and expression – could convey the true meaning of a communication in a manner not remotely possible by written word, or even rote recitation. Myths notwithstanding, the origin of the art was obscure, though there was little doubt that it developed from a battlefield skill. Amongst the Caddoran, being able to trace a line of descent in the general direction of some famous hero was a matter of great pride. Only a few generations ago, in less civilized times, that same kudos would have been gained by tracing the line back to some more legendary figure.

Yet the art was deeply strange. Though training was required, it was pointless unless a strong natural aptitude was present, and while this tended to run in families, it was wildly erratic, sometimes skipping several generations then producing two or three at once, sometimes jumping from the male to the female line. Then the talent would appear spontaneously in a family with no history of it. Thyrn had been one such. Though many theories had been offered, the progress of this necessary trait through the generations defied all analysis.

Thyrn proved to be more than just another unexplained example of the appearance of the talent. He had been exceptional, showing such aptitude that he was accepted for training by the Caddoran Congress while only five years old, instead of the normal twelve. Subsequently, at the age of fifteen, he had become a White Master, the highest possible grade and one which many Caddoran could not even aspire to. Prior to Thyrn, the youngest White Master had been twenty-seven. Not only did he have a gift for memorizing and reproducing messages which awed his superiors, he seemed to sense intuitively what the message sender wanted to say at such a deep level that on transmitting his message, the recipient would feel himself in the presence of the actual sender. Inevitably he became the personal Caddoran to the Wardens' Senior Commander.

Yet, in many ways, he was still a child. It was as if his talent took so much of him that the remainder could not fully develop. This, however, merely made him odd company when not on duty. It in no way lessened his value to Vashnar who, though he schooled himself obsessively in self-reliance, made the mistake he was now ruing, of growing to be too dependent on him for the carrying of his many sensitive and confidential messages. Nor did it concern Thyrn's parents who basked in the glory of their son's high employment and who, though he lived in the Moot Palace now, still 'advised' him on the disposition of his not insubstantial remuneration. It did concern his father's brother, Nordath, though, whose family pride in the young man was far outweighed by his affection for him and concern for the pain that he could feel emanating from him. In Thyrn he sensed the Caddoran that he had nearly been, and for some reason he could not avoid a feeling of guilt that he had been spared the burden.

'He needs friends of his own age. Ordinary friends. He's too different to get on with even the other Caddoran novices,' he had frequently told his brother. 'He needs friends he can talk to, wrestle with, get into trouble with.'

But it had been to no avail. Thyrn's parents had drawn a protective curtain about him: there was no saying what corrosive influence other children might have on their son's precious – and lucrative – talent. The boy's career had to be considered.

Despite their 'protection' Thyrn had returned Nordath's affection and turned to him as friend and adviser.

Thus it was that Nordath had one day rushed to his door in response to a frantic hammering, to find Thyrn standing there, white-faced and shaking.

56

Chapter 5

'*What?*'

The disbelieving cry came simultaneously from Rhavvan and Adren. Nordath and Thyrn looked at Hyrald in bewilderment.

'Back to Arvenshelm?' Rhavvan echoed. 'Are you crazy?' He thrust a finger in the direction that Oudrence and Endryk had taken. 'There could be scores of Wardens out looking for us. Those two who came with Oudrence won't be the only ones looking to catch Vashnar's eye, and if they found us, others can. And what are we going to do when . . . if . . . we manage to reach Arvenshelm alive? The crowds might have gone for now, but they'll come back soon enough.'

'I know, I know,' Hyrald replied defensively. 'But what are we going to do anyway? Think about what Endryk said last night. How are we going to be able to get the Death Cry rescinded if we're in some foreign land? Think about it *now*, he said, and he was right. We've been so busy running, hiding, surviving, we haven't stopped to think what we're doing, or why. Not once.'

'But . . .'

'But nothing. It's true. You know it.' Hyrald began pacing up and down, talking as much to himself as to the others as he struggled to clarify his thoughts. 'We're Wardens, for mercy's sake. The service isn't perfect, god knows, but on the whole we keep the peace, we're respected men. And we've got – we had

57

– good lives. So what are we doing here at the back end of nowhere, off the edge of any map I've ever seen, running like frightened dogs – and having to kill our own?' He put his hands to his temples. 'I can't believe we did that – right or wrong. And look what happened on the shore. We know the streets, the people, but out here? We're lost. The way that tide came in!' He closed his eyes and blew out an unsteady breath as, for an instant, he was crashing across the raging stream again. 'So fast! Faster than we could gallop, for pity's sake. I can feel it pulling at my horse right now. It's the purest chance that we'd got horses, that Endryk was there and that we weren't all killed.' He became emphatic. 'And if we get across the sea, who knows what kind of people we'll find out there?'

'People are the same everywhere, Endryk said.'

Nordath put a restraining hand on Thyrn's arm, but Hyrald merely dismissed the remark, albeit with a sneer.

'Yes, they are,' he said simply. 'They're dangerous.'

Thyrn persisted despite Nordath's silent plea. 'We must go on. Away from here. Away from Vashnar. There's a great city up there . . . everyone's heard about it – so big you can't see all of it no matter how high a building you climb. We'll be safe there. We can hide, we can . . .'

His voice faded as Hyrald stopped pacing and turned a searching look on him. When he spoke however, it was softly and slowly. 'We don't even know why we're here. We don't know *why* Vashnar called the Death Cry, and we don't even know why he wanted you in the first place.'

'It's a Caddoran matter,' Nordath said, edging forward to stand by Thyrn.

Hyrald's hand gently paddled the air, motioning him to silence. The gesture was both placating and menacing. 'You've said that before,' he replied, without taking his eyes off Thyrn. 'But it's not enough now.' He turned to Adren and Rhavvan. 'We've known one another for ever. We trust one another. We've been in some difficult places together keeping Arvenshelm's good citizens safe in their beds and on the streets, but this is beyond anything we've ever known. It's time to stop running before we run out of luck. Time to think. Time to find out the *why?* of all this.'

'It's a Caddoran matter,' Nordath said again, more forcefully.

Two birds flew over the group and disappeared into the trees beyond the shelter, their wings noisy and urgent. Hyrald shook his head.

'Nordath, I've known you for a long time too. No more of this. Thyrn gossiping about Vashnar's private messages is a Caddoran matter. Us unofficially tracking him down on Vashnar's behalf is a Wardens' matter. But Vashnar unearthing the Death Cry; us escaping from Arvenshelm by the skin of our teeth, thanks to some loyal friends and no small amount of luck; and us careening across the country, stealing food and hiding from village Watch patrols and would-be manhunters, killing our own, is a different matter altogether. Before we go anywhere, I . . . we . . . need to know what Thyrn's done. I've no great affection for Vashnar, but I know him as well as anyone does and I respect him. And I've never known him do anything without a reason.'

Nordath cast an uncomfortable glance at Thyrn whose expression was becoming increasingly desperate.

'It's difficult,' he said weakly.

'These past weeks have been difficult,' Hyrald retorted caustically. 'Yesterday in particular.'

Abruptly, Nordath's protective manner slipped away and uncertainty pervaded him. He turned unhappily to Thyrn and seemed to have to drag words from some great depth when he spoke. 'You'll have to tell them . . . us,' he said. The last word was almost inaudible, but the three Wardens heard it.

'Us!' exclaimed Rhavvan. 'You mean *you* don't know?'

A gesture from Hyrald silenced him. The sudden change in

Nordath's demeanour as Thyrn's guardian was disconcerting in itself, but now he saw Thyrn's eyes glazing over. For a moment he thought that the young man was going to collapse. As did Nordath, who reached out to support him. Despite this change, Rhavvan pressed his question.

'You mean, *you* don't know what all this is about?'

Nordath, recovered now and looking intently into Thyrn's face, tried a half-hearted negotiation. 'No, I don't,' he admitted bluntly. 'But the fact that Vashnar's proclaimed the Death Cry against *you* is enough to tell you it's something really bad he wants hidden, isn't it?'

Adren intruded quickly between Rhavvan's wide-eyed indignation and Hyrald's scarcely veiled anger. 'The seriousness isn't in dispute, Nordath,' she said quietly. 'Hyrald's right. We're here through a mixture of good luck and sheer panic, but we can't carry on like this, we need to know why we're running if we're ever going to be able to stop. You must tell us what Thyrn's done, Caddoran matter or not. You're not bound by any oath just because he might've broken his and told you something. If you want to help him, you'll have to tell us.'

As she spoke, she was helping Nordath to lower Thyrn into a seated position against the wall of Endryk's shelter.

'What's the matter with him?' Rhavvan asked.

'I don't know.' Nordath straightened up. 'He goes like this sometimes – when things are too much for him. He usually just comes out of it after a while, as if nothing had happened.'

'Running away, eh?'

Nordath turned on Rhavvan furiously, obliging the big man to take a step backwards. 'You judge this lad when you've walked a mile in his shoes, Warden. Caddoran aren't like ordinary people. They're strange, special. Almost impossible for the likes of us to understand. And Thyrn's special even amongst them. How do you think he got to work for Vashnar at his age?' He slapped his hand on his chest. 'I don't know why, but I'm the only person he's ever been able to turn to like an ordinary human being – a friend. His parents – my blessed brother and that shrew of a wife of his – just see him as a milch-cow. The other Caddoran of his age are too intimidated by his talent to treat him as an equal, while the older ones are for the most part either jealous of him or wanting to shine by reflection from him. And Vashnar cares for nothing and no one except his position and the power it brings him.'

Rhavvan recovered. 'We still need to know what's going on!' he shouted.

Nordath nodded briefly, but his anger was spent and he sagged. 'I know, I know. I'm sorry, I didn't mean to . . . I know none of us wants to be here. I realize we're a burden to you. I'm grateful . . . we're grateful.' He fell silent and sat down wearily beside Thyrn.

Prompted by Adren, Hyrald crouched down in front of him. 'Is Rhavvan right? Do you really not know what Thyrn's done?'

Nordath did not reply immediately, but fidgeted nervously, rubbing the palm of one hand with his thumb. 'No, I don't,' he replied eventually. 'When he came to me he was frantic – hysterical. I couldn't get two coherent words out of him. I've seen him in lots of moods, learned a lot about him over the years, even got some inkling about how he thinks, but I've never seen him like that before.' He recalled the thunderous pounding on his door, and yanking it open to have the terrified lad tumble, white and shaking, into his arms.

'It took me a long time just to get him quiet,' he went on soberly, 'and I soon learned that asking what had happened just set him back to where he'd started. I've never felt so helpless. Then, you three were there looking for him, and . . .' A shrug encompassed the gasping Warden who had brought the news of the Death Cry, and the subsequent confusion and flight. 'I haven't asked him since – not that we've had a chance.' He turned to the still distant Thyrn. 'But in any case, I haven't dared. Rightly too, by the look of him now.' He levered himself up, reluctant to continue talking about Thyrn as though he were not there. He lowered his voice. 'I don't even know if he can hear what we're saying when he's like this. And you're right, Rhavvan, he *is* running away, but what from, and where to . . .' He shrugged again.

'All of which leaves *us* where?' Rhavvan asked, though his manner was softer.

'No worse off, I suppose,' Hyrald replied resignedly. 'But, Nordath, we must try to find out what he's done – you can see that. Can you speculate – guess at what might have happened?'

Nordath shook his head. 'No. I told you, Caddoran think in different ways to the rest of us – especially Thyrn. You've seen how he is – nice to be with, more often than not, with an innocence about him and always wanting to know – like a child. Then other times he's so serious and intense it gives you a headache just looking at him. All I got from him were odd words like "darkness" or "blood". And he kept covering his eyes and curling up, as if he'd seen something he didn't want to.'

'Touched him. Deep.'

It was Thyrn, his voice distant and strained. As the others looked down at him, he let out a long, hissing breath and folded his hands tightly over his head. Hyrald knelt down in front of him, bending low in an attempt to look into his face.

'What did you say, Thyrn? We didn't hear you.'

A slight whimper keened out of the young man's tightly closed lips. Hyrald could feel the fear that prompted it rippling through him.

'Don't be afraid, you're safe with us, here. You—' He stopped with a startled cry as Thyrn's hand shot out and seized his arm. It drew him forward until there was scarcely a hand's width between their faces.

'Everyone be afraid,' Thyrn said, his voice soft and still strained. 'No one's safe. No one, anywhere. Darkness.'

Then the grip was gone and Thyrn's hands were covering his face. Hyrald looked up at Nordath for advice.

'I'll make him talk,' Rhavvan said, before Nordath could speak.

'I doubt it,' Hyrald said. 'I agree with Nordath. From the look of him I'd say he's scared out of his wits.'

Rhavvan bent forward, clenching his fist menacingly. 'Just another unco-operative witness. Make him more afraid of us than whoever else is frightening him.'

Hyrald noticed a slight twitch in Thyrn's face at this remark.

Part of you is still here, then, he thought. Listening, learning, watching. What goes on in that Caddoran mind of yours?

Once again, almost as though Thyrn had reached out to him, he sensed the young man's leaking terror.

He spoke directly into Thyrn's face as he eased Rhavvan's proffered fist aside. 'Difficult to do that, I'd judge. A push too far from where he is and, like some of our witnesses, we'll lose him completely.' Besides, despite the lad's irritating ways, as Nordath had claimed, he couldn't help liking him, not to say feeling sorry for him. 'I think right now he needs our help more than we need his.' He put his hands on Thyrn's shoulders.

'Thyrn.' He spoke softly. 'I know you're afraid. We're all afraid. It's understandable after what we've been through. But you've done well. You've run with us, hidden with us, eaten and slept with us. Done better than many a Senior Cadet.' He paused and searched into Thyrn's eyes for signs that he was being heard. But he could read nothing.

'We're safe here for the moment. Safer than we've been since we started. But we have to think what to do next. And to do that we have to know why we're running.' He became confidential. 'I don't want you to break your Caddoran Oath. I wouldn't ask you to do that. I know it's very important to you. But we've all got to help one another. Even if you don't want to help yourself, think about your uncle. He . . .'

A hand on his shoulder stopped him.

'No,' Nordath said firmly. 'He's had nothing but that off his parents and his teachers all his life. Let me speak to him.'

Hyrald looked into the unfocused eyes again. He felt guilt well up inside him. 'I'm sorry,' he said, patting Thyrn's arm. 'I made a mistake.'

Nordath took Hyrald's place in front of the immobile Thyrn. Rhavvan made an impatient gesture and strode off. Hyrald motioned Adren after him.

Nordath's hand fluttered uncertainly, then, a little awkwardly, he put his arms around Thyrn. 'Go where you've got to go, Thyrn. Come back when you're ready. We'll be here, waiting for you. We'll take care of you.'

Equally awkwardly he released his nephew and stood up, rather self-consciously.

'We will take care of him, won't we?' he said to Hyrald.

Only years as a Warden prevented Hyrald from showing his doubts as he met Nordath's gaze. It had occurred to him more than once in the days immediately following their flight from Arvenshelm that perhaps surrendering Thyrn might be a way of having the Death Cry against him and the others lifted. He was honest enough to admit that it was only the unexpected ferocity of the response to the Death Cry that had prevented him from doing this. As they had moved further away from Arvenshelm, the clamour and urgency had lessened but the day-to-day needs of hiding and surviving had remained and the option of surrender had faded away as the group gradually became five instead of three and two.

'Yes,' he replied. 'We've taken care of you so far. We won't stop now.'

But some time later, as he abandoned Nordath to his vigil and joined Rhavvan and Adren on top of a nearby rise his mind was awash with doubt.

'Why so fierce?' he said. Rhavvan frowned and Adren looked at him blankly.

'Why were the crowds so fierce when the Death Cry was announced? If we hadn't been warned – given that little extra time – we'd have been . . .' A sideways cutting action of his hand finished the sentence.

Rhavvan shrugged airily. 'Not everybody loves a Warden,' he declared mockingly. 'The ordinary Cry doesn't exactly bring the best out in people, does it? You know how long it takes us to get the streets quiet after one.'

Hyrald looked down at Thyrn and Nordath by the ramshackle shelter, then at the surrounding landscape. The view beyond the shelter was restricted by gently hilly terrain, lush with trees and shrubs, but in the other direction the colour gradually faded until it ended in the pale line of the dunes. In a dip between two of them, Hyrald could just see the bright line of the sea. It was good here. Open, undisturbed, even the air was different – so very different from the soiled and oppressive streets of Arvenshelm. Yet too, it was frightening. It was empty and lonely. It left him feeling exposed and vulnerable, thrown totally on his own resources. And the glint of the distant sea at once lured him and repelled him, filling him with vague images of great and alien spaces.

'I don't know,' he said, returning to his friends. 'It wasn't just the ordinary mob. It was as though . . .' he searched for the words '. . . as though something fearful had been released. There was a real bloodlust in those we saw when we were hiding in the Old Park.' He shivered at the memory, then he became thoughtful. 'I wonder how many people got killed in all that, in the general crush, by mistaken identity?'

'Not to forget the score-settling. There's always some of that in any Cry. I should imagine a lot were hurt. It's just one of those things. Anyway . . .' Rhavvan threw a suddenly cheerful arm around Hyrald's shoulders, making him stagger. 'What's the problem? People are bastards at the best of times, you know that. Whack you as soon as look at you if they thought it was to their advantage. They have to run amok from time to time. It's enough for me that we got away.'

'You're cynical.'

'I'm a Warden, and I see people for what they are.' A jabbing finger emphasized his point. 'As do you, normally.'

'Maybe,' Hyrald conceded reluctantly. 'But there was still something more. Worse than I'd have expected – realist or no.'

'You're right.' It was Adren. 'I hadn't thought about it until now, but it *was* worse than the usual mob that comes out for the Cry – much worse.'

Rhavvan threw up his hands, dismissing the two of them.

'It's been brewing for months,' she went on. 'Perhaps years.'

'What has?' demanded Rhavvan, increasingly exasperated.

'Trouble,' Adren replied simply. 'Year on year since I joined there's been more violence and discontent. And we've had more drunks, more beatings, more crowd flare-ups, more everything this last year than ever before – you know that. It's as though there's something in the air – like a storm coming.'

'Horse manure,' Rhavvan declaimed. 'That's all there is in the air – horse manure. And the warm weather always makes people fractious.' He slapped the purse on his belt. 'A nice heatwave's always good for business. More overtime, more fines, voluntary contributions, and the like.' He laughed.

The sound should have lightened the mood of the group a little, but the clink of coins in Rhavvan's purse had a dull, funereal timbre to Hyrald, reminding him that money was of no value to them now. Here it was only something more to be carried – another burden. And Adren was unconvinced by Rhavvan's airy analysis.

'There's a restlessness about,' she insisted doggedly. 'I don't know what it is, but something's falling apart. And all this business about the Morlider and what's going on in Nesdiryn hasn't helped. In fact, I think that's . . .'

A loud cry from Nordath cut across her.

Chapter 6

It was Close of Moot. Early today. The last few grains of sand in the hourglass which stood by the Throne of Marab had to be encouraged on their way by a surreptitious flick of Striker Bowlott's middle finger but if anyone saw, no one was interested in raising any elaborate procedural points about it. As usual, most of the Senators were only too anxious to be away to fulfil their various social and business commitments. Being a representative of the people was demanding work.

The current speaker froze, gaping in mid-word and mid-gesture as the end of Bowlott's staff struck the floor. An audible sigh of relief passed around the Moot Hall, dappled with the sounds of various Senators waking suddenly. The doleful peal of the Moot bells carrying the news through the corridors of the Palace seeped into the hall.

As he always did at close of Moot, Bowlott sat motionless until the sound of the bells faded into the general mumbling background of the hall, then his beady eyes scanned the noble assembly before him two or three times before, very slowly, he began to lever himself upright. Krim's deputy creaked forward to take the cushion that had been supporting Bowlott's head, lest it slip forward and mar the dignity of the occasion by entangling itself in his robes like a workman's pack, or by slithering down behind him and nudging his backside. It was a heavy cushion and its urging had more than once caused Striker Bowlott to waver unsteadily on his footstool at this juncture.

Today, however, there was no such lapse, though Krim's deputy, compounding Bowlott's malicious slowness with his own natural frailty, stretched out the ending of the day's business even further as he meticulously performed the ritual of the storing of the cushions. It was then his duty to escort the Striker from the hall. This involved walking down the long central aisle and was made all the slower by his tendency to drift from side to side, thereby, on average, increasing the length of the journey by about a third.

Eventually, however, they reached the entrance to the hall and the Assistant Cushion Bearer concluded his duties by executing a series of formal bows – another ritual, but one during which he invariably became confused and opted for starting again with much apologizing and sighing. When he finally reached the end, Bowlott turned and exited the hall with unusual speed for fear that the old man might be confused enough to begin bowing again. It was a relief to stride out freely for a little while – it was not easy following the Assistant Cushion Bearer even for someone of Bowlott's physical ineptitude. He really did not appreciate Krim missing the Close of Moot.

He had not gone far when he heard two sets of footsteps approaching from behind. He closed his eyes as he recognized both of them.

'Striker Bowlott, can you spare a moment?' Two voices, a droning tenor and a shrill descant bearing an unmistakable eastland accent confirmed his identification.

Bowlott surreptitiously increased his pace so that they had to scurry to catch him. 'Inner Senator Welt, Inner Senator Bryk,' he acknowledged, stopping suddenly as they reached him and watching their stumbling halt. 'How may I help you?'

Though there were many little cliques and cadres in the Moot, there were three major factions. The Keepers, whose members were drawn mainly from the families of the larger merchants and traders, came predominantly from Arvenstaat's cities and thus tended to dominate the Inner and Outer Moots. Then there were the Deemers who, typically, were clerks, lawyers and academics. As individuals, some of the Moot Senators were quite able, but a peculiarly incestuous blending of the Moot's ancient procedures and traditional loyalty to particular factions, subverted ability utterly and grievously detached the Moot from reality. Of the three factions, the Deemers were by far the furthest away. The third faction consisted of the Strivers, its members drawn from Arvenstaat's small traders, artisans and farmers. Confined for the most part to the Moot General, they were much given to pompous and impassioned rhetoric liberally sprinkled with earthy metaphor. Most of them affected intimate knowledge of a rugged working lifestyle though their manicured hands and expensive, well-tailored robes usually gave the lie to this.

Senators Welt and Bryk were the respective leaders of the Keepers and the Strivers, for the time being allies against the Deemers. Both were effectively permanent members of the Moot and both were unlovely. Bryk's bulging eyes and pursed mouth reminded Bowlott inexorably of a large, bad-tempered fish, and it was only with the greatest difficulty that he did not openly wince when his high-pitched and penetrating voice pierced its way through the Moot Hall's dull air. Welt's voice, by contrast, was profoundly soporific. Indeed, it was not uncommon for wagers to be made between the more frivolous Senators about the number of members that Welt would lure into sleep over any given time. He walked with a pronounced stoop but was still taller than Bowlott, and he had the look of a sad bloodhound.

They each took one of Bowlott's elbows and bent forward intently.

He raised silencing hands before they could begin to speak. 'Senators, I think I know why you wish to speak to me, but I have a pressing meeting on a most urgent matter.' He looked from one to the other taking some pleasure in seeing them exchange a glance, and watching their curiosity displacing their fawning confidentiality. They would not question him directly – that kind of thing was just not done; part of the art of the Moot debate was the ability to ask questions without seeming to, and also not answering questions while seeming to. Under normal circumstances Bowlott would have enjoyed seeing how Bryk and Welt played this scene but he was genuinely anxious about his pending meeting with Vashnar.

Although there were extensive informal working arrangements between lower ranking Wardens and equally low ranking Moot Officers, the relationship at the top was starchily formal. The two institutions which governed Arvenstaat each tacitly understood what was expected of them and took great pains to provide it without trespassing on the other's domain to any great degree. However, with Vashnar's proclaiming of the Death Cry and the consequent stirring up of the people, this balance had been disturbed and Bowlott had been placed in the invidious position of being seen to be 'doing something'. His immediate anxiety was not that he did not know what to do – that was normal – it was that he could not begin to start drafting a form of words that would look as if he did know. Vashnar's action had been far too practical and conspicuous for that. Worse, unlike these two dolts at his elbow, he hardly knew the man.

What were his weaknesses? Vashnar couldn't be ambitious, for where could he rise to from his present position? Greedy? Possibly, but this post carried many privileges and was well rewarded even excluding the Gilding – the long-established network that directed into his hands 'gifts' from grateful merchants and others who received particular protection from the Wardens. Perhaps he was vain? But that was unlikely to be a powerful lever even if he was. Lecherous? Women, men, boys?

The latter in particular was a weakness amongst certain high-ranking Wardens, but it was a dangerous trait, very unpopular with the people, and even if Vashnar was so inclined, Bowlott reasoned that he would be far too cunning and well placed to leave any chance of exposure open for discovery. Added to which, for what it was worth, he was married. It was a serious problem. He would have to make judgements about him as they spoke. This was something he quite enjoyed when meeting newly appointed Senators, full of enthusiasm and foolishness and easily crushed, but the Senior Commander of Arvenshelm's Wardens . . . ?

Despite these circling preoccupations, Bowlott could not resist tormenting his two companions by satisfying their curiosity while at the same time adding to it.

'I've asked Commander Vashnar to come to my office at Close today, and I'm sure you'll appreciate, it would be very discourteous of me to keep him waiting. However . . .' He set off walking again, startling them both. 'We can talk a little about your problems on the way.' He kept his eyes forward and maintained an unexpectedly rapid pace as the two men flapped after him. 'If I'm not mistaken, Senator Bryk, your members have been complaining about the number of their electors coming to speak to them about these Morlider rumours.' He did not wait for a reply. 'Tiresome business altogether. I sympathize. It's hard enough running the country without having electors bothering you every day with their petty problems.' He made an airy gesture. 'They do not have our breadth of vision, you see, gentlemen. And you, Senator Welt, have the same problem, because of the decline in trade with Nesdiryn. One can understand this a little more, but again, merchants, traders, well-meaning souls though they be for the most part, have little grasp of the problems we have to wrestle with, eh?' He looked expectantly at his entourage. 'Indulge me, have I read the times correctly?'

71

To his satisfaction there was quite a long pause before either replied. He could almost hear the clatter of confusion as their thoughts, 'Vashnar. What does he want to see Vashnar for?' vied with the need to answer his question.

Welt recovered first. 'Indeed, Striker,' he droned. 'As ever, you have your ear against the heart of the Moot.' Bowlott inclined his head modestly. 'But, if something has occurred of such importance that it requires you to meet directly with Commander Vashnar, we will, of course, not trouble you any further. Our concerns dwindle into insignificance.'

Bowlott waited.

'However,' Welt continued, 'as Senator Bryk and I are here with you, fortuitously – the greater part of the Moot as it were,' he made a peculiar rumbling sound which, even after many years of dealing with the man, Bowlott had to strive to remember was supposed to be a comradely chuckle, 'then perhaps we may be of assistance to you in your discussion with the Commander?'

Bryk, fish mouth seeking air, nodded in agreement.

Bowlott was surprised. This was a remarkably direct approach, especially from two such experienced Senators. Then again, he mused, they wouldn't be the first Senators to become a little strange as a result of being obliged to talk to their electors. Such people could be very unsettling: they brought in the pettifogging irritations of the outside world like a cold draught.

He pretended to ponder Welt's suggestion.

'I appreciate your gesture, gentlemen, especially as I know you're both very busy, but it would be . . .' he stretched out the pause '. . . inappropriate for you to become involved at the moment.'

That was enough, he thought. Keep them fluttering. He rapped his staff on the floor before either of them could pursue the matter. Out of habit, the two men stopped and bowed their heads at this signal of dismissal. Bowlott nodded to both of them and continued on his way. He allowed himself a peevish smile at the sound of scuffling and whispering behind him as the two men scurried off.

The smile vanished abruptly as just ahead of him Vashnar emerged from an adjoining passage. The Commander's leisurely but purposeful stride carried him in like a dark cloud, and Bowlott had the impression that the pictures, tapestries and statuary that decorated the walls of the long hallway were drawing away from him watchfully as he passed, while at the same time, paradoxically, Vashnar's bulk made everything look smaller. Involuntarily, Bowlott cringed. It was not an experience he was used to and it brought an immediate reaction. This was *his* domain. It was *other* people who cringed around here! Vashnar might be the Senior Warden Commander, but he still had things to learn about the Moot.

'Commander,' he called out, forcing himself to hurry forward.

The cloud paused and turned. Bowlott straightened as black eyes searched through him. His little eyes reflected the stare back.

'Striker Bowlott,' Vashnar acknowledged.

'Thank you for your promptness, Commander.'

Vashnar had Bowlott's message in his hand; he indicated it significantly. 'Close of Moot you . . . ordered . . . Striker. And Close of Moot it is.'

Aah. That hesitation. That quiet edge to the voice. Defensive about his position. A useful hint of weakness. A good starting point. Bowlott had to make an effort not to smile. He transformed the muscular impulse into a puzzled frown.

'May I?' he asked, reaching for the message. He was reading it and shaking his head as they came to his office.

Opening the door he ushered Vashnar into the ante-room ahead of him. The two Pages jumped to their feet, knocking over their board game.

'*Page*.' Bowlott's voice was stern; he waved the paper ahead of him like an irritable moth. 'One does not *order* the Senior Commander of the Wardens. By Request, is the ending for such a message. *By Request*. You should both know this by now.'

'But Striker . . .' The protest ended abruptly as a left foot swung rapidly up behind a right leg to deliver a kick without in the least disturbing the kicker's posture and demeanour.

'I . . . I apologize, Striker . . .' the protestor stammered, accurately reading his friend's suggestion and just managing to suppress the urge to reach down and massage his bruised leg.

Bowlott gazed skywards and directed a hand towards Vashnar.

Increasingly flustered, it took the Page a moment to understand the gesture. 'I apologize, Commander,' he managed eventually. 'I . . . made a mistake in interpreting the Striker's message. The blame is mine entirely. No offence was intended.'

Vashnar gave a non-committal grunt. With a parting glower at the two Pages, Bowlott motioned Vashnar towards the door to his office. The guilty Page rushed to open it, knocking the spilt remains of the board game across the floor on his way.

As he closed the door behind the two men, he simultaneously grimaced, bent down to rub his leg and mouthed a silent oath to be shared equally between Bowlott and his companion. Still rubbing his leg, he hopped over to join his friend, now standing by the voice tube, his expression gleeful.

Though the deep, tunnel-like doorway was high enough to accommodate him comfortably, Vashnar could do no other than stoop as he passed through it. The urge to remain stooped stayed with him as he emerged from the cave entrance into the heart of the Striker's world. The lamplit pallor, the grey oppression, the faded but almost total disorder, heightened by the occasional splash of tidiness, all conspired to ignite long-

74

forgotten memories of childish dreams when suffocating walls and ceiling would close around him until he jerked violently awake, shouting and gasping and beating the bedclothes. Though transient, the impression was disturbing and for a moment Vashnar could not move. Bowlott, still flushed with noting the Commander's sensitivity about his position, and his success in transferring the blame to the Pages, did not notice this demonstration of a far greater weakness.

All signs of Vashnar's momentary discomfiture had vanished completely by the time Bowlott had reached the central massif. He picked up a chair and placed it on the same side of the desk as his own. This would demonstrate his awareness of their equal status and further deflect blame for the 'By Order'. Vashnar looked at the chair warily before he sat down; it creaked uneasily under his bulk. The sound made him cast an equally wary glance around the over-burdened shelves as though it might signal the onset of a catastrophic avalanche of books and papers.

Bowlott misinterpreted the movement. 'You've never had the pleasure of coming to my den, have you, Commander?' He retraced Vashnar's glance around the room smugly. 'It rarely fails to impress. The collected wisdom of the Moot gathered here. Statutes, debates, precedents, modes of proceeding . . . everything is here. The heart of the government of Arvenstaat. The wisdom of the past enshrined for the guidance of the future.'

Vashnar had difficulty in not sneering outright. Part of him still wanted to choke. Dust, paper, disorder on a scale he'd scarcely have thought possible outside a natural disaster This could well be a metaphor for the way the Moot ran the country. And, continuing it, an inadvertent spark – perhaps from one of these lanterns – could end it all.

And out of the ashes . . .

He dismissed the thought quickly. Just as Bowlott did not

know him, so he did not know Bowlott other than by repute and through largely formal contacts. Whatever else he might seem to be, this fat clown now beaming proprietorially at him would be shrewd and capable, and quite probably ruthless in his own way. There was no saying how he might read a man.

'It's impressive indeed,' he said, confining himself to the comparatively safe ground of the truth. 'A marked contrast to my own office.'

Bowlott nodded understandingly. 'Yes, I imagine. The world of the man of action . . . austere,' he said, just avoiding the word 'simple' at the last moment. 'Constantly dealing with the immediate – with the misdeeds of the bad and the foolish. While we here must struggle with the more ponderous responsibilities of guiding the state through the years.'

Idiot. Get to the point.

There was a brief, awkward silence, then Bowlott leaned forward confidentially.

'Still, Commander, I've not asked you here to discuss our respective obligations. We both know what they are. Under your capable leadership, the Wardens fulfil their duties admirably, leaving the Moot free of disturbance to fulfil its duties in turn. Generally speaking, all is as it should be.' He gave a reluctant shrug. Seeing no other choice he would have to plunge right in. 'However, your declaration of the Death Cry has unfortunately caused . . . ripples.' He raised a protective hand before Vashnar could respond. 'I appreciate that your action was perfectly in order. There's no difficulty there. The Cry has never been a matter for the Moot, nor would any of us wish it to be. But the Death Cry, Commander – and against fellow Wardens.' He allowed himself raised eyebrows. 'I'm sure you're more aware than I am of the stir that it's caused – a stir that's now spread so far as to be felt even here. Hence my request for our unprecedented meeting.' As was usually the case, once he had started talking, the way ahead became clearer.

'To be honest, I'd thought the Death Cry moribund. I've never known it used before, but . . .' He gave a dismissive wave. 'My ignorance of such matters is of no consequence. Obviously you chose to use it because some extremely serious offence had been committed, but I felt that in the light of such seriousness, perhaps the Moot might be able to play a part in helping you resolve the affair.'

Vashnar shifted a little, making his chair creak again. Had Bowlott's opening remarks been in any way challenging to his authority, he would have had no compunction in discreetly telling him to mind his own affairs and walking away. The Moot was nothing without the Wardens to implement its will and no consequence would follow from such an action. He saw now however, that he had underestimated Bowlott's ability to slither around events – a foolish mistake. A deep self-anger threatened to stiffen his jawline. It was a pillar of Vashnar's vision of himself that he never did anything without careful thought and meticulous planning. So what in the name of sanity was he doing, making such an elementary error of judgement? It served only to compound the other foolish mistake he had made recently – the real cause of his anger – the proclaiming of the Death Cry against Thyrn and, worse, Hyrald and the others. It took him some effort to force the clamouring questions into silence and he achieved it only by making the resolution that this day – once he was free of this dust-choked lair – he would gather together his every personal resource, scattered since all this had started, and determine precisely why he had done what he had done. Then, and only then, could he set about reconstructing the plans of years which he had so strangely jeopardized.

He felt an ironic twinge of gratitude towards Bowlott. Had the wretched little man not inadvertently forced the issue, it is possible that he might not have steeled himself to this task until far worse consequences had ensued. And they *would* have ensued! Now there was merely the immediate problem of dealing with Bowlott's insinuating inquiry.

'I understand your concern, Striker Bowlott,' he began. 'And I appreciate your offer of assistance. Moot and Wardens are rather like draught horses . . .' Quoting the Treatise, eh? Bowlott thought, more than a little surprised. 'Independently, yet together, we draw the state along evenly and smoothly.' Vashnar risked extending Akharim's analogy. 'But sometimes the road is . . .' He hesitated.

'A little bumpy?' Bowlott offered incongruously.

Vashnar shook his head. 'Worse than that. The road is . . . no longer there. Swept away. Gone.'

Bowlott blinked and stared.

'Then one of us has to continue alone. Find a new way.' Like Bowlott before him, Vashnar was gathering confidence now that he had started. 'This is what has happened here. I can't tell you more at the moment, because I don't yet have the full measure of it – not yet found my way, as it were. Certain matters – Warding matters – have still to be resolved. But suffice it that something of the utmost seriousness has indeed happened and I shall advise you fully about it as soon as I can.' He let out a resigned breath. 'I'm afraid there's no way in which the Moot can help. I'm sorry if the incident has caused problems for any of the Senators, but please assure them that the matter is being pursued with the utmost vigour, and I've every hope that it will be concluded very shortly.'

Used to equivocation, Bowlott saw that he had done sufficient for the moment. That Vashnar was sitting in his office saying anything at all about the Death Cry made a strong enough point for the time being. The Commander now knew that the Moot had taken an active interest in his actions and that eventually, one way or another, he would have to give an account of them.

'That's most reassuring, Commander,' Bowlott said,

standing up. 'I'll pass it along to those Senators who've been asking about it, and we'll all look forward to your reporting on the matter in due course.'

Slightly unsettled by Bowlott's abrupt abandonment of the questioning, Vashnar also stood up. The chair let out a squeal of relief.

'Once again, my thanks for taking the time to come and discuss this with me, Commander. I appreciate it. You will remember to call on me at any time if you feel there's anything the Moot can do to assist, won't you?' Bowlott's arm directed Vashnar towards the cave entrance.

The two Pages were at their desks and working with studied diligence as Bowlott escorted Vashnar silently through the ante-room.

Walking through the corridors of the Palace, Vashnar felt strangely detached – his mind in one place, his body in another. The encounter with Bowlott had been no problem, but that dreadful room seemed to have numbed him. It was indeed like the heart of the government of Arvenstaat. Grey-edged, decaying and subtly menacing in its disorder, it was like something out of a nightmare. It confirmed the rightness of his own long-planned intentions, intentions already made more urgent now with increasing rumours of the Morlider islands appearing along the coast and hints of invasions from Nesdiryn in the west.

By an irony which eluded him, it was a diplomatic visit to Nesdiryn which had crystallized a long-felt dissatisfaction into a clear determination. He had merely glimpsed the two strange brothers who had ousted the Count, though their disturbing presence had been almost tangible as they scuttled through an audience chamber surrounded by their equally strange entourage. He had, however, met their Lord Counsellor Hagen and seen the Citadel guards and been impressed, almost over-awed, by both: Hagen, a powerful, frightening presence, single-mindedly ruthless in his determination to fulfil the will of his masters and to bring order to the land; the Citadel guards efficient and unquestioningly obedient and in conspicuous control of the streets.

Hagen it was who had given him the ring he now wore on his right hand. 'The Lords have noticed you, Commander,' he had said, fixing him with a penetrating gaze that Vashnar had had difficulty in meeting. 'They see things far beyond the sight of others, but even I can see you are one of us.' He leaned forward, the intensity of his gaze redoubling. 'Our time is coming. Above all things, there shall be order.' The quotation from his grandfather's Commentaries made Vashnar start despite himself.

How . . . ?

Before he could speak, Hagen had taken his hand and was placing the ring on his second finger. 'They offer you this gift. It is very special. It has been crafted to their design and their spirit enshrined in it will keep them ever watching over you.'

Circumstances had allowed Vashnar to make only a formal expression of thanks, but the gift and Hagen's manner had had a profound effect on him. The ring itself was simple and exactly to his taste, in so far as any form of personal adornment was to his taste. A stout black band held a small crystal set in a plain, highly polished, background. It fitted perfectly and he had worn it ever since. The thought of removing it unsettled him in ways which he felt ambivalent about and, after a while, the idea stopped occurring to him. Occasionally, when alone, he would stare at it. He thought that from time to time the crystal changed colour slightly – now faintly green, now blue, now clear – but it was the polished background that held him. It reflected images more clearly than any mirror he had ever seen, and years of wearing the ring had never diminished this. Once, standing in front of a mirror and casually raising a hand to his forehead the ring had reflected itself and, for an instant, he had seemed to see an infinitely deep well opening before him. It was full of lights and sounds and voices – calling out to him, reaching for him. The vision was gone as quickly as it had appeared and, just as quickly, he dismissed it.

Since that time, albeit for no apparent reason, the borders with Nesdiryn had gradually closed and the already infrequent diplomatic exchanges had been replaced by rumours carried by random travellers. Nevertheless, the memory of Hagen lingered powerfully with Vashnar and he continued to wear the ring.

He was thinking about Hagen and gently rubbing his thumb over the ring as he found himself entering his own office. He paused as he closed the door behind him, suddenly aware that he had no recollection of his journey after leaving Bowlott. He frowned and tried to recall the route he had followed, but nothing came. He had no memory of the long corridors, the stairs, the hallways, the people who would have stepped aside from him. There was just his formally polite parting from Bowlott, then nothing – only emptiness – until he was here. His frown deepened. None too soon had he made the resolution to pull himself together, to review the events that he had set in train and that seemed to be slipping away from him. The grey cobwebs from Bowlott's room formed around his mind. He shook his head to clear it then, opening the door slightly, called out to his aide: 'See that I'm not disturbed!'

The cobwebs returned, weighing in on him. Breathing heavily, he sat down at his desk. He was aware of his hands moving two writing tablets a little, then moving them back again to their original positions.

But they were a long way away . . .

At the end of a tunnel . . .

The cobwebs returned, closing over his eyes. Tighter and tighter, darker and darker.

Vashnar's fingers, resting on the desk, fluttered as if trying to brush them away, then his head slumped forward.

Chapter 7

Darkness.
Only darkness.

He was alone in it. He *was* it.

Darkness, motionless, yet rushing, tumbling, carrying all with it.

From nowhere, to nowhere, circling and spiralling. Forever.

Ever?

Time did not exist here.

Here? Nor was there here, or there.

Endings were beginnings; beginnings, endings. All things were one.

And nothing.

Yet terror was all about him. His . . .

And not his?

A wordless cry formed. It went rippling through the darkness, struggling with it.

For it did not belong. Nothing belonged. This place should not be, could not be . . .

Place?

This was all places, no places.

Darkness.

Nothing.

Nothing, and the terror, like cobwebs, folding and stirring the darkness, reaching through it, wrapping around it, clinging, choking.

And him. An awareness that knew itself now as Vashnar, though the knowledge rang emptily and without meaning. The cobwebs drifted apart at the touch of the terror that was his, a black wind amid the darkness.

What is this place?

Where is this place?

The questions too were meaningless. But they could do no other than be asked, just as the far-distant hands that were not his could have done no other than unnecessarily order his desk.

When had that happened?

He should know, but . . .

Other questions, darker ones, hovered.

Who am I?

What am I?

They must not be asked. They could not be answered. Not here. For cobwebs would surely leak into the emptiness that would follow. And then . . . ?

The darkness was ringing with the terror that was beyond doubt not his. Shrill and mindless like that of a child alone in the dark, save for the deep and cruel knowledge that had been laid down in ancient days when unseen and terrible hunters were always stalking beyond the light, at the edge of the vision.

Its call stirred its own kind within Vashnar, but he forbade it any rein. That much of him was tremblingly whole now. And this was not the cry of a child, for though it carried no words, no sign, he recognized it. It had touched him before, scattering everything that had bound his life together. Leading him to confusion and doubt. Bringing him to this.

Rage filled the darkness.

Thyrn!

The fear poured into him.

'Leave me be, demon, leave me be.'

Thyrn!

'Blood, fire, glittering blades, horror, mark your path. Let me be. Let me be free.'

No!

'Let me be!'

Such anger. Such fear.

Vashnar reached out in denial. This spirit – this spirit above all – must be bound. Its soaring freedom was a deep offence.

And a threat.

No! Two wills clashed, wringing and choking, like warring serpents.

From somewhere came a blow that racked Vashnar, fragmenting and scattering his tenuous awareness. The darkness itself shuddered under the impact, throwing him again into a tumbling emptiness.

Sinking, fading, a slow spiralling dwindling down towards . . .

Nothing.

Save a faint quivering line which questioned.

Was this all?

A quivering line, unbearable to look at.

A quivering line that was a sword-slash brightness cleaving through the darkness, turning silent desperation into a distant cry.

A wash of fear and hope – a flickering image of a longed-for haven – a vast teeming city, spanning from horizon to red-skyed horizon. But it was gone, and a face was staring at him intently, concerned, familiar. There were others with it. And a bright blue sky behind them.

Hyrald? The question boomed and echoed through his mind. As it swelled, the sky brightened, filling his eyes painfully and swallowing the faces.

The afternoon sun, low and searching, shimmered, rainbow-brilliant, off the polished facets of the crystal ink-stand that formed a centrepiece to the strategic array on his desk. It shifted, drawing him forward giddily. Instinctively he caught the edge of the desk to steady himself. Something fell wetly on to his hand. It was dark in his bleached vision. He became aware of his nose running. Another dark drop fell. Eyes blurring, he watched as it ran off his hand and formed a small, misshapen pool on the glistening wood.

Thyrn jerked forward violently into the waiting arms of Nordath, almost knocking him over. Nordath held him tightly. 'You're all right, you're all right,' he kept repeating desperately, as he restrained the struggling young Caddoran. 'You're safe. Don't be afraid.'

Hyrald and the others came running to them, alarmed, but Nordath motioned them not to interfere.

It was some time before Thyrn became calm enough for Nordath to risk releasing him.

'What happened?' Hyrald asked.

'I don't know,' Nordath replied.

Hyrald addressed the same question to Thyrn, who gazed up at him blankly. Though he appeared to be recovering, he was still pale and trembling. Hyrald saw that no matter what the answer to his question might be, Thyrn had just suffered a genuine fright. He used the insight to continue his interrogation. Whatever had happened to Thyrn and whatever condition he was in, this strange episode merely added to the many questions that had to be answered before they could continue their journey. Crouching down, he took Thyrn's arm.

'You gave us a fright. Particularly your uncle. Are you all right now?'

It took him some effort to affect a quiet concern, but it seemed to settle Thyrn further, though he replied only with a tentative nod of his head.

'Has anything like this happened before?' Hyrald pressed gently.

The nod became a shake then a nod again. Hyrald managed an encouraging smile. 'Is that a yes or a no?'

Thyrn lifted a hand as if to deflect the inquiry, then leaning on Hyrald, he stood up unsteadily. He looked younger and frailer than his years, but his voice was unexpectedly steady when he spoke. 'Something . . . similar has happened before but I can't talk about it. It's a Caddoran matter.'

Hyrald felt Rhavvan bridling and Adren shifted uncomfortably. He stepped close to Thyrn. His posture was confidential and protective, but his voice was quietly determined.

'I don't want to know anything about your Caddoran affairs, Thyrn, I've told you that. But there are things we need to know. We've travelled through some dangerous times these past days, and whatever we decide to do, there'll be more to come for sure. It's not been easy for any of us and you've handled yourself well, but if you're suddenly going to pass out without warning you can see that might be a problem, can't you?'

Thyrn turned away from him. 'I have to go north,' he said, gathering resolution from his questioner. 'Away from here. Away from . . .' He put his hands to his temples, though it was not a histrionic gesture. 'I have to get away from Vashnar. There are lands up there where we can hide. A great city . . .'

Despite himself, Hyrald could not disguise his irritation. 'Hiding, hiding. We can't spend the rest of our lives hiding.' He pointed to Rhavvan and Adren. 'We're Wardens. We, above all, know you can't hide for ever. No one can. Sooner or later, fugitives are always caught. Either that or they die dismally somewhere, alone, forgotten. Not to mention the fact that we've all got lives to live. Homes, friends, families back in Arvenshelm.'

He stopped. None of them could afford the self-indulgence of fretting about what they had left behind. That would merely add to their burdens. He forced himself to renew his assault as calmly as he could.

'As for this great city you keep talking about, it may just be a myth.' He pulled a sheet of paper from one of his pockets, unfolded it and smoothed it out noisily. 'We're still in Arvenstaat, but even *this* place isn't on the map. Look.' He tapped the paper. 'As for up there, there's no saying what there is, what dangers we might be walking into. Great cities, magic castles, lands full of gentle people carving, tending horses. All tales. And there are just as many tales of blasted lands, full of mists and swamps and tribes of wild creatures – scarcely human. And vast forests that no one who enters ever comes out of.' He managed to soften his manner. 'A few years ago – you're probably too young to remember – the gossip was all about a great war that was supposed to have been fought in the lands to the north. But that's all it was – gossip. The fact is, nobody knows anything about what's up there.'

Thyrn turned to his uncle but found no aid. For a moment Hyrald thought there was going to be a repeat of his mysterious collapse.

'Tell us what's frightening you,' he said urgently. 'Until you do that you're going to be a fugitive whether you stay here or keep running.'

Thyrn put his hands to his temples again and his face stiffened. 'I broke away from him. Pushed him out.' The words came out with great force, as if suddenly overcoming an obstacle. He looked both surprised and pleased with himself.

'Broke away, pushed who out, what do you mean?'

'Vashnar – broke away from him.'

Hyrald looked at Nordath for clarification but none came. 'When?' he asked, in the absence of greater inspiration.

Thyrn was down to earth. 'Now. Just now. When he tried to take me back. I pushed him out.'

Hyrald could only repeat, 'I don't understand. What do you mean?'

This time it was Thyrn who looked irritated. He spoke as to

a pestering child. 'When he came for me, just now. Tried to take me back. I got away from him.' Then he smiled, surprised and pleased again. 'Hit him, I think. Somehow.'

Noting the expressions on the faces of the three Wardens, Nordath intervened. 'How did he try to take you back, Thyrn?'

Thyrn tapped his head. 'In here. He's in here.' He was gaining confidence.

'He's nuts,' Rhavvan hissed to Hyrald. 'No wonder Vashnar wanted him brought in. Ye gods, we've been . . .' Hyrald motioned him to be quiet.

'You'll have to explain to us,' he said. 'We're not Caddoran, we don't understand.'

'Neither do I,' Thyrn said, abruptly angry. 'Not any of this. I don't even understand how I can do what I do. None of us do. We just do it.'

There was an uncomfortable pause. Hyrald risked the obvious. 'But how can Vashnar be in your . . . head . . . here, now?'

'I told you, I don't know. But he was here. The Joining I had with him . . .' Fear lit his face again.

'Joining?' Hyrald tried to make his query encouraging.

'Explain to them,' Nordath intervened. 'Tell them what a Joining is – that's no Caddoran secret, is it?'

Thyrn thought for a moment, eyeing his questioners, then let out a noisy breath. 'It's what happens when we're remembering messages. We just become very quiet inside, so that we can feel what a client wants – become like them – *become* them, to some extent – hence, Joining. I can't explain it any better than that.' His tone was final.

Hyrald gave the accepting shrug of someone who is none the wiser but grateful and anxious to press on. 'Tell us about "Joining" with Vashnar, then.'

Thyrn's manner changed again. As he spoke, he began to gesticulate and his voice became more emphatic, as though he was now anxious to explain himself fully. 'For some reason, what I do is much deeper – more intense – than for most other Caddoran. So I'm told anyway – I wouldn't really know, would I? Anyway, it's something like that, and that's why I'm so good at my job. That's why I got the job with Vashnar.' He wrinkled his nose in distaste.

'Caddoran to the Senior Warden is a much coveted post. Normally there's fierce competition for it within the Congress,' Nordath added by way of explanation.

Hyrald, however, was struggling with what Thyrn was saying. In his fairly limited dealings with Caddoran he had reached the commonly held conclusion that they were all 'a bit odd', but in so far as he had ever thought about how they worked he had imagined that they simply listened, remembered and repeated, like trained birds.

'You say, you almost *become* your client when you're taking their message?'

'Yes.'

'And when you're passing the messages on?'

'The same.'

Hyrald closed his eyes and thought for a moment, unconsciously imitating the Caddoran technique of feeling into the intention of the young man standing in front of him. When he opened them again, the sunlight, the shelter, the trees, everything, seemed a little brighter.

'And you became Vashnar?' he asked carefully.

Thyrn's confidence faltered. 'Vashnar's . . . strange,' he said, though the hesitation was more telling than the description. 'He gave me the creeps from the start.' The confession was almost blurted out. 'When I made my first Joining with him, it was like going into a dark cellar.' He shuddered. 'I got used to it, of course. I'd been told that some people are peculiar to deal with and because of what I am – what I do – I'd be more susceptible to such things than most. I had to be detached, professional. Get on with my job. They spent more time telling me that than teaching me anything. I mustn't let the Congress down, they said. It was a great honour to be given such a position so young. And good money too.'

Hyrald could not help smiling at the incongruous mixture of mature man and immature youth that Thyrn presented.

'But it didn't get any easier. In fact, it got worse the more I worked with him. There was always something frightening about him. Like something in the darkness, lurking there. Waiting to spring.'

'Monsters under the bed,' Rhavvan snorted, unable to contain himself. Hyrald angrily gestured him silent, but Thyrn did not respond to the jibe. He simply looked straight at Rhavvan.

'No, I'm not a child, afraid of shadows,' he said. 'I'm a Caddoran and a good one. I know my job. This was real. Very real. Very . . . disturbing. And it was there when I related the messages too. You could see it in people's eyes sometimes. Fear. Nothing bad in the message that I could hear, nothing in the words, but something behind them. Something that came out when I spoke them. Something of Vashnar's.'

There was silence. A light touch on his leg made Hyrald start. It was Endryk's dog sniffing at him. The shoreman was standing nearby. He made a gesture to indicate that all was well. His arrival, however, was a reminder to Hyrald that time was against them. It had been a risk allowing Oudrence to leave, but with Endryk to guide him on his way, the alternative of abandoning him here was peculiarly repellent. However, there was no saying how soon the young man might make contact with other Wardens and what the consequences of that might be. And too, for all Endryk's protestations about their indifference to events in Arvenshelm, the local villagers could yet prove to be a problem.

Thyrn began speaking again. 'It didn't bother me too much

at first. A job's a job. Don't get involved. Nothing bad was actually happening, after all. I tried to make a game of it – would this message be a frightener or not? That kind of thing. But as I said, it got worse. In the end I couldn't do anything but try to ignore it – pass the messages on as quickly as I could. Get rid of them.' He waved his hands as if shaking something off them. When he spoke again, he was weighing his words carefully, as though thinking aloud. 'The thing is, I think it might have been working both ways. He used to look at me very strangely sometimes. As if he'd picked up something from *me*.' He turned to Nordath. 'I wonder if he's part Caddoran?'

Nordath's eyes widened, but he did not reply, other than to answer Hyrald's unspoken question.

'Whatever faculty it is that enables Caddoran to do what they do, they don't practise their techniques on one another,' he explained. 'Strange things can sometimes happen to them when they Join to their own kind. Bad things. They get entangled in some way – can't separate. It's very bad. Caddoran have gone insane in the past, just experimenting. It's not something that's widely known. The Congress prefers to keep quiet about it. Hardly good for business if word gets about that using a Caddoran might drive you mad, is it?'

Hyrald was genuinely surprised. Like all Wardens, he prided himself on being worldly-wise, on knowing something about everything and he was always a little affronted when this proved not to be the case. It reinforced the prejudices that as a member of a closed group he had for other closed groups. 'I'd say, not widely known is a considerable understatement,' he retorted acidly.

'This is getting us nowhere,' Rhavvan intruded bluntly. He had interpreted Endryk's return as Hyrald had.

'Rambling off into the blue beyond isn't going to get us anywhere either,' Adren spoke up, untypically forceful. 'We need to know what's going on and Thyrn's the only one who can tell us.' Hyrald was glad of his sister's intervention. He would wish for no one better than Rhavvan at his back in a crisis, but patience was not one of his stronger traits and he was always inclined to act in preference to thinking.

'I'm sorry, Rhavvan. It's all my fault, isn't it? I did something wrong.' The apology came quietly and unexpectedly from Thyrn. It took all of them by surprise. Already faced down once by the young man, Rhavvan gaped. An odd sound emerged which eventually slithered into, 'No, not really. It's just that . . .' before fading away into a vaguely reassuring gesture. The others too, responding similarly to this unsought offering, eased forward hesitantly, making a protective ring about Thyrn. Endryk watched the group keenly.

Hyrald took back the initiative. 'It's Vashnar's fault,' he said categorically. 'Don't think otherwise for a moment. Whatever you did wrong – if anything – didn't warrant even the Cry, let alone the Death Cry. And the rest of us have done even less than you.' A momentary anger at their situation burst out. 'Besides, nothing warrants the Death Cry, for mercy's sake, not these days! We're supposed to be civilized. We don't hunt down people like animals. We don't—' He stopped himself. 'Anyway, what we have to do now is find out what happened so that we can decide where we go. Try to tell us why you ran away from Vashnar. It's very important.'

'It's difficult,' Thyrn said in a low voice. 'It wasn't just one particular thing. It had been building for a long time. The sense of menace I felt whenever I Joined with Vashnar gradually got worse – and it was obviously leaking into his messages, judging by the responses I was getting from listeners. I think I was telling them much more than he intended.' He straightened up. 'I must have been. He began asking me about my Oath. Did I understand what it meant – confidentiality? Did I understand what happened to Caddoran who were indiscreet? Those black eyes look right through you, you couldn't hide

93

anything from him even if you wanted to.'

He shivered. 'I told him, yes, of course I did. It's hammered into you incessantly at the Congress. But I could feel his doubt.' His eyes flicked around the watching group and he took two very deep breaths. 'Then, one day, we were sitting in his office. He seemed to be very relaxed. Jolly almost. As if something very good had just happened.' Rhavvan and Adren exchanged a look of conspicuous disbelief. 'He was giving me a routine message to one of the District Commanders. Nothing special. Something about moving men from one patrol to another . . .'

'Speak it,' Nordath suggested.

Thyrn waved his hands agitatedly. 'No, no. It's all one. It'll bring it back.'

'It's all right,' Hyrald said hastily. 'The message probably isn't important. Besides, we really don't want you to break your Oath. Carry on with your tale. And don't be afraid.' Thyrn looked at him fearfully. 'Nothing around here can hurt you,' Hyrald added, waving a hand across the rolling green countryside.

Thyrn took another deep breath. 'We were sitting there. Very relaxed. The sun was pouring in through that big window he has. Then . . . no warning . . . it's dark. There's a dreadful smell. Stinging smoke, a rancid rottenness.' He put his hand to his stomach. 'And something like burning meat – but it wasn't meat – it was people.' He shuddered and looked desperately at Nordath. 'How could I know that, Uncle? I've never smelt anything like that.'

'Don't worry, tell your tale, get it out. We'll talk about it all afterwards.' Nordath's voice was as strained as his nephew's.

'I knew everything that was there. Not how it came to be, you understand. But like in a dream. It makes no sense but you recognize each part.' He stopped.

'Darkness,' Hyrald prompted. 'You were in the darkness.'

Thyrn shook his head. 'Not completely dark. There were

flames all around. Lighting up great columns of smoke. Lighting up the clouds. The city was burning, the whole countryside was burning. And terrible cries. All around, terrible cries. People screaming – in fear and pain – awful sounds. But worse than that, I was filled with terrible feelings – feelings I shouldn't have – that no one should have. Feelings there aren't any words for.' He leaned forward, face intense and finger jabbing accusingly. 'And Vashnar was at the heart of it. Willing it on. Willing on a great tide of destruction and pain. Sweeping everything aside. Crushing everything underfoot. And delighting in it – delighting in it.'

Thyrn's manner and voice had changed completely. He was no longer a confused and inadequate young man. He was a commanding presence. And so vivid was his telling that Hyrald could almost feel the vision taking shape inside him.

'He was there? Vashnar? You saw him?' he asked.

'He was everywhere. The vision wasn't his, something he was thinking – it *was* him. The essence of him. There was no mistaking that. Blood, destruction, horror. Something out of control. He'll make it happen. He'll not stop until it's everywhere. It's what he is. Even if he doesn't know it.'

Despite himself, Rhavvan was as held by Thyrn's transformation as the others. To steady himself, he searched for the ordinary. 'Perhaps it was just your imagination – a dream – drowsing in the sunshine. Vashnar can frighten hardened criminals. It'd be easy for you to misunderstand him.'

A slow gesture from Thyrn dismissed the suggestion. 'I know my inner ways, Rhavvan. I mightn't be able to wield a sword, but I can focus my mind as sharp as any blade. I told you, I'm good at my job. I don't nod off, drift away, least of all when I'm working, any more than you do. And if I dream, I know I'm dreaming, and I control what's happening.' His voice was unequivocal.

'How long did this go on?' Hyrald asked, though the

inadequacy of the question rang through the words even as he spoke them.

Thyrn ignored it. 'Then it was over. I was in his office again, in the sunlight. Vashnar was staring at me. His face was demented: I've never seen anything like it. Every line of it shone with what I'd just seen. As if it were just a mask – like a piece of paper thrown on a fire – alive and charring before bursting into flames. And he was going to kill me. I was still Joined with him enough to feel myself dying at his hands.' He became increasingly agitated. Both Hyrald and Nordath reached out to support him. 'He had the excuse already – a knife put in my hand – he was just thinking how to do it, analysing the quickest, the cleanest way. I don't know why he didn't do it. I couldn't move. But he just sat there, as if he was paralysed – or something was holding him there.' He stopped, then looked at Nordath, realization in his eyes. 'He *is* part Caddoran! He was experiencing my fear at the same time as I could feel him working out how to kill me. That's why he couldn't move.' The thought seemed to calm him and he nodded to himself as if to confirm it. 'And suddenly I was free. I remember a great clattering – my chair falling over, I think – and Vashnar's voice, slow and echoing. Then nothing but running, running, confusion – until I was at your house, Uncle.'

There was a long silence.

'Which leaves us where?' Adren said eventually.

'I don't know,' Hyrald replied. 'That's everything?' he asked Thyrn.

'That's everything,' Nordath replied on his nephew's behalf. He seemed to be the most disturbed of the group.

'What do you think it means?' Hyrald asked him.

Nordath grimaced. 'It means what it means, Hyrald. You'll have to excuse me a moment. I don't know what Vashnar is, but I know I'm part Caddoran, and being so close to Thyrn when he told us that has . . .' He turned away hurriedly, bent forward and vomited. Endryk's dog backed away, ears flattened against its head.

Adren moved to help Nordath, but was waved aside for her pains.

'Sorry,' Nordath said simply, when he had recovered. 'I didn't realize how involved I was getting. I should've been more careful.'

'This is all beyond me,' Rhavvan said, torn between his impatience and concern for the patent distress of Thyrn and Nordath.

'It's beyond all of us,' Hyrald said.

'But it's what happened,' Nordath said. 'Make of it what you will. Thyrn's answered the question you asked him, and answered it honestly, I can vouch for that. It's not his fault it makes no sense. But I'll tell you this much, there's certainly something seriously wrong with Vashnar.'

'Or Thyrn,' Rhavvan suggested.

Nordath shook his head. '*I* felt Vashnar here just now,' he said. 'The only thing that's wrong with Thyrn is he's frightened witless. And so am I now – and by more than having the Death Cry called on me. That's why I threw up.'

'Which leaves us where?' Adren repeated her question.

'Still at the back end of nowhere and not knowing where to go,' Hyrald replied sourly. Thyrn's explanation had disturbed him. At one time even he thought he had felt Vashnar's presence. He was satisfied that, at the very least, Thyrn believed what he was saying and he had known Nordath long enough to know that he too was telling the truth as he saw it. Yet he could make little of this fevered vision of Vashnar. He knew the man to be intense and obsessive and even in the ordinary contacts he had with him in the line of duty, there was always an aura of restrained violence about him. But that was not uncommon amongst senior officers. Most of them, himself included, had risen to where they were by virtue of their effectiveness in keeping the peace on the street, and that invariably meant both proficiency with fist and baton and perhaps even sword, and a ready willingness to use all three. But this explanation was not enough. Thyrn's extraordinarily vivid telling seemed to have stripped layers of his own vision of Vashnar, exposing him as . . .

As what?

A madman?

A madman filled with dreams of wanton destruction?

That still did not sit easily with even his grimmest view of Vashnar. If he was filled with anything, Hyrald would have judged it to be the bringing of order to everything, not the chaos that Thyrn had described.

He veered away from the topic.

'Did you see Oudrence safely on his way?' he asked Endryk.

'Yes,' the shoreman replied. 'Got him some food from the village and set him on the right road. I don't think he's going to enjoy himself walking and sleeping rough, especially with that bad shoulder, but he's got a better chance than if he'd started from here. He's young and tough enough, he should be all right.'

'And the villagers? What did they have to say?'

'Nothing. They never saw him. I took him around the village.'

Hyrald's eyes narrowed. 'Why? You weren't concerned about what the villagers might think yesterday.'

Endryk shrugged. 'Went with my instinct. Your tale – Wardens all the way up here – killings. Something serious has obviously happened. Perhaps best the villagers didn't know anything about you being here. That way, if any more Wardens come, they can tell the truth. They've seen nothing.'

Hyrald's scrutiny of the shoreman intensified. 'Why are you helping us?'

Endryk smiled broadly. 'I saved your lives, I'm responsible for you now.'

'Or, some would say, we belong to you.'

'Whichever – I want neither burden.' Endryk gave a clipped, military bow. 'You're all free to go.'

'You're avoiding my question.'

Endryk's expression became serious. 'If I'd needed a reason for helping you I'd have left you on the shore. But I'm entitled to look at what I've dragged ashore, aren't I? Three law-keepers of sorts, a city dweller and a . . .' He looked at Thyrn. 'And him. All of you lost, floundering.' Rhavvan scowled at the expression, 'of sorts,' but did not speak. The dog moved to Endryk's side. 'There's harshness in you three, for sure, if needs be, but I can see no deep malice in any of you. I told you, I use my instinct. There's a stench of injustice about you – perhaps something worse after what I've just heard.'

'Your instinct could be wrong.'

Endryk laughed softly. 'Indeed it could. But I use my head as well.'

Hyrald's brow furrowed.

'If you'd been fugitives from justice you'd have killed Oudrence on the beach and me as soon as you were safe ashore.'

Hyrald started slightly, disturbed as much by Endryk's simple, matter-of-fact tone as by what he said. He did not know what to say next.

Not so Thyrn. 'You're not Arvens, are you?' he announced abruptly. 'Where are you from?'

Endryk looked at him enigmatically. 'Far, far away,' he said quietly.

Thyrn pointed at him. 'You're from up there, from the north,' he said triumphantly, looking round at the others.

Though it made no sound, the dog slowly curled its upper lip to reveal a row of powerful teeth, bright in the sunlight.

Chapter 8

Vellain's slender nose followed the line of her forehead, giving her a stern profile. She had a rather small mouth with lips that were so clearly defined they might have been shaped by a master carver. They were more voluptuous than they tended to seem at first glance. Her dark brown hair was short, immaculately groomed and unmoving. It never changed. She was not particularly tall for a woman, but the way she carried herself made others think of her so. Yet it was not just a straightness of posture or a carriage of the head; she had some other quality that sustained this illusion, perhaps aided by her brown, searching eyes. But whatever it was it remained with her even when she was in the presence of her husband, despite the fact that he was conspicuously taller than she was.

As she came into the room, her glance dismissed a hovering servant. Neither she nor he made any concession to the deep silence pervading the room and the purposeful sound of their intersecting footsteps on the polished wooden floor echoed unashamedly through it as the servant left and she moved straight to a chair at the side of the wide fireplace. Though upholstered and comfortable, the chair nevertheless had a spartan, utilitarian look about it, as did almost everything in Vashnar's house.

On his appointment to the position of Senior Commander of the Arvenshelm Wardens – the highest position in the Service – Vashnar had declined the official residence that went with the post. As was his way, he had given no explanation, though Hyrald, who had been his aide on the day he had taken possession of the building, had noted a slight movement of his mouth which said everything.

'Didn't like it one bit,' he told his colleagues authoritatively when he returned to his own district. 'I didn't think he would. All that luxury the old man used to go for. Plush chairs, carpets you have to part with your hands to get through, paintings, statues, tapestries, fancy furniture littering the place. Not for Vashnar at all. Mind you . . .' He allowed himself a significant pause and a knowing expectation lit up his audience. 'He seemed more interested in the mirrors in the master bedroom than I'd have thought.' Applause and loud laughter greeted this revelation. Then: '"I shall remain in my present house. This place isn't suited to my needs. It'll serve for official functions, guest accommodation and the like."' Amongst his near equals and well away from his Commander, Hyrald could safely imitate Vashnar's voice and the characteristically curt gesture that accompanied his pronouncement.

Vashnar did not move as Vellain sat down and silence returned. He was sitting directly opposite the wide, empty grate, staring at the stark, heat-marred ironwork, unhidden by any decorative summer screen. He had been there since he returned home.

Vellain did not speak. She was waiting for a sign which would tell her the reason for his unusual silence. Instinct told her that it was probably something to do with Thyrn and the Death Cry, though what it might be she could not hazard. There were many questions that she needed to have answered about that business, but it was no longer a major topic of the moment and she had already made her own resolution to wait patiently for an opportunity to ask them.

Not that she was too concerned about this present silence. She had complete faith in her husband. Not blind faith by any means, for Vellain was not a woman to follow anyone. More correctly, her faith was in her husband and herself. She had assessed the rising young Warden from their first meeting as being one who could go far, with the right kind of guidance. At the same time she had determined that she was the only one who would provide that guidance. And she had. Moulding his stern, ambitious character, discreetly sustaining him on the rare occasions when he had looked like faltering, and generally making good in her own image such faults as manifested themselves as they grew together.

And too, she loved him. That part of her was blind. The sight of him at that same first meeting had been like a physical blow. One which had redirected her life and from which, for all her clear eye and calculating nature, she had never fully recovered.

Nevertheless, the past weeks had been more difficult than any other time she could remember. The proclaiming of the Death Cry had surprised and shocked many people, but it had disturbed Vellain badly. There was an arbitrariness about the act which was quite unlike her husband, but worse by far was the explanation she had eventually forced out of him on the night of the deed.

'He was in my mind, Vellain. Inside it. And more. He seemed to take possession of me. I could feel thoughts being drawn out of me. Thoughts I didn't even know I had. He must know everything. Everything!'

As the words had stumbled out she had felt the foundations of her life shudder. This pillar of a man, her creation, the centre of her life, had gone insane. Kneeling beside him, she gripped the arm of his chair as though that might somehow hold back her rising panic. Condemnation of her husband's unbelievable folly rose up inside her like vomit. Then, on the verge of voicing her disbelief and fury, a saving image formed amid the turmoil and stopped her. An image of Thyrn.

The young Caddoran had routinely brought her personal messages from Vashnar and whenever she had listened to him, she had always had the feeling that it was her husband addressing her directly. That was the art and skill of the Caddoran, of course, a matter for applause and appreciation, though with Thyrn the sense of her husband's presence was far more intense than anything she had ever experienced before. With most Caddoran there was always some element of studied mimicry: subtle inaccuracies in gesture, posture, facial expression that distanced the sender from his messenger, albeit only slightly. But not with Thyrn. She had always felt uneasy about the way he brought the totality of her husband to her. His youth served only to compound this disturbing impression.

The recollection of Thyrn's strangeness brought calmer thoughts in its wake, reminded her of the certainties in her life. Vashnar had the qualities of a great leader, but even in madness he would not have had the imagination to think of something like this. And his manner now was not, after all, hysterical, still less deranged. Then too, he had said what he had said, knowing what it must sound like, when he could equally well have fabricated some plausible lie to explain what had happened. He had turned to her with the truth, or with what he perceived to be the truth, knowing he could rely on her support absolutely. He needed her.

Her anger vanished. She must be strong for him now. She must be strong for both of them. Looking at him as she reached this conclusion it came to her, entwined around the image of Thyrn, that her husband was the way he was now because he must be struggling with something he had never known before. Something had happened which was not only frightening but which he did not begin to understand. His obsessive nature would not respond well to that.

Threads of clarity began to form in the confusion. Obviously, they told her, whatever had occurred had been deeply strange, and Vashnar had misinterpreted it; grievously so, by the sound of it. Exactly what it had been she would have to discover but that would need a quieter time. For now, it would probably be better for her to focus on the action he had taken, and its likely consequences, and determine how these could best be turned to advantage.

Forcing herself to calmness, she spoke to him like a parent seeking clarification of a serious misdeed from a normally well-behaved child. 'And you've proclaimed the Death Cry against Hyrald and the others as well?' Vashnar seemed grateful for the tone of the question.

'No choice, Vellain. No choice. It was a mistake to send them after him in the first place. I realized that almost as soon as I'd done it.'

That was good. He had never been afraid to admit an error to her; he was rational and at least trying to take command of himself.

'The look on his face, Vellain . . .' He shook his head. 'No, not just the face. More than that. His thoughts. They swept over me in a great rush. I felt them, just as if they were my own, but I could tell they weren't. Don't ask me what was happening, but that's what it was. And he'd seen something he shouldn't have and he knew it. He even knew I was going to kill him – then and there – at the very instant I was thinking about it.'

He fell silent.

Vellain was staggered by this last revelation. She knew her husband was capable of extreme violence, it had been a necessary part of his job in the early years. Indeed, she found it not unattractive. But even to have contemplated so public an assassination was more startling than the proclamation of the Death Cry itself.

'But?' she prompted after a moment, controlling her voice with difficulty.

Vashnar frowned. 'Something stopped me. I couldn't move. Couldn't move! As though part of me were terrified.'

Vellain waited.

'Then he was gone.' The events having been forced into words, Vashnar was slowly becoming his normal self. 'Fortunately there was no one in the outer office, because I don't think I could have moved if they'd come in. And I don't know how long I sat there.'

'So you sent Hyrald and the others after him?'

Vashnar grimaced. 'Yes. They were the nearest. Handle it quietly, I thought. I don't know what possessed me. I mustn't have been thinking properly.' He straightened up. 'I *wasn't* thinking properly. I knew he was going to blurt out what had happened to anyone he met – Caddoran Oath or not. I knew it. Rhavvan wouldn't be a problem. He's just a plodding Warden, he'll do as he's told. But Hyrald would have been suspicious at the least, and you know him, he never gives up. Too much of a street Warden. It's a shame, but we'd have had to deal with him sooner or later – and that sister of his.' Vellain nodded; it was a matter they had discussed in the past.

'Hence the Death Cry for all of them.'

'For all of them,' Vashnar confirmed. 'There wasn't time to have them dealt with discreetly. I'd no one immediately to hand who could've done it. The idea of the Death Cry just came to me out of nowhere.' He gave a bitter grunt. 'One of the advantages of my assiduous study of our history, my dear. Ideal, I thought. The mob would do the job before Thyrn or the others had a chance to be heard.'

But while none of the fugitives had apparently spoken out, the mob *hadn't* done the job, Vellain mused as she sat watching her silent husband staring into the dead grate. Hyrald was not only able, he was popular. Almost certainly someone had warned him, and more than a few would have helped him. The only redeeming factor of his escape was that he was now probably far from both Arvenshelm and help. The latest rumours were that the group was fleeing north. All in all, it was a better conclusion than it had promised to be, not least because it removed Hyrald from any opportunity to oppose Vashnar's plans. And too, she reflected, the resurrection of this ancient form of justice had brought an uneasiness – a tension – to the streets, which she was sure could be used as an excuse for Vashnar to recruit new Wardens and increase his already considerable power.

It concerned her a little however, that since that day, she had been unable to persuade her husband to discuss in more detail what had happened during his encounter with Thyrn. Something told her that it could not be allowed to lie, to fester unseen. Who knew what harm might come of it, mouldering in the darkness? But a range of approaches, from the oblique to the very direct had failed to elicit anything other than an offhand dismissal.

'Some other time, my dear.'

In the end, sensing that further effort might serve only to build up resistance, she had resolved to retreat and to watch and wait. Sooner or later, an opportunity would present itself and she must be ready.

Could it be now? she wondered. Vashnar had arrived home unexpectedly and had been unusually silent. Something bad had happened, she could sense it, and though the only outward sign of anything out of the ordinary had been a bloodstained kerchief, she could not shake off the feeling that Thyrn was involved in some way.

'Trouble with a prisoner?' she had asked as casually as she could, though she knew that Senior Wardens rarely had anything to do with prisoners. Her concerns were confirmed when she received only a cursory headshake by way of reply.

Now, long into his silence, she tried again.

'Reading the coals?' she asked with a smile.

Vashnar turned to her blankly.

'Reading the coals?' she repeated, still smiling. It was a game they played in the winter months: watching the progress of the flames hissing and spitting through a landscape of glowing coals; wagering which crag would be the first engorged, which valley filled and choked, which sheer face would suddenly spall and crash to fill the black air with bright fleeing sparks. The whole like a distant and terrible battlefield where weapons beyond imagining were being used, and where all led inexorably to a great levelling and a dull grey death.

He glanced back at the dead grate, but did not respond to her irony. It gave her the opportunity she needed. She reached forward and laid a hand on his arm. 'What's the matter?' she said simply.

Vashnar met her gaze. It urged him on. He patted her hand then placed the ends of his fingers against his forehead. 'Thyrn,' he replied.

'Has he been caught?' Vellain asked urgently, torn between exhilaration and fear that perhaps the errant Caddoran had made public what he had discovered.

Vashnar frowned and closed his eyes. 'No. I've no idea where he is, except that Hyrald's still with him – and presumably the others – and that he wants to flee, to hide.'

Vellain's brow furrowed. 'How do you know?' she asked, suddenly anxious. 'Has someone seen them, spoken to them?'

Vashnar pressed his fingers into his forehead again, harder, as he shook his head. 'No. He . . . touched . . . me again. Got into my mind.' His face was angry when he turned to her but she could tell that the anger was not directed at her. 'Everything we know tells us they're somewhere up north by now, but somehow he reached out and got into my mind – just as he did when he was sitting opposite me.'

His eyes hardened and his jaw set. 'I think, in due course, we'll have to curtail the entire Caddoran Congress as well. We don't want to risk any more like him.'

Vellain's original concerns for her husband's sanity returned to full force at this further alarming revelation and it was only with a desperate rehearsal of her previous reasoning that she managed to keep her voice calm. 'That's a detail,' she said quickly. Shocked though she was, she had sufficient presence of mind to note that whatever had happened it had brought the subject out into the light again and it must not be allowed to slip away, as well it might if her husband retreated into the reassuring practicality of his future intentions. She must concentrate on the simple, immediate reality. 'But that's for later. Much later. Let's deal with the present, now. Tell me exactly what happened. All of it.'

Her manner jolted the tale out of him, but his voice became increasingly clipped and dismissive, as if the words were an offence to him. He fell silent for a moment when he had finished, then added hesitantly, 'I wonder if I'm going mad.'

Without hesitation, Vellain spoke the answer she herself had reached before. 'No. You haven't the imagination. You're as sane as I am. And you're right, we'll have to deal with the Caddoran Congress eventually. They're a peculiar crowd at the best and there was always something *very* odd about Thyrn. Having him here, reciting your messages, was like having you here in person. As if he'd stolen part of you.' She shuddered. It was a genuine reaction. 'But listening to you, it seems he wants to have nothing to do with you. All he wants to do is run away. Perhaps he doesn't want this linkage any more than you do. But perhaps he has no control over it.' She felt calmer. Her voice became authoritative and confident. 'He won't come back. In fact, I can't see any of them trying to come back. Not in the immediate future anyway. And if they do come back in due course, it won't matter, will it? It'll be too late. I think you should just forget about him. Either they'll leave the country or they'll be found, and if they're found they'll probably be killed.'

'And if they're not?'

Vellain's hand tightened around his arm. 'If they're not, then who's going to believe Thyrn? A demented Caddoran, thrust into too responsible a position at too young an age. Encouraged to breach his Oath by a doting relative and three corrupt Wardens.' She brightened, ideas flowing now. 'It may even be better if he does come back. It'll give you a first-class opportunity to start discrediting all the Caddoran. They've been grossly negligent, after all, putting so frail a creature in so sensitive a position. They did virtually thrust the lad on you.' She slipped out of her chair and knelt by him conspiratorially. 'They might even have done it as a deliberate act to discredit you, or spy on you, for who can say what sinister motives? They're such strange creatures, aren't they?'

Vashnar freed his arm and put it around her head, drawing her close to him.

'We do well, you and I,' he said.

'Indeed we do,' she replied.

They were silent for a while. Then Vashnar leaned back and closed his eyes. 'But why did this happen? How did he do it? It can't be possible to just . . . get into someone's head, take their thoughts like that.'

'Why does a cat land on its feet when you drop it? How does a fly land on a ceiling? Who knows?' Vellain was witheringly dismissive. She abandoned her prayer-like attitude and dropped back into her chair. 'Who cares? There'll always be more questions than answers. Leave them to the academics, the teachers, it'll stop them worrying about other things. You live in the real world – a world in desperate need of the order you can bring as Dictator. Morlider off the coast, menace from Nesdiryn, the Moot in decay – that's all you need to concern yourself about.'

'But if it happens again?'

Vellain shrugged. 'It happens. What's a headache and a nose

bleed? You've had worse than that in your time. If anything like it happens again, just tell me. We'll talk about it for five minutes – see if anything's to be learned from it – then get on with more important matters. Tell me what Bowlott wanted.'

But Vashnar was not prepared to let the subject go so easily. 'No. It's not that simple. You don't know what it was like – you can't. Lost, floundering in the dark, not knowing who I was, where I was, even *if* I was. What if it happens when I'm out on some public duty or in the middle of a meeting?'

It was a difficult question but Vellain bounced back an answer before she even thought about it. 'Why should it? It hasn't happened before.' She paused. 'But I don't think it will. Not while you're busy, your mind occupied. I think you had to be alone and quiet, and maybe he had to be the same, wherever he is.'

'But . . . ?'

Vellain was dismissive again. 'But if it does, if you pass out in the middle of something, so what? We'll say it's something you ate. Even a Senior Commander of the Wardens isn't immune to a stomach upset, is he?' She became intense. 'This is all working our way. Tension on the streets, Hyrald and his sister – always a potential problem – gone, Senators beginning to scuttle about. All to the good. Now tell me about Bowlott.'

Her manner lifted Vashnar out of the lingering remains of his dark reverie.

'Nothing much,' he said. 'Impertinent little goat actually *ordered* me to come and see him, then blamed it on some Page.' He screwed up his face in distaste. 'He's a wretched creature. And that office of his – it's appalling. I thought I was going to choke to death with the dust. There must be things in there that haven't been moved since Marab's time. And not a vestige of daylight. Dreadful place – typical of the whole Moot. The sooner the torch is put to the lot, the better.'

'But what did he want?'

'Just being nosy, that's all. The Death Cry's none of his business but he wanted to know if he – the Moot – could help.' Vellain chuckled unpleasantly. 'Help! As if they could. I'm surprised any of them can even get dressed without a committee to tell them how. They've had people coming in and wanting to talk to their Senators, that's all. You know how that upsets them – reality washing around their feet.'

Vellain smiled then laughed. All was well. Thyrn and his strange connection with her husband was unsettling, but there were bigger clouds in the sky and while Vashnar could tell her about it, she deemed it unimportant. As for Bowlott's sudden interest, that was no problem. The man was a cipher like all of them, a relic of times long gone – and not even a quaint relic at that. Soon they'd all be gone. Every last one of them.

Chapter 9

Endryk reached down and touched the snarling dog gently. 'Easy,' he whispered. 'It's all right.'

Rhavvan's hand was moving towards a knife in his belt.

'Don't,' Endryk said, softly but urgently. Rhavvan hesitated and Endryk's free hand extended to emphasize his command. 'Nals isn't a pet. He's neither trained nor tame, he does what he wants. And he knows about weapons. He's also afraid of nothing and if he goes for you I won't be able to stop him. He'll hurt you badly even if you kill him.'

There was no challenge or threat in Endryk's voice, just quiet and patently sincere advice, and Rhavvan made no further movement. Nevertheless he could do no other than demand to know, 'What's he doing that for, then?'

'My fault, probably,' Endryk replied. 'For some reason he's very protective of me. He sensed trouble.'

'Why? No one threatened you.'

At a further touch from Endryk, Nals grudgingly stopped his silent display and lay down. His head sank forward on to his paws, but his unblinking eyes moved relentlessly back and forth across the watching group.

'Thyrn startled me with what he said, that's all. Caught me unawares. Nals probably picked it up. Does the lad read minds?' Endryk's eyes belied the half-joking note in his voice.

'Are you from the north?' Hyrald asked, ignoring the

113

question. 'Your accent's different from ours, but I just took it to be a local one.'

'I'm here because I want to be,' Endryk replied, ignoring Hyrald's question in turn. 'Where I come from is no one's affair. Suffice it I don't want to be reminded of the past.'

Hyrald looked at him. 'And I don't want to intrude,' he said after a moment. 'Not after everything you've done for us – we're already considerably in your debt. But you know our position and if you can tell us anything about what there is to the north that could help us, I'd welcome the benefit of your experience.'

'I told you, I'm not accepting burdens. You owe me nothing.'

'But you *are* from the north?'

'I'm here.'

Thyrn's trembling voice intruded. 'We must get away from this place, from Vashnar. He's going to make dreadful things happen. He's—'

'For pity's sake, be quiet!' Hyrald snapped angrily, rounding on him. Everyone froze at his unexpected ferocity. To avoid their collective gaze he looked upwards and blew out a noisy breath.

The sky was clear and blue, open and wide.

It would be thus when they were gone.

Beautiful and indifferent.

Large white birds were wheeling in wide graceful circles high above. Their freedom seemed to sharpen his sense of his own bonds.

And yet? Something inside him shifted. 'I'm not accepting burdens,' Endryk had said. The simple statement seemed to ring through the arching sky, echoing louder and louder, subtly changing, until finally it became a question.

'What binds you?'

It jolted him.

In the inner silence that followed, Hyrald knew that the

asking of the question was its own answer. And one he already knew. One he had learned a long time ago. All things were as they were and must be accepted as such. Anything else was folly – sometimes dangerous folly. Getting through life safely and sanely was primarily a matter of deciding what could be changed and what not, then dealing with the former and letting the latter go, both wholeheartedly.

His spasm of anger vanished into depths of the sky. 'I'm sorry,' he said to Endryk. 'We've disturbed you long enough and now we've obviously woken an old pain by way of thanks. There's nothing up north for us, is there?'

Endryk opened his arms. 'People, places, bad, good. Who knows, for you. Not for me, certainly. Not yet. Not for quite a time, I think.'

Hyrald nodded, then spoke directly to Thyrn. 'It ends here,' he said, his voice both grim and pained. 'I can see no peace in exile, still less in continual flight – for any of us. Apart from the fact that we've done nothing wrong, we're Arvens. I wouldn't say we belong here no matter what, but everything I know tells me we'll be lost beyond recall if we just carry on running in the hope of finding some strange land to hide in.' Thyrn made to speak but Hyrald stopped him. 'Listen to me, Thyrn. Grasp this. Whatever made you what you are, whatever brought you to this place, has happened. It can't be changed or run away from and nothing but hurt is going to be achieved by denying that. You need to understand that.'

'But Vashnar's going to—'

'No! I said listen to me.' Hyrald became insistent. 'No one knows what anyone's going to do. I don't know what you've touched on in Vashnar, something bad without a doubt, but it's not the future. No one can know the future. Only in children's tales and ancient myths.' He scuffed the sandy ground with his foot scarring it dark brown and raising a small flurry of dust. Some of it spilled up on to the toe of his boot, while the rest slowly dispersed in an unfelt breeze. 'Who could have foreseen what I just did or where each tiny part of that dust would fall? And every least action makes the future. We're all practical people here, Thyrn. We plan, we think, we anticipate, but always we know things will turn out otherwise – sometimes a little, sometimes massively. And either way, in the end, we have to accept and deal with the reality that comes to pass. That's one of the differences between children and adults – though a lot of people never come to understand it, believe me. All of which leaves me with the knowledge that I don't think I can run any further. Not now it comes to it. I don't think any of us can. Too many ties. You're free to go on wherever you like, but I – we . . .' He glanced round at the others. 'We have to find another way.'

Thyrn stared at him, wide-eyed. Nordath stood pale and silent.

'Besides, whatever problem you've got with Vashnar is indeed a Caddoran matter, and quite beyond anything any of us here can help you with.'

Thyrn made to speak but Hyrald pressed on, earnest and encouraging. 'Think about this. Somewhere inside you is a resource that will help you deal with what's happening. You're the Caddoran, not Vashnar – at least he's only part one, perhaps.' He laid a scornful emphasis on the last word. 'Not only that but you're one of the best there's ever been – so everyone tells me. You've all the advantages even if you can't see them at the moment. If you meet Vashnar in this strange way again,' he tapped his head, 'remember that it's *your* territory. You can deal with him there. Don't keep fretting about running away. That's a sure way both to cloud your own vision and to bring a predator after you. It's usually better to face what's behind you than crash into some future that might well be worse and find yourself trapped between the two. Trust yourself, Thyrn, you've more in you than you know. I've seen that for myself.' He became matter-of-fact. 'Besides, it seems to me that this mysterious connection you have with Vashnar has nothing to do with distance. If you can somehow come together with you here and him in Arvenshelm, then I've a feeling that putting a sea between you won't make any difference.' He stopped, taken by an unexpected but obvious thought. 'And he must be very afraid of you,' he said, half to himself, half to the others. 'Why else would he have gone to such an extremity as proclaiming the Death Cry? And against his own kind, too?'

Thyrn's expression too, became thoughtful as Hyrald's harsh summary impinged on him. 'I did push him out,' he said. 'I don't know how, but I definitely fended him off. And I think he was as lost and frightened as I was.'

Rhavvan grunted. 'I don't think Vashnar's ever been frightened in his life,' he said, though to no one in particular.

'He was afraid, I'm sure of it,' Thyrn insisted, adding with an uncharacteristically bold stare, 'As you would've been, too.'

Rhavvan gave him a dark look but did not reply to this unexpected challenge. 'More to the point, which way are we going? North, south, where?' he demanded, avoiding it.

'What do you think?' Hyrald asked him directly. Rhavvan was taken aback. It took him a moment to gather his wits. 'I don't fancy going back to Arvenshelm or anywhere where people know about the Death Cry, that's for sure. Even if things have quietened down by now they could flare up in a moment. We were damned lucky to get away, to say the least.' He stopped, but no one spoke, forcing him to continue. 'On the other hand, you're right, we've done nothing wrong and we are Arvens, this is where we belong. We can't run for ever. Apart from anything else, I've no great desire to be struggling to make a new life in a strange land, if only because I'm not sure what I'm fit for – or any of us for that matter. We've no trade, no craft. And like you, I've got – I had – a good life

117

here and I'd like it back. But . . .'

He concluded with an unhappy shrug.

'There's something else.' It was Adren. 'I agree that whatever Thyrn's seeing when he Joins with Vashnar can't be the future – we've dealt with enough market fortune-tellers who didn't manage to see their own arrest coming, to know that, but it could be something Vashnar's thinking – perhaps something he intends to do. And, as you said, proclaiming the Death Cry confirms that he's afraid of Thyrn – very afraid – which in turn confirms that Thyrn's probably telling the truth as he sees it. We all know Vashnar's a bit odd – obsessive about things – but it sounds to me as if he might be coming unhinged. If he is, in his position, there's no saying what harm he might do. Perhaps that's another reason for going back. To find out what's going on and do something about it.'

'What?' Rhavvan exclaimed. 'Trying to get back to civilization is going to be hard enough, but walking into Vashnar's office and asking him if he's gone insane! That's brilliant.'

Adren flicked her thumb towards Hyrald. 'Thyrn's just had a sermon about not running away, about facing reality,' she said angrily. 'Time we all did it, I think. If Vashnar's coming apart we've got a duty to do something about it. We can't just ignore it. We are Wardens, after all.'

'We were Wardens!' Rhavvan burst out. 'Or have you forgotten we're hunted criminals now, despite doing our "duty" for years!'

She bridled. 'We're hunted, certainly. But none of us are criminals. I'm still a Warden and not only have I had enough running and hiding, I want to know what the devil Vashnar's up to if half the stuff that this lad has picked up from him is true. Not to mention the duty we've got to the people who look to us for protection.'

Rhavvan was scornful. 'Duty again, eh? And to the people,

no less! This is getting worse. I don't know about *Vashnar* going crazy.' He waved a dismissive hand. 'Then you always were a bit on the pious side.'

Adren stepped towards him menacingly.

Hyrald moved quickly between them, arms extended to keep them apart. 'You're both right. Perhaps Vashnar has gone mad. Even without what Thyrn's told us, he's hardly acted rationally, has he? But what we can do about it, I don't know, duty or not. And right now we still haven't decided whether we go north or south. We—'

'It'll be west for a day or so, in either case,' Endryk interrupted. 'South directly from here will send you back the way you came, and north will see you drowned in less than half a day.'

Hyrald threw up his arms and abandoned Rhavvan and Adren. 'I'd forgotten,' he said, relieved by Endryk's reminder. 'So we don't have to decide right away, after all. We can talk some more as we travel – and sleep on the matter.' His manner lightened noticeably at the prospect and he smiled at Endryk. 'If I could impose on you for one more thing – a description of the way we need to go, as far as you know it. I don't want to do anything that would leave us at the mercy of that tide again, but we mustn't stay here any longer. There's no saying whether there are any more of our "colleagues" searching for us, or how long it'll be before Oudrence reaches the first decent-sized community, or what'll happen when he does.'

Endryk looked at him silently. Nals stood up and wandered off. Rhavvan and Adren moved further apart as he walked between them, head low, eyes watchful.

Hyrald waited, loath to press his involuntary host for a reply.

'I'd be happy to,' Endryk said after a long, preoccupied pause. 'But I've been thinking that I could do with a change myself. I've been feeling restless lately. It's been interesting, but I don't think I'm really cut out to be a shoreman after all –

that shore is frightening even when you know it. And I didn't realize how much I missed having people to talk to.' He looked at each of his listeners in turn. 'Besides, I'm intrigued – about you, about what's happening here. If you don't mind an extra hour on your journey, I'd like to pick up some things from my cottage and then travel in your direction for a little while.'

The suggestion both surprised and disturbed Hyrald. 'Your help would be appreciated. We're city people, as you've gathered – not at our best out here, by any means. There are far too many surprises for us. But we *are* fugitives with the Death Cry proclaimed against us. If we're caught, you'll probably be fighting for your life before you get a chance to explain who you are. I don't know what a shoreman does to survive in this place, but I doubt fighting's one of them. I'm afraid we're not a happy find for you and we may well be unhappier company.'

'That's for me to judge,' Endryk said, with an odd smile. 'As for the fighting . . .' He opened his arms expansively. 'A little care should avoid that. There are plenty of vantage points and hiding places even here, and there are more as we move inland. And if any of your colleagues should come after you, don't forget, they know the country no better than you.'

Hyrald was not convinced. They owed too much to Endryk already. Whoever he was and wherever he came from, he could have no idea of the risk he was taking.

Endryk took his arm. 'It's time for me to move on,' he said soberly. 'I think I made that decision yesterday when I helped you off the shore – or it was made for me, I'm not sure. Anyway, as you rightly instructed your charge before, change is as unavoidable as its effects are uncalculable. It's my decision and I'll take the consequences.'

His manner was quite resolute and Hyrald found he had no more arguments to offer. Thus, shortly afterwards, he was walking beside Endryk, following his lead. The others rode behind. Nals too, joined them, though he kept well to one side like a cautious flank guard.

Endryk's cottage surprised Hyrald. His anticipation had been coloured by the disorderly construction of the shelter in which they had spent the night. What he saw now was radically different. Two storeys high, circular in plan with a steep pitched conical roof of heavy interlocking tiles and walls of well-pointed stonework, the building was not one he would have described as a cottage. It had the feel of a miniature fortress and looked peculiarly out of place amid the rolling landscape. Though no student of architecture, Hyrald tried to think where he had seen anything like it before, but without success. It reminded him vaguely of some of the towers that decorated the Moot Palace, but none of those had the solid purposefulness that this possessed. Still less were they bright and well maintained with orderly gardens at their feet. He could not resist expressing his surprise.

'Did you build this?' he asked, rather self-consciously.

Endryk laughed. 'No. I didn't even build the shelter, though some of the running repairs are mine.' His laughter faded. 'This has been here since before any of the locals can remember. No one even knows where this kind of stone comes from. It's certainly not from around here. The last occupant was a real shoreman, the old man who found me on the beach and took me in, helped me, taught me the ways of the shore. I keep the place in good order for him.'

'He's away?'

'He's dead.' He pointed to a small fenced area nearby. In it was a small, neatly tended tumulus at the head of which was a wooden stake topped with an iron ring.

'I'm sorry, I didn't mean . . .'

'It's all right. It was quite a time ago. And he died as well as any of us can expect to. Excuse me.' With that, he pushed open the door and stepped inside. Though uninvited, Hyrald was

121

contemplating following him when a nudge against his calves unbalanced him and pushed him to one side. As he recovered, he saw Nals circle a couple of times before draping himself across the threshold. Hyrald joined the others.

It was some time before Endryk reappeared and when he did it was from the rear of the building. He was wearing a sword and carrying a bow and leading two horses. One was a fine tall animal while the other was smaller and more solidly built, with the look of a good packhorse. Both were saddled and carried bulging saddlebags.

The three Wardens exchanged looks. Hyrald felt an unexpected twinge. He sensed that this was a man who could take his leadership from him. The thought shocked him a little. He had not imagined himself so petty. Nevertheless, and despite a stern inner word of self-reproach, it proved surprisingly difficult to lay the idea aside.

'Sorry I took so long,' Endryk said. 'I had to leave a note for my friends, my neighbours.'

'Are you sure about coming with us?' Hyrald asked, concerned, his momentary discomfiture gone. 'It seems to me that you've got a good life here.'

Endryk looked at the cottage. 'It is a good life. But it's not mine, and I can see it's over now. I have to move on.'

'But your friends?'

'A manner of speaking. They're friendly people – fairly friendly, anyway. They know me and they've accepted me as much as villagers accept anyone who hasn't got ten generations behind him in the one house, but they're not really my friends. None of them will miss me too much. In fact, they always seem a little surprised that I'm still here whenever they see me. I think they understand who I am better than I do.'

'Have you locked the place properly?' Rhavvan asked.

Endryk smiled. 'No. There's nothing worth stealing. Besides, in a way, the place belongs to everyone. The next person who wants to be a shoreman will just move in.'

Rhavvan scowled. 'I don't understand,' he said.

'Don't worry about it. As you said, you're city people. You're a long way from everything.'

Rhavvan's scowl deepened, but he did not reply.

Endryk became practical. He patted one of the saddlebags. 'I've got all the supplies I have in here, but there's fresh water around the back if you want to water your horses and fill your water-bags. We shouldn't have many problems with either food or water on the way, but we should start well.'

Nordath and Rhavvan took his advice and led their horses in the direction he was indicating. While the others were waiting, Nals left his post across the doorway and walked over to Endryk. The shoreman crouched down and began talking softly to the animal. As he did so, Hyrald noted the quality of the clothes he was wearing and the weapons he was carrying. They were simple and practical, and even though he could not examine them in detail he could tell they were well made. And his horse too, was one which would have turned heads in Arvenshelm. A twinge of jealousy flared briefly again but he stamped it out ruthlessly, marking its demise with another stern inner commentary. Whoever Endryk was he had saved their lives and done nothing but help them, and he had shown no indication that he wanted any part in the making of their decisions – quite the contrary. A calmer conclusion followed. A leader was a leader only for those who cared to follow, and fitness could determine everything. And beyond doubt, Endryk, with his local knowledge, could serve the group now better than he could. He felt suddenly easier, as if some shadow disturbing the edge of his vision had passed.

Nordath and Rhavvan returned. Endryk finished speaking to the dog and turned to Nordath. 'Could I suggest that you and Thyrn take my other horse and let Adren take yours,' he said. 'He's better able to carry the two of you.' He looked at

123

Hyrald. 'But we should walk as much as we can. Use the horses sparingly – keep them fresh in case we have to run.'

'We've been walking since we started,' Hyrald replied. 'We'll manage a little further, I think.' He motioned Endryk to lead the way.

Just before they lost sight of the cottage, Endryk turned and looked at it for a long moment. His face was unreadable. The others went ahead a little to leave him alone. Then he saluted and turned to join them again. Nals walked alongside the group as he had before.

It was not long before the undulating green terrain became dry and sandy again. After a brief but calf-tugging passage through some particularly soft dunes they found themselves once again on the hard-packed sand of the shore. They stopped without a command and looked out at the shining line of the sea in the distance.

Hyrald found his eyes turning up to the bright sky again. Whatever had been, whatever would be, this was a beautiful place. An inner resting point in the turmoil into which he had been sucked.

'So clear, so sharp,' Nordath said. 'The horizon, parting sea and sky. Straighter than any time I've ever seen.'

Hyrald looked and saw it for himself. He cast a quick glance at Endryk, wondering what he saw.

'Let's mount up,' Endryk said. 'We can make some worthwhile progress while the light holds.'

As they mounted, the mood of the group became less expansive. Rhavvan bent forward and, with a significant look towards the sea, asked Endryk, 'It's safe, here, is it? We won't suddenly have to run for it again, will we?'

Endryk indicated the dry dunes a little way to their left. 'Tide doesn't come much beyond where we are now, and not particularly quickly.' Then he turned and pointed behind them, out to sea. 'You were right out there.' He shook his head and chuckled to himself. 'You are *so* lucky. Those sand-bars are never the same two days running. *I* was taking a risk being out there. Maybe that's why I'm coming with you – you're lucky people.'

'I'd hardly call the Death Cry and being attacked by our own, lucky,' Adren joked.

'True,' Endryk conceded. 'But then, you did win, didn't you? Lucky the mist was with you.'

'Lucky we were listening,' Rhavvan intruded caustically. 'Talking of which, what's that noise?'

Endryk inclined his head, puzzled. Then: 'Oh, it's only the sea – and the birds.' He pointed again to the distant water's edge.

Rhavvan squinted along his arm. 'I can't see anything,' he said.

'They're much further away than you think,' Endryk said. 'You won't be able to see them from here if you don't know what you're looking for. But there's so many birds out there, they're like clouds of smoke blowing in the wind when they take off. It's quite a sight.'

'It's a lonely sound,' Thyrn said.

Endryk pursed his lips and nodded. 'Haunting, I think I'd say, rather than lonely.'

They moved on in silence towards the sinking sun.

Vashnar slowly stretched first one arm and then the other. Then he stiffened his shoulders and let them go. He looked at the dead hearth in front of him. There were no tell-tale lines of dust to indicate negligence on the part of the household staff and everything was in its place – pokers, tongs, rakes, all the fireside paraphernalia, even the wood carefully stacked in different sizes in readiness for ease of lighting on the return of the still distant winter. Yellow lights reflected brightly from the highly polished implements and from the equally polished wooden seats which stood on each side of the grate. Vashnar reproached himself. Surely he had not been asleep? He did not think so, for he felt no lingering drowsiness. But certainly he must have been deeply absorbed, he decided, for he had not heard the servants entering the room to light the lanterns in strict accordance with the dictates he had long since determined for the running of his house. Adding an edge to the reproach was a small, hard glint of anger and fear that this routine intrusion had indeed occurred without his noticing – a kind of carelessness that could prove fatal in other circumstances. But the anger did not seriously mar his sense of well-being and he shrugged it aside: it was the remains of a habit formed in days long passed, sharper days, when he had patrolled Arvenshelm's dark and dangerous places, and indeed, he took some pride in the fact that he still had it. But it was not needed here. Now, everything was the way it should be. This room, its meticulous order, its buffed and polished surfaces, reflected not only the silently lit lanterns, but his will. It was good. Vashnar detested disorder, loose ends, straggling details, those strands of darkness which could emerge unseen and unforeseen, to tangle silently about him and bring him down.

He nodded as if completing an internal conversation and wherever his thoughts had been, they returned immediately to his confessional discourse with Vellain.

Her blunt response to his problem with Thyrn had been refreshing. As ever, it had been shrewdly judged. He was particularly taken by the opportunity she had seen to discredit the Caddoran Congress. That, he had missed. Not for the first time, she had shifted his view of events, and now she had jolted him out of the blinkered unease into which he had settled. Nevertheless, he decided, she had not been right to dismiss the problem of Thyrn so casually. Then, of course, she could hardly be criticized for that. She was necessarily unaware of the complexity of the many intricate details that locked together the structure of pending events and of which he was the sustaining force. Two simple facts clearly condemned Thyrn. No matter where he was, he could not be allowed to wander free knowing what he knew, especially as, by now, he would surely have passed it on to Hyrald and the others. And as for his reaching out and entering his mind again . . . that was wholly unacceptable! Vashnar shrank away from what he could remember of the anonymous nothingness he had become and rooted his decision in more solid ground. The incident had been random and uncontrollable, and the effect of another occurring in a more public venue than this afternoon – of his collapsing like a clumsy schoolboy, his nose bleeding incongruously – could not be calculated. Other ideas began to form and when he spoke to his wife it was as if no silence, no taper-bearing servants, had intruded in their conversation.

'But Bowlott can be troublesome and matters are at a delicate stage: it would be politic to keep him unsettled. And having Thyrn and the others wandering abroad is too dangerous, no matter where they are. We can't risk some random coincidence of events jeopardizing everything at this stage – a tale told to a wandering tinker, an inn-keeper, anything.'

Vellain noted her husband's tone. Her eyes narrowed and she craned her head forward slightly, anxious not to miss some nuance.

'I agree with you that perhaps Thyrn's ability to enter my mind is something I should not preoccupy myself with, but it is still too dangerous.'

He fell silent, making no mention of the terror that the encounter had inspired in him. Faint household sounds drifted reassuringly into the room as the servants pursued their prescribed duties. Vellain waited.

'I think several ends will be served at once if we send the Tervaidin after them.'

Chapter 10

In the Beginning was the Burning of the Great Light, though there are those who say that this was not the true beginning but a Shaping again of that which had gone before. Be that as it may, from this terrible incandescence four figures emerged, bright beyond imagining, and such was their joy at being that for time without measure they danced and sang and used the Power that was the essence of the Great Light to Shape the world and fill it with wondrous things beyond number. Then they rested and looked on the wonders they had created and it came upon them that others should share their joy of being. Thus it was that they sang and danced again and wove from the mysterious fabric of nothingness their greatest creation, forming it in their own image and calling it life. And great was the rejoicing of all things that lived.

Yet in what they had done, Those who Shaped came to see a mystery beyond their understanding, for they found that the depth of the nature of life was without end. And they asked themselves how this might have come to pass. But no answer came save a silence, deep and profound. And so they searched, even into the heart of their own natures. But there they found only a greater question: how had they themselves come to be?

Knowing then that they were ignorant, they resolved to Shape no more until they had answered this question. And seeing that all about them was good and that all things knew the joy of being, they moved into the place which lay beyond and between the essence of this world, where floated the shifting dreams of unknowing and where neither time nor place was. All save one, the greatest of them, who remained in this world, deep in contemplation, to seek another way.

And knowledge of them faded from the minds of many, though the wisest amongst all creatures remembered them and revered their memory, rejoicing always in the gift of life which had been bestowed by them.

But in the fading of the Burning of the Great Light, other, lesser figures had emerged also, red and awful, carrying with them only the will to corrupt and destroy. And one among them was powerful indeed, equalling in His vision and will, Those who Shaped. But He remained still and silent, brooding darkly as Those who Shaped worked their mysteries and celebrated the Shaping of the world and all things in it, for He both feared them and their greatness, and despised their work, deeming it flawed and imperfect, especially that which was called life, though in that which was called man He saw the instrument of His own intent.

And thus is was until Those who Shaped, save the one, passed from this world.

Thence, free from all fear, He took on the form of man. And making Himself fair of face, and with great stealth and cunning, He moved amongst them, slowly corrupting with false words and filling them with His own malice until the joy of being slipped from them, like water through a grasping hand. And as they fell under His sway so He taught them envy and greed and, as He grew yet stronger, He taught them also war and its unending forms of treachery and cruelty. For Those who Shaped, knowing not the unfathomable depths of the nature of life, and of man especially, had made it curious and eternally questioning. And men above all proved the most apt and thorough pupils, amazing even Him.

But some saw beyond His words and His fairness of face and knew Him for what He was. And they spoke out, denouncing Him and His way. But those whom He had corrupted knew no restraint and put in thrall and to the sword all those who so spoke, making even greater His sway. Yet though enslaved, those who saw the truth would not yield to Him but began also to study His teaching, seeing, to their dismay, that in it lay their only salvation. And there came about the Wars of the First Coming and the world was dark with the fires of degradation and destruction and the air was filled with cries of despair and lamentation.

And so great was the clamour that the greatest of Those who Shaped was awakened from his contemplation, and looking about him he was filled with both horror and shame, despairing of what he saw and fearing that this had come about through the darkness of his own ignorance. Yet he saw too, that His hand was there, for he knew Him and the knowledge greatly troubled him. And taking the form of man himself he rallied the failing armies of those who still remembered him and after many and terrible battles, drove Him to an awful fastness in the north. And there, in the ninth hour of the Last Battle, faltering under the burden of His sins, He fell to the arrows and spears of men. Though with His final cast he slew the greatest of Those who Shaped.

Yet, some say that neither were truly slain, but were translated into another place and that He may come again should He be forgotten and the vigilance of good men fail.

Thus went the story of the Beginning and the Wars of the First Coming.

There are a myriad lesser tales of that time.

One such tells of a noble people, the Arvensfolk, who, cruelly dispossessed and dispersed for opposing His will, joined the many and fearful wanderings of peoples seeking respite from the Wars of the First Coming. Of the fate of the greater part of the Arvensfolk, nothing is known, but a weary remnant found refuge in the land that was to become Arvenstaat. Yet even here they were persecuted and enslaved by other peoples in that land who, though having been persecuted and driven from their homes themselves, were more numerous and greatly tainted by His teaching.

But the Arvensfolk would not yield and withstood the torments of their enemies, as they had stood against Him, until, when it seemed *all hope was gone, a great leader arose amongst them and filling them with his strength he led them against their oppressors, overthrowing them and sweeping them from the land.*

So goes the most common of the legends of the founding of Arvenstaat, though other versions add that, in gaining victory, the Arvensfolk became so like their oppressors that the man – or some say, woman – who led them, walked into the mountains, grieving, and was never seen again.

Written testimony, such as it is, tells a more prosaic, less creditable tale, though in many ways similar in essence: a fugitive people given shelter who rose up under a brutal and shrewd leader to overwhelm and enslave their hosts and seize their lands and properties.

By tradition, no name is ever given to this leader, but from him – or her, for even in the written testimony, this is still not known – came the rule of the Dictators. What had been the evil necessity of war became the commonplace of peace and the will of the Dictator came to be accepted as absolute. For while the first Dictator ruled with great brutality, he was nevertheless both respected and held in awe by his subjects, and his excesses were not seen as such. However, it is in the nature of power that it corrupts, and in the nature of leadership that it is a random not a hereditary quality, and while subsequent Dictators emulated the brutality of the first, they lacked his subtle understanding of the mood of his people who, in their turn, knew ever less of the benefits that he had brought to the Arvensfolk. Thus, to maintain the obedience of their subjects, the Dictators were obliged to resort increasingly to the use of armed force, gathering about them a body of guards who were given privileged positions in society and ever-increasing power and authority – the Tervaidin.

As is invariably the case with such guardians, the Tervaidin gathered so much power to themselves that in time they became the effective rulers of Arvenstaat, appointing and unseating Dictators as the whim took them. Ironically, because they too became corrupted and weakened by power, their final choice of Dictator, Koron Marab, was able to divide them amongst themselves and very effectively reduce their authority. Yet by a further irony, this triumph was short-lived, for it was this same division that enabled Akharim to enlist sufficient of the Tervaidin to act as passive witnesses to his own rise to power. Only when he had killed Marab did the Tervaidin fully realize that Akharim, in affecting to rule through the Moot, had judged the mood of the people very finely, and had left them no opportunity to deal with him as they had done with his predecessors. Following their honoured tradition of self-interested opportunism they therefore swore allegiance to him. Thence, over many years they were gradually transformed into the force that became the Wardens.

Long before the time of Akharim, the Wars of the First Coming had faded into legend, and, no further cataclysms shaking the world, its many peoples went their own ways – some would say degenerating into surly mediocrity, others would say moving inexorably, if unsteadily forward to ever quieter, more peaceful times. Whatever the truth, it was indisputably the case that the Arvens knew little real tyranny and still less menace from beyond their borders for many generations and, in the course of reaching their present condition, they came to regard the times of both Marab and Akharim as colourful and romantic – a gloss made possible only by virtue of the distance of the brutal reality of those times. Thus in those discussions concerning the repairing of the perceived faults of governance which featured regularly in taverns and hostelries throughout the land, voices could often be heard declaiming the virtues of the 'good old days of the Dictators'.

Caught also in the spurious glow from this distant time, the

Tervaidin too were usually seen indistinctly, invariably being represented as a disinterested professional elite, full of soldierly virtues and working only for the good of the people. Many fine and stirring stories had been written about their valiant adventures. That they had never been this and had fallen progressively further from even their original state was well documented but ignored in popular culture. Almost certainly, this rainbow view started with Akharim's manipulations to ensure that he retained both the protection of the Tervaidin and control over them, he knowing full well that myth can be far more potent than reality, not least for those being mythologized. Whatever the reason, the name rang well in the ears of the modern Arvens and thus Vashnar chose it for his own guards. It was more appropriate than he would have cared to admit for he intended them to fulfil the functions of the original Tervaidin and, like them, they were a mixture of thugs, opportunists and fanatics.

Vellain knew there would be no point in questioning her husband's decision. His tone told her that it was final. Nevertheless she did allow her considerable surprise to show. 'Earlier than you'd envisaged,' she said.

Vashnar stood up and began methodically stretching himself again. He was unusually stiff. A frowning glance at a tall clock clucking darkly in the corner told him that he had been sitting in the chair for some hours – much longer than he had thought. It disturbed him a little. 'You've delayed our meal,' he said.

'You needed time to think, without disturbance,' Vellain replied, then she reached out and tugged on a bell-pull hanging by the fireplace. A distant tinkling was followed almost immediately by a marked change in the tenor of the household noises that discreetly pervaded the room.

'And now I need to eat?' Vashnar said.

Vellain smiled. 'And now you need to eat,' she confirmed,

standing up and linking her arm in his. 'And you need to answer my question.'

'You haven't asked one.'

She gave him a provocative glance. 'My implicit question,' she said, with heavy emphasis, leaning on him. 'Earlier than you'd envisaged, I said – using the Tervaidin. Only a day or so ago, you said you were concerned they weren't ready yet.' She led him over to the window.

Vashnar yielded to her and gave a conceding nod. 'I still am. But circumstances change and we must move with them. We've never had a precise schedule for the latter part of our plan. By definition, it was something we prepared for against the time when an appropriate moment would arise. As for deciding when it had come, that was always going to be a difficult judgement.'

'And?' Vellain prompted, catching the note in his voice.

'And I think now that we might be much nearer than we realize. I think that perhaps we might even be able to engineer that moment.'

She squeezed his arm, pressing her question. 'But the Tervaidin . . .'

'Need to be tested. In the field. In action.'

'But they're all experienced Wardens. You picked them yourself, trained them.'

Vellain went to open the tall glass door that would lead them into the now darkened garden – they often walked there in the evening. But Vashnar stopped her. As she looked up she found herself the object of close scrutiny by her reflection in the night-backed window. The presence of this hollow image with the lamplit room in the background, like a mysterious identical world beyond, ever watching, unsettled her for some reason. She drew the curtains quickly.

Vashnar answered her question. 'I've no serious doubts about them, but their role is crucial and it won't be like anything they've done before. I need to test them in action. *They* need to test themselves in action.' There was a hint almost of excitement in his voice. 'And this is an ideal opportunity. We'll find out how obedient they are, how effective, working as a group, how reliable. And as well as testing them, mobilizing them now will serve other useful ends. We'll see how they're greeted on the streets, which is important – very important. And it'll keep Bowlott quiet – stop him fretting about the Death Cry too much. He'll probably be pleased actually – a new guard regiment for the Moot Palace, specially selected from our most experienced Wardens to protect the Senators should the rumours about Nesdiryn or the Morlider prove correct – or even from over-enthusiastic electors. It'll pander to his inflated sense of his own importance.'

'But Hyrald and the others are Wardens. Do you think your people will have any difficulty in . . .' Vellain made a vague throat-cutting gesture '. . . dealing with them?'

'None at all,' Vashnar said without hesitation. 'That, I've no qualms about. They all know where we're going, and what it means to them and they'll not allow any misguided old loyalties to stand in the way.'

Vellain loved her husband.

There was a single sharp rap on the door and a servant entered to announce that their meal was ready.

'I see no reason for delay,' Vashnar went on as they walked down a long uncarpeted corridor, their footsteps softly martial. 'The longer this business with Thyrn persists, the greater the risk. I'll send for Aghrid first thing tomorrow. Twenty, mounted, should do. He can pick them. They should be on the road by late afternoon.'

'Shouldn't you speak to the others?'

'I'll tell them at the same time. I doubt they'll disagree. The matter's clear-cut. Thyrn's got to be—'

'You can't tell them about Thyrn,' Vellain said urgently.

136

Vashnar smiled slightly. 'He was young, corruptible. Broke his Caddoran Oath. Discovered too much about our intentions. As you said yourself, he was probably spying for the Congress.'

Vellain reflected his smile back to him as he rehearsed his pending arguments.

They paused at the entrance to the dining room. 'A long, strange and interesting day, wife,' he said, routinely casting a critical eye over the formally laid table. 'For the first time since this trouble with Thyrn began I feel as though I'm seeing the way ahead again, clear and decisive.'

Vellain laid a sustaining hand on his arm as she moved past him. Had she been looking at his face however, she would have seen a hint of fear in his eyes. For though he had told her the truth, he had not told her all of it. He had not told her that for all his regained clarity of vision, he could still sense some part of Thyrn in every dark part of his mind – persistent and clinging, like the dust-laden cobwebs in Bowlott's office.

As Endryk guided Hyrald and the others along the shore through the latter part of the day, the clumps of vegetation in the hard sand became increasingly more dense until the shore ahead became a continuous sheet of dull green, streaked with patches of brown and grey, and the shining line of the sea became ragged and broken. The distant sound of birds had gradually grown much louder. It surrounded the riders, forming a relentless chorus to their journey across the long-shadowing landscape, at once desolate and reassuring.

'What's that?' Adren pointed towards the horizon. As she did so, a dark cloud, thin as smoke, rose up in the far distance against the reddening sky. It shifted, folded, moved from side to side as no cloud could, then, as quickly as it had appeared, sank and vanished.

'Birds,' Endryk said. 'Like I told you.'

Adren gaped. 'Birds?' she said uncertainly. Endryk nodded.

Adren's eyes widened with wonder and for a while she stared fixedly at the now motionless horizon. 'What a sight,' she said eventually. 'I've seen birds flocking in the city in the evening, but never anything like that. There must be so many. How can they move like that – so quickly?' She shook her head slowly in disbelief then pointed again. 'But that wasn't what I was looking at. What are those?'

Endryk followed her hand then glanced quickly at Thyrn. 'They're the tops of the hills on the other side, north,' he said, mouthing the last word silently. 'You'll see more as we move further inland, as the estuary narrows.'

Thyrn however, either did not hear or was too rapt in thought to note the first appearance of his long-sought goal. Adren acknowledged Endryk's discretion and said nothing further.

They rode on in silence for a little while until Endryk announced, 'We'll have to move off the shore now, it's nothing but marsh up ahead. Fine for the birds but hard going and very dangerous for us.'

'Tide dangerous, is it?' Rhavvan asked, anxious to use his slight knowledge of this alien place.

'No, not here,' Endryk replied. 'Not usually, anyway. But there are areas of soft mud here that could swallow an entire regiment in minutes – horses and all – and leave no trace.' Rhavvan reined his horse to a halt and stared at him as though he might be joking. 'They shift and change with the tide,' Endryk explained casually. 'I can't guide you through them. No one can.'

'The sooner we get back to civilization, the better,' Rhavvan sighed, looking down uncomfortably at the indentations his horse's hooves were making in the sand as he realized that Endryk was simply telling him the truth. 'This place has far too many bad surprises for my liking. What else are we going to find here?'

Endryk dismounted and began leading his horse towards

the trees that fringed the shore. The others followed him. 'A few insects, maybe, and some swift rivers,' he replied. 'Plenty of plants to sting and poison you if you're foolish enough to sit on them or eat them. A few animals to steal your food in the night, if you don't stow it properly. And, of course, starvation and exposure if you really don't know what you're doing. But plenty of food, water and shelter if you do.' His lip curled. 'And no thieves, murderers, drunkards, streets choked with horses, waggons and quarrelling people scrabbling to go nowhere special. No armies, no swords, no . . .' He stopped and grimaced. 'Sorry,' he muttered.

'The apologies are ours,' Hyrald said, watching his guide's face carefully. 'We've brought the memories and the swords back into your life. And I suppose there's a risk of more coming.'

'Yes,' Endryk said, his agitation gone as quickly as it had come. 'We'll have to talk about that.' Then he was fully himself again. 'There's a good place for a camp not far away. We've made as much of the day as we can, we should use the rest of the light to tend the horses and set up for the night.'

Within the hour it was dark and they were sitting around a small fire looking unusually contented. The Wardens who had attacked them on the shore had come well-equipped, leaving them not only with a welcome addition to their rations, but also two small tents to complement one they had stolen on their journey. Erecting them had proved a little problematical, but finally Rhavvan was able to declare, 'Quite spacious,' as he stood back and examined their joint handiwork. 'A marked improvement on the past weeks.'

Endryk, by contrast, had swiftly and skilfully rigged himself a shelter with a piece of rope and a sheet.

'Do you do any training in this kind of terrain?' he asked tentatively.

The three Wardens stared at him blankly. 'What for?' Hyrald asked.

Endryk shrugged. 'I thought perhaps as part of your basic training – for emergency survival?'

'No.' Hyrald's tone was disparaging. 'Survival for us is a matter of stick, sword, good information and having the wit to know when to run.'

'And your friends,' Rhavvan added, to common agreement.

'Why would we need to know how to live out here?' Hyrald went on. 'As you said yourself, there are no thieves and rogues about here, and if any of them want to run away from the city so much the better. Less trouble for us. Let *them* get poisoned and stung and die of exposure.'

Endryk nodded wistfully. 'Yes, of course, foolish question.'

'I gather *you* did – train to live out here,' Hyrald said, glancing at Endryk's neat and simple shelter.

'Different needs, different ways. Foolish question, as I said.' Endryk was obviously anxious not to pursue the matter.

There was little further talk around the flickering fire, everyone seeming to take to heart Hyrald's earlier advice that decisions about their future were perhaps best made after a night's sleep. And too, the gentle crackling of the fire and the shadowy vigil of the trees about them was more conducive to silence than debate. Only one topic stirred them before they retired to their respective tents.

'We must . . .' Endryk paused as he sought other words. 'I think it would be a good idea to post a guard.'

This provoked yet more blank looks, but this time Endryk did not retreat. He lowered his voice. 'People – hunters – have already found you once. As you pointed out, you're as far from Arvenshelm as you can get, here – off the map, I think you said. Yet out of this whole country they knew which way you'd gone and came straight to you. So if your own kind – city people – could follow you so easily, you've obviously left a trail like a runaway haycart.' The three Wardens looked at him darkly, unhappy at the reproach and uncertain where it was leading.

Hyrald made to interrupt but Endryk pressed on. 'If you decide ultimately to go north perhaps it won't matter, but if you go south, you'll be heading for trouble and you'll have to be much more careful about how you move and how you cover your tracks. Even now you've got two, maybe three, days in Arvenstaat before you decide which way to go and if you're found again, you may not have the mist on your side, or only three to deal with.'

Hyrald exchanged looks with Rhavvan and Adren as if seeking inspiration that would enable him to denounce or laugh off the notion of further pursuit and conflict. But nothing came. Endryk's quiet logic was indisputable – and frightening.

'You're right,' he said eventually. 'It's just not a way any of us think.'

'You need to start. Right away.'

Again Hyrald felt a hint of resentment at Endryk's command of events, but again it faded before his unaffected manner and the simple, if cruel, truth of what he was saying.

'Yes, I can see that.' He looked at Thyrn and Nordath. 'I suppose we all need to start thinking differently if we're going to survive this. Let go of our old lives if we're to get them back, as it were. We got through the first rush as much by good luck as anything else, but we can't rely on that holding for ever.' His manner became grim as his own words opened up the implications of their position. 'We've got a lot to learn. We're only going to get one try and one mistake could be our last.'

The mood of the group darkened and only the faint hiss of the fire disturbed the night silence. Then it spluttered and shifted, sending up a small flurry of sparks and lighting the solemn faces. Hyrald clapped his hands.

'We'll stand guard in two-hour shifts,' he said briskly. 'Nordath, will you do the first? Then Adren and Rhavvan. I'll do the last.' No one argued.

'What about me?' Thyrn asked, unexpectedly indignant.

'You're too young,' Hyrald replied, adding feebly, 'you need your sleep.'

'And me?' Endryk asked before Thyrn could argue further.

Hyrald looked at him. 'You've done more than enough for us. And this isn't your fight. If anything happens – if we're attacked, any time – run for it, save yourself, with our thanks.'

Endryk stood up and stretched. 'I'll stand my turn tomorrow night,' he said categorically, walking over to his shelter. 'Good night to you all. Sleep well.'

'And so will I,' Thyrn added, copying his tone. He nodded to the three Wardens. 'Good night.' Then, young again, to Nordath, 'Good night, Uncle.'

Hyrald stared after them. 'Well, I'm glad we got that settled,' he said sourly under his breath.

Nordath was chuckling to himself at Hyrald's caustic manner as he mounted guard. It felt strange. There had been precious little to make him laugh since Thyrn had tumbled, hysterical, into his house and plunged him into this waking nightmare. He was too old for all this hiding and fleeing. His quiet, humdrum life had been torn apart. Only affection for Thyrn had kept him going. Indeed, only affection for Thyrn had kept him sane. That and a burning anger which he never voiced but which co-existed with his almost constant fear. None of this should be. Vashnar, like all in his position before him, had been entrusted with the authority of the people to protect them from arbitrary justice, from mob rule. Now here he was, fomenting it. He *must* be crazed. But the implications of this didn't bear thinking about.

He leaned back against a tree and gripped Rhavvan's borrowed staff with all his strength – a futile measure of his impotence against Vashnar's corruption. Then, suddenly, he was quite calm. He began passing the staff gently from hand to hand.

'Don't sit down,' Endryk had discreetly whispered to him.

'You'll fall asleep very quickly. Keep something moving – just slow and easy and quiet. Keep looking at different things.' It seemed like good advice, Nordath reflected, as a pervasive yawn swept through him. He was just levering himself away from the tree when something nudged his leg making him suddenly very awake and on the verge of crying out. Nals' eyes glinted up at him, green in the starlit darkness. Nordath cleared his throat softly. 'Good dog,' he said, unconvincingly.

No incident disturbed the sleepers that night, other than the grumbles of those being awakened for guard duty, though each of them in turn had to cope with the stealthy footsteps, the rustling undergrowth, the strange grunts and squeals – some near, some far – that told of the lives of the countryside's night creatures. These, and the regular inspections by Nals, were the subject of some amusement the following morning as they breakfasted on their former colleagues' supplies.

Endryk's quiet education of the group began with the breaking of their camp. The fire was well doused, the ashes scattered, and the turf which he had removed before he lit it was replaced. Such damage as the tents and the horses had made was also covered or repaired and, to the untutored eyes of his pupils, the small clearing seemed to have been quite untouched by their stay.

Endryk was less sanguine. 'It'll have to do,' he said, though not unkindly.

'No Warden's going to notice, that's for sure,' Rhavvan told him confidently, proud of his new-learned skills.

Shortly after they left the camp, it began to rain – a steady vertical drizzle.

'This is set in for the day,' Endryk said, hitching on a long cape and pulling the hood forward. 'Not much fun.' He looked at the others and smiled. 'Well, I see the Wardens have good waterproof capes,' he said.

'Oh yes,' Rhavvan said. 'Standing for hours in the rain is

143

something we *do* know about. And I doubt it's any wetter here than in the city.'

For the rest of the day, a hunched procession moved steadily westwards, following the line of the shore. The terrain varied a great deal – sometimes flat and open, sometimes hilly and confused – a mixture of woodland and grassland with ragged stretches deep in ferns and shrubs, and an increasing number of rocky outcrops. But it presented them with no serious problems and they walked and rode equally, accepting the rhythm set by Endryk.

For the most part they travelled in silence, though on two occasions Endryk stopped so that he could show them some edible berries and roots. His dripping audience's attention was polite but unenthusiastic. He patted the saddlebags. 'Wait till you're hungry,' he said. 'This lot won't last for long. And we'll have to catch some livestock soon.' Thyrn gave his uncle a plaintive look as they moved off again.

Whenever they were in the open, Thyrn's gaze would be drawn inexorably northwards, but all he could make out through the rain was the dull green of the marshes fading into greyness.

Towards evening, the rain stopped and they finished the final part of their day's journey in the light of a low, warm and yellow sun which cut long shadows through the steam rising from them. They camped amongst trees again, though this time in the shelter of an overhanging rock face. After tending the horses and lighting a fire to dry themselves, they dined on a mixture of their own supplies and some of the roots and berries that Endryk had picked.

'A good day,' Endryk said, nudging the fire with his boot. 'We've done well.'

'That's a relief,' Hyrald said. 'I wouldn't have liked it to be a poor one. At least I can be exhausted with a clear conscience now. I didn't realize how tired I was until I sat down.'

Endryk looked a little guilty. 'I'm sorry,' he said. 'I forgot you're not used to travelling like this. I should've been more careful with you.'

'We'll live,' Rhavvan said, without conviction, his head slumping forward.

Endryk looked even guiltier. 'Before you get too settled, I need to show you how to lay some traps.'

The idea was greeted by a subdued chorus. 'What?'

'Traps – if you want to eat.'

It was dark when they returned from this reluctant exercise, but Nordath and Thyrn had kept the fire high and cheerful and this, added to their exhaustion, precluded any reproach to their guide.

'I'll do the first guard shift,' Thyrn said, by way of greeting.

'And I the second,' Endryk added quickly, while judiciously quietening the blazing fire.

Hyrald raised his hands in surrender.

There was little conversation after this and, as on the previous night, the topic of their ultimate destination was avoided.

Thyrn found his duty shift alarming, but gave a manful acknowledgement to Endryk when he was relieved. Wriggling gratefully into his tent he fell asleep immediately. Then, after what felt like only moments he was awake again. Someone had a hand over his mouth.

Chapter 11

Though the hand over his mouth was purposeful and completely effective in preventing him from making any sound, there was no threatening strength in it and Thyrn sensed rather than saw, in the dim light, a finger being applied to lips, warning him to be quiet.

'Don't be afraid – it's me, Endryk,' came a whisper.

Thyrn's wide eyes picked out only a faint silhouette, but Endryk's accent was unmistakable.

'Gently now. Don't wake the others. Come with me,' he said. 'I want to show you something.' The hand slipped from Thyrn's mouth and patted his shoulder conspiratorially. The silhouette slipped through the open flap of the tent, beckoning.

As he emerged, Thyrn took a deep breath. The air was cool and moist and had a quality about it quite different to anything he had ever known in the city. It felt good. Looking up he saw that the sky was greying.

'What time is it?' he whispered in some dismay as Endryk took his elbow and motioned him away from the tent.

'It'll be dawn soon,' came the reply. Thyrn felt his limbs go leaden. His mouth dropped open as a precursor to a loud exclamation. Endryk clamped his hand over it again. 'Don't wake the others,' he hissed. 'Especially your uncle, he needs his sleep. He's a lot of heart but he's too old for this kind of life.' He pointed into the gloom and Thyrn was just able to make out Nordath dutifully guarding the camp. He was sitting against a tree and was fast asleep. 'Don't worry,' Endryk said. 'Nals will keep guard until we get back.'

'Get back? From where? Where are we going?'

The hand on his elbow led him further away from the camp, then it released him and gestured to him to follow. Curious now, he obeyed the instruction almost without hesitation. He needed no injunction to silence. This was not only implicit in Endryk's posture, it was commanded by the heavy stillness of the surrounding trees.

After walking for a few minutes, Endryk stopped. In a gentle, sweeping movement, but keeping his hands low, he opened his arms in a slow, expansive gesture and then brought them together again. Thyrn watched him, bewildered. He had a momentary urge to copy him.

'What are you doing?' he risked.

'Just breathing. Feeling the morning,' came the unhelpful reply. 'It's important to remember that really there's only now.'

Thyrn frowned and let the matter go. 'Where are we going? What've you got me up at this time for?'

Endryk's smile showed pale through the greyness.

'So that you could feel the morning as well.'

'What!'

'Sh!'

A gesture brought the silence of the forest to Endryk's aid and then he was moving again, soft and easy. Thyrn followed, blundering and awkward by comparison, dew from the disturbed undergrowth dampening his boots and dark staining his trousers.

'Where are you taking me?' he asked after they had been walking for a while.

'We'll be there soon, but I wanted to talk to you alone.'

'To talk to me? What for?'

'Oh, lots of reasons. Not the least being the fact that you're at the heart of this business, and as I've allied myself with you

I need to know more about you.'

'I can't tell you any more than I told you the other day. If I could, I would. I don't know why Vashnar's . . .'

Endryk stopped him. 'I understand that,' he said. 'But it's not particularly important at the moment. It's sufficient for now that Vashnar's a pursuing enemy. What we've got to do first of all is make sure that we can survive out here indefinitely.'

'Indefinitely?' Thyrn stopped. 'You mean – for ever?'

Endryk did not reply.

'I hadn't thought about it like that,' Thyrn said after an uncertain silence.

'You hadn't thought about it at all,' Endryk said, walking on. 'None of you had. Somewhere in all your minds is the vague idea that sooner or later, everything will be as it was again.'

'No,' Thyrn protested loyally.

'Yes,' Endryk replied unequivocally. This time it was he who stopped. It was lighter now and Thyrn found himself transfixed by a penetrating gaze. 'Everyone thinks like that in an emergency. I've done it myself many times. It's what keeps you going in the first instance. Then, eventually, a quiet time comes and reality starts to impinge on you.'

'And?'

'And you change. Sooner or later you respond to that reality. And sooner's always a lot less painful than later, believe me.' His gaze released Thyrn and he pointed. 'Over there. Look.' He was indicating a tree about twenty paces away. At first, Thyrn could not make anything out, but as they drew nearer he wrinkled his nose in dismay. Hanging from a thin branch driven into the ground was a rabbit, a noose tight about its neck. It was twitching slightly. Before he could say anything, Endryk had deftly released the animal and struck it a powerful blow with his hand. Thyrn jumped at the impact. It seemed out of character for the man.

149

'Thank you,' Endryk said to the dead animal before thrusting it into Thyrn's hand. 'Does this bother you?' he asked as he bent the branch down and re-set the snare.

'I'm not used to animals,' Thyrn said evasively, holding the rabbit at arm's length.

'I can see that,' Endryk replied, standing up and taking it from him. 'Which means you won't be able to skin this either, I suppose.'

'Skin!' Thyrn shrank a little and mouthed the word, as if speaking it aloud might offend the dead rabbit.

Endryk took the animal from him, at once businesslike and fatherly. 'This is one of the things I need to talk to you about. I don't know what it's like being a Caddoran, still less someone as special as you seem to be, but it's very important that you understand that your former life is gone. Gone for ever. Perhaps you might get back to something like it one day, I don't know, but what I do know is that if that's to happen, you need to survive, and to survive you need to accept things the way they are, here, now, and to learn. Above all, you need to learn. You're a long way from anywhere here, and there's no one – *no one* – to help you if you get into trouble. Do you understand what I mean?'

'I think so,' Thyrn replied unhappily.

'Let's look at the rest of the traps,' Endryk said. 'Tell me about your journey as we walk.'

It was not a long tale, though Thyrn, having been terrified for most of the time, was vague about much of it. As far as he could recall, the warning from Hyrald's friend had enabled them to escape the mob, and they had spent some time hiding in a variety of empty properties. He did remember Hyrald saying that they should use the places that the mob had already searched. Then there had been a confusing collection of hushed discussions about scouting the streets, gathering supplies, dark figures coming and going, followed by a night-time cart ride hidden under old sacks, with stern instructions about silence and stillness. Then walking, and riding – he could not remember where the horses had come from or why they had been abandoned – sleeping in barns and outhouses, stealing food and various other things until they had eventually arrived on the shore.

Endryk did not press him on any part of the story, though he interrupted him as they came to each trap. They found one more rabbit, but the others were empty. This time Endryk showed Thyrn how to re-set them and made him do it. 'We'll check them again when we leave.' At the same time he pointed out why he had positioned the traps where he had, showing Thyrn rabbit burrows and signs of regular traffic. Then he showed him how to skin and clean the rabbit, a proceeding that both fascinated and appalled Thyrn and which included also instruction in how to sharpen a knife when, teeth bared unhappily, he attempted the same exercise with his own knife. 'You'll cut your head off with a knife this blunt,' was Endryk's horrified verdict as he examined the offending tool.

'Why did you thank the rabbits?' Thyrn asked as they set off back to the camp.

'We took their lives so that we could eat, the least we could do is thank them, isn't it? Honour their gift.'

Thyrn looked at him to see if he was being made the butt of some strange joke, but he saw that Endryk was quite serious. In fact, he was very serious. 'Survival is about awareness, Thyrn. You're a part of the land and everything in it, not separate, a passer-by untouched and untouching, even though you might feel like that. Everything connects to everything else, every action has consequences most of them not calculable – but you need to know that that's the way things are. You must honour the things you use. If you don't you're dishonouring a part of yourself and that prompts the question deep inside you, is it worthwhile, your surviving?' He looked intently at

Thyrn and then smiled broadly. 'You don't know what I'm talking about, do you?'

'A little bit, I think,' Thyrn replied, adding ruefully, 'I certainly understand about connections.'

Endryk looked rueful in his turn. 'Yes, of course you do,' he said. 'I'd forgotten.' He began to walk a little more quickly, levering his mood into cheerfulness. 'You've done well,' he said. 'You pick things up very quickly. Far quicker than I ever did.'

'It's my job,' Thyrn retorted quite unselfconsciously.

Endryk laughed softly at his manner and held up a placatory hand. The sun was above the horizon now, shining brightly through the leafy canopy above them and throwing a confusion of long dancing shadows everywhere. Endryk looked at his pupil and drew in a noisy breath. 'As I said before, it's important you learn as much as possible about how to live out here, Thyrn, for all our sakes. We all have to help one another, and there's no room for passengers. Your uncle concerns me. He's the one who's going to feel the strain first. The time's come now when you have to look after him, not he you. Do you understand?'

The question obviously disturbed Thyrn and he avoided Endryk's gaze for some time before grimacing guiltily. 'Yes, you're right. I've really hurt him, haven't I?' For an instant he seemed to be on the verge of tears. 'He's probably the only real friend I've got, and I dragged him into all this. All he wanted was to enjoy his quiet life – books, music, talking with his cronies.'

Endryk intervened, concerned by the response he had evoked. 'You turned to him for help. Don't reproach yourself for that. I'm sure he doesn't blame you. It's not your fault that Vashnar did what he did. You certainly couldn't have foreseen it. I meant . . .'

'I know what you meant. I've got to shape up and not be a burden any more, haven't I?' Thyrn took a gasping breath. 'I love my uncle, I'll do anything I can to make things right for him again, but I don't know what to do. I'm . . .' He took another breath before forcing out the words, 'I'm afraid.'

'You'd be a rare fool if you weren't.'

Thyrn blinked at Endryk's blunt response.

'Being afraid is the way you should be right now. Hyrald and the others are, you can rest assured.'

'But . . .'

'But nothing. They are, trust me. You can't have a lunatic tell an entire country to kill you and not be afraid.'

Thyrn looked at him in silence, uncertain what to do with this statement of the obvious.

'I want it to go away.'

The words hung in the waking morning air, simple and sincere and free from the tremulous self-pity that would have provoked disdain or anger.

Endryk put a hand on his arm, 'Yes, of course you do,' he said with equal simplicity. 'Fear's wretched. No one wants it. But it's part of what we are and there are times when we need it if we're going to survive. The others back there are Wardens; one way or another they know that. They're used to it – it helps.'

'My uncle's not a Warden.'

'No, but he's damned near a parent and that can be really frightening.'

There was a hint of a smile about his mouth and Thyrn gave him a suspicious look.

'He cares about you – about what happens to you. He feels what you feel,' Endryk said.

Thyrn looked down at his dew-sodden boots and trousers. Pollen and fragments of leaves and grass were clinging to them. 'I understand what you're saying. I want to shape up, to help, to take care of my uncle instead of being a burden. But I'm only—'

'Only! Only what?' Endryk's grip tightened about Thyrn's arm. 'You are what you are. Don't give me *only*. A little while ago you were someone who had a very special skill – a skill which enabled you to be of valuable service in Arvenshelm. And to command payment that others your age would kill for. You've still got that skill, but now you need others as well – skills to help you survive out here, on your own. You've already got some.' He pointed to the two skinned rabbits.

'But—'

'But nothing.' Endryk bent close to him. 'When you feel doubt and inadequacy gnawing at you, remember what you've already achieved, and remember your uncle. It's your turn to carry him now. You'll find resources in you you never dreamt of. And while I'm with you, I'll teach you whatever I can. Just watch, listen and, above all, think. And if you want to know something, ask.' His voice became urgent. 'That's important, Thyrn. Not only for you but for the others, because when they see you learning something, they'll learn it themselves.'

Thyrn looked puzzled. 'But what do they need to learn? They're Wardens.'

A laugh, not altogether kindly, burst out of Endryk, but he cut it off sharply. 'They seem like good people to me. Decent and honourable in their own way. And Hyrald's certainly getting to grips with what's happening. But my past experience of Wardens hasn't always been happy. They're not particularly well-disciplined or well-trained, and as an organization they leave a lot to be desired. I soon learned it was best to avoid them if possible.'

'You've had trouble with Wardens up here?'

Thyrn's open curiosity deflected Endryk. He became reflective. 'No. I travelled all over Arvenstaat before I ended up here. When I first arrived I was going to go south for ever – just for ever.' He paused, his eyes distant. 'But by the time I reached the southern mountains I was exhausted, inside and out, and I couldn't face them. And it was coming up to winter.'

'No one ever goes south,' Thyrn said knowingly. The impassability of the southern mountains was a given truth for

154

the Arvens. It was also false, though the mountains were not for the faint, the feeble or the inexperienced, and few travelled them.

'Where are you from?' Thyrn asked abruptly.

Endryk waved a hand in the direction of the unseen shore but otherwise ignored the question. 'So I ended up wandering around, taking odd jobs here and there for my keep. I spent quite a time in Arvenshelm. Learned a lot about this strange country I'd found myself in, with its farce of a government in the Moot, and the Wardens making up the law as they went along.' He shook his head. 'It's not a good way for a country to be, Thyrn. Something bad will come of it eventually.' He shrugged. 'Still, that's not our immediate problem, is it? Come on. Let's rouse the camp.'

'How did you get back up here?' Thyrn asked.

Endryk frowned, then sighed. 'Well, I did tell you to ask, didn't I? I came here the same way you did – fleeing an enemy. But unlike you, my enemy was in my head. I carried him with me all the time, and he drove me from every place I went to. I'm not sure I'm totally rid of him even now.' He waved a hand to forbid any more questions on the subject. 'But as I told you before, there comes a quiet time eventually and reality starts to make itself felt. In my case, it was when I was on my hands and knees out on the shore and an old shoreman was dragging me to safety.'

He stopped and stood silent for some time before clearing his throat and looking accusingly at Thyrn.

'But we're talking about you, aren't we? Not me. My enemy's long given up the chase – though I suspect we only have a kind of truce. But I've a feeling that yours hasn't really begun his pursuit yet. And to be ready for him, you and the others need to learn a lot more.'

Thyrn's loyalty reared again. 'I don't think Hyrald and the others have much to learn about looking after themselves.'

This time Endryk did not laugh. 'Yes they have, believe me. I've no doubt they can look after themselves very well in Arvenshelm – dealing with drunks and thieves and the like. Certainly they can fight well. They dealt with those others on the shore splendidly – it's no slight thing to stand your ground against a mounted attacker. But here . . .' He made an expansive gesture, encompassing the small sunlit clearing they were walking through. 'Here you can die of starvation, of thirst, of cold, through eating poisonous vegetation, maggoty meat, drinking foul water – most unheroically, like an animal – slowly, dismally, eaten by rodents and insects while you're still alive but too weak to move . . .'

He stopped. Thyrn's eyes were widening and the blood was draining from his face.

'Sorry,' he said unsympathetically. 'But there are things you need to know out here and Hyrald and his friends are no wiser than you about them. Their problem – *our* problem, actually – is that it's more difficult for them to admit their ignorance than it is for you, so if you act as a willing student it'll give them a chance to learn without losing face. Can we agree on that – our secret plot?'

He held out his hand. Thyrn shifted the rabbits to his other hand and grasped it warmly. 'Yes, I want to help – my uncle especially.' He was suddenly full of enthusiasm. 'Teach me everything you can. I can learn faster than anyone you've ever known.'

As they came in sight of the camp they saw that Nordath was awake. He was struggling to light the fire amid a cloud of smoke. Endryk looked upwards as it escaped through the canopy.

Thyrn hailed his uncle, waving the rabbits high. Nordath gave a cry and jumped to his feet unsteadily, patting his chest and coughing.

'You startled me,' he said, rubbing his watering eyes. 'I

thought you were still asleep.' He focused blearily on the carcasses dangling from his nephew's hands. 'What are they?' he asked in some alarm.

'Food,' Thyrn announced with great relish. 'Endryk showed me how to catch and skin them.' He mimed the operation. Nordath's expression ran a gamut of emotions until, seeing his nephew's patent delight at his achievement, he settled for sharing it with him. 'Very good,' he said, as encouragingly as he could.

Endryk in the meantime was attending to the fire, blowing on it gently and carefully feeding twigs into the glow that Nordath had managed to create. Discreetly he signalled Thyrn to watch. 'Not bad, Nordath,' he said. 'Not bad at all. But your kindling's a bit damp – hence the smoke.' Glancing at Thyrn he made a swift series of cuts in a thin twig, shaving back the wood like feathers. 'It's drier inside,' he explained, then he pointed to a dead branch hanging from a nearby tree, before adding the twig to the burgeoning fire. 'But standing deadwood's better, if you can find any,' he said casually.

'A bit of smoke won't hurt, will it?' Nordath retorted in a mildly injured tone before being convulsed by another fit of coughing as the smoke swept round and enfolded him.

'I think you've answered that for yourself,' Endryk replied, laughing. 'It's all right if you want to keep the flies off, but not for cooking, warmth, or a peaceful fireside.' More serious, he added, 'And it'll tell an enemy exactly where we are.'

'Enemy, what enemy?' It was Rhavvan emerging from his tent. He was dishevelled and scratching himself freely.

'Don't worry. We're just having a lesson in country crafts,' Nordath said, not without some heavy irony. Rhavvan grunted and disappeared into the bushes.

'That's another thing we need to talk about,' Endryk said to Thyrn, softly but very significantly, nodding in the direction Rhavvan had gone.

Breakfast proved to be quite a cheery affair with much claiming of credit for the capture of the rabbits by the previous night's reluctant trappers. In the course of it, Endryk conspicuously explained to Thyrn many things about the trapping and eating of animals and birds. He touched again on the grim ways of dying that lay in wait for the unwary, to which Thyrn nodded sagely, while the other listeners fell oddly silent. When Endryk had finished he added a discreet wink to his pupil.

'Can't live on rabbits for ever, of course,' he concluded. 'Not on their own anyway. They don't have everything we need. But they're tasty enough and they'll get us through the day. We'll collect some roots and leaves as we travel. Add a little extra to our fare.'

After they broke camp, they visited the traps again and Thyrn was able to demonstrate his new-found skill with a further catch. It provoked more banter, but they were all quietly impressed, not least Endryk. 'You do learn quickly, don't you?' he said as he helped to dismantle the remaining traps.

'I told you, it's my job. I watch, I copy,' Thyrn replied simply. Then he looked at Endryk with an unusual intensity. 'I'm also starting to think.'

The weather that day was overcast but mild and well suited to walking and leisurely riding. The terrain became a little more sparse, with fewer trees and more long stretches of exposed rock. The most conspicuous feature of their journey was the gradual appearance of the land to the north which was clearly visible whenever they travelled close to the shoreline. The open sea was slowly being transformed into a wide river. Thyrn, however, seemed to be less distracted by it than on the previous day, his attention being focused much more on Endryk who continued with his instruction of the entire group by stopping several times – ostensibly for Thyrn's benefit – to pick various plants and leaves and to unearth a few edible roots. This time it was Hyrald who kept glancing northwards whenever the opposite shore was visible. A decision would have to be made soon. North or south? North into the unknown, abandoning everything they had ever known. South into . . . ? He did not relish arriving at the end of this particular journey and unashamedly shunned the topic whenever it came to him.

'I'm afraid I've got a confession to make,' Nordath said as they camped that night. 'I dozed off when I was on guard last night – this morning.'

'We saw you,' Thyrn blurted out with a laugh but immediately regretting his inadvertent treachery. 'But Nals was keeping an eye on things,' he added hastily.

'Don't worry about it,' Rhavvan said dismissively. 'To be honest, I don't see any point in losing sleep just to stand listening to animals and insects doing whatever it is they're doing. It gives me the creeps. And it's ridiculous. No one's going to come after us now. Not all the way out here.'

Hyrald glanced at Endryk, who gave a slight shrug. 'They've come once, they could come again,' he said. 'But you know your own kind best. There's nothing else I can say, except that just listening to you all, gives me the feeling that your Commander won't give up until he's caught you. He doesn't sound like a man who willingly leaves loose ends about his affairs.'

Hyrald stepped towards the looming decision.

'That's true enough,' he said. 'Vashnar's nothing if not obsessive about details. And if we go south we'll have no alternative but to go carefully – very carefully. I know it's something we're not used to, but that can be said about this whole business. For what it's worth I think we might as well keep the habit going now we've started. Of course, if we go north, that's another matter.'

He looked around the firelit group questioningly, but while Rhavvan was shaking his head in silent disapproval, no one seemed disposed either to dispute the idea of continuing the guard shifts or to take up the debate about which way they should go. Their unwillingness to participate annoyed Hyrald. He turned to Nordath. 'Don't worry about this morning. No harm's been done. But – no disrespect to you – this is much harder on you than the rest of us.' He tried to find words that would enable him to relieve Nordath of the need to stand his turn as guard, but nothing came that would not also relieve him of his dignity. 'So I'd like you to take the first shift – and just for an hour. Is that acceptable?'

'Yes, it is,' Nordath replied. 'Thanks for the thoughtfulness. I did find it very hard this morning.'

'Tomorrow we decide,' Hyrald said starkly to the others. 'North or south. As we ride. Before we get too tired. We've slept on it long enough. Now we're just avoiding it.'

The next morning found them developing the beginnings of a routine under Endryk's covert instruction and Thyrn's conspicuous example-setting, and the campsite they left behind was markedly better repaired than their previous ones. They also added two more rabbits and a squirrel to their supplies.

Despite Hyrald's injunction of the night before however, none of them showed any willingness to discuss their future destination – least of all Hyrald himself.

Gradually the ground began to rise and eventually the trees petered out completely, though not before Endryk had brought down a large plump bird with a sling shot. It was a sudden and impulsive action and it impressed even him. 'Haven't used this in years,' he said as he retrieved the bird. 'I must get my eye back in again.' He reloaded the sling and swung it again, this time stopping the hissing pouch and missile in his other hand with a loud slap.

'Hope those never find their way on to the streets,' Adren said anxiously.

Endryk gave her a puzzled look. 'I don't understand.'

'Criminals, street thugs, the kind of riff-raff we have to deal with,' she amplified. 'Armed with those, they'd be lethal.'

The answer did not enlighten Endryk. He held up the sling. 'Hardly the work of a skilled craftsman, is it?' he said. 'If your riff-raff aren't using these already, I doubt you've anything to fear. It's not because they can't make one, it's because it takes a long time and a lot of practice to become a good slinger – just as it does with a bow or a sword. I can vouch for that on all counts – and I'm only average with all of them. If you're facing anyone who can use one of these properly, then while he might be a criminal, you'd be making a mistake to think of him as riff-raff. He'll probably be a trained soldier and you'll have serious problems with him no matter what he's carrying. Of course, if he can't use one then you can be reassured by the fact that he'd be as much at risk as you.' He laughed.

Adren seemed inclined to pursue the debate, but Hyrald intervened. 'You'll have to excuse my sister,' he said, laughing. 'I'm afraid she's got a bit of Vashnar in her. She thinks that laws can change people – and worse, that we can control them.'

'That's not fair,' Adren protested. 'Sensible laws, properly discussed . . .'

Rhavvan looked skywards and Hyrald snapped his fingers. 'Exactly,' he said triumphantly. '"Restraints so gentle and moderate that no man of probity would wish to see them set aside", etc etc. But not the kind of laws the Moot spews out talk about a tenuous grasp on reality. If we tried to enforce half of them, we'd be fighting a war within a week. You know well enough we can only do our job because most people let us.'

'This sounds like an old familiar debate,' Endryk said before Adren could reply. 'I'll stand outside and watch if you don't mind.'

But it was Thyrn who ended it. 'Can I try that?' he asked excitedly, reaching out to take the sling.

'Maybe later,' Endryk said, hastily pushing the sling into

his belt. 'In the meantime, you can pluck this bird.' He demonstrated then threw the carcass to Thyrn. 'Keep the feathers somewhere safe, we don't want to leave any more of a trail than we have to.'

Thyrn caught the bird clumsily. 'I can do *this* later,' he muttered.

'Now,' Endryk insisted. 'While it's warm.' A flick of his hand and an encouraging nod indicated that Thyrn should pick up the feathers that had spun into the air as he caught the bird. He did so without comment.

Nordath noted the exchange and seemed quietly pleased by it.

'You still think someone will follow us?' Rhavvan asked.

'I just think it's a risk, from what you've told me,' Endryk replied. 'But it's good manners to leave the trail as we find it anyway.'

'How long before there's a safe crossing?' Hyrald asked, as the turn of the conversation brought him back to the relentlessly avoided topic of their final destination.

'It's been a long time since I've travelled this way, so I can't say exactly,' Endryk replied. 'Tomorrow – midday, probably.'

'Where will you go?'

Endryk started at Thyrn's unexpected question. 'I don't know,' he said.

'I'd like you to stay with us,' Thyrn said.

The reply drew all eyes towards Endryk.

'I'll keep that in mind when we've to decide,' he said.

As they walked and rode through the day, the ground continued to rise and what had been a wide flat sea separating them from a distant shoreline, gradually became a noisy tumbling river at the bottom of a steep-sided valley.

'It doesn't look any different over there, does it?' Hyrald said, as avoiding a large outcrop brought them within clear sight of the far side of the valley. The group came to a halt spontaneously and stood staring across. The air was filled with the noise of the river echoing up from below. It was an intimidating sound, obliging them to raise their voices to be heard above it. It also lured them forward, until they were looking down at a sight which was equally intimidating. A jagged cliff dropped through a dense tree line to reveal a river that was both wide and foaming white with violence.

They moved off in silence.

After a while, the light beginning to fade, Endryk pointed to the skyline ahead. 'We'll camp on the far side of that ridge,' he said. 'Wake up to a downhill walk.'

As if the words had been trapped by the primeval din of the river and then released by Endryk's simple statement, Thyrn said, 'I think we have to go back home. I think we have to find out what's happening.'

Endryk was slightly ahead of the others but like them he turned to Thyrn sharply. As he did so, he noticed something in the distance.

He closed his eyes for a moment and lowered his head. Then he opened them and pointed.

'Look,' he said flatly.

The country they had traversed lay spread out behind them. In the distance a column of smoke was rising from the trees.

Chapter 12

The column of smoke rose like an unnatural sapling from the green shadow-streaked canopy. Its lower reaches were dark and ominous while higher up it became a pallid grey at the touch of the early evening sun before bending and twisting erratically and finally dispersing into a soft haze as though striking an unseen ceiling.

'What is it?' Hyrald asked.

'A camp fire,' Endryk replied, not without a hint of surprise that such a question should even be asked.

'Someone from the village?' There was an element of clinging to hope in Hyrald's voice. It was immediately dashed.

'No, nor from any of the villages in this region. No one needs to come out here. No one does. Grazing, hunting, farming, they're all better to the south. Not many even come as far as my cottage. Whoever it is, isn't local.' He shook his head. 'And they're as experienced at surviving out here as you are.'

Hyrald looked at him questioningly but it was Nordath who answered. 'They're making too much smoke,' he said, recalling Endryk's comments about his own fire-lighting efforts the previous day. 'I understand what you meant about an enemy seeing us, now. I never realized.'

'No reason why you should,' Endryk replied, without taking his eyes off the rising smoke.

'Who is it, then?' Hyrald asked.

'I don't know. But our wisest plan is to assume they're after us – you, anyway – and act accordingly.'

'We could go and find out,' Rhavvan suggested, raising a clenched fist. 'Sneak up on them. I'm getting heartily sick of running.'

Endryk shook his head but did not argue. 'I sympathize,' he said quietly. 'But it's much further than it looks – the best part of what we've covered today. And that's no small fire – there could be quite a few of them. Plus the fact that you'd lose your line of sight as soon as you got back down into the trees. You'd get lost.'

Rhavvan scowled and grunted but said nothing further.

'Assuming it is someone chasing us, what should we do?' Hyrald asked.

'Carry on as we were intending,' Endryk replied uneasily. 'Just take more care covering our tracks, keep a good guard at night and watch our backs all the time. For the moment we have the advantage. We know where they are, but they don't know where we are, or even that we're here. We must keep it that way.'

He motioned the group upwards towards the ridge. 'We'd better hurry. It's getting dark and we don't want to be using lights to find our way.'

The final ascent proved to be longer and steeper than it had seemed from below and it was a sweating and freely panting group that Endryk finally hustled over the ridge. Thyrn supported his uncle while the others led the horses. Endryk made them hug the edge of an outcrop and for the first time since they had set out, he showed some real urgency, constantly looking back and discreetly both keeping them together and urging them forward. He relaxed only when they were safely over, then, telling the others to rest, he went back up to the ridge and, crouching low, spent some time watching the still climbing smoke.

'Why the rush all of a sudden?' Rhavvan asked when he

returned. 'I thought you said they were almost a day away.'

'It was just in case they knew what they were doing and had a lookout. A good man up a tree might have seen us against the skyline, especially if he had a glass.'

Rhavvan closed his eyes and blew out a frustrated breath. 'Give me a couple of thugs in an alleyway any day,' he said, patting the long staff fastened to his horse. 'This is *not* my kind of country.'

'It will be soon,' Endryk said, unexpectedly serious. 'You'd wit enough to hear those men on the beach coming and courage enough to deal with them. You'll survive here if you keep your heads clear – watch, listen, think, learn – like Thyrn here.' He pointed back at the ridge. 'Arvenstaat's got no army or even a military tradition, so if that's someone looking for you – and it probably is – they won't be some trained elite, they'll be your own kind. And this won't be *their* kind of country either. In fact, looking at the state of that fire, it certainly isn't. They'll be lucky if they don't burn their own camp down.'

'Do you want to press on while there's some light?' Hyrald asked, unsettled by Endryk's remarks. 'Get further away from them?'

'No, I don't think so,' Endryk replied after a little thought. 'On the whole it'll be safer if we can see where they are. If we get the chance, we'll lay a false trail tomorrow just in case they are following us. We'll camp here tonight, near the top. That way we can keep an eye on them through the night and particularly first thing in the morning.'

The weather, however, worked against them. They were roused the next day by Endryk to be greeted by a damp, grey mist as they emerged from their tents. Endryk had already lit a small fire and cooked a rudimentary meal. He was unusually brisk. 'Eat up quickly,' he said to his shivering and reluctant charges. 'There's nothing to be gained by waiting around here. I don't think it's likely but we've got to assume your friends are already under way and we need to get out of this.' An airy wave encompassed the greyness about them. 'I think it's in for the day, but it's probably fairly local. With luck we should move out of it as we drop down.' Under his urging, the meal was eaten while the horses were being saddled and the camp broken. The only delay he allowed was in ensuring that all signs of their presence were meticulously removed.

Infected by Endryk's subtle pressure, Rhavvan became impatient to be off. 'They'll never see those,' he exclaimed disparagingly as Endryk carefully disposed of the scarred rocks that he had used as a fireplace.

Endryk continued unmoved. 'Never underestimate the effects of the small action, Rhavvan,' he said. 'There are demons in the details.'

'You sound like Vashnar.'

Endryk paused and smiled briefly. 'I'm sure he's not without some charm.'

'Come on. Let's be off.'

Endryk straightened up and gave the site a final glance before turning to leave. 'People don't come out here, Rhavvan. We're intruders – oddities – and we're as conspicuous as a herd of cattle in the Moot Palace square. Don't ever forget that.'

For most of the morning they trudged on in gloomy silence, surrounded by the mist and the sound of the nearby river. However, as Endryk had hoped, the mist gradually yellowed and eventually they came out into a bright sunny day. White clouds littered the blue sky. Drifting slowly, they had the purposeful look of a stately armada. The countryside was little different from that which they had been moving through previously, though its dips and rises were more pronounced, its woods darker and more dense, and its vegetation generally had a tough, hardy look to it. One new feature was the proliferation of boulders and large rocky outcrops. Some, spiky and jagged, looked as though they had been thrust through the ground by some act of violence far below, while others, weathered and rounded, looked as though they had been scattered at random by a vast and careless hand. Occasionally, isolated trees and bushes could be seen clinging to sheer rock faces, like determined siege engineers bravely challenging the vaunted invulnerability of a castle wall.

The mood of the group lightened in the sunlight, though the knowledge that others were behind them hung about them like a cold remnant of the morning mist. From time to time, each of them would look back, though it was not often that the ridge they had camped on could be seen.

As they moved along, the river rose to meet them, its steep valley sides disappearing and its location becoming less immediately apparent, though the sound of it was unremitting. Eventually they found themselves standing on its bank.

Despite being so easily hidden by the terrain, it was very wide. It was also very fast and turbulent. In all it was an intimidating sight.

'I'm coming to the end of the territory that I've travelled before,' Endryk said. 'And I have to confess it's been so long since I've been here that much of the way I've only recalled as we came to it.' He pointed upstream. Just above the trees, steep rocky walls could be seen. 'But this I remember clearly. We'll have to move south for a little while to find a place to get over those, but once we're over there's a place where it's possible to cross — at least it used to be. After that, I've no idea. If you choose to carry on west after that, you'll encounter the Karpas Mountains eventually. I imagine there'll be other places to cross on the way, but . . .' He shrugged and clicked his horse to move on.

As they continued, Hyrald pulled alongside Thyrn. 'Last night, before we saw that fire, you said you wanted to go back home. We didn't get a chance to talk about it after that, but is that still what you want?'

Thyrn glanced at Endryk leading the group as if the man's back might offer him inspiration. Then he looked north. The river was no longer visible. There was just the same hilly countryside that lay in every other direction.

'It's no different from here, is it?' he said.

Hyrald did not know how to reply. Thyrn put his fingertips to his temples. 'I can still feel part of Vashnar inside me. It's dim and distant but it's there, without a doubt. I don't know what it is, or why it is, but it's not changed since the other day, and I don't think it's going to.'

Hyrald's expression became concerned. He was about to call Nordath, but Thyrn stopped him. 'Don't worry. It's not a threat – to me, or to any of us. It just is. Like my aching legs and sore behind. I suspect Vashnar can sense me too. It's probably making him very afraid – he's not used to what the mind can do. At least I know a little. Perhaps that's why there's suddenly someone behind us – his fear.'

Hyrald found himself leaning forward, listening intently. Almost in spite of himself he had grown to like Thyrn as they had made their frantic flight across the country. Though he would perhaps have been hesitant to phrase it thus in front of his colleagues, where a certain worldly cynicism was traditional, it offended him deeply that this awkward but talented and fundamentally harmless young man should be driven from his home and hounded across the country without any semblance of legal process. It offended whatever instincts had originally turned him into a Warden – a protector of the ordinary people. That he and his colleagues had been subjected to the same treatment merely reinforced his sense of offence.

But the Thyrn he was listening to now was different. He had changed. Even as the thought occurred to him, he realized that Thyrn had been changing since they had set out from Endryk's cottage. His curiosity was as intense as ever, breaking through in a childlike manner from time to time – the incident with the sling had been a case in point – but he was definitely different. Hyrald recalled the sight of Endryk plucking a few feathers from the bird he had killed and then throwing it to Thyrn, who completed the task with only a minimal objection and as though it was something he had done all his life. He saw too, the brief exchange of looks between the two men. Other small incidents came to him – Thyrn asking conspicuous questions and Endryk drawing in everyone else as he answered, Thyrn doing his guard shift without complaint, and quietly supporting his uncle as they clambered up the last ridge.

He recognized the symptoms – Endryk had taken Thyrn in charge. He had done the same himself before now for the benefit of cadet Wardens. And Endryk's motives were probably the same, a mixture of the altruistic and the selfish. There would be a genuine desire to help someone learn easily what had taken him much time and effort to acquire – a thank you to his own teachers – part of the endless drive to improve which threads through the generations. Then there would be a childish impulse to demonstrate one's own knowledge and superiority – to boast. As Thyrn had done, he looked at Endryk at the head of their small procession. There was scarcely a vestige of the occasional resentment he had felt towards him at the outset. Now he was profoundly glad to have had his guidance throughout this venture. Hyrald had no doubt that it was he who was the junior cadet here and that under his own leadership, the party might have fared very badly indeed. This land might be beautiful and in many ways quietening to the spirit, but aside from any unknown dangers such as the tide that had nearly finished them, the isolation was deeply frightening. Being a capable and practical man, it gave him a particularly disturbing measure of his inadequacy, of his total dependence on others for the vital components of his life such as food and water, not to mentioned shelter and the countless other small services which were available in the city and whose existence he accepted so casually.

But Endryk was still an enigma. There were so many questions Hyrald wanted to ask him. He judged him to be about six or seven years younger than himself, which, from what he had already spoken of meant that he would have been little more than Thyrn's age when he came to Arvenstaat. What had sent him here? Had there indeed been some terrible war up there? Was he a fugitive, and if so, from what? It did not seem likely that he was a coward. Where had he learned this way of self-sufficiency? And Rhavvan's taunt had not been too far from the mark; he *did* have traits in common with Vashnar – an almost obsessive eye for detail and the consequences of any action. But while in Vashnar this was dark and brooding, in Endryk it illuminated, clarified.

'Arvenstaat's got no army, or even a military tradition,' he had said. The notion of an army was something that most Arvens had difficulty with, in so far as any of them concerned themselves about it. For most of its known history Arvenstaat had experienced only internal strife. No foreign army had ever marched across its borders or even menaced it. As a result, the very idea was inconceivable. True, the Morlider had been troublesome on occasions with their raids on coastal villages, but these had rarely been worse than the riots that tended to mar the peace of Arvenstaat's larger towns and cities from time to time as the Moot insisted on the implementation of some fatuous and irrelevant legislation. They had always been dealt with eventually by the good souls of the villages rousing themselves and combining to present a substantial and angry presence whenever Morlider ships were seen approaching. Further, however bad the Morlider incursions had been, it was always known that they would not last for long. The floating islands on which they lived were subject to the mysterious currents of the outer sea which sooner or later always drew them away.

172

Hyrald tried to imagine what a battle between armies would be like. The nearest he could imagine would be Wardens opposing Wardens, but even this he found difficult. A veteran of more than a few riots he was familiar with the procedure for dealing with an angry crowd – holding a shield line, cracking the heads of the ringleaders and leaving the rest plenty of escape routes. But here, in this random and unstructured landscape? It needed little imagination to see how a shield line could be outflanked or how the trees and undergrowth could shelter ambushes. And against a determined enemy, one that could hold a line as well as you, what then?

Hyrald wiped his hand across his brow. It was damp.

Had Endryk been trained to fight in such conflicts? Had he been in one? Was it that that had driven him from his own land?

So engrossed had he become that for a moment he was sorely tempted to ride up to Endryk and ask him outright. But, aware again of Thyrn by his side, he forced his attention back to his concerns. What had he said about Vashnar? 'Perhaps that's why there's suddenly someone behind us – his fear.' A strange remark. He took up the threads of their conversation.

'I can't pretend to understand what's happening between you and Vashnar, Thyrn,' he said. 'But it's important that you be clear about what you want to do.'

Endryk signalled that they should dismount and walk.

'I think we need to stop and talk,' Hyrald said. 'Decide what we're going to do when we reach the crossing.'

'Talk as we walk, Hyrald,' Endryk said. 'This place is too closed in. I'd like to get to higher ground. See if we can spot whoever's behind us before we relax too much.'

'I don't think there's anything to talk about,' Thyrn said abruptly, but motioning Endryk to continue. 'Not for me anyway. I've not changed my mind since last night. I've done nothing wrong. Not even broken my Caddoran Oath – you can all vouch for that. I can see it's not safe just to go blundering back into the city, but there's nothing to say we're going to be safe if we head north.' He shuffled his feet awkwardly. 'I know that's all I've been talking about since we got away from Arvenshelm, but I was frightened. I just wanted to get away – anywhere. I'm still frightened, but these last few days I've had a chance to think. Wherever we go we'll have to find food and shelter all the time, day in, day out. No disrespect to any of you but if we hadn't met Endryk, what state would we be in now? And where will we be in a few months' time when it's winter? And what if one of us is hurt, or takes ill?' He looked at Rhavvan. 'We've all got good lives back in Arvenshelm, you said, and you were right, and I'm going to go back to get mine – find out what's going on, somehow. Death Cry or not, Vashnar or not, frightened or not.'

He cleared his throat selfconsciously. The others stared at his flushed face, far from certain how to deal with this unprecedented outburst. Despite Endryk's injunction, they had all stopped. Anxious to avoid cross-examination, Thyrn moved on again, making Endryk step aside as he marched his horse purposefully forward.

Any immediate discussion was precluded however, by the fact that they found themselves facing a steep slope covered with tall and close-packed trees. Before they ventured into the silent twilight Endryk drew his sword and cut a long branch for Nordath to use as a staff. 'You'll find this a great help,' he said, as he trimmed it, using the sword as deftly as others might use a knife.

Once or twice, as they laboured up through the gloom, Thyrn stopped and cocked his head on one side.

'What's the matter?' Endryk asked, concerned. 'Can you hear something?'

Thyrn shook his head vigorously, though more as if to clear it than in denial. 'Just the leaves rustling, I think, but every now and then it seems to come together as if it made sense, even though I can't understand it – like a chorus of voices in the distance, or a crowd speaking in a foreign language.'

He looked at Endryk uncertainly as though expecting a laughing rebuke, but Endryk was staring at the trunks surrounding them. They tapered upwards giddyingly. 'It's like being in a huge building,' he said. 'They say that when the Old Forest spanned the entire land, the trees spoke to one another in some mysterious way and that there were some amongst men who could understand them. And these are old trees.'

'You're teasing me,' Thyrn protested.

'Maybe, maybe not,' Endryk said with a hesitant smile. 'But listening to your instincts is always a good idea; they're older than a lot of the things we use to get by with.'

Eventually, breathing heavily and blinking in the sunlight, they emerged from the leafy gloom on to a gentler slope. Without waiting for a command they all dropped on to the short, springy grass. Rhavvan and Thyrn sprawled out. The ridge ahead of them was clearly visible now. Endryk pointed to a dip in it. 'That's where we're going. If anyone's watching from down below, there's no way we can avoid being exposed as we approach it. We'll just have to move as quickly and as quietly as we can.'

'Quietly? Whoever they are, they won't be that close to us yet,' Rhavvan protested.

'I told you, we're intruders here,' Endryk replied. 'Voices are an alien sound and they can carry a long way, particularly if the conditions are right. A *long* way. Which reminds me, we should muffle the horses' tackle as well.' He frowned. 'I'm getting careless.'

'What!' Rhavvan exclaimed, levering himself up on to his elbows.

'Are you sure that's necessary?' Hyrald asked in more

measured tones before Rhavvan could voice his aggravation further. 'It seems a bit—'

'Yes,' Endryk replied categorically. 'We'll be ringing like a Spring Day procession.' He pointed back down through the trees. 'If those people are looking for us – for you – it's vital they've no indication where we are, or even that we're here. I'd dearly like to know where they are as well, but I think we'll have to settle for flight for the moment and hope that they'll expose themselves sooner or later. That col's very visible from the other side and it's the only way through for a long way. If they come over it carelessly we'll see them, providing we stay alert. If they don't they'll lose a day at least.'

'What if they're friends who've come to tell us the Death Cry's been rescinded?' Nordath asked.

Endryk laughed ruefully. 'I commend your optimism and your civilized thinking, Nordath. I can't comment – you know your own best. But even if they are friends we'll still need to know that for sure before we make contact with them. Let's rest for a little while so that we can clear the col without stopping again.'

This suggestion met with no opposition and the five relaxed back on the grass. Endryk, sitting higher up the slope, looked at them thoughtfully. Then he took the sling from his belt and, pursing his lips, nudged Thyrn with his foot. As Thyrn glanced up, frowning, Endryk spun the sling gently and looked at him expectantly.

Within a few minutes, the others were also sitting up and watching, for Thyrn was being given instruction in the use of the sling. They were not sitting for long however, as Thyrn's release proved to be problematical, making no particular direction safe from his errant missiles. Brought to their feet for safety's sake, and encouraged by Thyrn's initial ineptitude, the others soon joined in the lesson. Even Nordath was not immune to the competitive lure of the weapon. As it transpired, there being few boulders and attendant pebbles in their immediate vicinity, and with Nals looking disdainfully at Rhavvan's suggestion that he retrieve those that were thrown any distance, they ran out of ammunition before they ran out of enthusiasm. It was, however, a much more relaxed group that set off up towards the col than had emerged from the trees.

'People – soldiers – use these things?' Hyrald asked, handing the sling back to Endryk.

Endryk was silent for a moment. Hefting the sling, and with his eyes fixed on the rocky horizon ahead it was obvious that he was contending with many memories. Hyrald was about to withdraw his question when Endryk abandoned his brief reverie and pushed the sling casually into his belt. 'They can be used the same way as an arrow storm,' he said. 'To break up infantry, let the cavalry in – very frightening, very dangerous. And for dealing with sentries silently – providing you're good with one, that is. And, of course, they're good for hunting small game.' His voice was flat and empty and Hyrald found he could not ask any of the questions that the reply prompted.

Instead, it was he who was cross-examined. 'You all carry swords, staves, knives. Are you trained to use them?'

'We're trained more to *avoid* using them if we can,' he replied. The answer came out almost unbidden. It was the standard one for public consumption, rather than the true one. There was a difference between the formal written ideals of how the Wardens should contain violence, and the reality of it, just as there was with most Moot-inspired ideas.

'But you are trained in how to use them?'

Hyrald found the question disconcerting but he answered it nevertheless. 'The short staff mainly. Rhavvan's unusual, he uses a long staff – he's very good with it, even close in. It's not often we have to resort to swords, and then the theory is to use the flat of the blade if possible.' He raised a significant eyebrow as he imparted this.

'And the knives?'

'Knives are knives. They're working tools, not weapons. Not for us, anyway. Not remotely suitable for our kind of work. And if anyone wants to use one on us . . .' he patted the staff hanging from his belt '. . . give me distance and a big stick any time.'

Endryk nodded, then indicated the bow fastened to his saddle. Hyrald shook his head. 'Like your sling – not suitable for what we do. We're supposed to protect people, not kill and maim them – even the bad ones, as far as we can.' His brow furrowed and he spoke the question that had been building. 'Why are you concerned about how we're trained?'

Endryk cast a glance backwards, then shrugged. 'Just old habits coming back,' he said. 'I didn't realize they were ingrained so deeply.'

'You think we might end up having to fight these people, don't you?' Hyrald pressed.

Endryk answered reluctantly. 'I think it's a risk,' he said. 'It'd certainly be a mistake to ignore the possibility.' A cloud moved in front of the sun. In its shadow, Hyrald could feel the coolness of the slight breeze that was blowing. He suppressed a shiver.

'Adren, Rhavvan and I have got experience in dealing with riots, but generally we try to talk our way out of trouble. We're not soldiers. As for Thyrn and Nordath – I doubt either of them's even been in a fight worth calling one.'

'It's a long time since I've done any fighting and I've no desire to do any more, I can assure you,' Endryk said. 'But . . .' The cloud moved from in front of the sun as Endryk paused and he smiled as though reflecting the returned warmth. He waved a hand both to urge the party forward and to dismiss his concerns. 'Forget it. I'm being too anxious. As you say, we're hardly a fighting unit, are we? Nor liable to become one with a few hours' rudimentary training. We'll just be careful how we go, and keep a good lookout behind us – see if we can find out who's following us before we make too many plans.'

Hyrald did not feel as reassured as he would have liked. He could see that Endryk was deliberately not voicing all his concerns. Further, it was in neither his nature nor his training to run away from trouble. As a Warden, he was too used to taking charge of events and dealing with them. And he knew that, sooner or later, if they were being pursued, their pursuers would have to be faced and dealt with, whoever they were. Yet too, Endryk was correct, they were not in a position to do anything other than run or surrender.

After they had passed over the col, Endryk clambered part way up one side of it to obtain a better view of the land they had travelled over.

'I can't see anything,' he said unhappily, when he came down. 'We'll press on.'

And press on they did, Endryk setting the stiffest pace so far as they descended. Only when they had reached a more wooded area did he slow down.

'Sorry about that,' he said frankly. 'But I didn't want us to be caught in the open with them perhaps holding the high ground. We'll rest a little while if you like, before we go on to the river.'

'Is there any way we can watch the col as we travel?' Hyrald asked.

'No. Not now. Not unless you want to climb a tree every few minutes. I'm afraid that while they can't see us, we can't see them – whether they're getting nearer, falling back, or even following us at all.'

'We'll press on to the river, then,' Hyrald concluded. He turned to Thyrn. 'You still want to go back to Arvenshelm? Forget about going north?' he asked bluntly.

'Yes,' came an equally blunt reply.

An inquiring glance sought the views of Rhavvan and Adren.

'Thyrn summarized it well enough,' Adren said. 'I can't say I'm looking forward to it but, on the whole, I'd rather deal with trouble here than in some other country.' Rhavvan just nodded.

Finally, Hyrald turned to Endryk. There was a grimness in their guide's face that none of them had seen before as he replied. 'I'm not Arvens, and I've little interest in the affairs of your country. But I've lived here a long time and lived the way I wanted to, and to that extent I'm in your debt. And it was an Arvenstaat man who helped me when I needed it most.'

'I won't argue debts with you, Endryk,' Hyrald said. 'We can't begin to repay what we owe you.'

Endryk gently dismissed the acknowledgement. He spoke haltingly. 'I'm not sure that I'm ready to go back home yet. I've no idea what will be there now. The war was over, when I left, but the life I enjoyed – we all enjoyed – was destroyed. I lost some good friends. I don't know what to do.'

It distressed Hyrald to see Endryk's quietly assured manner racked thus, but he could say nothing. Abruptly, Endryk's face cleared. He looked surprised. 'Just speaking the words,' he said, though more to himself than the others. 'We slid into war because we each of us lived our "good" lives – turned away from petty injustice after petty injustice.' He looked at Rhavvan. 'Underestimated the effect of small actions – didn't see the harm that was being done because it happened slowly, quietly, piece by piece. Until suddenly there was a monster devouring our society from within and there were no acceptable choices left.' He closed his eyes. 'All that's needed for evil to prevail is for good men to do nothing. We all know that, don't we? Well, not again, not here – not anywhere where I can see it happening.' Opening his eyes he looked at the others one at a time. 'To do nothing in the face of what's happened to you will be a betrayal of far more than yourselves. *You're* without acceptable choices now. I'll come with you if I may. Help you find justice before injustice overwhelms everyone. Maybe then I can go home.'

The relief of the whole party was almost palpable, but Hyrald felt the need to press him. 'You're sure about this?' he asked soberly. 'This isn't your problem and you've—'

'Yes it is.' Endryk cut across him. 'It's—'

He stopped suddenly and held up his hand.

Into the silence came the distant sound of a raucous voice shouting commands.

Chapter 13

Though it was not possible to hear what was being shouted, the harshness in the distant voice told Hyrald and the others about the nature of the men following them more vividly than any amount of speculation.

'It doesn't sound as if they've come to bring us good news,' Adren said to Nordath, who nodded unhappily.

Endryk looked round quickly then dismounted and ran across to a tall tree, signalling Rhavvan to follow.

'Help me,' he said, pointing to the lowest branch. It was well above his head but with his foot supported in Rhavvan's cupped hands he managed to swing up and catch it. The others stared after him as he began clambering upwards. They remained thus even when he had disappeared. More shouting reached them as they waited.

He was not gone for long. 'Wardens, I think – uniformed anyway,' he said, as he dropped back down. His face was flushed. 'I never did like climbing trees,' he grumbled, wiping his hand irritably. 'They're mounted and riding fast. Too fast for this country, I'd judge. And I have to agree with Adren, they look more like a hunting party than a rescue team.'

'How many of them are there?' Hyrald asked fearfully.

'About ten.'

'Ten?' Hyrald echoed in disbelief.

'That I could see,' Endryk confirmed. 'The view wasn't ideal and they were milling about our camp site.'

'How would they know we've come this way?' Rhavvan asked.

'Maybe they met Oudrence and he told them. He knew we were going to go west,' Nordath offered.

'More likely it was the same way as those who found you on the shore,' Endryk said. 'I told you, you must have left a trail across the country like a haycart – I'm sure you could've followed it in their position.'

Rhavvan was more injured than indignant at this reminder of their wild northward dash. 'But we've been careful since we left your cottage.'

'True. But, as I said, people are out of place here. Our passage makes a disturbance that's virtually impossible to disguise.'

'It's irrelevant anyway,' Hyrald said, ending the debate. 'They might just have worked it out for themselves that the only way we could go was west.' He swore under his breath and put his hand to his head. 'The point is, they're here. We can't risk meeting them until we know for sure whether they're friend or enemy, though how we're going to find that out I don't know. It seems to me the only alternatives we have are to hide or outrun them.' He looked at Endryk. 'I know it's a long time since you've been here, but you still know this country better than any of us. Have you any suggestions?'

'We'll have to do a little of both,' Endryk replied. 'Just hiding a group this size around here is problematical to say the least, and if we run for it, that'll tell them exactly where we are. Also we've no idea about the condition of their horses. I can only imagine that to be riding the way they are, they've got reserve mounts somewhere. They could be very fresh.'

'And with a larger party behind them,' Rhavvan added.

'Quite possibly.'

'I'd like to see who it is,' Rhavvan said menacingly.

'So would we all,' Hyrald agreed. 'But we can't afford the luxury of getting close to them. What do you mean we'll have to do a little of both?' he asked Endryk.

'We'll keep on towards the river, find a good place to change direction, then leave signs to keep them heading north while we turn west and move slowly and quietly.'

Hyrald looked doubtful. Shouting drifted to them again.

'Do it,' he said.

Endryk spoke softly. 'You know now how sound can travel out here so make sure all your tackle is well muffled,' he said. 'And no talking unless it's essential – and I mean *essential*. And then confine yourselves to whispers. Keep strict single file. Keep your eyes and ears wide open – particularly your ears. I know it's not easy, but stay as relaxed as you can. Rhavvan, you listen well – take the rearguard.'

Rich forest scents pervaded the procession as it moved silently through the trees. Dancing sunlight dappled over and around them, endlessly shifting and changing, and the air was filled with birdsong and the gentle discourse of the leaves as they swayed to the touch of a scarcely felt breeze. To less troubled minds, the scene would have been idyllic, but the riders were prey and could know no tranquillity until they were free from the fear of their predator.

Thyrn, in his new secret role as protector of his protector and conspirator with Endryk, seemed to be the most at ease, though perhaps more by virtue of his youth rather than any deeper wisdom. The three Wardens were noticeably on edge. It was against their nature and training to retreat from threat and they were filled with too many questions. Further, having instincts that were tuned to the sights, scents and dangers of the city, everything about this place served to distract and disturb them so that the heightened awareness that circumstances had given them served not to clarify but to add only fretful confusion. Rhavvan, whose hearing had saved him more than once in Arvenshelm's darker places, found the constant noise particularly troubling and he kept stopping, his head cocked on one side and his eyes half closed as he sought amid it for sounds of pursuit. Nals came and went to needs of his own, frequently bolting off into the undergrowth.

After a while Endryk halted them. He dismounted and gently moved some hanging branches to one side. He studied the area beyond them then pointed. 'Wait over there,' he said. 'I'll lay a trail towards the river. I won't be long.' Nor was he, though to the waiting group his absence seemed much longer than it was. It made Hyrald, in particular, feel acutely aware of his inadequacy as their leader in their present position and he was openly relieved when Endryk returned. Endryk spent some time carefully removing all signs of their change of direction, finally adjusting the hanging branches. Rhavvan watched him with an expression that gradually changed from impatience to grudging respect. Then Endryk was silently directing them to move off again.

Their uneasy journey continued. At their head, though he gave no further orders, Endryk's presence continued to forbid all sound and cautioned them against the distracting lure of the sunlit calm of the woods despite the absence of any sign of pursuit. Even Nals was quieter now, spending most of the time loping soberly alongside Endryk.

Eventually they came to a break in the trees. Endryk halted some way from the edge. 'Stay in single file,' he whispered. Ahead of them was an expanse of open ground filled with tall ferns. It sloped downwards to the right. Beyond it lay more trees. They were darker and less inviting than those they were presently sheltering under, but still more welcome than the ground they would have to pass over. Endryk dismounted and moved forward a little way. The river could be seen at the bottom of the slope.

He was frowning when he returned. Everyone leaned forward as he spoke, very softly. 'We've no choice but to cross this and to cross it slowly. There's no saying what the ground's like under these ferns, but there'll certainly be streams and wet rocks. We can't risk hurting the horses by hurrying. We also can't do anything about the tracks we'll leave. We'll just have to hope the false trail was good enough and that they don't come this way.'

As they emerged into the clearing, each of them in turn looked upwards at the bright blue sky and the still passing army of white clouds. After the comforting shelter of the trees, they felt very exposed. For Rhavvan, the troublesome noise of the trees was replaced by the equally troublesome noise of the distant river.

It needed no sensitive hearing however, to hear the cry that rang out when they were about halfway across. It tore through their studied silence, jolting them with its harshness. Thyrn let out a brief cry. Rhavvan swore. A group of riders was moving along the river bank. One of them was pointing and, after the briefest of pauses, they were drawing swords and urging their horses up the slope.

Rhavvan's lip curled. 'Well, that's clear enough, drawing on us. Without even a word of challenge.'

Then his eyes blazed and his hand went to his own sword. However, even as he did so, the reality of his position came to him: there were at least seven riders in the charging group. He released his sword and began to urge his horse forward towards shelter. The others were doing the same but Endryk held out a restraining hand. 'No! Keep walking, slowly!' he said powerfully. 'Let them charge uphill and take their chance in this terrain. We're nearly across. We can run when the horses can see where they're going.'

As he spoke, one of the advancing horses went down, throwing its rider. Some of the others stopped to help their comrade but three of them continued their headlong dash.

Still observing Endryk's injunction to walk quietly Rhavvan took his long staff and held it discreetly on the far side of his

187

horse. He nearly collided with Hyrald, who had stopped suddenly.

'Carry on,' Hyrald said urgently, motioning him to move past.

'But—'

'Don't argue. Go! I'll be with you in a moment.'

As soon as Rhavvan had passed him, Hyrald stood in his stirrups and pointed at the approaching riders.

'You there, halt!' he bellowed. 'What the devil do you think you're playing at?'

The command and the rebuke were forceful enough to make two of the riders falter. The third, however, continued. Very leisurely, and indicating extreme irritation, Hyrald turned his horse as though to descend to meet them. 'Are you deaf, you oaf?' he bellowed again. 'I said, halt!' The third rider, realizing suddenly that he was alone now, faltered in his turn. Hyrald pressed his advantage. 'You've got a man down! You know your duty – what kind of Wardens are you? Go and see if he's all right. Then all of you get back up here. I'll need to hear a damned good explanation of your disgraceful conduct if you're not to end up on charges.' He turned his horse away again and with a final, 'Now! *Move!*' that actually made the lone rider swing his horse about, he resumed his easy walk across the clearing. Rhavvan had stopped at the edge of the trees and was turning to meet him. Hyrald discreetly urged him back.

'I can't believe you did that,' the big man said when Hyrald reached him.

'I've been wanting to do it since this began,' Hyrald snarled. 'At least we know we're not dealing with the brightest. Let's move, it's only gained us seconds.'

It took them a little while to catch up with Endryk and the others who were already riding as fast as the ground and their ability would allow. It was soon apparent that it was the latter that was the greatest problem. The three Wardens were not particularly good riders and Nordath and Thyrn, riding on one horse, were severely handicapped. Endryk assessed the situation with a single backward glance. Slowing down, but without stopping, he moved alongside Nordath and Thyrn and with a combination of encouragement and cajoling managed to transfer the older man to his own horse. Then he swung over to sit behind Thyrn and with a cry to Nordath of, 'Just hang on,' he took both sets of reins and spurred his horse to a fast canter.

Though Endryk did not seem to be suffering, it was a difficult, bone-jarring ride for the rest of them. Hyrald managed to pull alongside him. 'We can't go on for long like this,' he gasped. 'Nordath can't take much more and Thyrn doesn't look '

He stopped. Endryk's expression was frightening.

The sound of their pursuers could now be clearly heard, harsh and triumphant.

'The intention of these people is murderous?' Endryk asked starkly.

Hyrald's reply was pained. 'They look like Wardens but they've drawn on us without any form of challenge like those on the shore. It's not done. The Death Cry's still in place. Yes, they're murderous.'

'Bad odds, Warden,' Endryk said. 'But no choice.' He shouted to the others. 'We're going to have to stand. On my command, dismount and prepare to deal with whoever comes first.'

'Dismount?' Hyrald exclaimed.

'Horses are no advantage in this space. Especially for you. Do as I say.'

Even as he was speaking he was reaching round Thyrn and drawing the youth's knife from his belt. He pushed it into his startled hand. 'Keep this out of sight but if anyone gets too close and you can't run, lunge.' He thrust Thyrn's hand out by way of demonstration. 'To whatever part of them's nearest – throat, face, anything. Don't look into their eyes, you'll hesitate and get yourself killed. Keep stabbing until you're safe.'

Thyrn stiffened. 'I can't do that.'

'You can, you will! You'll have no choice if it happens. And you must protect your uncle as well as yourself. When we stop, help him down, and keep the horses together.' He tightened his grip to emphasize the urgency of his words. 'This is a bad lesson for you, Caddoran, but learn it well and learn it quickly. You're here through no fault of your own and you're entitled to survive. Do you understand? You're entitled to survive! Where we are now, everything is that simple.'

Endryk's tone allowed no debate as he pushed the knife back into Thyrn's belt.

Hyrald glanced quickly over his shoulder. Their pursuers were in sight.

Endryk was shouting. 'Now!'

As he swung off his horse, Endryk took Thyrn with him, thrust both sets of reins into his shaking hands and pushed him towards his uncle with a final command, 'Your uncle and the horses.'

Thyrn was vaguely aware of catching Nordath as he slid from Endryk's horse and shouting, 'Get the horses,' at him. Then everything was confusion and terror – a mosaic of sounds and images that moved at once with desperate slowness and violent, jerking, speed.

There was Nals, blurred and leaping, teeth fearsome.

And Endryk, eyes both frightening and frightened, drawing his bow.

It creaked deafeningly . . .

Bending the fabric of everything around it . . .

And the echoing, echoing, wind-rush of a flying arrow . . .

It struck the horse of the leading pursuer. Hooves flailed

and a high-pitched scream filled Thyrn's mind as the animal reared, white-eyed, unseating its rider and bringing down another.

Swords and staves were rising and falling . . .

The scream of the horse became a wavering background to a tangled cacophony of fury and terror.

A second arrow struck a rider . . .

Something twisted deep in Thyrn, a re-shaping, a re-ordering. The sound of the arrow's flight swelled to overtop everything clse. It stretched giddily backwards from its fateful strike to the very creaking of the bow.

Wrong . . .

Wrong way . . .

But it was the way it was.

It was the sound of a black sword falling through the darkness between . . .

Falling?

No . . .

Yes . . .

But from when to when?

It was gone.

He was Vashnar, mouth agape, staring down at his glistening, ordered desk, seeing everything, knowing everything.

Then he was Thyrn again. Scarcely a heartbeat spent. Trapped in the mosaic. Part of it. Still watching the arrow strike.

Endryk's target, moving his arms upwards to complete their futile attempt to deflect the arrow, tumbled backwards out of his saddle. A thrust from Rhavvan's staff was unseating another. Others had already been downed.

Then the hunters were retreating, as noisily as they had come, Nals barking after them.

'Gather the horses!' Endryk was shouting as he kicked the arms from under one of the unhorsed riders who was trying to rise. 'Stay where you are if you want to live.' He moved to the screaming horse, stroked its head gently then drew his sword and killed it with a single quick thrust. Thyrn heard himself gasp.

Silence flooded deafeningly over the scene.

Endryk pulled the arrow from the dead horse.

As if released by this, the sounds of the forest began to force their way through the silence. At their ragged edge was the dwindling echo of the crashing flight of the attackers.

'Damn you all!' Endryk shouted, turning his sword towards one of the downed riders. 'Bringing me to this again.' For a moment it seemed that he was going to kill the man as quickly as he had killed the horse, but instead he pushed his sword into the ground by his terrified face and placed a foot on his chest. Adren moved to the man that Endryk had shot, though her Warden's caution kept her blade levelled at him. The arrow had struck him in the shoulder and was swaying like an admonishing finger as he breathed. His eyes were wide and shocked.

'Horses, Thyrn.' It was Nordath nudging his nephew from behind. 'Come on. And empty the saddlebags on that dead one.'

There was a sudden scuffling and two of the unhorsed riders were on their feet and running.

'Let them go,' Hyrald said, as Rhavvan and Adren made to run after them. 'They're no use to us and it won't be long before the others re-group and come after us again. We've been lucky but we're still out-numbered, don't forget.' He moved to the man pinioned by Endryk's foot.

'Who are you? And why are you chasing us?' He bent forward, frowning. 'And what kind of a uniform is that you're wearing?'

The man's mouth was trembling too much for him to speak coherently. 'Orders. Vashnar's orders. Death Cry. Don't kill me, please.'

Hyrald drew his knife, knelt down by the cringing figure and cut off an insignia from his tunic. He glanced at it, puzzled, then pushed it into his pocket before seizing the man's face and turning it towards him.

'How many more of you? The truth now, or . . .' He indicated the watching figure of Endryk, looming above him, leaning on his sword.

'Only us,' the man blurted out. 'Nine. Lost some on way.'

'Who's in charge of you?'

'Commander Aghrid.'

Hyrald started and there was an audible response from the other two Wardens.

'*Commander* Aghrid?'

The man nodded, his eyes desperately urging the truth of what he was saying. Hyrald's face filled with questions.

'No time,' Endryk said, seeing them and laying a hand on his shoulder.

Reluctantly Hyrald stood up. 'Take your wounded friend and get out of here while you can. And take a message to whoever sent you, Warden.' He put a withering emphasis into the last word. 'We've done nothing wrong, but as soon as we can find a river crossing we're going north, away from Arvenstaat until some kind of sanity returns. You come after us again like this – *anyone* comes after us – and we'll defend ourselves.' His anger suddenly spilled out. 'And remember this, you drew on us without challenge! A civilian's taking a chance when he does that, but a Warden's breaking every unwritten law we live by.' He bent over the man viciously. 'So remember that we didn't kill you when we were more than entitled to. Remember that especially when you watch the sun go down tonight. Remember it every day for the rest of your life. Now *go*!'

For a moment he looked as though he were going to strike the man, then he stepped back, face set. The man clambered shakily to his feet, his eyes moving fearfully around each of his assailants in turn. He took a step and clutched at his leg with a grimace of pain. It evoked no response from his audience.

'Your friend,' Hyrald said coldly, pointing towards the rider that Endryk had shot.

'Wait,' Endryk said. He moved to the wounded man. 'Your lucky day,' he said, kneeling down beside him. 'Lucky it wasn't a battle arrow, lucky it was clean, and lucky I missed what I was aiming at.' Then, with the same abrupt briskness with which he had killed the horse, he pulled out the arrow. The man arched and his mouth gaped but no sound came. Endryk patted him reassuringly, then helped him to his feet with unexpected gentleness. 'Is there a healer with you?' he asked. The man shook his head. 'Well, do your best to keep the wound clean and don't use that arm too much.' He draped the man's uninjured arm around the shoulder of the limping man.

As they hobbled away, menaced by a returning Nals, Endryk turned to Nordath and Thyrn. 'Are you all right?'

'No, not remotely,' Nordath said, with unexpected force. 'I've just aged ten years, and my heart's beating enough to break my ribs, but I don't think I'm hurt and I can still ride.'

'Me too,' Thyrn said weakly.

Endryk looked at the others. 'The rest of you? Anyone hurt?'

Hyrald and Rhavvan shook their heads.

'Shaky. Very shaky,' Adren said, holding out her hands to demonstrate the point. 'But it'll pass. And you? How are you?'

A flicker of surprise passed over Endryk's face but he did not reply other than with a cursory nod. 'Two more horses, I see,' he said brusquely. 'And a few more supplies, I presume. That's good. In fact, it's excellent.' He stroked one of the horses. 'But they're in a sorry state. They look as if they've been ridden out. Still, we can take it steady for a while. Let's go.'

'All of them looked as if they'd been ridden out,' Adren said as they rode away from the sunlit battleground.

'All?' Endryk queried.

'The horses, the men. They all looked exhausted. As if they'd been riding for days.'

'I can't say I noticed, to be honest, I was too busy aiming,' Endryk replied. 'Though those two were even more travel-stained than you are. You could be right, they could well have travelled a long way very quickly.' He smiled appreciatively. 'Still, so much the better. They're three horses down now and with at least two injured men to tend to – one badly if that wound becomes infected. That plus exhaustion should slow them down radically.'

'What do you make of this?' Hyrald said, handing the insignia he had cut off the man's tunic to Rhavvan.

Rhavvan held it against the insignia on his own tunic. 'It's certainly not one of ours. It looks familiar, but I don't know where from. Come to think of it, there was something odd about their uniforms. Apart from being the worse for wear like ours.'

'They were black,' Endryk said. 'It brings back bad memories for me – black uniformed thugs policing the streets. Yours are very dark blue – or were before you set out.'

Adren took the insignia from Rhavvan and studied it intently. After a moment she began clicking her fingers in an attempt to conjure up an old memory. 'Two lightning flashes and a single silver star,' she said. 'I know it from somewhere. It's old.'

'It's the symbol of the Tervaidin,' Nordath said quietly. 'The old Dictators' bodyguards. Your ancient precursors.'

Hyrald leaned across to examine the insignia again. Adren gave it to him.

'You're right,' he said, frowning. 'What the devil's going on? Wardens wearing a Tervaidin symbol. It's . . .' He left the sentence hanging.

'Were they Wardens?' Endryk asked.

Hyrald looked at the captured horses. 'The uniforms were

the same, as far as I could tell, bar the colour and this badge. And the horses and tack are ours.'

'I recognized one of the ones who bolted,' Rhavvan said. 'One of Vashnar's own command, I think.'

'And *Commander* Aghrid,' Adren said, significantly.

'None of this makes any sense.' Hyrald scowled. 'Aghrid can't possibly be a Commander. He's a disgrace to the entire Warding. He should've been locked up, not just thrown out.'

'I don't think the man was lying,' Endryk said. 'And he did say Aghrid, quite clearly.'

Hyrald was clutching for reason. 'Anyway, there's no Commandership vacant.'

Adren cleared her throat significantly.

'Except yours.' Rhavvan spoke her meaning.

Hyrald glowered at him. 'Our men wouldn't accept Aghrid, you know that,' he said indignantly. 'Besides, I doubt he'd have the nerve even to go near the House. He was lucky someone didn't take a staff to him one quiet night.'

'He was lucky someone didn't take a sword to him,' Rhavvan added.

'This man is known to you?' Endryk asked diffidently.

Hyrald pulled a sour face, as though the words themselves were distasteful. 'He was a Deputy Commander – same rank as Adren and Rhavvan . . .'

'Acting Deputy Commander,' they both interpolated defensively. 'And to a minor district.'

Hyrald gave a conceding wave. 'Acting Deputy Commander,' he emphasized. 'But he was corrupt and violent.'

'In my limited stay in Arvenshelm I gained the distinct impression that corruption and violence amongst Wardens was endemic,' Endryk said bluntly.

Hyrald turned to him angrily. 'No!' he protested, but Endryk outfaced him.

'No shopkeepers and tradesmen, "doing favours"? No

"summary fines" in lieu of more physical retribution?' he said. Hyrald turned away unhappily.

'We're not perfect. And there are certain . . . traditions whereby citizens show their gratitude for what we do. That's always happened. But it's kept at a sensible level – there's never any threat. It's not officially condoned, and there's certainly no "summary fines" – not by any of my men, anyway.' He was wilting under Endryk's continuing gaze. 'Occasional "summary justice", I'll grant you. A cracked head perhaps, instead of burdening the courts.'

'But Aghrid was different?'

Hyrald searched the comment for some hint of sarcasm, but there was none. 'Yes, he was,' he replied, thankful to be on safer ground. 'Very different. He *did* intimidate and harass. How he ever got into the Warding in the first place defies me, let alone how he became an Acting Deputy Commander. He was completely out of control, getting greedier and more violent by the week until he half killed some poor shopkeeper who stood up to him. He was dismissed from the Warding eventually.'

'And the shopkeeper and his other victims?'

Hyrald clenched his fists at the memory. 'Duly recompensed,' he said, unsettled again. He turned to his colleagues for support. 'He *can't* be a Commander. It's not possible.'

'It's what the man said,' Adren replied unhelpfully. She was patently distressed herself. 'Aghrid and Tervaidin. None of this makes any sense.'

'The Tervaidin were an elite bodyguard who eventually took over the running of the state, weren't they?' Endryk asked, addressing the question predominantly to Nordath.

'Never overtly,' Nordath replied, his voice unsteady. 'They were astute enough to keep the Dictator conspicuously in the eye of the people so that he would carry the blame for anything

197

bad that happened. In the first place they were, anyway. Later, they just became corrupt and greedy – like Aghrid.'

'Corrupt and greedy. How about tyrannical and brutal?' Endryk said.

'That as well, certainly,' Nordath said. 'It's strange. They're generally thought of now as heroic – brave protectors of the land and people. Even though there's no doubt about what they were really like.'

They came to a clearing. Endryk reined his horse to a halt and held up a hand for silence. There was no sound of pursuit. Just the rustling of leaves and the sound of the river. It was not as loud now. The sun was low and the sky was purpling. The pristine whiteness of the slowly drifting flotilla of clouds was being transformed into a fevered redness tinged with leaden grey shadows.

'I've no idea where we are,' Endryk said. 'But I think we should move on westwards for as long as possible. Nice and steady. Use lanterns if we have to, they won't give our positions away while we're in the trees. And we'll have to post a double guard tonight.'

No one said anything, but the Wardens were grim-faced while Nordath and Thyrn looked distracted. He addressed their concerns.

'I'm sorry,' he said, clicking his horse forward. 'I'd forgotten. That must have frightened both of you very badly.' They looked up at him, but he did not wait for an answer. 'It frightened us all. Fighting isn't something you ever get used to – not fighting like that especially, where your life is threatened. There's an intensity to it – a focus – that leaves scars for ever. Changes you. Even Wardens, who deal with a lot of violence, don't often get threatened like that. My only advice is that if you want to be sick, or faint, or whatever – do it, get rid of it. But . . .' He looked at each of them in turn. 'Remember this, and cling to it. No matter how bad you feel, *you survived.* Not only that, in this instance you weren't even hurt. And know this, those people who came against you will be feeling far worse.'

'I'm still shaking.' The words tumbled out of Thyrn as if he had indeed been holding them back like vomit.

Endryk held out his hand, imitating Adren's earlier gesture. It was trembling slightly. 'It's the way your body looks after itself. Before and after. Don't be afraid to be afraid. It's not pleasant, but it's in your best interests. Don't hide things from yourself. I'll tell you this, too. You did well, both of you – very well. We'd have been in a sorry state if the horses had scattered.' He cast a glance at Hyrald and the others. 'In fact, we all did well. Though I'll have to get some archery practice in. Hitting that man in the shoulder like that.'

'You were aiming to kill him?' Adren asked hesitantly.

Endryk smiled ruefully. 'No. I told him he was lucky I missed just to catch his attention. I was aiming for the horse.' His smile turned into a laugh. Despite its grim origin his laughter lightened their mood as they rode from the clearing into the premature gloaming of the trees.

It was not long before it became too dark for them to ride safely and they were obliged to dismount. The dancing light of a solitary lantern held by Endryk led them on, filling their world with dusty flashing shadows, bright flickering moths and a snowy rain of flitting insects which left Rhavvan growling.

They walked for a long time and were very tired when they finally camped – too tired for any of them to be able to stand guard.

'They'll be in a worse state than we are,' Rhavvan protested to Endryk as his concern about this became apparent. 'We won't need a guard.'

'I'll remind you of that when you wake up tomorrow with your throat cut,' Endryk said uncompromisingly.

In the end he had them lay trip lines around the camp. 'Do

be careful when you get up in the morning,' he said, laughing again.

None of them slept well that night, Thyrn least of all as troublesome dreams full of terrible blood-soaked injuries plagued him. Only towards morning did some semblance of the control that he normally had over his dreams begin to return, but he was ill-at-ease when he finally woke to a dull, overcast day. There was some solace in the damp freshness that filled the air but none of them save Endryk and Nals seemed to find it.

As they ate, Hyrald was anxious to make and discuss plans for the rest of their journey, though his immediate concern was the intention of their pursuers. By common consent and at Endryk's prompting, they postponed any debate about the Tervaidin symbol and the mysterious re-appointment and promotion of Aghrid.

'With luck, they'll believe what I said about going north,' Hyrald said.

Thyrn cleared his throat noisily. 'It doesn't matter,' he said, louder than he had intended. 'I told Vashnar that we were coming back.'

Chapter 14

Vashnar clasped his hand over his mouth and nose. Panic filled him.

He had not felt the tell-tale welling of pressure which announced a nose-bleed but it was the first thing that came to mind after he realized he had once again been drawn into Thyrn's mind. Though he was alone in his office, there was something so peculiarly repellent to him in such a spontaneous haemorrhaging that he could do no other than glance quickly round as though a circle of jeering witnesses might have appeared just as spontaneously.

Vashnar accepted that there were many things over which he had no control and he had learned to ignore, tolerate, or use these to his advantage as circumstances dictated. But his body and his mind were things over which his control should be absolute and the sudden nose-bleed, unheralded, unprovoked, somehow struck towards the very foundations of the unseen inner supports that sustained him. It should not have happened. To be subjected to such a thing was both unacceptable and disturbing. And it brought with it a shame almost akin to that he might have felt had he wet his bed – a childish shame unreachable by reason, be it Vellain's easy common-sense dismissals or his own obsessively rehearsed arguments to be used if need should arise. No trite reply could answer the question that loomed before him. What would have happened if someone had been present? The bleeding had all the sinister qualities of one of those trivial events that lead inexorably to catastrophe.

It was thus some time before he managed to quieten himself sufficiently to turn to the truly unsettling aspect of what had just happened. Even then, this primal preoccupation gnawed at him and had him tentatively touching his nostrils and examining his fingers for signs of blood while at the same time he had to fight back a clamouring and mindless panic that was constantly threatening to overwhelm him.

Grim-faced with effort, he forced his thoughts back to what he had been doing just moments earlier.

It was the routine paperwork which still lay in front of him. He ran a hand over it gently, as if to confirm that it was really there. He had been relaxed and easy, with nothing in particular troubling him. Since sending out Aghrid and his special Wardens with their black uniforms and sporting the Tervaidin symbol, he had been, in many ways, more settled than at any time since his first fateful encounter with Thyrn. He usually felt that way when a decision had been made – when conjecture gave way to action.

His mind drifted after Aghrid racing northwards. The reports he had received so far were good. Indeed, they were very good. He had had to balance risks in telling Aghrid to move with the utmost urgency. While Thyrn and the others had to be dealt with as soon as possible, mounted patrols of Wardens were not common and would inevitably attract attention as they passed through the towns and villages which lay on the quickest route north. Would the appearance of the Tervaidin's symbol be noted? Would it provoke an adverse response? As it transpired, the symbol had been noted and though there had been adverse comments reported to him, the response was predominantly favourable. Unusually so. Indeed, on more than one occasion, people had come running to cheer the passing riders. It seemed that the brief fire the Death Cry had lit was still smouldering. That intrigued him – could it be that he had actually *underestimated* the discontent that was bubbling through the country? He set the thought aside for later consideration – it carried many implications. For now he was content to note those places where there had been a good response. He would have done the same had the responses been bad. Either way, it identified possible friends and enemies; it was useful information.

As if he had momentarily lowered his guard, panic suddenly washed over him, sweeping him along violently. Abruptly he was back at his desk, writing again. Not with the leisurely sensation of recollected thought however, but with the vertiginous vividness of actually having been dragged back through time to relive the events as they unfolded once more. He heard an echo of himself drawing in a gasping breath as the word he was writing seemed to unwrite itself, coiling from the page and back up the pen.

As suddenly as it had come, the intense immediacy was gone, and the image before him became just a memory again. He found himself gripping the edge of his desk. He was sure he had seen what he had seen. No, not merely seen – felt. His whole body, his consciousness, had seemed to slide backwards in some way. It was as terrifying on recollection as it had been when it first occurred, but he clenched his teeth angrily and forced himself to move on. It must have been nothing more than a momentary dizziness precursing Thyrn's attack. For attack it surely was. He remembered screwing his eyes tight shut in an instinctive attempt to stop the slithering unreality of what was happening on the page. Then he had felt the Caddoran displacing him, intruding into him effortlessly. He could offer no resistance. And when he had opened his eyes, he was Thyrn – choking on the young man's teeming terrors – clutching desperately at flying reins – reaching out to protect his uncle – aware of a terrible purpose in the knife in his belt, a lesson just learned. His head was ringing with screams and cries. Swords and staves were rising and falling, hooves were flailing, there was a rushing like a malevolent wind. And then he was himself again, hand clamped across his face, thoughts incoherent with panic and flooding questions. Almost incongruously he noted through the turmoil that the word he had been writing was whole again.

What had happened? Increasingly calmer now, the futile question pounded him mercilessly. As did the answer – the same as had happened before.

Yet it was not the same. He had not been plunged into a timeless nothingness, a dreadful darkness where he was and was not, and which had wrapped itself about and through him like a myriad spiders' webs. Even the memory of that still chilled him. And too there was no pain in his head. Nor a wretched, staining torrent from his nose. He examined his fingers again, then absently ran his thumb over his ring.

Leaning back in his chair, he pushed the front legs off the floor and began rocking gently. He recalled Vellain's remark that he and Thyrn might perhaps have to be in the same mood for such a . . . contact . . . to happen, but this patently was not the case here. He had been relaxed and at ease with himself, while Thyrn had been frantic with fear. The intensity of Thyrn's fear returned, momentarily overwhelming him. In its wake came a fury at his own powerlessness before Thyrn's intrusion. It gathered inside him, twisting tighter and tighter, searching for an outlet. Then, running before it, like a fleeing straggler, came a simple question.

How long? How long had he been . . . possessed?

He dropped his chair forward and looked at the paper he had been writing on. The word – the word that had unwound itself and equally mysteriously become whole again – was untrammelled by any sign of careless penmanship. There was no errant line, no sprayed blot – nothing to indicate that his hand had been disturbed in the least.

It must have lasted for less than a heartbeat. Far less. For a heartbeat could be a long time – long enough to scream and die in. Perhaps, it occurred to Vashnar, it had taken no time at all. Perhaps it had existed outside time.

This bizarre conclusion seemed to unwind the growing rage and he became aware of other matters fluttering tantalizingly beneath his awareness – or was it Thyrn's awareness? With an effort he forced all other questions aside and returned to the memory of the event again. He had no doubt that what he had experienced was true. He had once again touched and been touched by Thyrn. The how and the why of it he was reluctantly obliged to accept as being beyond his knowing, but there were certainties in it that surely precluded hallucination or self-deception?

Thyrn and his companions had been under a violent attack – by Wardens, he thought he detected. Despite himself he felt a glow of satisfaction. Perhaps even now Aghrid and his men were finishing off their business and preparing to return. He shunned the notion. It was too premature and there was nothing in what he had seen and felt that encouraged such a conclusion. Of course, the linkage with Thyrn could have been broken by Thyrn's death, but he sensed not. It would have to be sufficient for the moment that the fugitives had been found and engaged. That being the case, the matter was almost certainly finished but it was better that he did not anticipate it. A spasm of dark humour intruded. If his new Tervaidin couldn't deal with such a motley group, that would leave him with far greater problems for his future plans than any damage that Thyrn could do in betraying them.

He leaned forward and, resting his elbows on the desk, dropped his chin on to his interwoven fingers. An ill-formed idea floated into the confusion. What power would he be able to seize if this ability to see events so far away could be controlled? For an instant he regretted that he had insisted on

Thyrn's death, for what resource might he be destroying there? The idea shrivelled almost immediately in the light of colder, practical reasoning. However he had become linked with Thyrn in this way it was beyond his control and that was totally unacceptable. It could not be ended too soon. And the Caddoran Congress would definitely have to be dealt with in due course. There must be no chance of such an individual as Thyrn arising again.

He returned to his memory of the encounter, closing his eyes and forcing himself into quietness. There was something important there, he was sure. Something hidden under the clamour.

Horses, swords, staves – vivid but fleeting and confused images threaded around that frightening, hissing rush – what *was* that?

Let it go.

And beneath the images, what?

Despite his terror, he – Thyrn, Vashnar – was changed. Though still bewildered and uncertain, he was more assured than he had been. Lessons had been learned. And there was a hint of determination there.

Vashnar started.

He was not fleeing any longer. He was going to return! Return to the life that was his.

Vashnar stiffened, his eyes wide. Thyrn's memories were abruptly flushed from him by a surging fear of his own as he felt the edifice of his long-laid plans falter and shake under this simple but direct assault.

'No!' he gasped. But he was trembling, his body giving the lie to his words.

It was some time before he began to calm down sufficiently to tell himself that this response was wholly disproportionate. So, Thyrn had ambitions to return. What would that avail him? Even if by some miracle he survived the encounter with Aghrid it would only be as a more demented fugitive than before. At best he had only days left. But even as Vashnar pieced together these reassurances, faint tremors still shook him. And he knew that they would not go away. Thyrn had suddenly become an obstacle which would have to be destroyed before he could move on.

He had to know for sure what had happened to Thyrn!

But how? How was he to find out where he and his protectors were? He presumed they were somewhere in the uncharted north of the country. That was where rumours about them had pointed and where he had sent Aghrid, seemingly successfully, but . . .

He banged his fist on the table. He had to know!

But he couldn't go charging over the country like a crazed thing. Yet equally he could not do nothing.

He became aware of an urgent knocking.

'Enter,' he called out, hastily composing himself and checking his nose again.

The door was opened by a man wearing the black uniform of the Tervaidin. Although the Tervaidin were his chosen men and had been secretly preparing for their new role for a long time, Vashnar had introduced them into the Warding by affecting to appoint an Emergency Command in order to deal with the fugitives. That had always been the intention, only the pretext being left to circumstance. Now, it fitted well with the many rumours that Vashnar had encouraged following the proclamation of the Death Cry. At the same time he had taken the opportunity to place them in useful administrative positions as well.

The man was agitated. He saluted and held out a stained travelling wallet. 'This just arrived, sir. A rider from Commander Aghrid.'

Vashnar motioned him to place the wallet on his desk. He was loath to reach out for it for fear that his hand might begin to tremble again. 'Is he here, now?' he asked.

'No, sir. He's unconscious – exhausted. Both he and his horse could hardly stand when he arrived. Said he'd ridden one horse to death already before he passed out.'

Vashnar nodded and dismissed the man.

Only when the door clicked to did he pick up the wallet. His hands *were* shaking as he broke the seal and fumbled with the buckles. Inside was a solitary and badly creased sheet of paper. He flattened it on the desk before trying to read it. The writing was small and untidy and had obviously been written at speed and on an uneven surface. Nevertheless it was legible and Vashnar scanned through it quickly before returning to the beginning to read it more carefully.

It was a report of the progress that the patrol had made. Vashnar glanced at the map on the wall as he read. Aghrid had been heading into unknown territory when he wrote it and he had been making fearsome progress. Vashnar was impressed, though he was a little uneasy about the number of men who had failed to keep up with the killing pace and had been abandoned along the way. Still, that was a detail. More important was the fact that Aghrid had obtained clear evidence about the route the fugitives had taken and was gaining on them rapidly. It concluded: *We are told that they will run into the sea within a day or so if they continue north and that they can then turn only westward along the coast, all other ways returning them south eventually. From thence the sea becomes a river which they may seek to cross if they are intending to continue northwards. Wherever they go, we shall find them in accordance with your orders. Our resolve and loyalty is undiminished. We draw nearer to them by the hour.*

Vashnar looked at the map again. North into the sea, then westward? In common with most of the Arvens, he had little or no idea what lay to the north of Arvenstaat. There had never been any trade in that direction and he had never met anyone who had travelled there. In so far as he had thought about it, he presumed that progress northwards could be made uninterrupted. There were supposed to be other countries up there – somewhere. He deduced from Aghrid's report however, that the sea must turn inland. One day he would attend to the proper determining of the country's borders, he decided.

He continued staring at the map. Where were they now? Where had they come together in that violent confrontation that he had just been drawn into? He turned again to Aghrid's report then tried to estimate the position of the sea and how far he might have travelled along the coast had he maintained the same progress. He placed them well on their way towards the Karpas Mountains which, he presumed, continued north off the map. But the calculation merely unsettled him.

'You're becoming too preoccupied with Thyrn and the others,' Vellain told him later. Her tone was stern. 'All that matters is that he's out of the way and being pursued. Think about the Tervaidin – they've been introduced into the Warding with a minimum of opposition. Certainly much less opposition than had Hyrald still been here. He was always going to be a serious obstacle. You forget how we fretted and planned about that, and now it's happened almost without comment. And, for the most part, the people are taking to them, which is an unexpected advantage.'

However, she could not keep the concern from her voice when he reminded her of his second contact with Thyrn. 'Nothing's to be done about it,' she decided unhappily after she had interrogated him at some length. 'It's beyond any understanding and there's no point struggling with it. As you say, it's probably over and done with by now. Even with his reduced numbers, Aghrid will have had no difficulty in dealing with four men and a boy.'

'Three men, one woman and a young man,' Vashnar corrected her off-handedly, prompting a head-shaking smile. But he was not sanguine. 'I think I'd know if Thyrn was dead.

Don't ask me how, but I've got the feeling that there's a part of him with me all the time. And when he dies, I'll know.'

Vellain looked at him. Though she controlled them, tiny flickering doubts about her husband's sanity persisted in making themselves felt despite the crushing weight of reason and instinct she buried them under.

Beyond understanding – no point struggling with it, she repeated inwardly to herself until they were gone again. But it was not easy.

She put her arm around his neck. 'All's well here, isn't it,' she said. 'Nothing needs your immediate attention. Why don't we take a little time to ourselves? Break the routine – relax. A rest will be good for both of us.' She tightened her arm promisingly. 'We could go north. See for ourselves how the Tervaidin were accepted. Check on our old allies and find out what new ones the appearance of the Tervaidin has brought to light. Who knows, we might meet Aghrid on his return!'

Normally Vashnar was reluctant to be away from Arvenshelm, but Vellain's suggestion attracted him. If nothing else it would help to satisfy his irrational desire to mount up and charge after Aghrid to discover Thyrn's fate. It troubled him that for all Aghrid should have swept aside Hyrald and the others effortlessly, he had had no inner sign that Thyrn was gone. Also, though he made no mention of this, should he find himself touched again by Thyrn, he would be in the presence only of his wife.

That evening, the Senior Warden Commander's coach with an escort and a small retinue of servants left Arvenshelm and headed north. As was the tradition, many of the people doffed their hats as the coach passed. Many did not.

Thyrn was suddenly the focus of the group. 'What do you mean, you told him we were going back?' Rhavvan demanded. Thyrn shifted uncomfortably then told them of his brief contact with

Vashnar in the middle of the skirmish with Aghrid's men.

It was greeted with silence at first then Nordath spoke. 'Are you sure it wasn't just imagination? You didn't pass out like before. I was watching you all the time.'

'It was different,' Thyrn admitted. 'Just a strange kind of dizziness, then I was Vashnar – in his office – looking down at that damned immaculate desk of his. And then I was back here, scrambling for the horses.' He looked round at the three Wardens. 'I know it's hard for you to believe, but that's what happened. For an instant, both of us were in the other's place, each knowing what the other knew – sharing thoughts somehow.'

As before, Hyrald found himself struggling to accept what Thyrn was telling them but also as before he found he had little alternative. Vashnar's proclamation of the Death Cry was no less crazy than anything that Thyrn had said, and as the young man's strange linkage with Vashnar indisputably lay at the root of this whole business it behoved him to keep as open a mind as possible. But it was not easy, and he did not know whether it helped or hindered that the Thyrn now speaking was subtly different – more mature – than the one with whom they had set out.

'Did you have any visions of the city burning – of the destruction you saw when this all started?' he asked, as much for something to say as for any other reason.

Thyrn shook his head. 'No. Just humdrum thoughts. Stuff I don't understand. A quarterly report to the Moot. A request for more money, and more . . .' He paused, before querying, 'Delegated authority?' with a shrug. Then he closed his eyes tightly as though he were listening for a distant sound. 'In the background, the flames – the destruction – are still there somewhere: I can feel them. But I don't think he's even aware of them. Nearer the forefront there are confused images of the Tervaidin – or what the Tervaidin will be – spreading across the country, setting aside and replacing the old order of

Wardens.' He opened his eyes. 'Vashnar's pleased with what's happened so far, with the ones he's sent out. They've been well received, apparently.'

'You said you told him we were going back,' Rhavvan prompted.

Thyrn gestured vaguely. 'I didn't talk to him, if that's what you mean. It's just that he thought my thoughts, and I thought his. We were one person for an instant. He'd see the fighting. He'd . . . just a moment.' He sat up very straight, took in a long slow breath and released it even more slowly, noticeably relaxing as he did so. His companions watched in silence. 'He'd know I was trying to catch and control the horses – and look after Uncle. He'd feel everything I felt then.' He gave a short scornful laugh. 'And good luck to him. I hope he nearly messed his trousers too.' The concentration returned. 'He might well have noted my intention to return. It was near the surface. It depends on how sensitive he is, of course. It could be that the shock of our Joining may have jolted everything from his mind. He was definitely disturbed. But on the other hand, if he's part Caddoran . . . I don't know.' His expression darkened. 'It doesn't matter anyway. Whether he felt it directly or not is irrelevant. The thought's in there somewhere now and he'll act on it sooner or later.'

'What do you mean, the thought's in there?' Hyrald asked.

'Just that,' Thyrn replied. 'Most of our thoughts are below the surface, most of the time, aren't they? We drag them up as we need them – or they come of their own accord. The point is, when he's thinking about what you might do, he'll have the answer already even though he doesn't know it.'

'It'll guide his planning knowingly or unknowingly,' Endryk said.

'Splendid,' Rhavvan said sourly. 'It was going to be hard enough getting back to Arvenshelm anyway without him knowing we were coming.' He threw up his hands in annoyance.

'What am I talking about? I don't believe any of this nonsense. Exchanging minds – reading one another's thoughts. It isn't possible!'

'Believe what you like, Rhavvan,' Thyrn said angrily. 'I've spent my life doing something which I'm only just beginning to realize defies all explanation, so I understand your doubts. But I owe my life to you all and I'm telling you what's happened so that you'll know as much as I do. Make of it what you will. The knowledge might be difficult to deal with, but it's a damned sight better than ignorance.'

Hyrald and Adren both turned a look of amused expectancy towards a wordless Rhavvan as this outburst concluded. Endryk smiled openly at the big man's discomfiture then spoke to Thyrn.

'Is it possible that you could control this contact you have with Vashnar?'

Thyrn's face softened. 'No, I don't think so. It didn't announce itself in any way whatsoever. It just came, and then went. Very quickly.' He frowned. '*Very* quickly,' he emphasized. 'Almost as though it took place without time passing.' He shook his head and stood up, dusting down his trousers. 'This is as bewildering to me as it is to you. Worse, in fact, I can assure you. If it's any consolation I think Vashnar may be coping even less well. I never realized how disciplined I was – what control I had over my mind – until I touched his. Quite a revelation. I'll need to think about it. Anyway, all I can do is tell you what happened and I've done that now. I think we should move on. I'll go over it all again as we travel. If anything else occurs to me, I'll tell you.'

He looked expectantly at Hyrald who levered himself to his feet. His manner ended any further debate.

'Which brings us back to where we're going next, and what we're going to do about Aghrid,' Hyrald said, accepting Thyrn's decision.

'Maybe he'll give up,' Nordath said. 'They've three horses

213

less and at least one wounded man.'

'If our prisoner was to be believed, there are nine of them and they've lost others on the way here, whatever "lost" means,' Adren said.

'It means they've been riding like the devil, and that they've abandoned men on the way,' Endryk said darkly. 'You know this man better than I do, but I've a feeling he's not one to give up. Not everyone tends their wounded, by any means.'

'It's difficult,' Hyrald said. 'I've met him but I wouldn't say I knew him. From what I do know I'd say he's capable of anything – certainly abandoning people. But whether he's got the personal resources or the leadership to carry on pursuing us after yesterday, I've no idea. I wouldn't have thought he could get from Arvenshelm to here so quickly, to be honest.'

'Something's driving him then,' Endryk said. 'We'll have to assume that he'll keep coming after us.'

'Which means what?' Adren asked.

'Which means that we watch our backs, protect our night camps properly, and keep leaving him false trails.'

'Or wait for him and stop him,' Rhavvan said, punching his palm with his fist.

'Not yet, I think,' Endryk replied. 'We were lucky first time. They came recklessly and in a confined space and there were more of us than they thought. They won't do that again. And don't forget – they still outnumber us.'

Rhavvan seemed inclined to argue but Endryk anticipated him. 'But we will, if we have to,' he said coldly. He turned to Hyrald. 'West, is it, then?' he asked. 'Back to your home?'

Hyrald looked at each of the others in turn and received their silent assent. 'And you?' he asked Endryk. 'Are you still prepared to come with us?'

'Yes.'

Nevertheless, at Endryk's suggestion they set off not to the west but northwards towards the river. Reaching it they turned

214

west again and began moving upstream. The river was wide, fast and turbulent for much of the way, making a noise which prevented any conversation. Twice they had to move away from the bank and over rocky ridges as the river came plunging, white-foamed and even noisier, through narrow gorges. Towards midday they came to a place where the river broadened and became much quieter. Endryk halted and studied the terrain for some time.

'This should do,' he concluded eventually. 'We'll move into the water then head upstream until we can find a place to come out without leaving tracks. With a little good fortune, Aghrid will think we've crossed over and he'll either give up or go wandering off north. Either way, it'll win more time for us.'

Both he and Thyrn stopped and stared across the river as their horses entered the water.

'Can horses swim?' Thyrn asked.

'Yes,' Endryk replied. 'But it can be a bit alarming. Are you changing your mind about going home?'

Still staring across the water, Thyrn shook his head. 'No, whatever trouble's waiting back home, there's nothing over there for me.' He paused. 'Not until I can go there because I want to, anyway.' Then he shivered and hunched his shoulders. 'Men chasing after us like that. It's so frightening.' He looked at Endryk nervously and patted his stomach hesitantly. 'But there's all sorts of other feelings in here. Violent ones. I'm not sure what they mean – what to do with them. I've never hurt anyone.' He bared his teeth. 'Curse Vashnar and his crazed thoughts. The man's a lunatic.'

Endryk clicked his horse forward and they began moving upstream. 'You're suffering from a sense of outraged justice,' he said with a mixture of sympathy and humour. 'All you can do with those kinds of feelings is accept that they're there and focus them into a cold resolution to fight for what you know is right. As a friend of mine once told me, let the stomach drive and the head guide.'

'I don't understand.'

'Yes you do,' Endryk replied.

It was well into the afternoon when they came to a rocky section of bank on a bend in the river. Nals was waiting for them. He had been alternately swimming and walking along the bank.

'This'll do,' Endryk said, motioning the others to leave the water. 'Walk the horses up to that embankment over there.' He watched them go, then followed very slowly, carefully removing any signs of their passage.

As they waited for him, Rhavvan's expressions showed a mixture of impatience and curiosity. 'No one'll even see that,' he chafed as Endryk replaced a tumbled rock before finally joining them.

Endryk's rebuttal was matter-of-fact. 'You may be right. But if Aghrid gets this far, it means that he'll have learned how to live out here – or started learning, anyway. Which means in turn that he'll be even more dangerous than before.' He cast a final eye over the path they had taken across the rocks. 'I notice that while you obviously dislike this man, none of you have referred to him as being either stupid or cowardly.'

Rhavvan grunted. 'He's a city man born and bred, he'll not get this far. None of us would have without you. I'll wager he's scurrying back to Arvenshelm right now.'

Endryk acknowledged Rhavvan's oblique thanks with an inclination of his head but rejected his conclusion. 'Someone who's ridden so hard and abandoned men on the way has qualities which shouldn't be underestimated,' he said. Then, satisfied with the state of the shore he indicated that they should move off. 'But Aghrid or nor, we've a great many problems that need to be addressed if we're going to be travelling secretly through the country – the mountains, probably – for any length of time. I think it's time we had a council of war.'

Chapter 15

'Council of war?' Hyrald echoed uncertainly. 'What's that?'
'Precisely what it says, a council – an assembly – to discuss the war,' Endryk replied.

'What war?' The pitch of Hyrald's voice rose further than he intended.

'The one we're in,' Endryk retorted bluntly. 'Just because there isn't cavalry and infantry tramping the countryside doesn't mean there's no war going on. There is, and you need to understand that if you're going to survive. And that's only a start – a great many things will have to be thought about if we're to survive. Thyrn mentioned them the other day. How to live in this place – not for a few days but for months, quite possibly into the winter. How to cope with illness and injury. How to defend ourselves against Aghrid and anyone else who comes after us. How to find out what's happening back in Arvenshelm if you want to return there. And, not least, how to do something about it.'

His words hung uncomfortably in the dull, damp air as they walked along. No one spoke for some time.

'It's a grim list,' Hyrald said eventually.

'It is,' Endryk agreed. 'Grimmer than you know, I suspect, but unavoidable given the decision you've made to return – which, for what it's worth, I think is right,' he added hastily. 'Given that the alternative is fruitless – a wandering exile and no guarantee you might not be pursued even into that. Still, to

217

quote Thyrn, knowledge might be difficult to deal with, but it's a damned sight better than ignorance and while we accept the simple fact of our position we'll at least have a chance.'

'We've managed well enough so far,' Rhavvan said defensively.

'Well enough, yes,' Endryk agreed. 'But we can't carry on like this for much longer. That was just to keep us going day by day while you were recovering from your flight and thinking about what to do. Plus we've been lucky – with the weather, the terrain, even the supplies. That won't continue. But at least the situation's clearer now.'

'We've got a vicious enemy behind us, a definite intention ahead, and a long way to travel. We need to work out in detail what we're going to do, how we're going to do it, and who's going to do what.'

It was Adren. There was an edge to her voice. Endryk acknowledged her summary of their position with a gesture that indicated he had nothing further to say.

'Council of war it is, then.' Hyrald smiled ruefully. 'A planning meeting, I suppose we'd call it.' This inadvertent reminder of times now seemingly gone for ever, brought a long fretting thought to the surface. He looked at Endryk squarely and cleared his throat. 'Back home, these two,' he indicated Rhavvan and Adren, 'are my deputies, while Nordath and Thyrn would naturally yield to the authority of any Warden. But out here I've no illusions about my worth. Frankly, I'm lost. You've been our leader since we left your cottage. Will you continue to be?'

Endryk met his gaze and answered immediately. 'No. I appreciate what you're saying but we can't work like that. It's not appropriate. We're not a battalion with our own long-established support structure and lines of communication back to a battle centre somewhere. We're more what would be called a deep penetration group – a small patrol sent far into enemy territory to spy on troop dispositions, supply lines and the like – completely cut off from all external help, obliged to fend for ourselves totally.'

All three Wardens were looking at him, puzzled. 'We're not spying on anyone or anything. And this isn't enemy territory,' Rhavvan said. 'All we're trying to do is get back home.' He laughed tentatively but no one responded.

'Enemy territory is precisely what it is,' Endryk insisted. 'All of it, from here to Arvenshelm. Adren summarized our position exactly.'

'But what are we going to do if you won't act as leader?' Hyrald fretted. 'We have to allocate responsibilities and duties – decide who does what and when.'

'Yes, obviously,' Endryk replied. 'But we'll all of us need to make a deep change to the ways we think.' He looked at Hyrald. 'Warden, Caddoran, shoreman – they mean nothing out here. We're going to be totally dependent on one another. We need to know one another's strengths and weaknesses. And we've each got to be able to cope *without* the others. We have to become such that if one of us is lost, then that's all we lose – one – not the entire group because we were too reliant on that one person.'

'Sounds logical,' Hyrald commented, though the doubt in his voice said more than his words.

'Back to basic training, I suppose.' Adren was scarcely more enthusiastic.

'I'm sorry,' Endryk said.

'It's not your fault, is it?' Hyrald retorted. He stopped and stood silent. No one spoke and the soft stillness of the damp day closed about the group. It was very quiet. The sound of the river, hitherto ubiquitous, was faint and distant. Even the birds and animals in the surrounding trees seemed to be waiting for something.

One of the horses stamped its foot softly then shook itself.

'Damn Vashnar,' Hyrald said through clenched teeth. 'Damn him to hell.' He set off again. They walked for some time in silence until after a short rise they emerged from the trees to find themselves on the grassy shoulder of a hill.

'Let's see where we are,' Endryk said, pointing to the crest.

Hyrald spoke to him as they continued. 'I suppose what we're intending to do wouldn't be easy even if we'd been trained to it, would it?'

'No,' Endryk replied flatly. 'But I don't know that anyone could be trained for such a bizarre eventuality.' He paused thoughtfully. 'Yet Vashnar's position is no stronger than ours.'

Hyrald looked at him, puzzled.

'I hadn't thought about that before,' Endryk went on. 'Apparently he has all the advantages. He's safe in Arvenshelm with the Wardens and a mob at his back, while we're hunted fugitives alone in the middle of nowhere.' He paused, then nodded to himself as if reaching a conclusion. 'But that very safety might well be preventing him from standing back and assessing what's happening.' He paused again. 'If he's capable of such an action any more. He's a meticulous man, you say, obsessive almost?'

'Yes,' Hyrald confirmed. 'I don't know what he was like when he was younger, but even since I've known him, his skill as a planner – an anticipator of events – which is considerable, seems to have . . .' he searched for a phrase '. . . turned in on itself. Become self-absorbed. His plans can become very detailed – constraining. As though freedom of action unsettles him, particularly in other people.'

'His plans are becoming more important than the goals they're meant to achieve?'

'I suppose so, yes. At times.'

Endryk seemed pleased with the answer. He cast a glance at Thyrn and then the others. 'Well, it's not much, but we're a small group, determined, and not without resources. If we stay

220

careful, keep our thinking flexible, the more he plans like that, the better – assuming he's still capable of thinking rationally. Like us he's no experience with a situation as strange as this. It'll magnify any self-doubt he has, reduce his trust in others even further. And the more rigid he makes his schemes the more we'll be able to respond to anything he does – move around him, slip in under his guard.'

Rhavvan frowned. 'You sound as if you're going to attack him,' he said.

'Of course,' Endryk replied. 'One way or another you'll have to. You've no choice about that.'

Rhavvan stopped and his hands came out, palms forward, in a powerful gesture of denial. 'Whoa! That's not what I had in mind when I agreed we should go back.'

'What else did you have in mind?' Endryk's question was winding in its simplicity. Rhavvan stared at him. Hyrald and Adren watched both men uncertainly, their thoughts chiming with Rhavvan's.

'But we can't just . . . attack him,' Rhavvan managed uncomfortably after a moment.

'One way or another, I said,' Endryk replied. He tapped his forehead. 'But you need to be thinking about defeating him *all the time!* Nothing less is acceptable. It's either us or him and we can't afford the luxury of not accepting that; it'll eat us alive when things get rough. As far as I can see at the moment, probably the only tactic we can adopt is to run him to exhaustion – somehow. Flit here and there – crack those rigid plans of his – make him destroy the morale of his own people. But whatever we do, when he's down – in whatever fashion that occurs – *we move in.*' He made a direct stabbing motion to Rhavvan's chest.

'We can't kill him,' Rhavvan said, eyes widening.

Endryk was abruptly stern, angry almost. 'If it comes to that extremity, you will or you'll die yourself and don't think otherwise.' Rhavvan made to speak but Endryk gave him no

221

opportunity. 'But I'm not talking just about killing him. I'm talking about defeating him and the need for you not only to realize that that's what you're going to have to do, but thinking about how you're going to do it constantly.'

Rhavvan eyed him suspiciously but did not speak. Adren took him by the arm. 'I think we've just been given a cadet's morale roust,' she said sheepishly, looking at Endryk for confirmation. It was colder than she had anticipated.

'I said we'll all have to make a deep change in the way we think,' he replied. 'Be clear in what it is you're trying to achieve – to get your old lives back, or as near as can be. Cling to that. Forget everything else. While you're dithering because the details of some precious scheme are falling apart, someone might be cutting your throat.'

They were nearing the top of the hill and the grey sky was beginning to thin, frayed streaks of blue appearing. The mood of the group, however, had darkened. Hyrald addressed it and Endryk directly. 'Well, whether you want to be leader or not, you are, for the moment. We all of us want to know who you are and why you're here, but none of us are going to ask, are we?' He looked at the others significantly. 'But it's perfectly obvious that you've been a soldier at some time and that you've got more experience of this kind of life than the rest of us put together. Equally, as you pointed out, we're none of us without resources and experience of our own, and if you'll teach, we'll learn. You're right about where we're all going and why – we'll remember that. I think now we should start on that grim list of yours right away.'

They had reached the top of the hill. Without comment they moved quickly over the crest before stopping. The sky was continuing to clear, but the country ahead of them, like that behind, disappeared into a soft greyness before it reached the horizon. Thyrn and Nordath took charge of the horses while the others moved back to the shelter of a cluster of rocks on the crest of the rise from where they could view the land they had been travelling over without making themselves conspicuous against the skyline.

It was not possible to see the line of the river, though occasional shining hints of it glinted through the mixture of rolling forest and open land spread before them.

North and south, no difference, Hyrald thought, reminding himself of Thyrn's earlier remark. His reflections were interrupted by the sight of several grey columns feebly rising from the trees. All three Wardens reacted.

'Ye gods!' Rhavvan hissed. 'How many people are out there following us?'

'Don't worry. No more than before,' Endryk said reassuringly. 'Those aren't camp-fires, it's just moisture rising from the trees.' He pointed. 'See how it's dissipating – fading away vaguely. Smoke doesn't do that. It's denser – hangs together more. I think it's time for us to rest for a while.

Thyrn, tongue protruding, was practising with a makeshift sling.

'Your grim list,' Hyrald reminded Endryk.

'Will you show me how to use your bow?' Thyrn asked, turning to Endryk as he released a shot and causing some consternation as the stone went wildly awry.

'Very soon,' Endryk promised as he seized Thyrn's hand to demonstrate the correct action. 'Remember what I told you,' he said, not unkindly. 'You're supposed to be a menace to your *enemies*, not your friends.' He manoeuvred Thyrn a little way from the group and indicated a small rock some twenty paces distant. 'Hit that,' he said. Thyrn bent forward towards the rock, his eyes narrowed in disbelief. 'Do it,' Endryk commanded, before Thyrn could say anything.

The others sat down and relaxed.

'He's changed a lot,' Adren said softly as they watched Thyrn engrossed in his practice.

'And for the better,' Nordath said. A look of pain passed over his face. 'He's a remarkable young man. It's always distressed me to see the way he was treated by that dismal brother of mine and his wretched wife. But what can you do? It's family, isn't it? Not my business.'

'Did they knock him about?' Adren asked, as though she were making a formal Warden's inquiry.

Nordath's denial was unequivocal. 'Oh no, not physically. They're not brutes. Not like that anyway. But emotionally . . .' He shook his head. 'I've hardly got any memories of him as a child running, playing, laughing – getting into mischief. Just his solemn lost little face looking round at everyone. He used to play for hours with a ball I bought him – bright red it was. He'd throw it, catch it, easily, naturally. The way we do before we "grow up".' He pulled a sour face. 'But it "disappeared". As soon as his talent began to appear they kept him close, cherished him like some delicate plant – didn't allow him contact with other children, or precious little. And all for money – or to strut in front of their friends.' Adren winced at the bitterness and anger in Nordath's voice. 'But look at him now.'

It needed no great perception to see that Thyrn was enjoying himself. Nordath turned to Endryk. 'Don't think I haven't noticed what you've been doing.' Endryk looked like a man suddenly obliged to justify a guilty secret. Nordath laid a reassuring hand on his arm. 'I just wanted to say thank you while I had the chance. I'd never thought to see him like this – especially after the state he was in when he ran away from Vashnar. I thought . . . I don't know what I thought . . .' His voice had become husky and he stopped.

Endryk returned his comforting grasp. He was about to speak when Thyrn hit the rock for the second time in succession and turned to the others, arms raised in triumph. It earned him a generous round of applause, then Endryk called out, 'When you're hitting it more than you're missing it, use your left hand.' Thyrn clenched his fist by way of accepting the challenge.

Endryk turned to the others. 'All of you must learn to do that. And to make and use a bow. And to use a staff and sword properly. And a knife.'

Rhavvan bridled. 'What? What in the name of sanity would we want to learn all that for? Thinking about defeating Vashnar's one thing, but we're not going to do it with an army, are we? Besides, my staffwork's fine.'

'And so's my swordwork, thank you,' Adren added acidly.

'Yes, I've seen you, don't forget,' Endryk replied. 'I'll come to that in a moment. But you'll need to be able to use both bow and sling for hunting if you don't want to starve. And, sadly, there's every possibility that sooner or later you'll have to fight your own kind again. Only next time they'll know how dangerous you are and they won't be so reckless. The only way you'll survive that is by being both better and worse than they are.' Rhavvan and Adren looked set to speak but he did not allow them. 'Rhavvan, your staff fighting's very interesting – looks to me as if it's been derived from the ancient fighting school of hard knocks. I look forward to practising with you. I think we'll both learn a lot. Hyrald.' He was sympathetic. 'I'm afraid your swordwork's no more than adequate. We'll have to work on it.' This was not telling Hyrald anything he did not already know, and he merely looked at Endryk uncertainly as he pressed on. 'Adren, your swordwork's quite good, it'll make an excellent basis for developing a proper technique, and –'

'Quite good!' she spluttered before he could continue. Adren took a considerable pride in her skill with a sword and she did not respond well to this slight on her ability. 'Proper technique!' Her anger suddenly welled up. 'I'll give you proper technique, you son of a bitch.' She stood up and drew her sword. 'On your feet and see if you like the flat of my technique across your backside.' Hyrald and Rhavvan edged back, knowing from experience that there were times when Adren was not to be disputed with. She bent forward and held a beckoning hand in front of Endryk's bemused face.

'Up,' she said.

He turned to Rhavvan and Hyrald in appeal but received only regretful shrugs. Then he smiled and stood up. The smile did nothing to assuage Adren's mood.

'Maybe I phrased my remarks a little unhappily,' he said, conciliatory. 'I didn't mean . . .'

Adren's finger jabbed out towards his sword. 'I know exactly what you meant. Draw that. Put your blade where your mouth is or sit down.'

'Be careful, little sister,' Hyrald said warningly.

'Don't worry, big brother,' Adren retorted caustically. 'No one's going to get hurt, other than in their pride. Someone here's got to stand up for the Wardens.'

Seeing himself abandoned, Endryk drew his sword awkwardly. He did not present any form of guard, however; instead he let his arm hang loose by his side, his sword point resting on the ground, as if uncertain as to what he should do. Adren circled around him with slow easy strides, both her sword and her gaze levelled at him unwaveringly.

Hyrald watched with mixed feelings. Wardens did not often have to resort to using their swords, and on most of the occasions they did so, it was the terror that the action invoked and the liberal use of the flat of the blade that did what was necessary. Nevertheless, proficiency with a sword was a matter of some pride amongst them and Adren was generally acknowledged to be one of their finest exponents. There were very few Wardens who could face her and come away unscathed. She was legitimately proud of her skill. On the other hand, Endryk was their guide, helper and ally. There was no saying what his response might be if Adren fulfilled her promise and humiliated him. And too, he was a completely unknown quantity. Almost daily since their first meeting he had demonstrated skills that Hyrald had never realized existed. Further, this was not the time for such antics.

He had just resolved that he should intervene when Adren stepped sideways and forward and spun around. It was a manoeuvre intended to carry her suddenly outside her opponent's line of sight and which would conclude with the flat of her blade landing squarely on his rear. Having been the victim of it himself more than once, Hyrald knew that her abrupt disappearance was disconcerting enough without the indignity and implicit menace of the blow.

Endryk, however, somehow mirrored the move so that Adren's blade flew wide, unbalancing her slightly and leaving the two of them facing one another again. Though swift, Endryk's move had been done so unhurriedly that it drove Hyrald's immediate preoccupations from his mind as he tried to recall exactly what had happened. Endryk had still not raised his sword.

Adren recovered quickly and taking her swinging sword in both hands she suddenly spun the blade vertical as though to strike Endryk flat in the face. This time he did move with conspicuous speed, stepping back and sideways and swinging his own sword around to beat hers down. Again Adren responded quickly, retreating and raising her sword into its initial guard position. The challenge had gone from her face. Her expression was now a mixture of shrewd assessment and curiosity.

'That was very good,' Endryk said genuinely. 'I apologise for underestimating you. My mistake. I won't do it again.' He held out a hand to halt the proceedings briefly. 'But – if I may – you're using your sword as a punishment baton. You're going to have to think about using it to kill people with.' Adren stiffened. As did Hyrald. Oddly, Endryk's soft voice was more frightening than any screamed instruction. Adren had killed two people during her service with the Wardens. In both cases she had acted in self-defence and no reproach had been offered her either legally or morally. Indeed, she had acted with great courage. But the incidents were never far from her mind.

'I can do that, if I have to,' she said, her face suddenly drawn and her mouth taut.

Endryk looked at her for a long moment. 'Yes. I can see that. I'm sorry again. I didn't realize. I think we've both just made a mistake, don't you? We'll do this some other time.' He sheathed his sword.

Adren's face softened. 'No, it was my fault – I started it. The apology's mine.' Then some of her challenge returned and she cocked her head on one side. 'Still, no one's ever moved around me like that before. I'd be interested to know how you did it.'

Endryk seemed inclined to refuse, then he changed his mind. He addressed the entire group. Thyrn had abandoned his practice and was standing nearby, watching wide-eyed. Endryk tapped his stomach then his forehead. Hyrald suddenly had a vision of a line of teachers reaching back through time and doing the same.

'Survival lies in the mind and body being together. I can show you where to put your hands and feet, and why. And you can – you must – practise what I show you. But the will – the clear intention – has to come from inside. You must know about that from the outset, even if you don't understand. Let me show you something to think about.'

He turned back to Adren. 'Lunge,' he said, offering himself squarely to her. Adren frowned then hesitantly pushed her sword forward so that it stopped a little way in front of him.

Endryk looked down at it. 'I don't need to defend myself against an attack that's not there,' he said. 'This time lunge as if you meant it.'

'But . . .'

228

'And you shouldn't teach yourself not to attack. It'll get you killed one day.'

'But . . .'

Endryk looked into her eyes. 'We have to trust one another as you've never trusted before if you're to win your lives back. Trust me now. Lunge again. Properly this time.'

Adren still hesitated. She looked quickly at Hyrald but found no help there.

'Do it!' Endryk commanded. '*Trust!*'

Adren's hand twitched nervously around the hilt of her sword then, eyes both fearful and determined, she lunged again, this time advancing and extending fully. As before, Endryk's response did not seem to be hurried, but before Adren's forward movement had stopped, he was by her side, one hand gripping her leading sword hand and the other holding a knife across her throat. She gasped and her eyes widened in shock.

'Good,' Endryk said, releasing her and sheathing his knife. 'Very good. I see we've all got a lot to learn from one another. Thank you.' His arm looped around Adren's shoulders and embraced her briefly.

Rhavvan was on his feet asking the question that Adren was about to ask. 'How did you do that? That was amazing. You must show me . . .'

'All in due course,' Endryk said. 'I think we should be on our way. We don't know what's behind us yet and there's a lot of open country ahead. We should make what speed we can. Get where we're going as soon as possible.' He was pointing.

The others followed his hand. The sky was clearing rapidly and with it the mistiness that had been clouding the countryside.

On the horizon was the ragged outline of the Karpas Mountains.

Chapter 16

As the coach moved steadily away from the centre of Arvenshelm, Vashnar leaned back into its lush upholstery. Slowly his eyes closed.

The coach was a well-sprung and luxuriously appointed vehicle built at the behest of Vashnar's more hedonistic predecessor. On his appointment, Vashnar's immediate response, as it had been to much of his predecessor's handiwork, was to dispense with it on the grounds that its conspicuous lavishness was not appropriate to the stern office of Senior Warden Commander.

Both Bowlott and Vellain, however, had persuaded him otherwise, Vellain citing her own comfort when she accompanied him on official occasions, Bowlott citing both the cost of using an ordinary coach while that stood idle – 'It's not as if we could sell it' – and reminding him that, 'The tone has been set. The people and your own men – the Moot – all expect it.' Vellain had also insinuated more subtle touches such as the fact that it would leave him less tired and thus the better able to fulfil his duties efficiently at the end of a long journey.

It helped too that Vashnar genuinely appreciated the skilled craftsmanship and ingenuity of design that underlay the coach's smooth and easy working. Of late, it had come to him that similar vehicles, shorn of frippery, could be used to transport large numbers of Wardens very quickly to scenes of public disorder; indeed, it was perhaps possible they could be built to

231

serve as weapons in themselves. Though his thoughts on that were ill-formed he had nevertheless spent some time talking to the owners of the company that had made the coach, and they were gradually becoming clearer – and more attractive.

Vellain watched her husband carefully as the gentle swaying gradually relaxed him. The next few days were going to be important. Since learning of the details of Thyrn's first attack upon her husband – for, like Vashnar, an attack was how she perceived it – she had been anxious to lure him away from the daily demands of the Warding. She needed to have him where she and she alone could discreetly observe and counsel him. And she needed him to be at ease, in so far as such a term could ever be applied to Vashnar.

She was, however, far too aware of her husband's character to attempt simply to drag him away from his preoccupations by wifely persistence, and, after the initial shock, she was almost relieved when Thyrn's second attack occurred in that it gave her the opportunity to suggest this northwards journey. That she had been right to do so was confirmed to her by the ease with which Vashnar had accepted the idea and the considerable alacrity with which he had set it in train.

As she watched him, teetering gently between waking and sleeping, she briefly pondered the doubts that the past weeks had brought her then she wilfully set aside such of them as still lingered and asserted anew her faith in him. He and everything about him was hers, and greatness was to be his – he deserved no less. This was beyond dispute – a rock of certainty in her life – and she would ensure his destiny came to pass, no matter what the cost. Thyrn, or anyone else who opposed him would be destroyed, by one means or another. Even Vashnar's own weaknesses would be destroyed if they impeded this progress.

As these old familiar thoughts wove through her mind, her expression became so grim and determined that had Vashnar woken at that moment, he might well not have recognized her for his wife. Catching sight of herself in one of the carriage's mirrors, she hastily forced a smile. As if on cue, Vashnar opened his eyes and sat up, wide awake.

'What are you smiling at?' he asked.

The smile broadened. 'Just being here with you,' Vellain replied. 'Away from the relentless daily routines for a while. Time to think, to plan.'

Vashnar tried to frown though it was difficult in the face of his wife's open affection. 'Those routines are important,' he said heavily.

'And well organized – and in more than capable hands,' Vellain chided. 'More so now you've brought in some of the Tervaidin to attend to them.' She said tenderly, 'And who is it who tells his senior officers that they shouldn't allow the urgent to obscure the important?'

Vashnar leaned back again, defeated. The coach was more seductive than he realized. 'Yes, you're quite right. With all the flurry and strangeness of what's happened lately it's been difficult to stand back from events and assess them properly.' A gleam came into his eyes. 'But we're nearly there, my love. Nearly there. I'll sound out our allies over the next few days, then when we hear from Aghrid, everything tells me we'll be in a position to plan our final move.'

Vellain reached across and squeezed his hand.

A raucous voice from outside interrupted them and there was an abrupt change in the steadily clattering hooves of the escorting riders. Vashnar eased his wife's hand away and lifted back the light curtain covering the side window. Vellain did the same, just in time to see an unkempt figure being knocked over by one of the escort swinging his horse sideways. As the man rolled over, a large rock fell from his hands. He made a half-hearted attempt to recover it but a glancing blow from the rider's staff sent him staggering and he scuttled away quickly, hands raised to protect his head. He was soon lost from sight amongst the people thronging the busy shops and roadside stalls. There was a mixture of jeering and cheering from a few of the passers-by but most ignored the incident. The rider turned to see Vashnar watching him. He looked flustered and uncertain but Vashnar gave him a signal of approval for his action and motioned him to forget the man.

'Ousten district,' he said as he replaced the curtain. 'There are times when I'd like to raze the whole area – it's a sinkhole of thieves and troublemakers. It causes us more trouble than every other district in the city put together.'

'It also yields the most taxes,' Vellain reminded him, craning round as they passed by a brightly lit shop window. 'Not to mention the fact that it's also the biggest and liveliest district of the city and that some of its most successful criminals are also its most successful merchants. And don't forget the Gilding.'

'Yes,' Vashnar agreed reluctantly. The Gilding was never lightly to be set aside from any considerations. Legally questionable it might be, but it was deeply entrenched and it smoothed out many of the city's administrative tangles even more efficiently than Vashnar's coach smoothed out its uneven and rutted road surfaces.

'Still, something will have to be done about it when I'm in control.'

'We'll think of something,' Vellain said dismissively. 'There'll be plenty of time then. Anyway, I think the Ousten's the least of our problems. The people who matter here are businessmen not Moot Senators. They know what's in their interests and what's not, and needless trouble isn't. They'll keep order here for us themselves when they see how things lie.'

'You're probably right.'

'I am right.'

Leaving the sprawling and vibrant disorder of the Ousten district the coach passed on through one of the city's poorer but more reputable areas where tightly packed houses jostled crookedly with one another for the privilege of opening directly on to the streets. It was from such that Vellain had come, burning with ambition for as long as anyone had known her. Her expression was unreadable as they passed the ragged lines of houses with their unsettling mixture of struggling respectability and blatant neglect. Only when the coach reached the outer parts of the city, where the lavish houses of successful merchants and businessmen maintained varying degrees of stately dignity across spacious gardens and parklands, did her face soften.

She and Vashnar spoke very little as they finally left the city and set off along the north road. The evening turned to night and a bright moon silvered the landscape to light their way though neither of them saw it from behind the coach's drawn curtains. Even when they stopped at their accommodation for the night, it did not occur to either of them to look up beyond the dancing shadows of the lamplit courtyard as the proud householder ushered them into his home.

'It's good to see you again,' he repeated with over-hearty sincerity and for the third time as he showed them into a large, well-lit room. 'And you, Vellain,' he added, closing the doors softly behind them. 'So rarely we see you. But I can see why Vashnar keeps you to himself – beautiful as ever.' He took both her hands in his and looked at her with a licence that he would not have dared had Vashnar not been there.

The walls of the room were lined with decorative displays of highly polished weapons alternating with heavily framed pictures. Without exception these last showed either individuals posturing in elaborate and lavishly decorated uniforms, or frozen scenes of stylized battlefield violence. The glittering points and edges and the martial images contrasted oddly with the luxuriant carpet underfoot and the opulent and well-made furniture that filled the room, but the whole was redolent of great wealth.

'Good to see you, too, Darransen,' Vashnar replied. 'I'm sorry about the short notice, but . . .'

Like the room, Darransen, upright but overweight and with a florid complexion and a midriff which was winning the battle against a tightly fastened belt, was a mixture of self-indulgence and strutting orderliness. A fighting man gone to seed, Vellain always thought of him. Or a would-be fighting man, she was never sure.

He waved the apology aside. 'No notice is required for you, Commander. My house is yours any time, you know that. A room is always ready for you. As it is, your rider was here more than an hour ago so we have a meal for you if you wish.'

He lowered his voice and became confidential. 'I've also taken the liberty of calling together some of our . . . colleagues. Discreetly, of course. But with all that's happened of late – the Death Cry – the Tervaidin appearing . . .' He waxed briefly and his hand went out towards a picture showing the traditional representation of the Tervaidin, improbably brightly lit, fighting against a demented enemy equally improbably shaded by looming thunderclouds. 'What a sight they were. I never thought I'd see the day – splendid. Still, forgive me – as I was saying, with all that's happened lately I thought you might like to speak to some of your supporters. You know them all.' He recited their names. 'If I've been hasty, just . . .'

Only Vellain was sharp enough to detect Vashnar's momentary hesitation. Darransen was far too occupied with past and future events to notice the present.

'Of course,' Vashnar said, cutting across Darransen's reservations. 'As ever, I can rely on your judgement in these matters. A little talk will be timely, though . . .' he raised a cautionary hand '. . . I'm not yet in a position to discuss current developments in any detail. Far too delicate. Suffice it that circumstances are moving steadily our way, as intended, but perhaps somewhat faster than we had originally hoped. We must all remain both ready and patient.'

Later, Vashnar and Vellain sat alone in the room that Darransen had provided for them. Here, as throughout the rambling house, the decor showed an uneasy mixture of luxury and military bellicosity. 'I'm not sure I have your faith in Darransen,' Vellain said, looking around.

Vashnar followed her gaze. 'You mean all the weapons and the battle scenes? You think he plays at this. An armchair warrior.'

'Yes.'

Vashnar loosened his collar and began unbuttoning his tunic. 'He is and he isn't. I've known him a long time. He's never been a Warden or even a Watch Guard to my knowledge, and, to be honest, I don't think I'd trust him with anything much more dangerous than a knife and fork in a fight. But he's rich, shrewd, powerful and very capable. He's been invaluable in raising support for us and he'll do well when it's over – providing he doesn't get too ambitious. I certainly wouldn't want him against us at this stage. He's not to be underestimated.'

'A little indiscreet, bringing the others together at once, though.'

Vashnar shook his head. 'Not really. I told you, he's shrewd. Took me a little offguard, I'll admit, but he was right. He judged the moment well – and their mood, with everything that's been happening. They've gone away buoyed up – renewed.'

'Without actually knowing anything more about what's going on,' Vellain added.

'Knowing what they needed to know,' Vashnar corrected, with a hint of dark humour. 'And knowing the importance of both continued secrecy and obeying orders.'

'How long do you want to stay here?'

'We'll leave early tomorrow. If we stay longer, Darransen will start pressing for more information. He's not easily fobbed off and I don't want to offend him. Thinking he's near to the centre is important to him.'

Vellain moved behind his chair and, leaning forward, put her arms around him. 'You're probably right. But if he's too persistent tomorrow, tell him the truth.'

Vashnar started and half turned to look at her.

'The truth,' she repeated. 'You're taking time away from day to day affairs to plan the final details while visiting our friends to test their readiness.'

'Oh, that truth.'

Vellain bit his ear.

As it transpired, Darransen presented no problems. The weighty emphasis that Vashnar had laid at the meeting on the need for discretion at 'this very delicate moment' was more than sufficient to keep his observations about coming events to knowing looks. It helped too that Vellain was there, distracting him from 'business matters' with questions about his house, its furnishings, carpets, maintenance, servants and so on.

As they were preparing to leave, he disappeared briefly back into the house to emerge bearing a small box. He offered it to Vellain. 'A gift,' he said simply. Genuinely surprised, Vellain thanked him and held it up in the morning light. Made of polished wood, and unexpectedly heavy, it was undecorated apart from some delicate incised scrolling on one face. Turning it she could see no joints or any obvious means of opening it. Darransen reached forward and gently touched part of the scrolling. There was a faint click and Vellain's eyes widened as the sides and top of the box slowly unfolded to reveal a small statuette. As might have been expected, the figure was a warrior, though unusually, it was not holding some posture of proud defiance. Instead, it was of a sombre-looking young man wearing battered armour and leaning on a buckled and scarred shield. A hacked sword hung limply by his side. Vellain leaned forward to examine it more closely. As she did, a hint of sunlight broke through the grey sky only to fade almost immediately. Vellain gave a slight gasp. It seemed to her that at the touch of

238

the light, the stone figure had moved – his stance shifting and the expression on his face changing. She blinked as if to clear her vision and looked at it again intently. The closer she looked at it, the more she saw that it was a superb piece of carving, full of intricate and fine detail. Unexpectedly she heard herself saying, 'But I can't accept this, it's beautiful work. It must be worth a fortune.'

'For the sun in my Commander's life, nothing is too much,' Darransen said.

Vellain bounced back the heavy-handed compliment sternly. 'No,' she insisted. 'I really can't.'

Darransen, however, was not to be deflected. He turned in appeal to Vashnar who gave a friendly but disclaiming shrug.

'It's far too valuable for me to take,' Vellain said, carefully easing the sides of the box together. They began to close without her assistance once she had touched them. 'And besides, it's we who should be giving gifts to you after your hospitality and your continued help.' Again, as the light about him changed, the figure seemed to move.

Darransen took advantage of her momentary distraction. 'Expense is nothing to me, Vellain,' he said, his voice sober and quite free of the heartiness that had pervaded it for much of their stay. 'I have money enough to last many lifetimes, and I continue to make more – even though the loss of trade with Nesdiryn is proving a problem. Far more important to me is the work your husband is doing.' His voice fell. 'We need a Dictator more than ever now. It should have been done years ago. It will bring order to the people – sanity to our government – crush those whose pernicious influence is rotting us from within.' He took her hand and firmly pressed the box into it. 'I do what I can to help him, but you sustain him more than I possibly could. This is part of my thanks to you for that. I'll take no refusal.'

Vellain caught a slight nod from her husband.

'How can I refuse then,' she said. Darransen smiled and released her. There was a short, awkward silence following this acquiescence. Vellain ended it.

'Do you know who carved it?' she asked.

'No Arvenstaat carver, for sure,' Darransen replied categorically. 'I'm no great judge of carving, but even I can tell it's a remarkable piece. The more you look at it, the more you see in it.' That some of the things he saw in it he did not like, Darransen forbore to mention. The figure's aura of deep fatigue disturbed him in some way. 'A buyer I use came across it by chance, languishing on a shelf in one of his suppliers' warehouses. The owner thought it had come from somewhere up north – way up north, off the map – but it could've come from anywhere, I suppose.'

'I'll give it a place of honour,' Vellain said.

'In one of my rooms,' she said to Vashnar as the coach clattered out of Darransen's courtyard and turned northwards again. 'I know you and ornaments.'

Vashnar shook his head. 'Put it somewhere conspicuous,' he said. 'I don't want to have to remember niceties like that if Darransen has cause to visit us – as well he might. He's very odd about some things. Wouldn't say anything, but wouldn't take kindly to finding his gift anywhere other than in the centre of my attention.'

They travelled on in silence, Vellain occasionally looking down at the wooden box containing the statuette. During the day they stopped at three villages and Vellain watched as her husband spoke with local Wardens and Watch Guards and discreetly raised hopes and renewed old pledges and loyalties as he had at Darransen's. She made no demur. Slowly, as she had intended, he was shedding the tensions of his daily routine.

'Good?' she asked as he dropped on to the seat opposite her and the coach moved off again.

'Excellent,' he replied, acknowledging the parting salutes

of a group of Watch Guards. 'The Tervaidin moving through here has worked wonders. Apparently there's been some grumbling, but not much, and only from well-known malcontents. Our allies are with us more than ever and new ones are coming in every day.'

Vellain expressed some concern. 'We must still be careful. You said yourself things are at a delicate stage. This is no time for reckless cries in the street.'

'Our people know that,' Vashnar reassured her. 'And I reminded them of it as well.' He clapped his hands together. 'We were right to make this journey. It's not only bolstering our friends, it's reminding me how many we really have. When we finally move, few will want to stand against us and even fewer will be able to.'

Vellain took a chance. 'And Thyrn?' she said.

'Just another problem,' Vashnar returned. 'My problem. And maybe Aghrid's already solved it – we'll see. In any event, even if he escapes Aghrid and somehow manages to find anyone in authority who'll listen to him, with the way matters are developing it's unlikely any notice will be taken of him.'

'And Hyrald and the others? If they return, they'll have no difficulty attracting attention.'

Vashnar leaned forward and rested his hand on her knee. 'You're concerning yourself too much. The general acceptance of the Tervaidin has changed everything. I knew things were going well but actually speaking to Darransen and the others has given me an insight into matters that the written reports couldn't. The mood for change is stronger than ever now – I can almost feel it in the air. Anyone who opposes us is going to find it very difficult to make himself heard. And if Thyrn or Hyrald or any of them somehow manage to get back we'll just arrest them. A couple of months in jail waiting for trial and it will be too late anyway.'

Vellain took another chance. 'Have you thought any more

about what it was that Thyrn might have seen, to make him so frightened?'

'It's irrelevant now.' The reply was a little too brusque for Vellain.

'It's just that I still can't see why some kind of accidental insight into your plans would frighten him so badly.'

Vashnar shifted uncomfortably. He obviously did not want to pursue the matter, but the buoyancy of his mood carried him into it. 'I've stopped thinking about it. Whenever I did I got nowhere – it just unsettled me. Who can say what he saw, what he felt? All I can recall is terror – his terror – washing over me.' He closed his eyes and shook his head to dispel the memory. 'That, and the knowledge that somehow he'd discovered everything and was going to blurt it out everywhere. He was dangerous, out of control. He had to be stopped.'

Vellain was tempted to press him further. Thyrn's frantic response still concerned her. It was disproportionate. Shock there might well have been, but terror? Still, the Caddoran were a strange lot and Thyrn was strange even for a Caddoran. By all accounts he'd had an odd life, with his parents perpetually hovering about him, almost imprisoning him; he'd never really been a child. Small wonder his response had been disproportionate. And, of course, Vashnar, startled and angry, would frighten anyone. For a moment she felt a twinge of sympathy for the young man suddenly facing this terrifying figure. Enough, she decided abruptly. She must do as her husband had – let it go. The whole business was beyond anything she had ever known and as Vashnar seemed to have made his own peace with it she saw little to be gained by disturbing him further. Circumstances, as he said, had changed radically. The threat that Thyrn had apparently posed had turned into a catalyst for progress. It was good.

The heart of Vashnar's scheming, both practical and political, lay in Arvenshelm and the people he needed there he dealt with constantly. He had few reservations about these and it was generally accepted amongst them that if any opposition came from beyond the city it would not be serious and would almost certainly diminish with distance. Nevertheless, his obsessive nature had not accepted that risk and over time he had worked to win support where a lesser man might have thought it unnecessary. It always troubled him to some degree that he could not maintain the direct contact with his more distant allies that he would have liked. Was he neglecting them? How resolute were they? How reliable? How discreet? How prepared?

Over the next few days as he and Vellain travelled north he was able to answer many of these questions while at the same time revitalizing any flagging enthusiasm. Not that there was much, he found to his increasing satisfaction. Aghrid may have passed through most of these small towns and villages very quickly, but he had not gone unnoticed and the effects of his passage were rippling outwards still, stirring further the disturbance already caused by the Death Cry. The Tervaidin returned was an omen of great changes to come, surely?

Those that Vashnar met recited the tale he had already heard from Darransen. A little grumbling here and there by the constitutionally discontented but, on the whole, there was unconditional support.

Vellain basked in the glow of her husband's increasing confidence. Gradually, as they travelled, as they walked, as they lay together in the pleasant darkness of strange but friendly rooms, he began to prepare plans for the final part of his scheme.

Then they met one of Aghrid's men.

Chapter 17

The Karpas Mountains ran north to south down the centre of Arvenstaat. Legend had it that they were created during the Wars of the First Coming by one of the Great Corrupter's aides – a necromancer to whom He had given a portion of His power. Seeking to destroy an entire nation which was strong against his Lord, he tore a great island from its roots and hurled it into their land with such force that what had been a shoreline was crushed and buckled and thrust high into the air to become the Karpas Mountains. That this was patently true was demonstrated by the presence of sea shells in various places along the western edge of the mountains, now on the far side from the ocean and at a great distance from it. Arvenstaat's academics, burdened as they were with observed facts and rational thought, offered explanations for this phenomenon which were far more tentative and far less interesting.

Although sometimes referred to as the backbone of the land, and certainly splendid to look at, the Karpas Mountains on the whole were not particularly daunting and posed no serious obstacle to travel east and west across Arvenstaat. There were a few places where individual peaks and groups of peaks shouldered one another ominously, but at no point did they assume the daunting impassability of the southern mountains or even the rugged defiance of those in the west which separated Arvenstaat from Nesdiryn.

Hyrald and the others had reached the northern extremity

of that part of the Karpas range which lay in Arvenstaat. Hyrald found it oddly intriguing as they moved westwards that while the river dwindled and divided, making any passage to the north much easier, he was increasingly sure that they had made the right decision to end their flight and return south. Even the prospect of what would undoubtedly be serious difficulties in returning to Arvenshelm did little to diminish this certainty.

'How far north do they go?' he asked Endryk as they reached a vantage which showed the mountains extending to both horizons.

'A long way, I'd think,' Endryk replied. 'They've the look of the tail-end of a long range.' He pointed. As the range extended northwards, what they could see of it began to assume a greyer, colder aspect, its peaks higher and closer.

'You don't know what's up there, then?'

Endryk shook his head. 'No, Warden,' he said with a smile at Hyrald's untypically awkward prying. 'My land's further east. There's supposed to be a remnant of the Old Forest up there somewhere – to the west – bigger than the whole of Arvenstaat and unbelievably ancient. Not a safe place, they say. Not for people, anyway. They go in and don't come out. It's said to be surrounded by mountains. Perhaps that's where these go, I wouldn't be surprised. The world's a big place and a small place. However far you travel there's always somewhere else to go, new wonders to find.' He looked north then south along the mountains. 'And the same old things to discover anew.'

They were not the same group that had trekked along the river and fought off Aghrid's men, and they were markedly different from the group that had nearly drowned on the shore. Where Endryk had taught Thyrn surreptitiously, he now taught all of them constantly and openly. And too, he learned.

'We're like all the other animals around here. Free, but in constant peril, with only our wits and good fortune to protect us. It's a frightening feeling for people who've been brought

246

up in any kind of community, but we have to accept it. It's important we think of ourselves as being here for ever. We must be completely self-sufficient in everything; renew as we use – waste nothing.'

Unlike the animals however, he acknowledged, their needs were more complex and in addition to their surviving day to day, they also had to plan for winter and, eventually, their return to Arvenshelm.

'Whatever you've been, you're that no longer. You must live your lives at a different pace. Learn to relax into whatever you're doing. Take your time – concern yourselves with the here and now, be patient. Fretting about the future may break your ankle in the present, or worse, and drastically change the very future you were carefully laying out. The time to think and plan ahead is around the fire or lying in the darkness.'

'Be patient?' Rhavvan snorted. 'Then the next thing he's saying is, learn this, learn that, time's not with us, time's not with us.' He mimicked Endryk ruthlessly.

'Nor is it,' Endryk replied laughing. 'To go as slowly as we need to you'll have to learn quickly. You'll need all your Warden's skills if you're to leave your Warden's thinking behind.' He slapped the growling Rhavvan on the back.

The three Wardens were very keen to learn more about the fighting skills that Endryk had briefly demonstrated, as was Thyrn, though where the Wardens' interest was for the most part professional, Thyrn's was openly excited and heavily coloured by romantic myth and legend. It brought down a sober lecture on his head from Hyrald. Nordath was generally nervous of the subject and invariably diverted conversation away from it when it arose.

In any event, Endryk was not to be drawn, other than into telling them that relaxation and breathing were fundamental, underlying everything, a contribution which left Rhavvan in particular looking at him in open disbelief. The others tried to disguise their own doubts with polite nods.

'Trust me in this,' he said, noting their response with some amusement. 'As I was once told by someone for whom I had a great regard, how can you expect to control others when you can't control yourself? Cruel question. And if you can't control your own body, or even your own breathing . . . ?' He grinned and shrugged.

When Rhavvan pressed him strongly one night, he reiterated the point, adding, 'We'll look at this in due course. When we're more together. When it's more appropriate. There are more urgent things needing our attention right now.' He pointed to a bundle of sticks that Nordath had gathered and selected. 'Like feathering and pointing those arrows, for example. An army marches on its stomach and so do we. No food for a few days and fighting skills are going to be very low down on your list of what's important.'

For that same reason however, he did begin to show them how to use the bow and the sling.

'You need these for hunting.'

Even here though, his instruction consisted mainly of showing them how to make and care for their bows, arrows and strings. His pupils took to their learning very variably: Rhavvan constantly demonstrated his flair for impatience; Adren showed a remarkable natural marksmanship – her wilful flaunting of which further tested Rhavvan's threadbare patience, to everyone else's amusement; Hyrald and Thyrn plodded along diligently and dutifully. Nordath proved to be the most reluctant and least confident, having neither youth, fighting experience nor inclination on his side. He did, however, show an unexpected aptitude at shaping bows and finding wood suitable for arrows. Ironically, his enthusiasm for the task and everyone else's willingness to let him do it, prompted the nearest to an angry reaction that Endryk had shown since they first met him. 'Everyone does everything,' he insisted with unusual force. 'All the time. We want no weak links. If you're good at something, get better at it and help the others. If you're bad at it – keep doing it until you're not. And if you need help, in the name of pity, ask. Pride's inexcusable out here. I'll show you things as many times as it takes, but I can't teach you anything, you have to learn it.'

On the whole though, their journey to the mountains was filled with good spirits and enthusiasm.

The only incident of note during their plodding progress was the killing of a small deer on their last westward march. There was little excitement in the hunt itself which for the most part consisted of testing the wind, lying still, and keeping very quiet while Endryk slowly moved close enough to bring the animal down. As the heavy-headed arrow struck it, the deer ran for a few paces then stumbled. Endryk shot it again very quickly then, moving closer, finished it with two carefully placed arrows.

Though she was trying not to show it, Adren was obviously distressed when she emerged from cover. 'Couldn't you have killed it with your sword – like the horse?' she asked inadequately.

'Who would you rather tackle in an alley – a frightened man or an injured, frightened man?' Endryk replied. 'It mightn't be very big but, believe me, a blow from a deer's flailing leg can do a great deal of harm. And I'll remind you where we are.'

'You'll have to forgive me,' Adren said, wincing as Endryk cut out the arrows. 'I'm used to seeing dead people, but . . .' She stopped.

'You're just not used to seeing your meat killed.'

Adren ran her hand across the animal's head. 'It's a beautiful creature.'

'Yes,' said Endryk, drawing his knife.

'You thank it,' Thyrn said, anxious to help her. She looked up at him uncertainly. 'You thank it for being beautiful and for

249

the food it'll give you. You do it to anything you kill – for food that is,' he added uncomfortably.

'And there'll be more than food from this.' Endryk's tone approved Thyrn's intervention. He handed Adren his knife and without further comment began to instruct her in how to bleed and skin the animal. It took some time and was a heavy learning for her.

'That's because you're not hungry yet,' Endryk said, though his manner was sympathetic throughout. 'You did well. Very well. That skin will be shelter or clothes before we've finished.'

It fell to the watching Rhavvan and Hyrald to gut and butcher the carcass.

They were all quieter than usual as they finished that day's travelling.

They were less quiet that night when they were eating the results of their endeavours.

'This is amazing. I've never tasted anything like it.' Rhavvan's praise of the food met with general agreement and congratulations for the hunter.

'Fresh air and fresh meat,' Endryk told them. 'Not something you're used to in Arvenshelm, I'd imagine. Especially meat you've caught yourself.'

When the meal was finished and a string of Wardens' reminiscences had petered out, Hyrald remarked to Endryk that, 'This must be much harder for you than you thought when we set out.'

'Yes and no,' Endryk replied. 'Being Wardens has given you a greater aptitude than you realize. You listen, you think, more than many do.' He looked significantly at Rhavvan. 'Most times, you ask when you don't know. No, it's not difficult. In fact, I think it's slowly waking me up.'

'What do you mean?'

'I learned all these things years ago – with a damned sight greater reluctance than you're showing now, I can assure you.

Then some of them I had to use without thinking, just to get me from one place to another safely, quickly, my mind full of other things – frightening things. Now, faced with this – a long journey with no end in sight – and having spent years wandering and living alone, I see a value in what my old teachers showed me that'd make them smile if they could hear me admitting it. I'm surprised I'm remembering so much of it.'

'You were an officer in your army?' Nordath asked tentatively.

Endryk shied away from the question a little. 'No, just an ordinary soldier – but none of us were what you'd think of as soldiers really. It was just our way – part of our society – a military tradition maintained in memory of harsher times long gone, just as you have a tradition of having no army – only the Warding. We had no enemies. We lived in peace with our neighbours, in so far as we ever met them. As here, no one travelled much. We had all we needed. We were content.'

'How did you come to be fighting in a war, then?' Rhavvan blundered in. Hyrald scowled at him.

'We failed in our duty,' Endryk replied. His voice was unsteady, as if he had answered without wanting to. 'Relaxed our vigilance. Forgot how and why such a tradition had come about. Our enemy was within us . . .' He stopped and stared into the fire. His eyes were shining. 'I'm sorry, I don't want to talk about it.'

'The apology's ours,' Hyrald said, still scowling at Rhavvan. 'Asking questions is such a part of our job it becomes a habit. We forget that it's not always appropriate.'

'I'm sorry,' Rhavvan said, genuinely repentant. 'I don't always think before I speak.'

Endryk did not reply but just nodded and held out his hand to end the matter. The easy, relaxed atmosphere that the meal had induced gradually reasserted itself. Rhavvan casually observed that, 'I don't suppose he's eating as well as we are,' and the discussion fell to Aghrid.

Having been moving through open country for the last few days they had taken every opportunity to look behind them. But there had been no sign of any pursuit. Hyrald voiced the unspoken conclusion.

'I suppose he might have gone wandering off north, but I doubt it. I think we've bloodied his nose too much. I think he's on his way home.'

His analysis was tentatively accepted, but Endryk still insisted that they should continue posting guards through the night. 'We can't be sure yet, and it's too good a habit to break,' he said. 'We must be absolutely certain. There's a chance that perhaps he's learning too.' He did not sound too convinced by his own argument and the Wardens dismissed it.

Rhavvan was blunt. 'Aghrid's ruthless and crafty, but he's a street creature, like me, like all of us. He's lost out here. Three horses down and at least one man badly hurt. He's running for home.'

'According to the one we caught, he'd abandoned men on the way; he may have done the same with his wounded,' Endryk countered.

'Possibly, but I doubt it,' Hyrald said. 'I've been fretting about this Tervaidin business, and about Aghrid reinstated. It's frightening – I can't think what it all means. But the only men I can imagine running with Aghrid would be his own kind and they'd take only so much of that treatment. He's astute enough to know he'll get a knife in the ribs one night if he's not careful. He's gone, all right.'

'But we must be vigilant, always,' Endryk insisted. There was an earnestness in his manner and a resonance in the word *vigilant* that brought back their earlier intrusion into his past and the discussion ended abruptly.

'You're right,' Hyrald said. 'We'll keep the watch duties. I don't want to take the slightest chance that we might be wrong about Aghrid. And anyway, it'll be harder to start them again if we stop. Not to mention the fact that we don't know who or what else is out here.'

'No one lives round here,' Rhavvan said.

'You're sure about that, are you?' Hyrald retorted. 'Bearing in mind that there was an entire sea we knew nothing about only a few days ago.'

Rhavvan conceded the point unhappily.

The rest of the evening they spent following Endryk's advice and considering their future movement. Relaxed by the food, the soft light of the fire and the warmth of the night, the discussion about their route rambled freely over many topics. In the course of it, Nordath remarked, 'I've got family in the country in the west, and quite a few friends.' The greater part of Arvenstaat's population lay on the eastern side of the mountains. The western side was devoted mainly to farming and was viewed with knowing disdain by the sophisticated city- and town-dwellers to the east who gave little thought to where most of their food came from. 'They think city folk – and that includes me, now – and easterners generally, are all foolish and rather unpleasant. Not people to be trusted.'

This revelation provoked some banter about Nordath's antecedents but then Hyrald became serious and asked, 'How would they respond to the Death Cry, Nordath?'

'Difficult, that. At any other time I'd have said they'd have nothing to do with it, but after what happened over here, I don't know. I still find it all hard to accept.'

'But on the whole, they respond badly to edicts and injunctions coming out of the Moot?'

'Oh, yes. The Moot's held in even greater scorn than it is over here, if such a thing is possible.'

'And if memory serves me, there's only a couple of towns with proper Wardings,' Hyrald mused. 'Everywhere else will be the Watch.'

'Not much call for either Wardens or Watch Guards,' Nordath said. 'It's a quieter, more trusting place.'

Hyrald looked round the circle of firelit faces. 'That's perhaps the way we should go. Through the mountains and down the western side.'

'Forgive me, but it's not through, it's *over* the mountains,' Rhavvan said, arcing an extended forefinger significantly.

Hyrald turned to Endryk who shrugged. 'The further south we go, the more people there are. And the nearer we get to Arvenshelm, the more likely they are to remember the Death Cry from what you've told me. We're going to have to go into the mountains sooner or later, just to hide.'

'Do you think we can go over the mountains?'

'I was brought up in mountains far more severe than these,' Endryk replied. 'But I know enough not to underestimate even the most innocent-looking of hills. Given that we've got to go into them eventually, we might as well do it now, while the summer's with us and there's game for hunting and fodder for the horses.' He was about to add something else, then thought better of it. Hyrald pressed him. Endryk smiled a little guiltily. 'I was about to say it'll be even harder than what we've been doing, but then I remembered we were at war. Hard or not, we've no choice.' He patted his stomach. 'Deceptive stuff, good venison. Makes you too comfortable.' He sat up and stretched himself. 'Yes, I think you're right. We should go over to the western side as soon as we can. I've no idea of the way so I suggest we continue south until we come to the first likely-looking valley, then we'll have to take our chance.'

The next morning they woke to a thin drizzling rain. Endryk was irritatingly hearty. 'Good mountain weather,' he announced. 'But at least the visibility's not too bad.' He watched as they each examined their boots and clothes, then he repeated the instructions he had given before they had retired the previous night. 'Keep together. Once we start climbing, watch every step, especially now that it's raining. And if we're moving down – even more so. Whatever you do, don't rush. There's no urgency. We'll stop a lot – go at the pace of the slowest. Any problems, speak up right away.'

'And keep breathing and relaxing,' Rhavvan whined, to general amusement.

'More than ever,' Endryk confirmed in the same vein.

For most of the morning, their journey was little different from what it had been over the past few days. The rain came and went to its own rhythms and progress was for the most part silent. As they walked, Endryk studied the mountains. Eventually he stopped and pointed. 'There's no guarantee whether what lies beyond it is passable, but that valley there seems to be the most tempting.'

'Not too far,' Rhavvan said.

'It'll take most of the day,' Endryk replied. 'Distances, heights, they're all deceptive in the mountains.'

His estimate proved to be correct and it was late afternoon by the time they were entering the valley. As they drew nearer, Endryk stopped and turned them all round to look across the country they had just walked over.

'I thought my legs were telling me something,' Nordath said, rubbing his thighs ruefully.

'What a view,' Adren said, wiping her forehead. 'We're so high. I didn't realize we'd been climbing so long.' The rain had long stopped and though the horizon was lost in mist, the countryside was laid out before them in a rolling patchwork of hills and forests, laced here and there with white and silver streams and lit by a watery sun hesitantly making its way through the slowly clearing sky.

'It didn't seem to be so high when we set off,' Hyrald said.

'I told you – distances, heights – all deceptive in the mountains. We're very small things really,' Endryk replied. 'But let's make the most of where we are by spending a little time looking for our pursuers.'

'I can't even see which way we've come,' Adren said uncomfortably. 'I wouldn't know how to get back.' Endryk bent close to her and pointed out features that they had passed. 'Now we're in the mountains, that's something we need to be careful about. It's quite likely we'll have to retrace our steps at some time or other and things tend to look very different when you're travelling the other way. I'll show you how to mark a track without it being conspicuous.'

They spent some time watching intently, but there was no sign of anyone following them.

'Like I said last night, they've gone,' Rhavvan declared emphatically. 'Running for home with their tails between their legs.'

'You're probably right,' Endryk agreed finally. 'Besides, it'll be much harder for anyone to follow us through the mountains.'

'You don't seem particularly overjoyed at losing them,' Hyrald said.

'Just wondering what your Vashnar will do when he finds out what's happened to them.'

Rhavvan laughed at the prospect. 'I'm only sorry I won't be there to see it.'

Endryk did not share his humour. 'You miss my point. For whatever reason, he put enough urgency into them to have them exhaust themselves and their horses finding us, not to mention abandoning their colleagues – not something I presume even the likes of Aghrid would do lightly. So the questions now become who will he send next – how many – when – where?'

Rhavvan closed his eyes. 'Don't you ever give up?'

'Will *he*?' Endryk replied starkly.

Rhavvan had no answer.

They continued westward along the valley for the rest of the afternoon. It rose steadily but gently and was easy going.

Sheltered by the mountains, it grew dark prematurely and they were pitching camp while the sky was still comparatively light, the higher peaks turning pink as they caught the unseen setting sun.

As all hint of the sun faded, Rhavvan looked round at the dark silhouettes hemming them in, some wrapped about with scarves of dull grey cloud. 'I'm not sure whether I like this or not,' he said. 'It feels a bit too closed in for my taste.'

'It's not as closed in as the forest,' Adren said curtly, though she was hunched forward a little, her arms wrapped around her knees. Rhavvan contented himself with a grunt by way of reply.

The following days passed without incidents other than those inherent in travelling with horses through unknown mountain terrain. As they moved on, now west, now south, now along lush valleys, now through dense forest, up steep slopes and over disconcerting ridges, through endlessly changing weather, each of them was obliged to wrestle with the implications of their changed circumstances. Anger, elation, frustration, contentment, resignation, even some despair came to all of them in varying degrees at different times. There were angry quarrels, surly and resentful silences, earnest discussion, apologies, reconciliations, laughter and excitement. And throughout, the group slowly changed.

Adren maintained an instinctive female concern for her appearance which she used unashamedly to scorn the men into doing the same.

'There's not one of you suits a beard,' she inveighed one misty morning, her face wrinkling in distaste as she emerged from her tent and viewed the shuffling ensemble. 'And for pity's sake do something with your hair. You look like a sale of chimney sweeps' brushes – and second-hand ones at that.'

Her undisguised contempt provoked a robust, if brief, exchange:

'All the disadvantages of being married and none of the advantages . . .'

'Looking like that could cause a riot. I've arrested smarter-looking tramps . . .'

'The Death Cry at our backs and the Death Nag to our front . . .'

'Little chin too fragile for a blade, is it, dear?' Pat, pat.

Endryk, who had shaved regularly since they had set out, and taken the same quiet care of his appearance as Adren had of hers, excused himself from hearing any appeals and tried unsuccessfully not to laugh. Adren's onslaught was sufficient to make the offending males turn to him for instruction about how to sharpen their knives for such a task. Only Thyrn hesitated. Not having a mirror to hand he fancied the straggling growth tickling his chin was distinctly manly and he was secretly quite proud of it. A gentle tug on it by Adren and the epithet 'cute', however, was sufficient to make him hastily follow the example of the others. It proved to be a strained and bloody affair for all of them, but Adren sternly hid any pangs of conscience she might have felt about it.

It was one of many small turning points for the group. More soberly later, they all agreed the importance of striving to keep the appearance of Wardens.

Slowly Endryk was becoming less and less their overt instructor and leader. Hunting, trapping, fire-lighting, cooking, maintenance of equipment and clothes, tending the horses, all the many activities that were a necessary part of their continued progress, not to say survival, became both shared and routine and subject only to the passing grumbles of the moment – even the continuing nightly guard duties. None of the group hesitated to ask Endryk's advice when they were unsure, nor he theirs.

Though they still moved cautiously over skylines and maintained their watch for pursuers, it became increasingly obvious that Aghrid and his band had abandoned the chase. This, coupled with the developing daily routines eased the pace of their travelling.

Having increasingly less to tell his charges about the necessities of their lives, Endryk began to show them some of the fighting techniques which had manifested themselves in his skill with the bow and the sling and in his confrontation with the indignant, sword-wielding Adren. Ironically, the searching inquiries which this incident had generated at the time had faded away as the real nature of the group's day to day existence had become apparent. The interest was still there though, and of all the daily tasks that had to be done, practising with sling and bow were the least likely to be scowled at. The sling proved to be a demanding weapon and while all of them acquired a modest proficiency, none of them excelled. With the bow, the patterns set at the beginning were maintained. Adren became very fast and accurate, while the others became more than proficient. Nordath, never having had cause to handle any kind of a weapon before, was particularly proud of the progress he eventually made.

'It would never have occurred to me that I could learn such a thing at my age. It's oddly relaxing too.'

His unassuming pride illuminated all of them, particularly Endryk.

Rhavvan, inevitably, made himself a particularly powerful bow which sent a heavier arrow further than all the others'. Save Endryk's, that is. 'It's just a better bow,' he told the irritated Rhavvan as the big man tested its seemingly less powerful draw. Rhavvan's range and accuracy nevertheless became impressive, though the lengthy task of retrieving the far-flung arrows caused him as much irritation as it did amusement to his comrades. 'We should get that damned dog of yours to bring these back,' Rhavvan protested. He picked up a stick and threw it. 'Here, Nals, fetch.'

The dog's head did not move, but his eyes followed the flight of the stick then returned to stare balefully at the thrower before closing.

Endryk had no hesitation in teaching his companions the use of the bow and the sling because they were necessary for hunting and none of the group had had experience with them. The use of sword, staff and knife, however, had no such rationale, nor had unarmed fighting, and he was almost apologetic when he suggested that these too should be studied and practised. His concern was unfounded. The three Wardens had a genuine professional interest in what he had done to Adren and had not forgotten it, least of all Adren herself. And while Thyrn's youthful enthusiasm had been tempered by Hyrald's stem reproaches, Nordath's reservations had dwindled in the light of his success with the bow and his rueful acceptance of the reality of their circumstances.

Unlike the instruction he had given with the bow, Endryk did not teach directly. Instead he had the Wardens demonstrate their own ways, then made suggestions and debated strengths and weaknesses with them. He was particularly intrigued by Rhavvan's skill with the long staff. His work with the knife disturbed them all, as did his teaching on the ethics of fighting with or without weapons, which he was adamant were to be understood more deeply than any fighting technique.

'Don't start conflict. Avoid it if humanly possible. If it isn't, be clear in your mind, you've the right to survive and you may do whatever's necessary to ensure that. When you're safe, stop – perhaps help your enemy, if you can.' He addressed his remarks most strongly to the Wardens. 'This is deeply alien to you, more than to Thyrn and Nordath. But you understand, don't you? You've had to do it already. I'm not talking about trying not to harm disorderly citizens too much. I'm talking about dealing with people who intend to kill you, and if you hesitate, you'll die. *And your companions may die.* Don't forget that. Not ever. Your focus must be clear and unclouded.'

'We understand. But it's hard. As you say, it's not our way,' Adren said into a heavy silence.

'It is now,' Endryk replied coldly.

'It's horrible.'

'It is.'

There was some debate, but not much. Endryk's logic on all points was as impeccable as it was awful. He did not attempt to teach Thyrn and Nordath this kind of fighting, but left it to the Wardens, intervening only when complexity and elaboration began to bring confusion.

'Keep it simple. This is life and death. Avoid, and attack the centre. Your body's far wiser than you, let it do what it already knows. You've more resources than you realize when you have to fight.'

'*If*,' Nordath said.

Endryk did not reply.

As with everything he did, Endryk proved to be quietly relentless in his instruction. Practice was not excessive but it was regular and purposeful. Achievements were praised but they were always used as a step towards some further goal. It was a discipline that bewildered, even angered, all of them at some time, except, unexpectedly, Thyrn.

'There is no end. Abilities must always be stretched,' he said, quoting his erstwhile masters at the Caddoran Congress. 'Where improvement can be made, it *must* be made. Why else would it be there?' Thyrn's manner was both unaffected and peculiarly humbling and the need for continuing practice was never disputed again.

Thus the days passed. Occasionally there would be speculation about the future and what they should do when they reached the far side of the mountains, though it was accepted that no plans could be made until the mood of the people was known. Occasionally too, homesickness would come

261

like a hammer-blow to take its toll as some casual remark reminded them of the injustice they had suffered and the good lives they had been obliged to abandon. Weapons practice was the invariable cure for such attacks.

Then, one morning, Thyrn was gone.

Chapter 18

Degelham was a typically Arvens village – a random but not unpleasant muddle of one- and two-storey houses and cottages, each one identical to its neighbour only in its warped roof, heavily lintelled windows and crooked and twisted walls. A few, mainly towards the outskirts of the village, showed signs of neglect but most were in reasonable, if not good order, for Degelham was quite prosperous. It had a better than average blacksmith, an excellent saddle-maker and a peculiarly surly cobbler who, through a mouthful of nails, invariably advised his customers that their shoes would be 'ready tomorrow' independent of how long they had been in his safe-keeping. For the most part however, its inhabitants worked on local farms, their own small-holdings, or in the nearby town of Degelvak – Little Degel or Degel's Guardian, depending on which student of Old Arvens or particularly parochial resident of Degelham was being asked. The village also sported a small but thriving quarry and it was stones from this that covered most of the roofs and metalled the road which threaded a winding way through the seemingly randomly built houses. Here and there, dirt roads and pathways branched off this main thoroughfare to skirt past more reclusive dwellings before disappearing vaguely into trees or fields or rampant undergrowth.

Despite its prosperity, Degelham was not the home of anyone particularly important or powerful, and was thus of little interest to Vashnar other than being the last wayside stop before he and his entourage pressed on to Degelvak – the most northerly point of his progress. Even travelling leisurely and in luxury could become irksome and cramping after a while, and opportunities to rest and water the horses and for everyone to walk awhile were valued.

Being home to no special allies, Vashnar's messengers would have passed through the village almost without noticing it and, at most, all he expected was some more or less impromptu reception by the local Watch Guards, news of his coming having almost certainly preceded him. Thus as the coach came to a halt by the larger than usual green at the centre of the village he was not particularly surprised to see, in addition to various livestock and a handful of curious villagers, a nervously shuffling gaggle of men sporting the traditional black neckerchiefs of the Local Watches. He was, however, more than surprised to have the coach door opened by a Tervaidin Trooper and he hesitated momentarily at the sight of him, instinctively using the shade of the coach's interior to ensure that his features did not betray his response.

As he emerged into the bright sunlight he paused and looked about him before waving a purposeful acknowledgement to the waiting men. A glance and a touch on Vellain's arm dispatched her to speak to them. He wasted no such pleasantries on the Trooper.

'What are you doing here?'

'Commander Aghrid sent me, sir.'

Vashnar had already taken in every detail of the man. Although he had obviously made an effort to make himself presentable, his uniform was creased and showed signs of ineffective attempts to remove travel-staining. The sunshine highlighted deep lines of fatigue in his face. He was also blatantly nervous. Everything about him told Vashnar that he was not going to receive the good news he had been anticipating.

He held the man with an unblinking black-eyed stare.

'Why is Commander Aghrid not here in person, Trooper?'

The man cleared his throat. 'He's camped in the woods just outside the village, sir, with the others. There've been . . . difficulties.'

The word sounded like a knell and Vashnar's stomach, already tense from this unexpected development, felt suddenly leaden. The growing euphoria of the past days vanished instantly and, for a moment, his entire, carefully planned future wavered vertiginously. Then he was once again in the middle of the violent skirmish into which his last contact with Thyrn had plunged him.

A voice reverberated inside his head to bring him back to the village green. 'Difficulties?' he heard himself echoing.

It was taking him a considerable effort to control the turmoil swirling inside him, and some part of it must have reached his face for the Trooper almost flinched when he answered.

'The Commander will explain, sir. I don't know everything that's happened.' He made to distance himself from his Commander's failure. 'My horse was lost on the outward journey.'

Vashnar frowned, distracted. 'Lost?'

'Died, sir. Collapsed under me. Couldn't keep the pace. Nearly broke my neck at the same time.' A hand moved hesitantly to his ribs. 'As it was, I   '

'How far is this camp?' Vashnar cut across the pending reminiscence curtly.

'Only a few minutes, sir.'

Vashnar took a deep breath and nodded slowly. 'Wait here.'

It was some measure of Vashnar that despite the inner demons which were now frantically tearing at him, he walked over to the waiting Watch Guards currently being held in Vellain's thrall and spoke with them for several minutes before dismissing them with his thanks. To a man they were all

265

standing straighter when he left them.

'What's happened?' Vellain hissed urgently as they entered the coach again. A slight gesture and a look directed her both to silence and the watching crowd of curious villagers and noisy children that had grown larger during their short stay. The coach set off and she repeated her question even as she was smiling and waving to the spectators. A flurry of hens and a raucous duck scattered noisily out of the way of the clattering hooves.

Vashnar's face was stony. 'I don't know, but it's not good. Aghrid's camped somewhere outside the village.'

'What?' Vellain exclaimed.

'That's all I know,' Vashnar replied impatiently. 'We'll find out soon enough presumably.' His manner ended all questioning.

Sitting rigid and preoccupied, they might as well have been riding on a farmer's cart for all the comfort the coach's luxurious appointments brought them over the next few minutes. When it stopped, Vashnar jumped down before the door could be opened for him. The Tervaidin Trooper's nervousness had not lessened.

'We'll have to ride from here, sir. It's not far, but there's no path for the coach.'

Vashnar hesitated for a moment then motioned for both his own horse and Vellain's.

The short journey to Aghrid's camp had an unreal, detached quality for him. Sunlight was dancing joyously through the leafy canopy and the air was filled with bird song, the rustling of leaves and all the soft perfumes of the woodland. It contrasted disorientatingly with the dark and scarcely controlled concerns now racking him. An angry winter wind throwing stinging hailstones in his face would have disturbed him less.

They reached a small clearing. There was a general air of brisk industry about the place, with tents being taken down, fires being extinguished and horses being saddled and loaded. But there was also an uneasy edge to it. Both Vashnar and Vellain sensed it immediately and exchanged a look. All activity came to an abrupt halt as the three riders entered the clearing, and the uneasiness became almost palpable. Vashnar dismounted and moved forward. Aghrid emerged from a group of men standing by the horses. He strode across the clearing and saluted Vashnar. He gave an uncertain start as Vellain moved into view, then managed a clipped, formal bow.

Though only of average height Aghrid was heavily built and obviously powerful. He had a square, coarse-featured face marred by a broken nose and a scar over one eye. His manner exuded callousness and cunning in equal proportions. Anyone who had known him in his days as a brutally corrupt Warden would have recognised this but they would have noticed something else as well – a gleam in his eyes – the gleam of a fanatic. At some time, Aghrid had seen a great light. The gleam was to be found in the eyes of many of the Tervaidin. Vashnar took it as respect for himself and dedication to his cause but Vellain saw it for what it was, a disturbing mixture of personal ambition and dedication to Vashnar's cause only in so far as it allowed the shedding of all sense of personal responsibility for their actions.

Vashnar dismissed the Trooper who had brought them here, and signalled the others to continue with their work.

'You do not have good news for me, Commander,' he said very quietly.

Aghrid's eyes flickered towards the retreating back of the escort.

'He didn't have to say anything, Commander,' Vashnar reassured him coldly. 'His manner told me enough. As does your skulking in the woods here.'

Aghrid cleared his throat.

'Tell it quickly, accurately and without excuse, Commander,'

Vashnar said, with scarcely veiled anger. 'I'll determine blame, if any.'

'The fugitives escaped us, sir.' Aghrid stood very still. 'We obtained good information from local people about their route as we pursued them – thefts of stock and food – damage to fields – occasionally actual sightings. They were moving north all the time.'

Vashnar hurried him on with a curt gesture.

'Then we followed them off the map, to the sea – as I put in my report. It surprised us all. I was expecting just to continue north. But there it was, the sea, directly across our path. Fortunately we were able to pick up signs of where they'd gone and we followed them west along the coast.'

Vashnar set the distraction aside. 'And when you met them – fought with them – in the forest?'

Aghrid started visibly and his eyes flicked again towards the Trooper he had sent to escort Vashnar.

'Look at me, Commander,' Vashnar snapped. 'And don't concern yourself about what I know or how I know it. Your man said nothing other than what you told him to say. Just confine yourself to the truth.'

Aghrid's eyes widened almost in terror and for a moment he could not speak. Then, mingling with a renewed awe for this man he had chosen to follow, years of lying to officers and justices came to his rescue. Nevertheless, his mouth was dry when he returned to his rehearsed tale. 'It was difficult terrain, sir . . .'

'There were twenty or more of you, supposed to be amongst the best we can muster. They were only five of them – three Wardens, an old man and an ineffective youth!'

Still unsettled by his Commander's seeming knowledge of what had happened, Aghrid became defensive. 'These men *are* the best we have, sir. Chosen for their abilities and loyalty to you. But we were only nine then. The pace we kept up cost us men and horses on the way – we had to leave them or lose the fugitives. And the terrain up there's awful – hills, forests, rivers . . . it's not something any of us know anything about. We were exhausted, running out of supplies when we finally caught up with them.'

'And they weren't?'

Aghrid's jaw tightened. 'They had help, sir. A lot of help. A man who knew the area, and how to live in it. And he could fight, too. He used a bow – wounded one man and brought down a horse with two arrows. It was the trees and the undergrowth, sir. There wasn't the space to use the horses properly.' He took a deep breath and let it out noisily. 'Maybe I made a mistake, I don't know. I couldn't risk letting them get even further ahead. We were all stretched to our limit. It might have been wiser not to attack. But ' He hesitated. It would be a risk to allocate any of the blame to his Commander but he saw no other alternative than at least to hint at it. 'I knew how important their capture was.' That would have to do. 'I accept full responsibility for the failure. The men did as I told them and did it well.'

From time to time since it had happened, Vashnar had deliberately touched on the confused jumble of thoughts and terrors that he had lived through when Thyrn had last reached out to him – become him. It was not something he did lightly for it was no ordinary recollection; it was like edging towards the centre of a great whirlpool. An inadvertent step – a careless letting go – and somehow he felt he could be lost for ever, tumbling into the dark limbo that was neither him nor Thyrn.

As he listened to Aghrid's obviously practised account, he was allowed no such caution. Brief vivid flashes returned to him unbidden to confirm what he was hearing – the noise, the confusion, the confined space and, not least, hissing out of the soft rustling of the trees about him, the sudden rushing wind he had heard – full of danger and malevolence. It made him

269

flinch inwardly. To disguise the involuntary movement he straightened up and turned away from Aghrid as if thinking.

Yet, in so far as he had been able to learn anything from Thyrn's momentary possession of him there was nothing about a stranger – a helper. Or was there? There had been a quality about Thyrn's consciousness which said that he knew he was different. He *had* learned things, though what, Vashnar's uneasy touch could not fathom. And too, there was resolution, strength – a greater sense of self-worth in the young man which had the feeling of being newly gained. Where, or from whom, would these changes come? Not just Hyrald and the others, surely?

He fought down the memories as they threatened to overwhelm and choke him. But at least they had given a ring of truth to Aghrid's tale. Hyrald and the others should have been cold, hungry, fearful – like any pursued prey. They had been driven from Arvenshelm by a mob whose ferocity in response to the Death Cry had alarmed even him; it must have been profoundly terrifying for them. And they were none of them used to living in the country, still less fending for themselves there. Beyond a doubt, *something* had happened to enable them not only to turn and meet their enemies, but to prevail. This stranger would serve as well as any other possible reason for the time being. Vashnar did not relish the conclusion but, compulsively orderly though he was, he was also experienced enough to recognize the inexorable nemesis of all plans – the random, completely unforeseeable event.

'This helper – who was he?'

'When we turned back, we interrogated the people in the nearest village. Eventually they decided it was probably a man called Endryk – a recluse of some kind who lived out on the shore somewhere. Apparently he'd said he was leaving. He'd given his house away, or something – I didn't understand properly, they're a queer lot up there. But no one knew anything much about him, except that he spoke "funny". They thought maybe he was from the north.' His lip curled. 'I think they were telling the truth, they're a half-witted lot – too stupid to lie. But whoever he was and wherever he's from, he's dangerous and he's with them now – helping them.' His tale told, Aghrid came to what he hoped would be good news. 'It may be of no concern now, sir. We managed to follow them a little further before we decided to turn back. There were tracks leading into the river – they've probably crossed it and gone north as they were originally intending to.'

'No,' Vashnar said unequivocally. 'They're coming back.'

'But . . . ?'

'They're coming back, Commander. Be assured.'

Vashnar was finding it increasingly difficult to maintain an outward calm. The memories which had returned to him as he listened to Aghrid's tale had shaken him both physically and mentally and Thyrn's panic was now resonating relentlessly through him, threatening to make itself into his own. He kept reiterating to himself that Thyrn and the others were no longer a real threat, they could do little harm now – events had moved on. This analysis was beyond doubt correct but it did little to calm his deeper and growing emotional response. It did, however, serve to bring his mind back to his more immediate problems.

Though part of him wanted to scream at Aghrid and his men for what he perceived to be their blistering incompetence, he knew that nothing was to be gained and much would be lost by such intemperance. Not least because there was some injustice in it. Aghrid had, after all, pursued his orders with the vigour that had been demanded. That he and his men had made contact with the fugitives at all was no small achievement given the time that had elapsed before they had been sent in pursuit. These men were not his chosen – his Tervaidin – for any slight reason. They were, as Aghrid had protested, the best of all those under his command – capable and, above all, loyal.

And, as if in confirmation of their worth, their passage through the country had yielded unexpected dividends. Now he must repair any damage that had been done to them.

'Who knows about your return, Commander?'

'Very few, sir. I thought it best to return discreetly until we could contact you.'

'And the men you had to leave behind?'

'They're all back with us, sir. We picked them up just as discreetly. And we've had replacement horses from friends along the way.'

'And you've a wounded man, you said?'

'Yes sir, an arrow in the shoulder. He's weak, but he's recovering. This Endryk apparently removed the arrow before he released him.'

Vashnar made no comment. He looked thoughtful for a moment, then he nodded approvingly.

'You've done well, Commander,' he said. 'Very well. All of you. The outcome was merely unfortunate. Circumstances were against you. Nevertheless, much is to be learned. We have to rise above circumstances, however adverse. We'll talk more of it later. In the meantime, I'll speak to the men.'

As she had on many occasions, Vellain watched as her husband moved paternally amongst the men, at once both friendly and distant – always finding the right word, the right expression or gesture to raise morale. Yet too, she could see he was strained. She had heard Aghrid's account and had watched Vashnar intently throughout. Like her husband, she stumbled over the intervention of random happenings – the sea lying to the north – the interference of a complete stranger. Endryk? The name meant nothing to her. Who could he be? And what was he doing living up there? From the north? What did that mean? It was bad enough there were enemies to the east and west, were more to be found to the north too? The sooner this country came firmly under the control of her husband the better.

But she was not given to dwelling too long on what might, or should, be. What mattered was the present. Now, she knew she would have to use all her skills to learn exactly how her husband had been affected by what he had just heard. For it would be far more than he would easily show.

Even as she was thinking about this, Vashnar was ordering the immediate future. Aghrid and his men were to accompany them to Degelvak. Their mission would be declared a success, though questions about it were to be answered non-committally. Hyrald and the others were no longer a threat. They had fled north, treacherously aided by secret allies.

'Useful,' Vellain said as they sat once again in the coach. She was anxious to have her husband discuss his intentions. Only as his words revealed his thoughts would she be able to see what was truly troubling him. 'Treachery within and an unknown menace to the north. It'll help more people realize the value of strong leadership.'

Vashnar did not reply. Vellain affected to close her eyes, though in reality she was watching him intently. After some minutes he clenched his fist and drove it viciously into the yielding upholstery. She opened her eyes as if startled.

'What's the matter, my love?'

'Thyrn, damn him. Thyrn's the matter.'

'But he's just a—'

Vashnar's hand came up for silence. 'As long as I can remember I've known beyond any doubt that one day this land was to be mine – that I'd dispense with the Moot and lift it from its disordered grovelling ways into order and glory, that its people would bend to my will, that other lands would quail before us. Where does such a knowledge – such certainty – come from, Vellain?'

It was a rhetorical question. Vellain's eyes widened, both in excitement and concern at her husband's tone. He had never spoken of his ambitions with such stark openness before.

Vashnar looked around the interior of the coach as if he were viewing a vast sky with a sprawling landscape spread before him. Then suddenly he was almost whispering as though fearful of being overheard.

'Who can say what powers control events – control *us*, Vellain? Or is everything just chance – random events that we simply thread our way through, finding patterns where none really exist because to do anything else would be to fall into insanity?' He looked at his hand and flexed his fingers. 'We feel free.' His hands went briefly to his forehead and his voice rose a little. 'We are free. I am free. Surely? Free to follow the destiny which has been set before me – be it by chance or some power beyond any understanding.' Realization came into his expression and he smiled knowingly. 'Not that it matters where it comes from. Just as I test men to learn if they are fit to serve me, so wouldn't some knowing power test my worthiness too? And if there is no such power, just chance, then mustn't I look to struggle if order is to be imposed on chaos?'

Vellain was almost gaping. Both her excitement and her concern had grown proportionately. What was he rambling about? Had this business with Thyrn driven him over the edge – or even given him religion? That would be catastrophic! And yet, his voice, his manner, was thrilling through her.

'I . . . I don't understand,' she stammered.

'You don't need to, my love.' Vashnar's eyes were bright. 'It's enough that I do. It's enough that I see now where Thyrn belongs in all this. Whether he's a wilful testing or a whim of chance, he's here to impede my destiny and I must—'

Vellain leaned forward and took his hand urgently. 'You *mustn't* do anything. Thyrn's nothing,' she said, shaking him as though that might impel her will into him. 'Things have changed. He can't say or do anything that—'

Vashnar freed himself and enveloped her hands in both of his. He spoke to her as to a frightened child. 'No. You don't see

274

things as I do – you can't. This isn't the same as someone opposing me when I was making my way through the Warding, or Bowlott having the Moot raising fatuous objections to some proposal. Or even struggling to get the support of the merchants and businessmen that we need. This is different. True, it's unlikely Thyrn, or any of them, can *say* anything that will be of any consequence, but his opposition's deeper than that – much deeper. The sudden appearance of this stranger, Endryk, protecting him, is enough to show that. He's changed too. And he's coming back – deliberately. He's not going to go away. He has to be dealt with or everything will fall about us.'

Vellain sensed that she could have no effect on Vashnar's inner debate and his conclusions, but she had to try. 'I don't know what you're talking about. Perhaps you can see something in Thyrn that eludes me but I see no threat in him other than you making him into one. Leave him alone. Let him wander the countryside – let them all wander the countryside – fending for themselves. They'll not last long. They're all city bred. Can't tell a cow from a coach horse – and Nordath's no chicken. He can't possibly last long, living rough. Sooner or later some farmer will come across them and you'll find out where they are. Then you can send a few men out to finish them off once and for all.'

'You're forgetting about this Endryk who's been helping them.'

Vellain threw up her hand. 'Endryk, Endryk. He might be no more than a figment of Aghrid's imagination, conjured up to excuse some folly he's committed.' She jabbed a finger towards him. 'He was over-confident, I'll wager. Went charging in and got the worst of it. Hyrald and Rhavvan aren't fools. They'll have heard him coming and laid an ambush for him. And don't forget – they'd everything to lose. They'd be in no mood for idle chatter.'

Vashnar was shaking his head. 'No,' he said. 'I can

understand what you say, but you're wrong, trust me. Aghrid's telling the truth about Endryk. Thyrn's destiny is wrapped about mine inextricably. Just as mine is working to its conclusion, so is Thyrn's also – whatever's brought it all about. They've chased off Aghrid against the odds. They'll survive and come against me.'

'Four – five men, and one woman. Let them come!'

'Thyrn, Vellain. Not the rest. They're nothing. Footsteps in the dust of time. But Thyrn's part of me. He can reach out and touch me – unman me from inside. There's no saying what he'll become if he lives and begins to thrive out there.'

Vellain fell silent. Not only did Vashnar's manner indicate that nothing was to be gained by disputing with him, there was a chilling quality of truth about what he was now saying. The strange intrusions that Thyrn had made into his mind were beyond experience, common-sense or logic and Vashnar's remarks about a deeper power hidden from their sight briefly took on a vivid menace for Vellain. Then she rejected it utterly with a crushing contempt. She *was* free. Nothing manipulated her, and to think that it did was merely to seek confusion and doubt. There was simply reality, however strange, however improbable it might be. What was, was. The why, was irrelevant. And to this extent she could now accept Vashnar's continuing concern about Thyrn. Given that the cause of his linkage with Vashnar was unknown, there was indeed no saying that it might not change or grow, to her husband's detriment.

'Yes, you're right,' she conceded. 'He will have to be dealt with. I can see that now. It's too great a risk to have him wandering about loose. But how's it to be done? We've no idea where he is. And Aghrid's right, we don't have anyone who's trained to survive on their own in the wild, perhaps even in the mountains. Least of all on a chase that might last for months.'

The coach and its now extended escort rolled unhurriedly on through the afternoon sunlight towards Degelvak. Vashnar did not answer his wife's concerns immediately. Instead, he sat staring silently at the passing fields. Some were lying fallow, spiky with flourishing weeds. Others wavered gently as an unfelt breeze brushed long-stemmed grasses. Sheep and cattle grazed in yet others. Occasionally a worker or a chewing cow would look up and stare with blank curiosity at the passing cavalcade.

By inclining his head a little, Vashnar could see the flanking columns of the Tervaidin tapering back behind the coach. Though the men were still obviously tired, they were no longer the edgy dispirited group he had seen when he rode into their camp. Now they were riding tall and proudly. They were his men again. It had been a good testing. Much would be learned from it. Already a new direction had been pointed out to him.

He turned back to his wife and spoke very thoughtfully. 'Tonight, when all the business and the socializing is finished, we'll sit quietly, you and I.'

Vellain raised an expectant eyebrow.

Vashnar touched his temple delicately. 'And in here, I'll seek him out.'

Chapter 19

Thyrn had been doing the last spell on guard duty and, at first, he was not missed. There was a little ritual grumbling when the wakers emerged to an unlit fire and this was followed by a vague presumption that he had probably gone to fetch water from a nearby stream.

The fire was lit and breakfast was being cooked before it became apparent that he had been away a long time. Even then, there was no great concern. Though it was chilly, everything presaged a fine day, the sky was clear and the air was invigoratingly fresh.

'He's probably exploring up in the rocks,' Nordath said. 'There's a lot of him that never got past eight years old.'

Adren made a disparaging sound. 'Do any men?' she asked of no one in particular, gingerly snatching a piece of hot meat from the pan.

'Oh, going to be one of those days, is it?' Rhavvan observed with martyred resignation. 'Been sharpening your tongue all night, eh dear?'

There was a brief exchange of abuse between the Wardens before someone noticed that Endryk was looking anxiously up at the rocks at the top of the slope where they had camped.

'What's the matter?' Hyrald asked.

'I can't see him,' Endryk replied flatly. He stood up and looked around the valley. 'In fact, I can't see him anywhere.'

Hyrald shot a quick glance at Nordath before commenting,

with a rather forced heartiness, 'Maybe he's playing some kind of a game. All this business is hard enough for us, it's difficult to imagine what it must be like for him. As Nordath said, he's only a kid in many ways. He needs to be away from us occasionally.'

But Endryk was unconvinced. 'That's true, but I don't think he'd go far without telling us. And he certainly wouldn't leave the camp unguarded. He's very keen to do things correctly.'

The mood about the fire darkened. Slowly they all stood up to join Endryk in his searching of the valley. But Thyrn was not to be seen.

Rhavvan called out, startling them all. His voice echoed emptily into the fresh morning air, but no reply came back. He shouted again but to the same effect.

Nordath began rubbing his hands together. 'Could . . . Aghrid's men have taken him?' he asked nervously.

'No,' Endryk said unequivocally. 'No one's following us now. And no one's been into the camp. Even if Thyrn had nodded off, Nals would have woken us up.' For the first time since they had met him, he seemed to be completely at a loss. He turned to Hyrald. 'Perhaps you've more experience of this kind of thing than I do.'

'Perhaps,' Hyrald agreed. 'But not in a place like this or under these circumstances. Usually there's no real problem – a woman somewhere – too raucous a night with friends – a family quarrel. But none of those apply here. I'm afraid I'm as lost as you.'

Nordath's nervousness was turning into agitation. 'He must be somewhere nearby. He wouldn't just wander off.'

Adren took his arm, Warden's experience showing through. 'Don't worry. That's all he can have done. He's probably become engrossed in something and hasn't realized how far he's gone. He'll be all right. We'll find him.' She turned him gently so that he did not see the growing concern on Endryk's

280

face. She could not shield him from his voice however.

'If he's not replying to Rhavvan's call and he's not in sight he's either been gone for some time or he's injured himself.' Adren glowered at him and gave Nordath's arm a reassuring squeeze.

'Will you be able to find any tracks he might have left?' Hyrald asked Endryk.

'We can look, but I doubt there's anything to be seen. The ground's too hard.' He frowned. 'Check the horses and his pack. See if he's taken anything.'

A hasty search found everything intact.

'So all he's got is what he's wearing and probably a water bottle.' Endryk puffed out his cheeks and looked round none too hopefully at the valley and the enclosing peaks.

'This is a bad place to be lost?' Hyrald said very softly.

'It is,' Endryk replied, equally softly. 'What in pity's name could have possessed the lad?' He answered his own question. 'Maybe as you said, it's all suddenly become too much for him. He's borne up so well we might have missed something. Then again, I suppose with the kind of life he's led, keeping things to himself has become a habit.' He grimaced. 'Still, it doesn't matter. We'll just have to do our best and hope luck's with us. At least the weather is.' He rallied a little. 'And whatever else he is, he's not stupid. There'll be reasoning of some kind going on in his head.' He turned to the others. 'Adren, you're the most agile, you come with me, we'll look in the rocks up there. Rhavvan, Hyrald, you take the horses and start searching the valley. Use the camp as a centre, move out, across and back.' He pointed. 'Then continue the same pattern swinging across from there to there.' His arm traced out a broad arc. 'Go slowly and carefully. Keep your eyes and your ears open.'

Nordath was heading for his horse. Endryk stopped him. 'Nordath, I know you want to do something, but I'd like you to stay here in case he comes back while we're away. Make a smoky fire so that—' He stopped suddenly and closed his eyes in disbelief. There was a brief silence, then he said curtly, 'Forget all that.' He picked up Thyrn's pack and opened it.

'Nals,' he called.

Nals was lying by the fire watching the food cooking. Without moving his head, his eyes turned towards Endryk, examined him, then returned to watching the food. Endryk walked over and squatted down beside him. 'This one's his own dog,' he said over his shoulder to the others, 'but he's far and away the best here to find Thyrn – if he feels like it. Start breaking the camp anyway. He'll concentrate better when the food's gone.'

Nordath's hand fluttered. 'Break camp? But if he comes back?'

'We'll mark our trail clearly. Anyway, if Thyrn's nearby and unhurt he'll probably see us over this ground.' He offered the open pack to Nals. The dog looked at him suspiciously then tentatively pushed its nose into it.

'Find him for us, please. Find Thyrn,' Endryk said, his voice quiet and serious.

Nals withdrew his head from the pack and looked anxiously at the now disappearing food. Adren threw him a piece of meat which he caught with a rapid flick of his head.

'Find Thyrn,' Endryk repeated patiently, as soon as Nals had seen that all the food was gone. He proffered the bag again.

Nals took another desultory sniff at it then levered himself up and, after a prolonged stretch, began meandering slowly about the camp, sniffing the ground intently. At Endryk's silent urging, the others began quickly breaking the camp as he had instructed. Abruptly, Nals was moving away from them and down the slope in the direction they had intended to take that day. Endryk untethered his horse. 'Follow me when you've finished,' he said to the others. 'If we change direction before you catch up, I'll leave a clear sign.' Before anyone could reply he was running after the retreating dog, his horse trotting beside him.

Impelled by this unexpected development, it did not take Hyrald and Rhavvan long to pack the shelters and load the horses, while Nordath and Adren cleaned the site. Both Endryk and Nals were thus still in sight when they set off after them.

'Perhaps best if we don't hurry,' Hyrald said, 'at least while we can see them. We've got enough problems now without one of us taking a fall.'

It was good advice but it proved to be unnecessary. Nals was moving quite rapidly but he was also moving erratically, wandering from side to side and frequently pausing. It was not long before Endryk was joined by the others.

As they walked on, following Nals' eccentric progress, Nordath asked, 'Are you sure he knows what he's doing?' He glanced back towards the camp site. 'What if Thyrn's up in those rocks and we're walking away from him?'

'We aren't,' Endryk said categorically. 'Nals' sense of smell is better than either our sight or our hearing. Thyrn's been this way.' Nordath looked at him and then at Nals, uncertainly. Endryk pointed back the way they had come. 'And I've seen some signs myself. Not much – just some scuff marks on those rocks over there – but enough. No animal made them, that's for sure.'

This reassurance quietened Nordath a little though he was still preoccupied and tense.

Then Nals lay down.

'What's he doing?' Nordath demanded, eyes widening.

'He's lying down,' Endryk said.

'I can see that,' Nordath retorted crossly. 'I mean, what's he doing? Why's he stopped?'

'He's had enough for now. He's lost interest.'

'Lost interest!' Nordath shouted, suddenly beside himself. He leaned over and shook Endryk's arm vigorously. 'Get him moving, for crying out.' He made to dismount. 'Don't bother, I'll do it myself.'

Endryk jumped down from his horse quickly and moved to stop him. 'You stay where you are,' he said firmly. 'I told you, Nals is his own dog. He's a companion, not a pet. He's like the rest of us – neither trained nor tame. He does what he wants *when* he wants. And, believe me, he doesn't respond well to abuse. I'll try to get him interested again.'

It took Hyrald and Rhavvan edging their horses closer towards Nordath to keep him in his saddle, but eventually and with an ill grace, he agreed to remain where he was. Endryk took Thyrn's pack across to Nals and offered it to him again.

No one spoke as he crouched down and talked to the dog. The sounds of the valley closed around the watching riders, distant tumbling streams, whispering breezes rustling over short turf and rocks and scree, cold winds soughing around high peaks and boulders, all laced and interlaced, echoed and re-echoed, to become a shifting background murmur unlike any of its parts. It was punctuated occasionally by the creak of harness or a throaty croak from one of the black birds circling high above them.

'What's he doing?' Nordath whispered, lifting himself in his stirrups to ease the tension pervading him.

'More than any of us can,' Adren replied gently. 'Don't fret. Everything will be all right. Like Endryk said, Thyrn will have a reason for what he's done – he's not stupid. And at least you can be sure here he's not been abducted by some gang for ransom.'

'Or by some diseased inadequate,' Rhavvan added in as near a comforting voice as he could manage.

Nordath let out a noisy breath and fell reluctantly silent, though he was tapping his hand on his leg in a relentless tattoo.

Then, Endryk was stroking Nals' head and the dog was moving again. Adren gave Nordath a reassuring wink and the procession set off again, trailing raggedly after Nals' renewed search. It carried them steadily westward for a long time, continuing to follow the route they had intended to take. Gradually the valley narrowed and became rockier and bleaker until eventually they were obliged to dismount and continue on foot. At the same time Endryk began to point out more marks which indicated the recent passage of someone.

'It looks as if he's travelling quite quickly,' he said. 'He's certainly making no attempt to cover his tracks, so either he's expecting us to follow, or he doesn't care. Either way it's to our advantage.'

Their progress soon began to slow however as they found themselves leading the horses up an increasingly steep rocky slope. More than once Endryk had to caution Nordath for trying to move too quickly. Finally he was almost brutal. 'I know it's difficult for you, Nordath, but don't forget where you are. This place is dangerous. If you injure yourself then we'll really be slowed down. If you want to look after Thyrn, you'll have to look after yourself first. Be careful.'

Shortly after that Endryk called them to a halt. 'We're going too fast, anyway,' he said, wiping his forehead.

'You mean, I'm holding you up,' Nordath said. He was flushed and breathing heavily. 'You'd be moving faster without me.'

'We'd be moving faster if Thyrn hadn't run off,' Endryk said irritably. 'And we'd all be better off if the Death Cry had never been proclaimed against you, and worse off if Aghrid had caught us in the open. And so on backwards, for ever. Yes, we're having to move at your speed but that's not the same as you holding us up. The fact is, it won't make any difference if we find Thyrn in one hour or three. I've seen enough sign to know that he's not injured so far. Right now, we all need to rest and refresh ourselves. Then we'll move on again.'

Nordath sat down and leaned against a rock silently.

'I'm sorry,' Endryk said guiltily. 'I know it's difficult not to fret. We're all concerned about him but you really have to understand how important it is to stay in control out here.' He gave Nordath a look full of compassion. 'This is a cruel place and we're in a cruel predicament. Nothing's to be gained by looking at it otherwise. The only one of us really fitted to survive out here is Nals. The rest of us have got to work at it all the time.'

Nordath looked at the dog then clenched his fist. His face contorted. 'Damn this place,' he hissed. 'And damn Vashnar, and Aghrid. Damn all of them, with their swords and their staffs and their brutal ways. What are we doing here? Why couldn't we just be left alone? We weren't causing anyone any trouble.'

No reply was expected and none was offered as Nordath fell silent and dropped his head in his hands. Endryk reached out as if to comfort him then thought better of it. He looked up unhappily at the long uneven dip between the two peaks which headed the valley and towards which they were heading.

'This next part's going to be difficult. When we've rested a little longer, Adren and I will go to the top and see if we can find out which way he's gone. We might be able to find an easier route for the rest of you once we're up there.'

'No,' Nordath said, looking up at him. 'We'll stay together.' He heaved himself to his feet. 'I'm sorry about that little outburst. I wouldn't want any of you to think that I was anything other than deeply grateful for everything you've done. It's just that . . .'

'No apology's necessary,' Hyrald said, before he could finish. 'You only said what the rest of us were thinking, and thoughts like that are best exposed to the light where they can't fester.' He took Nordath's arm. 'As for Thyrn, I can't think what he's playing at, or why, and I won't tell you not to worry about him, but I will tell you not to give up. We *will* find him between us.'

As Endryk had said, clambering up the final part of the slope proved to be no easy task. The horses in particular found it very difficult and needed a great deal of careful handling. Nevertheless, they eventually reached the dip without serious incident. Endryk told the others to wait while he and Nals moved some way ahead, searching for further sign of Thyrn's passing.

In front of them now lay two valleys. The first, broad and open, was similar to the one they had just travelled through. It continued to the west. The other, despite the sunlight, was darker and bleaker in appearance and ran south-west.

Nordath gazed along it intently. 'He's gone that way,' he said, apparently to himself. A gust of cold wind swept over the dip as he spoke. He wrapped his arms about himself and shivered. Adren ushered him into the sunlit lea of a rocky outcrop. None of the Wardens questioned him about his comment though they exchanged significant glances when Endryk returned a few minutes later with the same information. They set off without any debate, scrambling cautiously over the broad sheet of shattered rocks that sloped down from the dip.

The valley which Thyrn had chosen was substantially narrower than the one they had been travelling along, and bounded by higher, more jagged peaks. Its floor was uneven and littered with boulders of all sizes, and such grass as grew there had a stunted and brittle look to it. A feeling of oppression soon began to pervade the group. Rhavvan voiced it first in his characteristically direct manner.

'This place gives me the creeps. What did he want to come down here for?'

'Well, at least he's still heading in the right direction,' Endryk offered. 'He could've decided he wanted to go north again.'

'That's no consolation,' Rhavvan said, glancing sourly up at the looming peaks.

Endryk told them to mount.

'We'll have to risk a gentle trot while we can. He's moving quickly. Without anything to carry he's probably been gaining on us steadily. I'd like at least to catch sight of him before nightfall.' His expression became worried. 'Whatever's driving him, it's not impossible he might carry on in the dark and we certainly can't do that.'

They rode on in silence for a long time, their pace being set predominantly by Nals who seemed to be warming to his task now. On occasions he ran a long way ahead of them, almost out of sight, but he always stopped to wait for them, tongue lolling and with a generally impatient demeanour. The bleak vista that the valley had offered at the outset did not change as they moved along it. Indeed it grew worse as the floor grew narrower and the scree-fringed sides became steeper, ramping darkly up to increasingly jagged ridges and peaks. The sun added little and a flaccid stream meandering reluctantly along with the riders brought none of the bustling liveliness that a mountain stream should have.

'More like the mountains in your homeland, is it – all this?' Hyrald asked Endryk in an effort to lighten the group's silent and increasingly sullen mood, but his forced geniality rang emptily.

'There are valleys and valleys, Hyrald,' Endryk replied, making the same effort himself. 'This one has little charm, for sure. Certainly not one that would be sought out for a pleasant day's walking. I suppose we should think ourselves lucky it's not overcast and raining.' He smiled, then chuckled to himself. 'Mountains and valleys are like adults – they reflect the way they were treated when they were young.'

Hyrald looked up warily as if in the presence of reproving parents. '*Young* mountains, eh? Can't say the life-cycle of mountains is anything I've ever thought about, to be honest.'

Endryk made an expansive, encompassing gesture. 'You should. Everything here's been carved out with ice and snow, wind and rain, summer heat and winter cold, pebble by pebble, crevice by crevice, over a span of years we can't begin to comprehend. The mountains were here and changing long before we even existed, and they'll be here and changing long after we've gone. Our entire lives are less to them than the blink of an eye is to us. It's good for one's sense of perspective.'

'Don't try to cheer us up any more than you have to, will you?' Rhavvan chimed in. 'I'm feeling small and inadequate enough as it is.'

'No, it's interesting,' Adren chimed in. 'I'd never thought about anything like that, not even when I was a kid. And I used to think some odd things. I used to plague my father with questions like, why can't animals talk, why can't I fly, why isn't rain blue like the sky where it comes from?' She laughed to herself as old memories washed over her.

Rhavvan muttered something derogatory under his breath to which Adren, still laughing, replied with a gesture quite at odds with her innocent childhood recollections.

'How do you know all this, anyway?' Rhavvan demanded of Endryk. 'Who can say how old a mountains is?'

'My people are just curious about things. They take a pride in discovery, in reasoning, in probing with the mind. Testing, rejecting, searching – and teaching.'

'Why?'

Endryk turned in his saddle to look straight at him. 'That sounds like one of Adren's unanswerable childish questions,' he replied, smiling.

It was Nordath who replied. 'They do it for the same reason you're asking the question, Rhavvan – curiosity. It's deep in our nature – discovering things, solving problems. And it's fun, isn't it, learning? Knowledge is always preferable to ignorance.'

Rhavvan drew in a noisy breath and looked at his colleagues. 'I'm not so sure about that, some of the things we've seen,' he said.

'I didn't say it was comforting or cosy,' Nordath went on. 'Merely preferable.'

'Nothing's to be feared, it's only to be understood,' Endryk said.

'Precisely,' Nordath agreed.

'Not my own words, I'm afraid,' Endryk admitted.

'Don't be afraid,' Nordath retorted and they both laughed.

Rhavvan's response was more caustic. 'I'll remember that little gem the next time some drunken oaf's swinging a sword at me.' He mimicked Endryk's voice. 'I understand what's happening so I don't need to be afraid. Very useful, that.'

Endryk was still laughing. He put his hand to his head in mock despair. 'I'd a feeling I was going to get a remark like that even as I spoke.'

The brief exchange eased the mood of the group a little and they trotted on in comparatively good spirits for some time, following Nals' still enthusiastic lead.

Then he stopped and began walking round in erratic circles. Endryk dismounted.

'What's the matter?' Nordath asked anxiously.

'I don't know,' Endryk replied. 'It looks as if he's lost the scent. Wait here.'

Cautiously he walked up to the circling dog and began looking intently at the area it was traversing. Then he motioned the others forward.

'It looks as if Thyrn stopped here for some reason.' He looked puzzled. 'But he didn't rest. In fact, he doesn't seem to have rested since he left the camp.' A flicker of concern passed over his face. 'It hadn't occurred to me before, but he must be exhausted by now. We'll have to find him soon.' He pointed. 'Look, there's part of a footprint in that soft ground there. And another over there, and here.' He glanced up at the surrounding crags. Nearby was the ragged scar of a small rock fall. Parts of it glistened with the persistent dribbles of water that had probably caused it.

Endryk moved towards it. The others followed. It needed no profound tracking skills to see more of Thyrn's footprints in the sodden ground. Endryk grimaced and swore softly.

'What the devil's he up to,' he muttered. 'We can't possibly get the horses up there.' He frowned and stood looking thoughtfully at Thyrn's tracks for a while.

'We're going to have to divide the party,' he said eventually. 'Adren, you and I'll go up to the top of this and see if we can find his tracks up there. The rest of you will have to stay here and wait. A rest won't do you any harm – and the horses need one, anyway. Feed and water them.' He delved into his saddlebag and withdrew a small lantern. 'We'll come back before nightfall, but set up camp and light a fire once the light starts to go – it'll be useful as a guide for us.'

There was some resistance to this decision, not least from Adren.

'I can't climb up there,' she protested volubly, to general agreement. 'Ye gods, look at it.'

Endryk scrutinized the rock fall again, his hand shading narrowed eyes against the bright sky. 'It's not a climb, it's a scramble, that's all,' he said. 'If it involved climbing I'd go on my own. It looks worse than it is. You're still not used to the scale of the mountains, that's all. Don't worry. Thyrn's done it.'

This did not reassure her. She cast a surreptitious glance at Nordath. 'Thyrn's . . . preoccupied,' she said with heavy discretion.

Endryk nodded. 'Yes, and when we find him he'll probably respond better to you than anyone else except perhaps Nordath, and he won't be able to get up there without plenty of resting and help, all of which will take time.'

Adren's mouth curled in defeat and she motioned him ahead of her up the slope. Nals ran in front of them both.

'You go first,' he said to her as they began scrambling up the fall. 'Same rules as everywhere else. Don't rush, and think about what you're doing. It'll be very slippery in parts. Tell me if anything's bothering you.'

'What about the dog? Is he coming too?'

'If he wants. Don't worry about him. I'll help him if he needs it.'

They were over halfway up the climb before Endryk spoke again. He looked up at Adren, her tongue protruding slightly as she planted a foot solidly and grasped the edge of a rock. He smiled. 'You're enjoying this, aren't you?'

She peered down at him underneath her arm. 'Certainly not,' she said firmly. Down below, the brief exchange reached the watchers quite clearly.

'I think we can stop holding our breath now,' Hyrald said, clearing his throat self-consciously.

'I could've climbed that,' Rhavvan announced, lips pursed in certainty.

'You might have to yet,' Hyrald retorted. 'You can carry one of the horses.' He slapped his comrade's arm. 'Speaking of which, let's get them tended and ourselves ready for a long wait. That, at least, we're good at.'

'Are you all right?' Endryk asked as he reached the ridge.

Adren was flushed and her eyes were shining. 'Yes,' she said, then she turned round, her arms open wide, all pretence at indifference gone. 'Look at this, isn't it splendid?'

This was the view. Sunlit peaks and rolling hills ranged in every direction under a cloudless sky. It would have been difficult to imagine a greater contrast with the lowering valley out of which they had just struggled.

'Beautiful, beautiful,' she whispered.

She waved enthusiastically to the watching group below and they waved back.

Endryk smiled then closed his eyes and took a slow deep

breath, opening his arms slowly in front of him, palms upwards. As he breathed out he brought them together again, palms down. It was a graceful, relaxed movement quite different to Adren's exhilarated embrace of the mountains.

'What are you doing?' Adren asked.

'Just breathing,' Endryk replied, smiling.

'You and your breathing,' she retorted, though the scornful tone she tried to affect turned into just a friendly jibe. 'Let's find our man. I noticed plenty of scuff marks on the way up, so he's breathing as well.'

'Yes,' Endryk agreed, his face darkening. 'Too many scuff marks. He's going too fast and he's getting tired. I can't see that he'll get much further without running into some kind of problem. We'll just have to hope it's not a serious one.'

Nals ran between them, bumping into Endryk's legs. Far from needing any help, the dog had scuttled and scratched his way up the rock fall with alarming alacrity and seemed to be even more excited at reaching the ridge than Adren. Endryk, however, ignored him and began searching for some sign of the way Thyrn had gone. It did not take long. He had followed the ridge, in the direction he had been taking along the valley. Endryk's brow furrowed as he looked along the route. The ridge rose steadily, curving round in a broad sweep towards a large peak which dominated the area.

'What's the matter?' Adren asked.

'Nothing much,' Endryk replied. 'It could have been worse, he could've gone down the other side and that would have really given us problems. But I'm trying to work out how long it'll take us to get up there and back.' He looked up at the sun. 'The light's going to hold well. We should be able to make that peak and be back before nightfall, but we'll have to mark the route as we go, especially this point, just in case we get held up. We'll also have to keep a careful eye out for where he's been. It might look narrow from here but there's plenty of places he could've gone. He could be just skirting round that peak for some reason.'

'Nals will help, won't he?'

'Possibly. When he's quietened down a bit. He's too excited to be any use at the moment.'

Adren stroked the dog and made sympathetic noises to it before giving another wave to the watchers below. Then they set off along the ridge.

They made steady progress; the going was not difficult and the warmth of the sun tempered the cold breeze that was blowing over the ridge. Gradually, Nals became more his old taciturn self again, loping ahead of them, head low over the rocky ground and con-firming the occasional physical signs of Thyrn's passing that they found.

They had risen perhaps a third of the way up to the peak, and the ridge had broadened out to become part of the wide, hunched shoulders of the mountain, when Nals stopped. His ears went up sharply as if he had heard something and, after an introductory growl, he barked. Adren could not recall having heard him bark before and the sound, harsh in the mountain silence, startled her.

Endryk crouched down by him and peered intently in the direction where he was staring. The dog's ears were still erect as if he were listening to something.

Adren pointed. 'There,' she said softly as if fearful of disturbing someone. 'On the skyline.'

It took Endryk a moment to make out the distant figure sitting on a ledge. It was motionless and its head was slumped forward.

Chapter 20

Adren put a gently restraining hand on Nals' neck and the dog sat down quietly.

Eyes narrowed, she leaned forward as if being that little nearer would enable her to see more. 'I can't make out any details clearly against the sky.' She was puzzled. 'Thyrn doesn't normally sit like that. He's very straight.'

'It's not likely to be anyone else, is it?' Endryk said. 'He's probably sat down for a rest and fallen asleep.'

Adren frowned. 'It's difficult to tell from here, but it looks as if where he's sitting might be a dangerous place to be sleeping.' She became instructive. 'We must approach him quietly and calmly, almost as if we were out for a casual walk. We don't want him waking with a start. And if he happens to be awake, given that something's the matter with him anyway, we don't want to startle him.'

She stood up. 'Stay by me, dog,' she said to Nals. Endryk could not forbear a look of surprise as the dog fell in behind her dutifully. He did the same.

Following Adren's advice, they began walking towards the motionless figure. Adren forced a casual pace on Endryk, and twice she had to put a hand on his sleeve to restrain him.

'I've seen people sitting quietly in high places like that before,' she said. 'Believe me, both charging in and skulking in can have disastrous consequences.' She did not elaborate but she did not have to restrain him again.

At one point they lost sight of the motionless figure as they dropped into a rocky cleft gashed across the ridge. Momentarily disorientated, they paused, unclear which way to go when Nal's ears shot up again as if he had heard something. He made a low uncertain sound, part whine, part growl.

'What's the matter with him?' Adren asked.

'I don't know.' Endryk looked puzzled. 'Maybe he's still a bit excited from the climb. He normally does that when someone's about and he hasn't made his mind up whether they're friendly or not.'

Nals fell silent, but seemingly still listening to something he abandoned Adren to trot ahead of them. Then he was jumping and scrambling his way up the far side of the cleft. In the absence of better guidance, Adren and Endryk followed him. As they reached the top, Nals was waiting for them, tail wagging. The figure on the skyline was directly ahead of them. Adren was about to set off towards it when Endryk turned sharply.

'First the dog, now you,' Adren said with exaggerated irritation. 'Have you heard something as well?'

Endryk ignored her tone. He was pointing hesitantly towards the looming face of the mountain. He took a few steps forward then paused.

'I'm sorry,' he said, after a moment. 'I thought I saw someone moving over there – someone small.' He shrugged. 'Couldn't be, I suppose. I certainly can't see anyone now. Probably a bird.'

As though in confirmation, a throaty 'Rrrk' floated down to them from a large black bird circling high above them.

Adren shook her head. 'Do they have anything called mountain madness in your country?' she asked acidly, setting off again.

'As a matter of fact, yes,' Endryk replied. 'I'll tell you about it one day. But this isn't it.'

Adren stopped and looked at him knowingly. 'You'd realize

if you were mad, of course?' she said.

Endryk slithered away from her taunt. 'Let's look to our charge,' he said, pointing to the still unmoving figure.

As they drew nearer they were able to distinguish first Thyrn's clothes and then his face. Both were reluctant to feel relieved however. Though he did not appear to be injured, the ledge on which he was sitting was dangerous, albeit not immediately perilous. An injudicious movement would send him rolling down a long rocky slope.

'He *is* asleep,' Adren whispered.

'Silly young man,' Endryk said, shaking his head. 'He should have more sense by now than to doze off in a place like that.'

'Come on.'

They succeeded in positioning themselves on either side of him. While Endryk braced himself to cope with any sudden flurry of waking anxiety, Adren shook Thyrn's arm gently. Somewhat to their surprise, he did not start violently, but opened his eyes slowly and then turned to each of them in turn with a smile – a guilty smile.

'Hello. Nodded off, did I? Sorry. I was waiting for you.'

Both Adren and Endryk stared at him blankly. Having spent an anxious and testing day presuming that Thyrn had been taken ill in some way, this was not the reaction they had expected. Thyrn rolled his shoulders and then his head. 'Mistake, that. I should've known better. My neck's stiff now.' He winced. 'And my behind.' He looked around. 'Still, isn't it splendid up here? So quiet, so majestic. I'd never have imagined such a place.'

Adren, still braced for a more fraught meeting, and unsettled by Thyrn's assumption of normality, scowled. 'Thyrn, what the devil have you been up to?'

'Where's the little old man?' The question, asked wide-eyed and frankly, left her gaping.

'Old man? What old man?' she spluttered.

'The one who said I should wait for you. He was going to fetch you. I say he was old but it was difficult to tell, really. But he *was* little.' Adren looked to Endryk for help but though he was obviously concerned, he could only shrug. Thyrn began to lever himself to his feet. He flexed his legs carefully as he stood up and nodded gratefully to Endryk who gave him a supporting hand. Adren composed herself and there was a conscious note of gentle humouring in her voice when she spoke to him again.

'We haven't seen anyone else, Thyrn,' she said, motioning him along the ledge and towards safer ground. 'Are you sure you weren't just dreaming?'

Thyrn's expression became thoughtful. As always when he was treating with anything that touched near his profession his expression changed from that of a young, often bewildered or lonely young man, to that of a mature and experienced adult. 'There was something odd about him,' he admitted. 'Something I can't put my finger on at the moment, but it wasn't a dream, no.'

'You've had a long and strange day, Thyrn, and very little to eat. The mountains can play peculiar tricks on you when you're not used to them.' Endryk took his tentative tone from Adren.

Thyrn shook his head and met his gaze quite straightforwardly. 'Yes. A stranger day than you can know.' He looked guilty again. 'And you have too, I imagine. I'm sorry, I owe you all an apology. I'll explain as best I can when we join the others – if I can. But the little man *was* here. He was neither dream nor hallucination. I mightn't be much of a fighter or a mountain dweller, but I know my mind and all the tricks it can play . . .' Then he was looking around, puzzled. 'I've no idea where he is now though, if he's not with you. He did say he was going to fetch you.'

'No one came for us, Thyrn,' Adren said, almost

apologetically. 'And we've seen no one.' She cast a quick look at Endryk.

Thyrn frowned. 'Odd, that. He was quite insistent I wait. Still, you're here, aren't you? That's all that matters.'

Adren could not prevent her Warden's interrogatory nature from coming to the fore. 'What was he like? What was he wearing?'

'I didn't really notice, I'm afraid. He was little.' He held out a hand level with Adren's shoulder by way of demonstration. Then he smiled. 'Bright eyes, he had. And he was full of life. With a sing-song voice – very calming, reassuring. Went right through me, like sunlight. He'd a pack on his back, I think, and he seemed . . . to belong here somehow.' His smile faded. 'It is odd though, now I think about it, meeting someone like that, up here of all places. I don't know why it didn't occur to me at the time. Everything just seemed to be quite natural, standing here, talking. We might have been in the middle of Arvenshelm.' He frowned. 'I'll have to think about it.'

Adren was about to question him further but Endryk caught her eye and shook his head.

'Let's get down to the others,' he said. 'They'll be getting anxious and I don't really want to tackle that rock fall in the dark.' He turned to Thyrn. 'Think about it when we're back at camp. For now, just think where you're putting your feet.'

Before they began the descent, both Adren and Thyrn stood for a while looking round at the mountains in their frozen march to the horizon. Endryk joined them when he saw what they were doing. No one spoke.

Nor did they speak much on the way down into the growing darkness of the valley. Hyrald and the others had set up camp a little way from the foot of the fall and a fire was burning, casting an odd light in the bright-skyed gloaming. They were not sat around it however, but had ascended part way up the lower reaches of the fall to greet the returning rescuers. They had been there since Endryk had called down to let them know that Thyrn was safe and unhurt.

When he had reassured himself of this personally, Nordath erupted in anger. The others stood back as his outburst swept their own clamouring questions aside.

'What the devil did you think you were doing, wandering off like that? No indication of where you'd gone – taking no food with you, no clothes – your guard duty abandoned.' This was an afterthought. 'What if the weather had changed, or if you'd had an accident? If it hadn't been for the damned dog we wouldn't have had the faintest idea where you'd gone.'

The anger faded almost as suddenly as it had flared up, as Thyrn visibly wilted under the onslaught. Uncle and nephew were left staring at one another in a pained and helpless silence. Adren broke it.

Taking Thyrn's arm, she said briskly, as to a child who had been on a special outing, 'Let's get something to eat, then you can sit down and tell us everything that's happened.' An unexpected motherliness in her manner coupled with an unequivocal and protective menace dispatched the men to their tasks and further postponed the squall of questions that had been brewing all day.

Gradually the valley darkened and bright stars began to appear in the purpling sky. Endryk struck his lantern to complement the firelight. Under Adren's stern writ however, the only sounds to be heard were those of the fire and the cooking food.

As they were all settling around the fire and beginning to eat, a signal from her prompted Thyrn.

'This is difficult,' he began, avoiding looking directly at anyone. 'I really don't know where to start. I know what I did was unbelievably stupid – caused you a lot of distress and difficulty and risked getting me lost or killed, but I won't apologize to you because a simple "sorry" isn't enough. I'm appalled at what I've done and all I can do is try to tell you what happened as honestly as possible.' He raised a hand to touch his temple. His face was serious when he looked up and met the gaze of each of his listeners in turn. 'I'm not certain why or how any of it happened, but in so far as it touches on my skill as a Caddoran, I *am* certain that I'll get to the bottom of it before I've finished. You'll have to trust me about that.' There was a note of determination in his voice that none of them had heard before and no one spoke.

'I was on guard duty, walking about to prevent myself from dozing off – Rhavvan had woken me from a very deep sleep and I was quite groggy. It was very quiet – the mountains aren't like the forest, are they, with all manner of things wandering about killing one another. And none of you were snoring for the moment.' This provoked some indignant looks but he continued before anyone could interrupt. 'Suddenly, I felt something . . . pulling at me.' He paused and, closing his eyes, took a slow breath.

'Pulling?' Hyrald queried cautiously.

Thyrn released the breath and opened his eyes. 'When a Caddoran Joins with a client,' he began to explain, 'he has to let go of whatever's going on in his own mind. Make a blank space, as it were, so that the client's intentions can be recorded accurately. The blanker the space, the more accurate the receiving of the message will be.' He smiled unexpectedly but there was an edge to his voice as he continued. 'It's not an easy thing to do by any means but, being "gifted", I can be very blank when need arises – that's what makes me so valuable.' He shrugged the observation aside. 'Anyway, this letting go is as much a physical thing as a mental one and it has physical effects. These tend to be different for each individual Caddoran. Some feel they're floating in water, some flying, some just diffusing into nothingness – all sorts of things. For me it's a sensation of being drawn – pulled – towards a client, or more correctly, towards his message and his intentions.'

'And this . . . pulling . . . is what you felt?' Adren prompted.

'Yes.' Thyrn was shaking his head as if reluctant to confirm his own answer. 'Very strongly. Stronger than I've ever felt it with any client – even Vashnar.'

Nordath waved his hands vaguely. 'But I thought you had to prepare yourself before this could happen – that it was something absolutely in your control.'

'So it is,' Thyrn replied, staring into the fire. Shadows danced about his face and he looked much older than his real age. 'So it has to be. Without control, what would there be? Just madness. A mind helpless – completely exposed – filling with everything around it.' He shuddered. 'Like a sewer.'

Few Wardens passed through their careers without having to go down into Arvenshelm's ancient and labyrinthine sewers in search of one of the many criminals who used them as a convenient underground road system and hiding place; Hyrald, Rhavvan and Adren were no exceptions. Thyrn's image disturbed them but they did not speak.

'But it was there,' Thyrn went on. 'Quite unmistakable. And, as I said, stronger than I've ever known.'

'Stronger – what do you mean?' Hyrald asked.

'The intensity is different for each client,' Thyrn replied offhandedly.

'I don't understand any of this,' Rhavvan said. He spat a piece of gristle into his hand and threw it into the fire.

'*You* don't understand it?' Thyrn said bluntly. '*I* don't understand it. I wouldn't have thought such a thing possible. In fact, I still have difficulty realizing that it actually happened. But it did, and that's what it was. A pulling stronger than I've ever known that came on without any preparation by myself and without a client – or anyone that it could be related to.'

He fell silent, staring into the fire again. Adren looked at him carefully. There was some fear in his eyes, but mainly there was anger. He had been affronted. He was feeling as she had when Endryk had casually overwhelmed her vaunted swordwork. Except that then Endryk had been there to rebuild and improve upon what he had destroyed. For Thyrn there was no one.

'Is it possible that somehow one of us might accidentally have . . . contacted . . . you while we were sleeping?' she asked.

Thyrn pursed his lips then turned to look at her. The look told her she was talking nonsense, but that he was grateful for the effort she had made. 'No,' he said. 'A Caddoran's art is really only mimicry. It's not mind-reading. It's strange – mysterious, intuitive, but there's nothing mystical or magical about it. The client doesn't really have to do anything except give the message he wants delivered. Everything else is up to the Caddoran and his discipline.'

'But you say this came from nowhere, without you doing anything?' Nordath's statement was a question.

'Yes,' Thyrn replied simply. 'I told you, I don't understand.'

'Go on,' Adren urged gently, sensing the beginning of a futile debate. 'Just tell us what happened. We can discuss the whys and wherefores after.'

Thyrn nodded. 'I'm not totally sure what happened next,' he said. 'I remember also feeling a great need in the pulling. Although I could see no one, everything else told me that I'd a client who needed a difficult and important message delivered urgently. I could do no other than move towards it.'

Suddenly he wrapped his arms about himself. 'I'm sorry. I was all right when I woke up, but the more I think about all this, the more it's bothering me – frightening me.' The last words came out reluctantly. As he looked round the listening circle he was a bewildered young man again. 'I know the tricks my mind can play; I can always end them even if I can't prevent them from starting.' His distress grew. 'But looking back, I can't think why I did any of what I did. How could I have felt the pull of a client without preparation, without seeing him? Why should I have thought that I could find the message-sender by looking for him when everything that was happening could only have come from inside myself? Why had I no control over my mind, my actions?'

Hyrald intervened quickly, leaning towards him and holding his gaze. 'Thyrn. Listen to me. None of us has control over everything all the time. Look at us, senior officers of the Warding, experienced in dealing with and controlling all manner of situations – frightening, horrific, chaotic, tragic situations. And where are we now? Sitting round a campfire in the middle of the Karpas Mountains, as far from our old homes and lives as if they'd never existed. Why? Because frightening, inexplicable things quite beyond our control have happened to us. You're forgetting that somehow, without you doing anything, you and Vashnar touched one another when you were more than half the country apart. I can understand you being afraid, but understand too, *you've survived.*' He gripped Thyrn's arm powerfully. 'And you've found skills and abilities in yourself over just these past days you'd never have thought possible. Everything's changed for all of us. Maybe your Caddoran skills are changing too. Developing in some way. Just trust yourself.' He drew the others into his plea. 'We trust you. And we'll support you if you slip. Just tell us what happened as well as you can then it won't catch us unawares again.'

Thyrn placed his hand over Hyrald's and nodded.

'You're right. I'm sorry. I'm not used to relying on other people like this.' He cast an anguished glance at Nordath.

'It's all right,' his uncle said, smiling. 'I understand what you mean.' He motioned him to continue. It took Thyrn a few moments to compose himself again.

'There's not much more to tell, really. The pull was so strong that I just had to keep following it.'

'Did you realize what you were doing?' Endryk asked.

Thyrn gave a feeble shrug. 'Yes and no. I knew I was walking away from the camp. I remember being careful how I walked in the half light. But I didn't realize how long I'd been walking. As I said, the pull was so strong. I just kept thinking, a little further and I'll find out what all this is about – who needs this urgent message sending – a little further, over and over. I remember scrambling up there.' He pointed to the ridge, now only a suggestion of deeper shadow against the starry sky. 'And I remember walking along the ridge. I didn't hesitate, didn't even see that marvellous view of the mountains – I just walked on. The pull was getting stronger. Then there was this little figure coming towards me. I think he was whistling, or singing, to himself.'

Hyrald, Rhavvan and Nordath all craned forward.

'Then there was a message-sender actually causing this?' Hyrald voiced the general anticipation.

Thyrn shook his head. 'He wasn't the message-sender. I don't know who he was. I got the impression he was just a traveller – someone passing by.'

'*What?*' Rhavvan's protestation made everyone jump. 'Passing by? Just like that – halfway up a mountainside, in a part of the country that most of the people don't even know exists?'

'Let him finish.' Adren reached out for silence. 'You're still sure you met this man, Thyrn? That you weren't dreaming? Because we saw no one and we certainly didn't get any message about where you were.'

'He was there.' Thyrn was as definite as when he had been on the ridge. He described the man again – little, bright-eyed, lively, infectious voice, though he could still remember little of what the man had been wearing, and he was hesitant about his age – old and not old. Rhavvan was patently sceptical but Adren's glower and taut jawline kept him silent.

'You are a Caddoran, Thyrn,' she said with just a hint of

reproach. 'You must remember. Exactly what did he say to you?'

The question obviously unsettled Thyrn and he did not reply for some time. He was frowning when he did. 'That's very strange. Even when I'm not working I tend to recall conversations quite well – especially if they're out of the ordinary. But I can only remember parts of this clearly.' He stared into the fire, silent again for some time. 'I remember the sound of his voice. It was strange – musical, seemed to pass right through me, but pleasant – reassuring, like everything about him.'

'Go back to when you first saw him,' Adren said.

'I am,' Thyrn replied, tapping his head. 'I'm going through everything thoroughly.' His hand came up as if enumerating items on a list. 'As we drew nearer to each other – I could see him smiling from quite a distance away – he just held out his hand; I took it. He seemed to be concerned about me. "A long way from home," was the first thing he said. Then he was asking me who I was, where I was going.'

'And what did you tell him?' Adren pressed, very gently.

'I think I told him everything,' Thyrn said doubtfully. His lack of recall was obviously troubling him. 'I don't think I could have done anything else, the way he asked.'

'You told him you were following this . . . pull?' Adren asked.

'Yes, I did, definitely,' Thyrn replied, certain now. 'Bits are coming back to me. I told him who and what I was – a Caddoran – and why I was up there – not about the Death Cry and all that, but the pull of a message-sender, yes.'

'And what did he say?'

Thyrn looked at Endryk, surprise lighting his face. 'Same as you did when you rescued us, when I told him what I was, but not so sarcastic. "Battle messenger or storyteller?" he asked. How strange. Maybe he comes from your country, although he didn't have your accent.'

'That was all?'

'Yes, though I can't imagine what he thought about it. Odd enough for him to meet someone out here without suddenly finding out they might be a lunatic.' He laughed. Despite the difficulty he was having remembering the details of his conversation, recalling even part of it seemed to put him remarkably at ease. His mood touched the others too. It was as though the sound of a distant and happy celebration was dancing in the firelight. Nals, on the fringes of the group, pricked up his ears and looked around briefly before returning his head to his paws to continue his scrutiny of his companions.

'You said he told you to wait?' Adren said. 'That he'd go and look for us?'

Thyrn became thoughtful again. 'It's really odd. Parts of what we talked about are as clear as if I'd just spoken them. Others are vague and blurred, like voices in the room below when you're half asleep. But, yes, he did say that. He seemed a bit worried when I told him why I was there. He said there's a bad place ahead – he'd come across it by accident, and it was very dangerous. I think he said something about a place of old power, or great power, I can't remember. I have images of cracks and schisms – a terrible focus.' He shook his head as if to clear it. 'But it was that that was drawing me, because of what I was. I wasn't to go any further, I was to sit and rest and . . .' He snapped his fingers. 'That's it! He wasn't going to go for you. He actually said, "I'll call them to you," and he pursed his lips as though he were going to whistle for you. It made me laugh. He said he couldn't wait, he had to be on his way. And, besides, he'd had enough of crowds for the moment. I don't seem to remember anything much after that. Just his voice filling my head – that and the fact that the pull had gone. I suppose I must have fallen asleep. I *was* very tired.'

He looked round at his audience. 'I *am* sorry about all this,' he said. 'I know it's a strange tale but it's the truth. And I've no idea why I can't recall all of it.' He looked at Endryk. 'Oddly, I don't seem to be as bothered about it as I did, although I suppose I should be. Perhaps, as you said, it was just fatigue and lack of food. I don't work well when I'm tired, I know that. But that's everything I can remember.'

'It's gone then, this pull – this sense of a distance message-sender?' Nordath asked.

'Was it ever there?' Rhavvan's sceptical query finally broke through Adren's silent restraints.

Thyrn turned to him. 'Oh yes, it was. I'm not that addled. It's still there now.'

This created a small stir.

'Don't worry. It's weaker, more distant – though I still don't know what it is.'

'Can you . . . resist it?' Nordath asked.

'Yes, Uncle. I'm curious about it, very curious, but when that traveller told me there was danger ahead, I could feel the truth of what he was saying and I'm not going searching for it again. It won't catch me like it did before.'

A little later, when Thyrn had retired to his tent, his tale was recounted and dissected around the fire.

'There was no sign of anyone up there?' Hyrald asked Endryk.

'We didn't see anyone although I thought I caught a glimpse of something – someone – moving at one point. And Nals kept hearing things. There's no reason why there shouldn't be someone living out here, I suppose – someone who really knows the place – someone a bit eccentric.' A thought made him smile. 'I lived on my own in the middle of nowhere for long enough. And I just happened on you when you were heading into danger. Odd as the lad's story is, I've got no reason to doubt it. He certainly believes it and he's not a liar.'

'He's no liar, but Rhavvan's still of the opinion he's nuts,' Adren said provokingly.

Rhavvan was unexpectedly candid. 'It's the easiest answer to everything that's happened, but we've all dealt with deranged people before and Thyrn's not like that. In fact, as you said, Hyrald, he's changed a lot since we set off from Endryk's cottage. He's matured – made a real effort to learn things, to pull his weight.'

'You don't seem to be too happy about it.'

Rhavvan grimaced. 'Well, if *he's* not nuts, maybe we are! Either that or there are some *very* peculiar things in these mountains.' He turned to Endryk. 'What did you make of that remark about a place of old power, great power? I noticed you reacted.'

Endryk looked uncomfortable. 'Nothing really. Thyrn might be right . . . maybe the man he met was from my country. According to our old histories, all things are no more than different aspects of the Old Power – the power that came from the Great Searing – or even created the Great Searing. You call it the Great Light, I think. It's not as fanciful as it seems, believe me. I've seen the Old Power used, both benignly and otherwise. It's very real.' He waved a hand agitatedly. 'There are said to be places where, for some reason, the Old Power is concentrated – focused.'

'Could there be such a place about here?' Rhavvan asked the question unhappily.

Endryk shrugged. 'I've no skill in using the Old Power. Few people have, fortunately. I probably wouldn't recognize such a place if I was in the middle of it.'

The conversation swayed back and forth until eventually it began to circle pointlessly.

Hyrald cut through it. 'We're not going to reach any great conclusions about this. I think we'd better get back to where we are. Today's been bizarre, to say the least, but I think Thyrn's told us the truth of it – as he sees it, anyway. And no harm's been done except that we've caught no food – something we'll have to concentrate on tomorrow. We'll just have to put this behind us. At least we've been moving in the right direction to take us home.'

'What about this little old man he met?' Rhavvan queried. 'What if he's still wandering about?'

Hyrald shrugged. 'Well, whoever he was – is – he doesn't seem to have been particularly menacing. Thyrn seemed to like him – and he did warn him about some kind of danger. There's no saying where Thyrn would be by now if he hadn't stopped. At worst the fellow was negligent, abandoning Thyrn like that. But, thinking about it – a traveller, hermit, whatever, on his own, miles from anywhere, I imagine he'd be far more frightened of us than we are likely to be of him. Either he's gone on his way, like he told Thyrn, or he's hiding from us. And I can't say I blame him. Look at us – ugly and armed to the teeth. He's just another mystery to add to everything else.'

'But what if Thyrn wanders off again?' Rhavvan's final question was met at first with silence. Then there was a brief, embarrassed discussion about how Thyrn might be discreetly restrained or at least observed, but this was abandoned after a brief swing into black humour.

'He's part of the group now,' Endryk said. 'We'll have to trust him. Whatever he is, whatever strange skills he has, even Rhavvan concedes that he's changing, learning, gradually becoming someone that any of us would be glad to be with in this position. We shouldn't even be talking about him behind his back like this.'

No one disagreed with this final summary and the conversation moved away from the day's events to discussing plans for the following day.

In his tent, Thyrn, drifting in and out of sleep against a background of faintly flickering firelight and the soft rumble of voices, punctuated by the occasional laugh, rehearsed again his unreasoned response to the strange pull he had felt. As he had admitted, it was still there, though its power over him had gone. He was determined to solve the problem somehow, but his duty now – a duty he was happy to accept – was to the companions who had brought him this far.

Just as he was slipping finally into sleep, he thought he heard the little old man's sing-song voice again, oddly clear and still reassuring. 'Light be with you, Caddoran,' it said, carrying him gently into the darkness.

There was dreamless stillness.

Then Vashnar was all about him.

Chapter 21

'I'll seek him out.'

Vellain's stomach had turned icy at her husband's words. Instinctively, her hand went out to catch his arm.

'No! You can't do such a thing – you mustn't. The risks . . .'

Her plea had faltered against his grim resolution. Vashnar could be as subtle and devious as Bowlott or any of the Moot's political creatures when he so chose, but his inclination was always to direct action, and not only did he not flinch from confrontation if he deemed it necessary, he relished it. Thyrn's distant shade, once merely the irksome buzzing of a night-time insect, had not changed in itself but, by some eerie metamorphosis in Vashnar's mind, had become like the tapping of an unseen sapper gnawing at the roots of a castle once deemed impregnable, or the faint wind-borne trumpet calls of a mighty army. It could no longer be ignored. It must be ended!

It is in the nature of power that those who hold it for a long time choose to consider from what or whom it is derived only when they sense that it is threatened. Then, through the distorting glass of their own deepest fears and self-doubts, they see only weakness and vulnerability, finding that what they had thought to be stout buttresses are flimsy and inadequate – easily susceptible to anyone, like themselves, with the insight to see them clearly and the will to assail them. Thus, inexorably, they begin the desperate garnering of more power, the building of ramping towers and bulwarks, each both overreaching and over-burdening the last, futilely striving for that which cannot be attained until eventually the whole tumbles into destruction, overwhelmed by its own unrestrained weight.

'What risks?' Vashnar said. 'A nosebleed? A headache? I think I'll survive those.'

Unusually, Vellain's naked doubts showed on her face. 'This is something we know nothing about.' She floundered for words, eventually blurting out, 'You're fighting on someone else's ground.'

Vashnar smiled patronizingly. 'And so are you, using military analogies.' He realized immediately that in his preoccupation he had made a mistake and that his manner would serve only to transform Vellain's doubting expression into one of anger. A rare anger – one directed solely at him.

'I've no choice,' he said hastily, before she could give it voice. To avoid looking at her for the moment, he massaged his temple with three restless fingers. 'So far, I've tolerated Thyrn's presence as a niggling irritation at the edges of my mind. I've ignored it, as something of no consequence. But that might have been a mistake. At the best it must be distracting me, however slightly – preventing me from giving everything that must be given to our cause.' He became earnest. 'Worse, I might be turning away from a threat, leaving myself open to some ambush as perhaps Aghrid and his men did.'

'You accept *that* military analysis, then?' Vellain said viciously. Vashnar took the blow without comment. He deserved it for such carelessness and he was glad it had come. He gave her an apologetic nod, relieved that nothing worse had happened.

'I told you, I've no choice.' He was grim again. 'Who knows what demented skills this youth has? For all we know, he may be aware of everything I do and intend to do. He may be completely in control of what's happening – just waiting for a suitable opportunity to bring me low. I don't think he is, but I can't risk it, not with everything so close. The country's ripe for the taking – this journey's shown me that more clearly than ever. His ground or not, I've got to find him and deal with him.' He leaned back into the coach's lush seat and became casually resolute. 'I've dealt with worse. When it comes to fighting, it's not strength, skill, or weapons that decide; in the end, it's the will.' He clenched his fists. 'The will to win, to crush your enemies. And I have him there – I have anyone there.'

Vellain made no response. It was a conclusion that no one who knew Vashnar would dispute. It lay near the heart of what had drawn her to him and what held her there.

The coach and its escort moved steadily on through the late afternoon sunshine.

Their reception at Degelvak proved to be better than any they had received on the entire journey so far. As everywhere else, amongst those who were swayed by such things, the Tervaidin had made a considerable impression on their earlier northward journey. Now that they were returned, tired but seemingly triumphant, and in the presence of their Senior Commander – the man who had resurrected their ancient and proud name – the number of people so impressed increased fourfold. At one point, towards the centre of the town, the procession found itself being cheered by passers-by. Excited children, gangs of young men and noisy dogs ran alongside the coach, providing an impromptu honour guard to complement the stern-faced Tervaidin.

'Excellent,' Vashnar said to Vellain while he was acknowledging the crowd. 'So much for the idea that the further from Arvenshelm, the less the enthusiasm for our cause.'

'But these people know nothing of your plans,' Vellain remarked, still uneasy about her husband's intention of seeking out Thyrn. 'At least, I hope not. Even at this stage, a wrong word in the wrong ear could bring everything down on us. Bowlott and the Moot are not *that* stupid, and more than a few of the Warding are of Hyrald's inclination.'

But Vashnar was not to be deterred. 'The mood is here. All around us. As it has been throughout. The need for change – for strong leadership. Look at them – just look at them. They'll be with us when the time comes.'

And indeed the mood of the crowd did persist. The good citizens of Degelvak seemed determined to confirm Vashnar in his opinion that support for his imminent bid for power would be almost universal, treating his arrival with general revelry. Even his chief ally in the town, the leader of the local Senate, expressed surprise as he looked round at the noisy diners filling the town's public banqueting hall that evening.

'Inspired, if I may say so, Commander,' he said. 'Bringing back the Tervaidin to pursue those traitors. Inspired. The town's been buzzing with it ever since they rode through.' He leaned confidentially towards his guest but had to shout just to make himself heard. 'And support for our cause has . . .' He did not finish the sentence but merely gestured upwards.

Vashnar nodded agreeably but made no attempt to reply. He had already learned that when he spoke other than to his immediate neighbour, a silence hissed out from him to fill the hall as the many talkers suddenly became many listeners. At one point he had had to clap his hands loudly into this emptiness and, with an indulgent laugh, tell them all to, 'Carry on eating, my friends, I was only talking about the weather.' The laughter had returned to him disproportionately.

Then it was over. The last of the 'useful' introductions had been made, the last hand had been shaken, the last of the important dignitaries and influential supporters gently and jovially dismissed. Vellain flopped heavily into a capacious basketwork chair in their bedroom. It creaked ungallantly. She kicked off her shoes. Though she had not been able fully to put aside her concerns about what her husband was intending to do that night, she too had been swept up by the general excitement. Her eyes shone as she watched Vashnar dragging off his boots. Untypically they lay where they fell as he removed his tunic and with unbridled relief loosened his collar.

He dropped back on to the bed and closed his eyes momentarily. Vellain's expression became wantonly purposeful but as she gripped the arms of the chair and began to lever herself upright, it creaked again and Vashnar turned to look at her. A denying hand reached out to stop her.

'Later,' he said with undisguised reluctance. 'This can't be delayed any longer.'

Vellain paused, then, with equal reluctance, sat back into the betraying chair and prepared for a final burst of opposition to her husband's intentions. 'What are you going to do?' she asked. 'How are you going to . . . find him?' She gesticulated vaguely.

'I don't know,' Vashnar replied. 'But I'll get no better chance to do it on my own terms than now. So many unspoken questions have been answered over these past days. The mood of the people is as I've always judged. They're weary of the fatuous antics of the Moot. They're crying out for leadership, strong leadership – *my* leadership. To deal with the Morlider. To prepare us for whatever's likely to come from Nesdiryn. To bring order back to the land. Whether Thyrn's contact with me is inadvertent or deliberate, I can't risk having him bring me down now.'

'But . . .'

The restraining hand was there again.

'Help me, Vellain. As you've always helped me.'

Vellain held his gaze for a long moment. Then, slowly, she lowered her eyes. When she raised them again she was his ally.

'What shall I do?' she asked.

Vashnar looked up at the rough-hewn timber beams, black stripes against the white ceiling. Various hooks and large-headed nails protruded crookedly here and there, painted black like the wood now, their original purpose long forgotten.

'Turn the lamps down,' he replied uncertainly. 'Then just watch over me while I try to find this wretch inside me.'

Vellain did as she was bidden and when she had finished, the room was suffused with little more than a soft candlelight, a new landscape of shadows bounding it. Vashnar nodded approvingly and closed his eyes. Vellain sat down again, choosing this time an upholstered chair which accepted her without a sound.

She waited.

Secure in her presence and with renewed strength in his purpose, Vashnar tried to focus his mind on the distant uneasiness that he identified as being Thyrn. It was no easy task. Plans, schemes, ideas, thoughts of things past, of things to come, trivial and important, but all irrelevant to the moment, appeared from nowhere and tumbled recklessly and without order through the darkness of his mind. For some time, as was his way, he tried to deal with them methodically, taking each in turn, examining it and then dismissing it, in the belief that so dispatched it would not return. But it soon became apparent to him that such an exercise was one of futility. It was like trying to part a way through water with his hands, for each thought so confronted led him a taunting dance down endlessly dividing ways, and a cascade of other thoughts swirled into his wake and demanded attention.

His face stiffened and he scowled as he fought against this seemingly endless and growing clamour. Vellain watched him silently. She sensed nothing untoward. This restless figure she was familiar with, but the balm she would normally offer him at such times was, for the moment, inappropriate.

Vashnar turned on to his left side. The pillow was cool on his cheek and at its touch, for a moment, the turmoil in his mind drained away. He heard a long breath leaving him and he felt his body softening. It came to him that he must not chase after the faint whisper that was Thyrn. It was like a distant star at the edge of his vision. To turn to it was to have it disappear. It was like a familiar name, momentarily forgotten. Pursued, it would burrow into the depths like a hunted ground creature. Left alone it would emerge unrequested.

He must trust himself. He must be patient. He must let Thyrn's hold on him reveal itself in its own way and its own time. Some of the eddying thoughts began to return but he ignored them. Logically he knew that none of them needed his immediate attention; intuitively he knew that plunging after them again would merely stir up further confusion and disorder.

Through the growing ease, he became aware of a source of comfort somewhere, almost childlike in character. It took him a little while to identify it as his old habit of rubbing his thumb against the ring on his right hand. Hagen's gift.

Hagen.

'You are one of us.'

His eyes flickered involuntarily. Amid the shapeless forms that danced with the colours behind his eyelids, something glinted. The light fragmented, almost painfully, in his blurred vision. Keeping his eyes almost closed he focused on it. For a moment he thought that he was looking at an evening sky, with a solitary silver star shining bright against the soft gold of a vanished sun. Then the golden sky became the back of his hand, resting close to his face and lit by the room's lowered lamplight. And the star in its turn became his ring, catching a light from somewhere and transforming it into this unexpected brightness. Vashnar made a cursory effort to think where the flame was that might be causing this but he could not remember where the room's lamps were. It was of no consequence.

Nevertheless, the brilliance in the ring held him and increasingly its seeming solidity reduced the image of the hand to something vague and distant, like a dull painting. More questions drifted to him idly. Was the light coming from the crystal or from that strange clear mirror-like mounting?

That too, was of no consequence. Let it go.

But the light *was* important. It seemed to be growing in intensity, swelling – the word 'blossoming' came to him – until it filled his entire vision, save for a darkness at its centre – small, circular and of a blackness so intense that he knew nothing could escape from it. That too was growing.

How was it that both the light and the darkness could simultaneously be so dominating?

He heard the question form as a low, mewling whine at the back of his throat, then it tailed off into nothingness and he was falling.

Vellain canted her head and leaned forward as she heard the slight sound, but she could make out nothing articulate. Her husband was lying like a child, with his right hand dangling awkwardly in front of his face.

Asleep, she diagnosed. Whatever he had gone searching for, sleep had found him first. It had been a long day and the needs of his body had overtaken the desires of his mind. Though she had in the end supported his intention, the prospect of his slipping into another mysterious trance and waking wide-eyed, bleeding and disorientated, unsettled her badly and she was more than relieved that he had apparently failed. For a moment she considered joining him on the bed, but though it had been a long day for her too, she was wide awake. More so than when she had first entered the room. There was no point taking her place by her husband; she would inevitably wake him and there was no saying what his mood might be if he found that his search for Thyrn had ended in his simply falling asleep. No, she would do as he had asked. She would watch him. At least until she fell asleep.

But far from that silent bedroom and his wife's dutiful vigil, Vashnar was still falling.

Falling?

The word hung about him, but though there had been a moment of terror, a feeling of all support about him disappearing, of tumbling headlong into a black emptiness – that had passed. Now, though he knew he was moving he could sense neither up nor down. Nor was there any rush of air tearing at him. Nor any fear, for that matter, as surely there should have been? Rather it was as though he was being drawn along, though he could feel no force pulling him. What was happening? Where could he be going?

The question made no sense. Ambivalence pervaded everything. He was and he was not, travelling. He was lying on the bed in his host's house, and he was somewhere else, being drawn to another place. Surprise curled through him as the contradictions – the impossibility of what was happening – failed to disturb him. Nor did any of the lights and sounds that were moving through and around him on his strange journey. Shapeless and indistinct, they came from all directions, in so far as directions existed in this place, if place it was. Yet there was some order here, he knew – a meaning behind them – if he could apply himself to discovering it.

Then there *was* fear. Though whether it was his own or someone else's, he could not tell. The lights changed and streaked in response, bursting into bright shards of iridescence that seared painfully through his mind. And the sounds pulsed and shook, buffeting him. A rhythm, subtly beyond his grasp, began to make itself felt. He reached out into the confusion, to steady himself and to wring the meaning from it.

No!

The denial – his denial – formed clearly, shaking all about him.

The lights circled and spiralled. The sounds swirled after them dizzyingly, coming together and breaking apart again. The darkness he had seen at the heart of the ring was there again, drawing all to it. Nothing could resist, nothing could escape. All was coming to an inexorable Joining.

Then he was himself and whole, blinking in a bright greyness. The journey was ended.

I am here and I am elsewhere, under the watch of my wife.

He tested the thought. It was insane. The imaginings of a madman. Yet too, it was not. Though it offended any logic he had ever used, it was nevertheless so. He was both here and there. What part of him was here his mind refused to speculate on.

Perhaps this is a dream? he thought, but he rejected the idea immediately. He did not dream – never had. What had happened – was happening – could not be so glibly accounted for. He was afraid, but less afraid than he thought he should have been. This place offered him no danger. This place had drawn him here: it wanted him. Yet there were terrible things here. But what kind of things?

And where was he?

He looked about him. He was having difficulty focusing though it seemed to him that shapes were struggling to crystallize in the greyness. Hints and suggestions of walls and doorways and strange high platforms and balconies formed wherever he looked, only to dim and fade at the edges of his vision. Images of a great echoing hall filled his mind. As if to help him, memories of some of Arvenshelm's finest buildings came to him – even the Count's Palace in Nesdiryn. But to no avail. Whatever this place was, none of them compared to it. Such as he could make out of it was like nothing he had ever seen before.

One thing was for certain, however. The place was enormous – and grey – a dreary, monotonous grey, despite the brightness. Slowly his eyes adjusted and, giddyingly high above him, he saw a vast domed roof. It was dotted with brilliant lights, splaying out in radial lines, each of them sweeping down to vanish into a misty distance. And still it was as though the building formed wherever he looked – as though this was all it could do; as though without him, it would not *be* at all. And even with him, it could not come wholly into existence, strive though it might.

Everything shifted.

And the sounds were about him again, though now they were unmistakably voices – rising and falling, chanting. He could not make out any individual words, though the whole sounded coherent and intelligible. And it was full of fervour and passion, with a stridency that thrilled him. He looked about him in search of its source, but nothing was to be seen other than the same vague images, struggling to come into being. He focused on one, a stairway leading to a platform or balcony – he could not make out which. He moved towards it. The flat sound of his footsteps reached him as he strode out, oddly reassuring. Unconsciously he adjusted his pace to merge with the rhythm of the chanting.

The stairway remained clearly in his view as he approached it. Reaching it he paused, then he grasped the metal handrail. It was solid and cool and he knew that if he ran his hand along it he would find it tainted with a faint but characteristically acrid tang. He resisted the temptation to test this. Sniffing his hand had a childish, even animal-like connotation; it was not fitting, least of all here. He glanced upwards along the spiralling stairway. The platform – for platform it was – loomed darkly over him. He should go to a high place. From there, he would be able to see more. He began climbing. The steps were as solid as the handrail but an awkward height for him and he found, as was often the case, that he had to take two at a time to walk comfortably.

The platform proved to be higher than he had thought, and he was aware of some strain in his legs when he eventually reached it. The stairway opened into the middle of it and as he emerged, he could see that it was a narrow oval in shape with almost pointed ends. A simple metal handrail like that of the stairway ran around it. He looked up again. For all the height he had climbed, the domed roof seemed to be little closer. He did notice, however, that the lines of lights converged directly over him. He was standing at the centre of whatever this place was.

He rubbed his thighs to ease the stiffening muscles. As he did so, a small spasm of fear shook him. How could he leave this place? For all he could not see it in its entirety, it was as real as the room he knew he was lying in. Could he be trapped here for ever, in this unsettling greyness?

As the fear threatened to well up and unman him, the awareness that he was both there *and* lying safely in Degelvak returned to him vividly, reassuringly. And with it came the realization that there was no hint of Thyrn's presence anywhere in this place. It was his and his alone.

Yet it was not, for everything here was beyond anything he could have wilfully imagined. He was no builder, but common sense told him that it was not possible to build anything so large, nor make lamps that shone so brightly. And what purpose could such a place serve? It was a freakish creation, the work of someone patently crazed. A colder thought came to him. Perhaps it was Thyrn's, after all. Perhaps the Caddoran had made this place specially for him, as a trap. Perhaps even now Thyrn was hiding – waiting in ambush as Vellain had conjectured.

He straightened up. If this was Thyrn's trap, so be it. Sooner or later, he would have to reveal himself. And when he did . . .

Whatever strange skills he might have, Thyrn did not possess the will to defeat him: Vashnar had no doubts about that.

He walked slowly to one of the narrow ends of the platform and, gripping the handrails, stared out over his eerie empire. As before, the building seemed to emerge only as he looked at it. He could make out other platforms surrounding the one he was on. For the most part they were lower, although six of them, some considerable distance away, he judged, towered high above. They looked to be dangerously slender for their height. Their shapes varied but they were laid out symmetrically around his platform to some pattern that he could not discern. What in Marab's name was this place meant to be?

The chanting was still all around him, rising and falling.

'Who are you?' he called out. 'Where are you? What is this place?'

Almost immediately the chanting began to fragment as a babble of countless different voices began to mingle with it. Still Vashnar could not make out any individual words, but where before there had been a united fervour and passion, now veins of confusion and doubt ran through it. The chanting filled the greyness but with it came questions – and recriminations.

Vashnar tightened his grip on the handrail. He felt his ring scuffing on the metal and automatically his thumb reached across to rub it protectively. He glanced down casually, but as he looked at the ring it seemed to fill his vision and, with a momentary spasm, he was looking out from the platform again, as though he had never looked down. He shook his head sharply to clear the impression.

The babble continued undiminished. He repeated his questions.

'Who are you? Where are you?'

A quality in the voices changed. Where before he had been an inadvertent eavesdropper, now he was becoming an object of attention. Though Vashnar could still distinguish nothing intelligible, momentary flashes of meaning began to come to him.

'Is this victory? Are the heretics destroyed?'

The babble washed to and fro, more and more questions rippling through it.

'Is this the Golden Land? The promised hereafter? The special place of heroes?'

The words were full of doubt. Then, in horror, 'We are defeated. We are without form. This is a place of darkness – we are cast down into the place of the apostates.'

Vashnar could do no other than raise his hands to his ears in an attempt to keep out the ululating shrieks of terror that rose up from this. But the gesture was fruitless. The sounds were in his head. Their mounting panic threatened to overwhelm him. He felt his knees buckling and, gritting his teeth with effort, he forced his hands down to grasp the handrail to steady himself.

'Silence!' he roared into the empty, screeching greyness.

The word boomed through the howling din like the wave from a rock fall tumbled into a mountain lake, sweeping everything else before it. It took with it the screaming, twisting it tighter and higher until it vanished into a plaintive and distant insect whine. The sudden silence made Vashnar lurch forward against the handrail. It took him a little time to recover and as he did, he noted that the clamour had been replaced by a pervasive susurration, like the sound of wind in the trees, or of many people breathing – listening.

And listening they were, he realized. Listening to him. Listening to the one who had commanded silence. The one who stood at the centre of all this. But were they listening, or was this Thyrn about to spring his trap?

Vashnar asked his first question again.

'Who are you?'

'Who are you?' The reply seemed to be both inside and outside his head, an unsettling, rasping chorus.

Vashnar tightened his grip on the handrail again. Whatever was happening here, however bizarre, he must see it through. Somewhere the hand of that damned Caddoran was to be found. All he had to do was wait.

'I am the one you called here,' he replied.

Bewilderment surrounded him. Vashnar felt his right hand becoming heavy.

'He bears the Sign – the Light that is the Way.'

'Are you the Guide? The one sent to take us to the Golden Land?'

Vashnar clung to his question. 'Who are you?'

Bewilderment again.

'We are the Chosen. The followers of the One True God. The Followers of the One Way. The Scourge and Destroyer of His enemies.'

Vashnar flexed his right hand. 'Who are His enemies?'

More bewilderment. Then realization.

'He teots us. He *is* the Guide.' Words hovered about him then surged forward. 'His enemies are those who follow not the One Way. Those who deviate from His Holy Words.'

Vashnar frowned. He had had to deal with one or two religious fanatics and their followers in his time and he recognized the reply. It was a rote answer, a talisman. Devoid of any real meaning, it and a plethora of others in the same ranting vein were to be uttered as definitive responses to almost any question that tilted at their belief, or as justification for any action, however foul. Was this part of Thyrn's ambush? Such people were at best a nuisance, but at worst they were appallingly dangerous. He must be careful. Best to maintain the interrogation.

'And they are destroyed?'

Even the soft murmuring fell silent.

Vashnar shook his right hand. It was becoming heavier and more awkward. The murmuring returned. 'We are the Chosen. We have . . . perished . . . in the final slaying of His enemies. The Golden Land is ours by His Holy Word. We are not to be examined. So it is written.'

There was some menace in the words. Strangely, Vashnar

felt more at ease. Threats were something he was used to. 'You would defy me?' he said, adding a menace of his own. His hand was beginning to distract him badly. Now it was becoming numb. He made to shake it again only to find that he could not move it. He looked down in some alarm, but his hand was still clutching the handrail. He tried again, but still it would not move. It took him some effort to stay calm. There appeared to be nothing wrong with it, nor anything unusual.

Except for his ring.

It was catching the lights above and scattering them in all directions in splintering shafts of brightness. As had happened before, as he peered at the ring, Vashnar felt a pervasive spasm then found himself looking across the grey hall. Though now it was transformed. The lights from his ring seemed to be rending open the grey dullness – dividing, slicing, separating it, rather than illuminating it. He was aware of a shifting kaleidoscope of images but he could bring no one of them into focus, try as he might. Then, though he could not have said from where the knowledge came, he knew that he was not looking at a mere optical illusion, like reflections in the splaying cracks of a shattered mirror, but at an unfolding array of many places – many times.

Many realities.

With his ring at the heart of them, an infinitely deep well from which they all poured.

Vashnar could do no other than watch, though he was more than just a spectator. He was part of all that was happening, just as everything was a part of everything else throughout all worlds. There were no words for what he found himself experiencing. Vast expanses of forest spread before and through him, cruel shimmering deserts, shifting, glittering ice mountains so bright as to scorch the eyes of anyone who looked on them carelessly. Raging oceans possessed him, and towering cataracts, and livid rivers of burning rock. Towns, villages, cities, were there too, some such as he might have known, some so strange in appearance that only his inner knowledge told him what they were. And, a bloody continuous scar throughout, countless, terrible conflicts – fields and mountainsides blackened with rotting corpses and fluttering carrion birds as far as the eye could see – lowering skies lurid with flames and carried on bloated columns of black smoke – crowds fleeing in panic, the old, the young, the weak, crushed under hooves and wheels – husbands, fathers, gentle lovers now warriors slaying all before them, wild-eyed and without pity.

The times and the places came ever faster, occasional impressions lingering fleetingly. A figure impaled with a spear tumbled from a horse, narrowly missing him. A bloodstained woman, clutching a child and screaming hysterically, fell on her knees in front of him. Blazing buildings crumbled over him. The sky darkened with arrows, glinting axes rose and fell, a terrifying concussion shook him, throwing severed limbs and arcing skeins of blood into the flame-filled air. A black sword fell through time, a strange device embedded deep in its hilt – two intertwined strands which stretched for ever across a star-filled void.

He could feel that which was him, slipping away. Though he was the centre of this hurtling turmoil, he was also the least of things, the merest mote. He thought he heard himself crying out, but nothing could be of its own essence in this broiling chaos.

The last part of him was fading.

A hand fell on his shoulder.

Chapter 22

The many realities were gone and not gone. Now they were no longer part of him, nor he of them but, though fainter and more distant, they were still boiling through the greyness of the hall as if held at bay by an unseen force. Once again Vashnar felt himself both here and in Degelvak. And his right hand was recovered. He was about to look at it, when some caution prevented him; the ring seemed to have some peculiar, disjointing influence in this place.

All these impressions filled his mind instantly and simultaneously, but the caution which informed the last rapidly transformed itself into a more familiar one as he responded to the hand on his shoulder. Seemingly, someone had restored him to what he was, saved him from being drawn into that swirling maelstrom of clashing worlds. But to be caught unawares thus both offended his Warden's pride and struck notes of alarm deep inside him. At the same time an unexpected question came to him: who could be sharing this world that should have been uniquely his?

He felt no threat in the grip, but it was only his momentary confusion at his sudden rescue that gave him the time to note this. Under other circumstances, whoever ventured such an act could have expected an immediate and violent response. Then again, he thought ruefully, under other circumstances, no one would have been able to do it.

Slowly Vashnar released the handrail and turned around.

331

The hand fell away, and Vashnar found himself facing a tall figure in a long dun-coloured robe. A deep hood completely hid the wearer's face. The figure was standing some way from him, as if it had stepped back rapidly when he turned, though it gave no indication of having made a hasty movement. It seemed to be the focus of a peculiar disturbance with an aura about it that shifted and changed, like air dancing over hot coals; giving the disconcerting impression that it was being constantly made and remade. There was nothing unsteady about the unseen gaze that Vashnar could feel searching into him, however. He met and returned it, staring unflinchingly into the darkness of the hood.

'Who are you?'

Both spoke at the same time. The figure's words chimed oddly with the inner sound of his own voice and carried the many resonances that Vashnar had heard when he questioned the unseen voices before. The figure inclined its head curiously. So did Vashnar. He still could not fully make out what he was looking at. The figure seemed real enough. And the hand on his shoulder certainly had been. But how far away from him was it? And how tall? He realized he had nothing to gauge it by. The wavering aura surrounding it even made it difficult for him to be sure it was standing on the floor.

Nevertheless, a slight sense of gratitude for his rescue curled through Vashnar's grim curiosity and prompted him into replying first. 'I am Vashnar, Senior Commander of the Warding of Arvenshelm.'

A hand hidden in a long sleeve gave a slight, dismissive wave.

'Labels, titles, vanities,' the figure said, still many-voiced. 'What are you, then?'

Vashnar frowned. 'I don't understand. I am Vashnar, Senior Commander of the Warding of Arvenshelm,' he repeated.

The figure leaned forward a little, as if intensifying its scrutiny of him. 'Ah,' it said, its voices full of realization. 'You are one of us. One of the Chosen.'

One of us. The words took Vashnar back to the Count's Palace in Nesdiryn and he was once again accepting the gift of the ring from Hagen. Feeling such control of events as he had slipping away from him he wrenched it back, taking a half step forward and drawing himself to his full height. 'I still don't understand,' he said again, though in a tone which clearly implied that this was the newcomer's fault. 'Explain yourself. Who are you? Why are you in this place – *my* place?'

There might have been a hint of a bow from the figure but it was still not fully of this place and Vashnar could not be sure.

'Answer me!' he demanded.

'You carry the Sign. You are the Guide,' the figure said. 'Where else could we be?'

Vashnar took another, more determined step forward, but though the figure did not move it brought him no nearer.

'Who are you?' he insisted.

There was a pause as if the figure were debating with itself.

'We are the servants of the One True God,' it said eventually. 'Why do you question us? We are not to be tested. It is written in the Holy Book that such as we, who die in Holy War, die righteously and will be admitted to the Golden Land without testing or purification.'

Vashnar's eyes narrowed; he had held this conversation once and, at best, he had little time for the gibbering of religious fanatics. He bared his teeth and extended a menacing right hand towards the figure. Light flickered from the ring and the figure flinched.

'Enough of this nonsense,' Vashnar shouted. 'You're some creation of Thyrn's like the rest of this place, and I'll have none of you. Go! Now! Tell your creator to come here and face me in person.' He turned round and bellowed, 'Thyrn!' several times.

His words seemed to take form in the grey air, and the

restrained shadows of the broken realities filling the hall became frenzied. But still they were no longer a part of him and he ignored them. Turning back to the figure challengingly he saw that the aura surrounding it was responding similarly, growing in both size and turbulence, while the figure itself was wavering and faltering. At any moment he felt that the robe would crumple, untenanted, to the floor.

Then he sensed a change. A conflict was under way, though he could neither see anything nor hazard what form it might be taking. But conflict it was. A powerful will was making itself felt – fighting for domination. The scrutiny he had felt reaching out from the dark hood was gone and was being directed elsewhere, and he had become again a mere eavesdropper to the distant and garbled voices that were now rising and falling around him.

Abruptly it was over. Both the noise and the wavering distortion about the figure came to some violent, self-consuming climax which made him turn his head away as if to avoid an impact. Then all was silent.

When he looked again at the figure, he saw that it was now clearly present, as solid in this place as he was. It looked around for some time, then long hands emerged to test the hidden face and be examined in their turn. Finally the figure turned towards Vashnar. He clenched his fists, expecting the hood to be withdrawn to reveal Thyrn. But the hood merely nodded slowly, as if satisfying itself about something.

'You are indeed one of us, Vashnar,' said the figure. 'It shines through you.' The voice was full, resonant, and commanding.

Vashnar did not speak.

'You are lost in this place, are you not? Its strangeness, its ambivalence unsettles you. Indeed, its very existence defies any logic you have ever known.' Vashnar sensed a smile in the shade of the hood. 'Yet this place, and all the others about you . . .' an arm swept over the turbulent greyness beyond the platform '. . . are there always for those who would seek, who would find the Way.' The head inclined in the direction of Vashnar's ring. 'Or have both the will and the key.'

Still Vashnar did not speak, though it was not for want of something to say. The figure's words and his manner of speaking them told him that he was dealing not only with someone used to authority and the wielding of power, but someone who knew about him. Silence was thus his best tactic. He must let this new arrival reveal himself with his own words before deciding how to handle him.

'Still, I would not reproach you for that. I see it myself now only in the light of my own . . . unusual experience. My view from a special vantage, as it were. The one I once was would not have come to this conclusion in an eternity of contemplation.' Then there was a grating note of barely restrained anger in the voice. 'But, it seems, he is long gone now. And his followers. And . . .' he looked around '. . . the world we knew.'

Vashnar risked his question again. 'Who are you?'

The figure lowered its head, as if in thought. 'Not a question I can answer,' he said after a long pause. 'Not yet, at least. There is a name I find lingering about me – a name for who I was, before I became . . . what I became. But that is without meaning now – a burr tangled in the great weave of time and the remaking we set in train.' A low, self-deprecating laugh emerged from the hood. 'I suppose it could be said that I am one who has been . . . born again.' The laugh rolled on, as at some ironic private joke, before dwindling into an introspective chuckle. 'Yes, born again – most apt. Now I am remade in my old image, by forces that I do not fully comprehend any more than a newborn child comprehends how he comes to be. Still, it is of no consequence. Whatever conjunction has brought this about, whatever coming together of strange and disparate events – including the spirit and will of Vashnar and the

335

mysterious key he carries – we are here, and the work is to continue.'

'Work?'

'Your work – our work – the bringing of order out of the meandering chaos that is humanity's way. That is your work, is it not?' The figure inclined its head. Vashnar felt a coldness passing through him. The figure let out a long breath of realization, before continuing. 'Though I see your horizons are limited.' The voice became scornful. 'Morlider to the east, Nesdiryn, silent and frightening, to the west. Your gaze is at the ground. You grovel in the dust when stars and suns shine bright around you.' The scorn became a hissing declamation. 'You have not the measure of either your worth or your ability, Vashnar, or even the extent of the ambitions that you harbour within yourself. But with my touch, you will.'

The coldness returned and Vashnar suddenly felt as though a shrouding veil had been torn away, exposing not only all his present plans and future dreams, but a far greater vision, one which saw the borders of Arvenstaat expanding relentlessly under his leadership – expanding until there would be no place where his writ did not run and his name not bring awe.

Part of him exulted in the revelation, but another part of him tried to turn away from it in fear. Two long strides brought the figure before him and two powerful hands held his face. The suddenness of the movement made Vashnar gasp despite himself. Staring into the depths of the hood he saw only a hint of light reflected in the distant eyes. Warm breath touched his face. He could not move.

'No!' said the figure, its grip tightening. 'Neither defy me, nor deny yourself. Look into the heart of your ambitions and see them for what they are, unbounded by mountains and shore and the petty limitations of your old ways. Know that with the power I command through you, nothing can prevail against your will.' The voice became passionate and driving. 'Vashnar,

336

Vashnar. You know the truth of this. Much of me is you. You are a necessary part of my coming to be again. You and the power of the faith of my erstwhile followers. Now this is yours. There is nothing you cannot achieve. Whole nations will bow before your armies, make obeisance to your flag. Strike! Strike now! Begin! For aeons I have been scattered, without form. Such an event as we find here – such a coming together – does not happen once in ten thousand generations. And you are at its heart. Cling to your old ways and all will slip from you and turn to dust. Your life will snivel to its dismal end in bitterness and whining self-reproach.'

The figure released him and stepped back. Vashnar clutched at the handrail for support, his mind reeling with the force of the emotions that had been unleashed within him. But some caution still lingered. He had dealt with enough convincing charlatans in his time to be deeply sceptical about wild and freely given promises.

'If you have such sight – such power – how is it that you're here, defeated?' he said.

There was a long silence, then the figure said, 'Now that it is about me again, I see that time is not with us – or with you.' There was a hint of anxiety in the voice. 'There is another – a powerful opponent – one who lies beyond my touching. He is aware of us. He must be . . .'

'Answer my question.'

There was another long silence. Vashnar sensed the voices returning and the figure swayed slightly. 'I cannot. How I came to be thus . . .' it made an airy gesture and the voices rose and fell with it '. . . I do not know. But our enemies are so, too. That I know. They too, were defeated. All that was, then, was changed – transmuted.' Its voice became strident. 'We had armies beyond your imagining. And engines of war beyond your imagining. Engines that would unravel the very being – *the very essence* – of our enemies. No living thing could stand against

337

us. Victory was in our grasp.' The voice faltered and became bewildered and uncertain. 'I see another conjunction – but one that should not have been. Our enemies must have . . .' The figure raised an arm across its hood as if to protect its eyes. 'I see a brightness moving across the land, across the oceans – moving through all that lived, moving scarcely at the pace of a walking man – but relentlessly growing, sustaining itself. And all fleeing its touch – believer and heretic alike.'

'And none escaped,'Vashnar said. The words came unbidden and chilled him to his heart with their certainty. He did not know where the knowledge came from.

'None escaped,' the figure confirmed softly. 'And then there was only a brightness beyond bearing – a re-shaping, a re-making. I . . .'

The figure fell silent and lowered its arm.

Vashnar did not speak for some time, and when he did, his voice was cold. 'And *you* – defeated – would offer me your help?'

The figure stiffened and Vashnar felt its scrutiny of him return. 'All were defeated, Vashnar. Our enemy's treachery brought about their own destruction.' The voice was wilfully restrained. 'That *I* am here – that the power of my followers is mine now as it never could have been before – marks my victory, not defeat.'

'I see no power. Only the antics of a market shaman gulling the public.'

The coldness touched him again and, unexpectedly, the voice became relaxed and easy. 'Yes. I forget myself. I forget the needs of your form must be met. Here is a touch of the power – a zephyr touch, light, caressing.' Something struck Vashnar in the chest. The force of the blow made him stagger backwards and almost toppled him over the handrail. With an oath he recovered his balance and started forward angrily. After one pace however, he found he could move no further. It was as though a great hand were effortlessly restraining him. He glowered at the motionless figure.

'No market shaman ever gulled the public thus, I think,' it said quietly, in reply to Vashnar's unspoken curses. 'And no greater effort would be needed to bind whole armies – to raze entire cities.' Vashnar felt the restraint slip away. He was momentarily tempted to advance on the figure and strike it down, but calmer counsels prevailed. He had been struck and then held by a force which he could neither see nor resist. That was indisputable. Further, his every instinct told him that the figure's last remark had been no empty boast. And throughout, the figure had not even moved.

'Do not ask how this can be,' it said, forestalling the question that Vashnar was just forming. 'It is beyond anything you could understand. Suffice it that it is, and that it is mine to command as I wish – or as you wish.'

Vashnar caught the faint hint of dissatisfaction in the voice. 'Why then do you offer it to me? No one relinquishes power voluntarily.'

The figure bowed slightly, like a teacher acknowledging the work of a gifted pupil. 'Circumstance constrains me to this half-place to which you have brought me, but, that changed, the nature of the power itself will still constrain me to your new-formed world. While you, with the will and the key to move in the worlds beyond, will find yourself constrained from using the power yourself. Only together can we achieve what must be achieved.'

The memory of the turbulent vision that the figure had drawn him from returned to Vashnar. 'What are these places? Why would you wish to travel to them?'

'Because chaos reigns there and chaos threatens all things. Only through order can perfection be attained and only such as we can bring order to these places. It is our destiny.' The fierce passion in both the figure's words and its demeanour swept through Vashnar. The voices returned, clamouring noisily.

Abruptly, they were silent and the figure was watching him again. 'But these plans are for the future. We must start where we find ourselves – nurture into a great tree the seeds that you have planted and tended here.' It held out a hand. 'Accept my help. Not the wildest of your ambitions can be denied you if you do.'

Vashnar reached out to take it, but then hesitated. 'You spoke before of another – someone beyond your touching, you said. A powerful enemy.'

The figure withdrew its hand. 'There is. I sense him both inside you and beyond – dark and menacing. He bears a remnant of our old enemy. It is dormant or weak, or both, but I cannot destroy it without destroying you too.' The figure looked around. 'This place is a shadow, Vashnar. Somewhere in your world is its true form or a lingering part of it. Find it and seek me out again when you are there. Follow the call I will leave you with. Our strength will be greater by far there.'

'But this enemy, is it Thyrn?'

'Names have no meaning for me. You know who it is. Follow the call of this place and he will come too. He can do no other. Then you can kill him.' The voice became commanding again. 'A word of warning, keyholder. Do not assail him anywhere other than in that place you think of as your world.' The hand was extended again, urgently. Vashnar grasped it without hesitation. For the briefest of moments he felt a warm muscular grip, then the figure was gone and the surrounding greyness was sweeping him away.

He rolled on to his back and looked up at the black-beamed ceiling.

'Are you all right?' Vellain said softly, as if afraid of wakening him. 'Has anything happened?'

Vashnar held up his hand. 'Give me a moment,' he said. He closed his eyes and went through all that had just happened.

Everything was quite clear. Wherever he had been, it was no less real than the bedroom he was now lying in. He had a choice now. He could fret and fume and denounce the folly of his senses for so vividly misleading him, or he could embrace without question the mysterious opportunity that had been given to him and listen to the faint call of the voices he could now hear within him.

He opened his eyes and, smiling, beckoned his wife.

Nordath started upright, wide awake. There was a little light in the tent from the remains of the camp fire and he could just see that Thyrn was also sitting up. He needed no light to know that something was wrong; he could hear Thyrn shaking.

'What's the matter?' he said urgently.

'Vashnar,' came the trembling reply after he asked again.

Nordath struggled in the darkness to find the small lantern that Endryk had given them. When he found and struck it, he drew a shocked breath. The mellow light of the lantern etched deep shadows in Thyrn's face, making him look haggard and old. His eyes were wide with fear.

'Vashnar?' Nordath stammered, instinctively reaching out to his nephew, at the same time glancing round the tent half expecting to find that the architect of all their troubles had suddenly manifested himself.

Thyrn grasped the outstretched hand desperately, making Nordath wince. 'Gently,' he pleaded. Thyrn not responding, Nordath wrenched his hand free and turned up the light of the lantern. In the increased brightness, Thyrn's eyes were still wide with fear and Nordath could see that his brow was slick with sweat.

'You're all right, Thyrn,' he said reassuringly. 'You're safe. You're in the camp in the mountains, remember? Rhavvan and Nals are on guard duty.'

Thyrn made no acknowledgement other than to nod his

341

head vaguely. Then he turned to his uncle. Nordath could not respond to the pain he saw reflected there other than to wrap his arms around the young man. They remained thus for some time. Thyrn's trembling gradually lessened, but it was a slithering interruption by Nals, curious about this unexpected night-time activity, which finally prised them gently apart.

'What's happened?' Nordath asked, as soon as he felt that Thyrn had composed himself sufficiently. 'Have you been Joined with Vashnar again? Or was it just a nightmare?'

Thyrn's hands were still shaking and he brought them towards his face. For a moment, Nordath thought that his inquiry had been too soon and that his nephew was going to drop back into the immobilizing terror out of which he had just clambered, but determination vied with fear in Thyrn's face and after a moment he forced his hands down. They massaged his thighs while he spoke.

'A Joining? Yes. No. I don't know! It was certainly no dream, and like nothing I've ever experienced with Vashnar. Though . . .'

'Is everything all right? I saw the light – heard you talking.'

It was Rhavvan, discreetly peering into the tent. He answered his own question with a knowing, 'Oh,' as he looked at Thyrn. 'Something's happened again, has it?' he said, more statement than question and unexpectedly concerned. 'I can soon build the fire up if you want to sit and talk about it. The night's mild.'

Thyrn hesitated. 'I don't know. I . . . I need to think. Clear my thoughts.'

'Whatever you want,' Rhavvan said understandingly. 'I'll build the fire up anyway.'

After he had gone, Thyrn looked about the tent, almost as though he expected to find himself somewhere else. The faint sounds of Rhavvan stirring the fire impinged on the two men in the heightened silence.

'I will go outside, I feel trapped in here,' Thyrn said eventually, his voice steadier. He pulled on his jacket and crawled out of the tent. Nordath followed him.

Rhavvan emerged out of the darkness beyond the firelight. Though he did not speak, his manner reflected both curiosity and anxiety and he gave Nordath an inquiring look. Nordath silently counselled patience. Thyrn gazed around into the night as he had in the tent. He seemed to be reassuring himself about something. Then he sat down by the fire and dropped his head into his hands. Nordath sat down beside him anxiously. Rhavvan stepped towards him and then crouched down to lessen his own intimidating presence. Thyrn's posture, however, was one of resignation rather than despair, as was confirmed by his expression when he looked up again and stared into the fire. Disturbed by Rhavvan's recent coaxing, a smouldering branch suddenly flared up, sending a flurry of sparks cascading up into the darkness, like frantic messengers from a battle catastrophe. Thyrn watched them.

'I wish all this would go away,' he said, to no one in particular. 'All I ever wanted was just to . . .' He stopped and his expression changed. 'Was just to . . .' He turned to Nordath, his face a mixture of surprise and mounting alarm. 'I don't know what I wanted.' He stood up. 'I don't know what I ever wanted. I thought . . . do as you're told – do what my parents want – please them . . . then the money . . . prestige . . . youngest White Master . . . Caddoran to the Senior Warden, but . . .' His voice faded then suddenly he gave a great wordless cry of anger and frustration. 'Now all this! What am I doing here, Uncle? Chased across the country like a wild animal. For what? I've done nothing wrong. I *never* did anything wrong. But here I am, in the middle of nowhere, living in a tent, hunting for food, washing in freezing streams or out of a cup, tending horses. Just because Vashnar—' He stopped abruptly. By now the impromptu gathering had been joined by Hyrald, Adren and

Endryk in various states of alarm and undress. He looked round at them, motionless figures in the flickering firelight. 'Someone tell me I'm not going mad.'

'Mad is the last thing you are.' It was Endryk. 'Troubled, frightened, yes. Like the rest of us. But mad, no.'

'Then why's this happening to me? Why me?' He blasted the question at all of them.

'Why not?' Nordath's reply was as brutal as it was unexpected. Thyrn gaped at him. 'Why did that particular deer have to die the other day? Why are some people born crooked and bent? Why do some get sick and die, scarcely your age? Why does someone get killed by a bolting horse while another standing next to him lives? And good fortune's no different. Why's Endryk – a stranger, a foreigner – here to help us? Beyond a certain point we just have to accept that there's no reason that we can hope to find, just an endless chain of tiny "if onlys", reaching back for ever, each link splitting into its own endless chains, and so on. Once you're at that point, all that matters is not, why? but what you do. Are you going to pick your way down those endless chains or are you going to forge your own links?' Despite the harshness of what he was saying, his voice was full of compassion. 'The difference between young and old usually lies in when and how they realize this and how they cope with it, Thyrn. I learned it slowly, gently, drip by drip. Endryk, I suspect, learned it the hard way – brutally, in battle. Rhavvan, Adren, Hyrald . . .' he shrugged '. . . who knows? Some people never learn it. Never have even the slightest grasp of the worth of their lives. You're learning it right now, like Endryk – brutally. But at least you're not on your own.'

Thyrn was still gaping at him when he finished. He made several attempts at speaking before managing, 'Damn you, Uncle. That's not what I want.'

'It's all I've got to give,' Nordath replied starkly. 'But you knew that, didn't you? It's not the first time you've asked that question. You mightn't be able to answer it, but you've decided what to do about it. You're going forward, aren't you? Why else would you have learned more from Endryk than the rest of us put together?' He did not wait for a reply. 'Just tell us what's upset you so much, then we can all move on. You said it was a kind of Joining with Vashnar.'

Thyrn looked at each of his companions in turn as if some answer to his original plaint might be lingering there, but found nothing.

'Sit down, Thyrn,' Hyrald said. 'You know by now that we're your friends and that we'll help you as far as we're able. But your uncle also loves you, and you can know *beyond any doubt* that anything he does for you is in your best interests.'

Slowly Thyrn sat down. Rhavvan put some more wood on the fire.

Thyrn closed his eyes. 'I understand what you mean, Uncle,' he said, after a long silence. 'But like almost everything else, I simply don't understand any of what's just happened – except that it was awful. And I don't think I can do anything about it. I think I'm the one who's going to fall under the horse's hooves.'

'Fortunately, none of us can know the future,' Nordath said. 'Tell us as well as you can. However it comes, dragging it into the open certainly won't make it any worse.'

Thyrn nodded reluctantly and paused for a moment to collect his thoughts. 'I was very tired. I remember listening to you all talking for a few minutes – I couldn't hear anything, of course, but it was a comforting sound. I was thinking about what I owed you all. How I should help more.' He cleared his throat self-consciously, then smiled. 'And I thought I heard the little old man again. "Light be with you," he said.' Endryk glanced at him sharply but did not speak. 'That was very odd. Not unpleasant, just odd. As if he was there with me and a long way away at the same time. Then, I must have gone to sleep. I don't remember you coming to bed, Uncle.'

'You were fast asleep,' Nordath confirmed.

Thyrn gritted his teeth and took a deep breath.

Chapter 23

'The next thing I remember is Vashnar – his presence all around me. Just as vividly as he was when all this started.' Thyrn looked at his listeners, easier now that he had embarked on his tale proper. 'But I didn't get swept up this time. I centred myself properly. Took control. Watched, waited. I mightn't know what's happening, but this is *my* territory, I thought. I'm master here and whoever intrudes will be subject to my will.' At another time this might have sounded like an empty youthful boast, but Thyrn's manner transformed it into a determined resolution. 'But it wasn't like any of the Joinings I'd had with Vashnar – or like any Joining I've ever had. It was as though I was there by accident – an inadvertent eavesdropper. Something else – *someone* else – was Joining with him. I was both there and not there.'

He stopped and brought up his hands to cup his face tightly. They were shaking again. For a moment it seemed that he was going to slip into the fearful despair he had shown before. He looked at Endryk. 'I'm not sure whether I'm frightened of this because I don't understand what I felt, or because I do.'

'You felt what you felt, Thyrn,' Endryk replied. 'Whatever it was, it's not here now, and there's no danger around this fire.'

'I'm not too sure about that,' Thyrn said softly, looking up at the enclosing mountains, hidden by the night and the glow of the fire. As he continued he seemed to be forcing his words out. 'Vashnar I recognized.'

'Recognized? You *saw* him?' Hyrald exclaimed.

Thyrn frowned and waved the interruption aside. 'I sensed him. Alone, defensive, hesitant. But though he was the brightest thing there . . . the centre, the source, of what was happening, there was something else there as well. Something drawn there by him or perhaps by me – I couldn't tell.' Suddenly his bared teeth were shining in the firelight and sweat was glistening on his forehead. 'But it was awful – an abomination. All those visions I had – burning buildings, fleeing people, fighting and bloodshed – they came from deep within Vashnar, but they were nothing compared to this.' With his foot he nudged a smouldering twig by the fire. 'Less than this is to one of the big Solstice bonfires – far less. It felt like something that had come from, I don't know – a different world almost. A different time – a time older than myths and legends, or beyond them.' He shuddered. 'Such black consuming hatred. Such lust for destruction and . . .' He thought for a moment. 'For power.'

His eyes widened as he spoke, reflecting the camp fire so that they seemed to be ablaze with the inner vision of what he had seen. He looked at Endryk again. 'And I understood it. It was human – a person.' He hesitated. 'Or perhaps many people –I can't tell now. It was like many people become one.' He nodded to himself, unhappy, but satisfied with this conclusion. 'But I felt the lure of it, like when we brought down that deer. But not so that we could eat – just the killing, the pain, the blood – for its own sake – and revelling in it, wild, completely without restraint.' He grimaced. 'I think I'm going to be sick.'

'Not here you're not,' Endryk said, stepping quickly across the fire and dragging him to his feet before the others could move. A few paces into the darkness, Thyrn bent forward and retched. He did not vomit however, and once the spasm had passed, Endryk returned him gently to his place. Adren had used the interval to fetch him a cup of water which he drank noisily.

'I'm sorry about that,' he said. 'It's just . . . I feel so ashamed, to take pleasure in such things.' He shuddered again.

Endryk laid a hand on his shoulder, his expression pained. 'But you don't, do you? Not really. Even the idea just made you sick.'

'But I did. I felt it. It's inside me.'

'It's inside all of us, Thyrn. All you felt was what you *can* do – what your body is capable of. What we're all capable of when need arises.' He turned Thyrn around and looked at him intently. 'But always there's a choice. Nothing compels you. And there are times, which I hope you'll never come to, when those feelings you describe – horrific though they are – give you that final choice: do you wish to live, or do you wish to die? Don't confuse the ability to do something with your moral worth.' He reached down and picked up a branch from the fire. The end was burning vigorously. 'Fire can keep us warm and comfortable, cook our food, dry our sodden clothing.' He pushed it back into the fire. 'And it can burn down houses, fields of precious crops, destroy animals – people.

'It's not the same.'

'It is. It just feels different, that's all. Just because you've learned to make a fire doesn't mean you're going to become a fire-raiser, does it? And just because you've discovered a dark ability in yourself doesn't mean you're suddenly going to run amok slaughtering people for no reason. But maybe,' he leaned closer to Thyrn, 'maybe because you've seen this, you might one day be able to kill someone to save your own life.'

Thyrn stared at him, his face riven with doubt and pain.

'Or someone else's,' Endryk concluded significantly. He released Thyrn and sat back. 'Finish your tale. Can you describe this presence that you felt?'

'No more than I already have,' Thyrn replied, his voice unsteady. 'There were images – sensations – that I've no words for. It was terrifying, and it was vast.' A memory returned to

349

him. 'Like those birds we saw when we were riding along the shore. Individual birds, but so many they were like smoke in the distance. This was the same, but much bigger – as though birds were filling the entire sky, shrieking and screaming. I sensed a malevolent power trying to unleash itself, to wreak destruction on everything. But something was restraining it. Something about Vashnar.' He snapped his fingers. 'It needs him. He's . . . a key. Something that will release them.'

'Them?'

'Them, him, it – all these things. That's not important; it's the extent of it all I can't convey to you.' He looked out beyond the fire. 'I was dwarfed by it far more than I am by these mountains.' He took several long breaths to calm himself.

'Are you sure this wasn't all just a dream?' Adren asked tentatively. 'You had a very peculiar experience yesterday.'

'It was no dream,' Thyrn said categorically and without any resentment at the question. 'It was real, and it was part of everything that's been happening. And it's only by clinging to you here, for support, that I can keep the real horror of it all at bay.' He clenched his hands together painfully. 'It knew I was there,' he said, his voice cracking. His eyes widened in fear again. 'It's me who's in their way. They'll have to destroy me to take Vashnar.' In a desperate flurry, he made to stand up but both Endryk and Nordath restrained him.

'You're safe here,' Endryk said but he had to keep repeating it and he was almost shouting before Thyrn seemed to hear him and became a little calmer. 'Whatever it was you experienced, it has no power out here.'

Adren, who had been watching Thyrn intently, leaned across to him and echoed Endryk's words. 'Whatever it was you experienced, it had no power over you in there, did it?' she said, emphasizing the last two words with a jabbing finger. 'It might have frightened you half to death, but if it knew you were there, and you were in its way, why didn't it do anything?'

Gradually Thyrn's panic began to slip away and a realization dawned.

'You're right,' he said, half to himself, his eyes becoming shrewd and angry. Endryk and Nordath cautiously released him. Endryk shot Adren a grateful look.

No one spoke for a while, then Thyrn said, 'I need to think about this again, quietly. Get it clearer in my mind. I'm sorry I disturbed you all.'

'You've nothing to apologize for,' Endryk said, patting him on the shoulder. 'Go back to bed. It's some time to dawn yet. We can talk again in the morning. Things usually seem less intimidating in the daylight.'

'Don't say a word,' Adren said to Rhavvan when Thyrn had returned to his tent.

'All right, all right, I know,' Rhavvan blustered. 'I like the lad as much as you do – he's grown on me, especially these past few days. But it's difficult, this Joining business. It makes no sense. It was bad enough accepting the idea that he and Vashnar were somehow in contact in his head, but now we've got monsters out of who knows where coming to haunt us.' He waved his hands helplessly. 'How can we be sure he's not just going quietly mad after all?'

'I suppose we can't be,' Hyrald said eventually. 'He's young and he's unusual, and what's happened of late could push anyone over the edge. But if he is mad, it's not like any other kind of madness I've ever seen, for what that's worth. We've all seen him change from being an irritating burden to becoming one of us – someone we could rely on, someone who pulls his weight. Nordath understands more about being a Caddoran than any of us, so I'm quite prepared to accept his word that Thyrn and Vashnar have become tangled together in some way. But this last business, and him wandering off like he did, meeting little old men that none of us saw, hearing him speak in the night . . . it's straining matters

351

for me.' He gave Nordath an apologetic look.

'It's all right,' Nordath said. 'I understand how you feel. I don't know what's happening either. But I do know that whatever it is, Thyrn believes it absolutely. There was no mistaking his fear when he woke up, or when he was talking to us.'

None of them disputed that.

'What do you think, Endryk?' Rhavvan asked, still subdued.

Endryk was staring into the fire. 'My stomach says, yes, it's all true. My head says, I don't know. I told you – I've seen such powers used before by *men*, which were far beyond anything I could begin to explain. And I know that there are old and fearful forces which are ignored or dismissed only at appalling risk – to everyone.' He looked at Nordath. 'As you've already surmised, it's because of that that I'm here. I've been through my own insanity and I'm loath to condemn Thyrn.' He tapped a burning log absently with his boot. 'I think we've no choice but to give him the benefit of the doubt – to accept his tale, and support him as much as we can. One way or another it'll resolve itself.' Suddenly he bared his teeth and his eyes shone, feral and frightening, in the firelight. 'One thing's for sure. If we ignore him, and he's telling the truth, it'll be the last mistake we ever make.'

No one spoke, but all eyes were on him. Then, the fearful mask was gone and he stood up, himself again. 'Anyway, it's my duty spell now, isn't it?' He slapped Rhavvan on the back heartily. 'Don't look so glum, Rhavvan. Whether in the end we're going to face your Vashnar and his thugs, or dragons and wild beasties, we've still got tomorrow to get through – food, walking, training.'

The remainder of the night passed off without incident. Rather to his surprise, Nordath found that Thyrn was already asleep when he returned to his tent. He was less fortunate himself and woke the next morning bemoaning the fact that he had 'only just got off'.

The preliminaries of the day were completed in comparative silence, albeit more strained than usual, and they were sitting eating before Thyrn spoke.

'I'm sorry about last night, but I was very frightened. Thank you all for helping me.' This brought a variety of awkward and dismissive mutterings which ended with Rhavvan asking him how he felt now.

'Still frightened,' he replied, causing a momentary pause in the meal. 'But I've been going over what happened. Thinking about it.' He cleared his throat nervously. 'I'm assuming that I'm not going mad – that something in my Caddoran nature hasn't gone askew and is leading me astray, as it were. But if that's so, then I have to say that something far worse is happening than just the Death Cry being proclaimed against us, or whatever it is that Vashnar's up to with his Tervaidin Wardens.'

His voice was compellingly calm and no one was eating now. He looked up at the surrounding peaks, forbidding and enclosing against an overcast sky. 'Somewhere, not far from here, I think – there's a place that's . . . significant . . . in this business. I think I was being drawn to it yesterday. Maybe if the old man hadn't stopped me, I'd . . .' His expression became preoccupied and he paused. 'I told you I could feel part of Vashnar with me all the time.' He looked at Rhavvan. 'I know that's difficult for you to understand, but it's so, nevertheless.' He turned to the others. 'Now there's something else. A call. A sign. Voices. Something to draw Vashnar here.'

'What do you mean?' Hyrald asked.

Thyrn shrugged. 'Just that. I can feel it – hear it, if you like. Whatever it was that reached out to Vashnar last night needs him to be closer – physically closer. The call that it left is for him to follow. And he will – even I can feel its compulsion. And it will bring him here.'

'Here? Right here?' Hyrald's finger pointed directly downwards.

Thyrn shook his head. 'No. Just into these mountains – but somewhere not too far away. As I said, I think perhaps I was being drawn to it myself yesterday.' He caught Rhavvan's eye. 'Don't you think I know how crazy all this sounds?' he protested angrily before Rhavvan could speak. 'Don't you think I'd rather we just broke camp and plodded on towards Arvenshelm in the hope that sooner or later I – we – would get a fair hearing in a Warden's Court, or something; that everything would be seen to be a regrettable misunderstanding; that we'd all be allowed back to our old lives as though nothing had happened?' Rhavvan made to speak, but Thyrn ploughed on. 'Maybe I'm wrong. Maybe I am going insane. I don't know. How could I tell? I don't feel insane. And what I'm sensing, for all it seems to be beyond reason, feels as real as this plate.'

Rhavvan managed to interrupt him as he paused for breath. He echoed the conclusion that Endryk had offered the previous night. 'You're right, it does sound crazy. And more than once I've thought you might be crazy yourself. But this whole business has been crazy from the start. And no matter what we all think of one another we've no alternative but to stick to Endryk's advice and work as a team if we're going to stand any chance of getting out of this. If it's any help, you might be having crazy thoughts, but you neither look nor sound mad and, like Endryk told you last night, none of us think you are. The least any of us will give you is the benefit of the doubt – innocent until proved guilty, if you like. There's no denying you were a pain in the beginning, but you're one of us now.' His large hands reached and engulfed Thyrn's.

Adren's eyebrows rose and she seemed to be weighing a tart response to this bluff admission, though in the end she remained silent. Endryk spoke as Thyrn eventually extricated himself from Rhavvan's grip.

'You were going to tell us something else about this call to Vashnar that you heard.'

'Am hearing,' Thyrn corrected. He hesitated. 'Something inside tells me that I should follow this call myself – move towards what seems to be the heart of all this.'

Endryk stared at him uncertainly, then, 'That's your judgement, Thyrn. I couldn't begin to advise you. But we've no route planned and if this call takes us south or west, I can't see why we shouldn't go wherever you want.' He looked round at the others, seeking their consent. No one disagreed, though there was concern in all their faces. He voiced it. 'But don't forget we're as bound up in this as you are. You *are* one of us now. Don't shut us out. Don't wander off on your own again. And if anything else strange happens to you, don't nurse it to yourself – spit it out straight away.'

'I will,' Thyrn agreed.

A little later they were trudging towards the rocky head of the valley. Thyrn had wanted to clamber up on the ridge again but Endryk had been unequivocal about not dividing the group. 'We stay together and we go where the horses can go,' he insisted. 'Not every valley's going to be as bleak as this, I hope, but generally, hunting around here's not going to be good and, apart from the horses carrying our equipment, if the worst comes to the worst, we can eat them.'

This brought an indignant denial from Adren, which Endryk brushed aside with a curt, 'You will when you're hungry.'

Reaching the head of the valley they found themselves overlooking another, wider and less intimidating than the one they had just travelled. Its floor and lower slopes were verdant and lightly wooded, and in the distance they could just make out the glint of a lake.

'Quite a contrast,' Hyrald said, glancing back.

Endryk nodded then looked at Thyrn. 'Which way do you want to go?' he asked.

After a moment, as if it were being lifted by some external force, Thyrn's right arm slowly rose. 'Along this side,' he said.

'South-west,' Endryk confirmed, looking at the pale disc of the sun trying to make its way through the clouds.

Then Thyrn's arm stiffened. 'There,' he said. He was pointing to a distant peak rising solitary above its neighbours. 'Yes, there, definitely.'

'We're not going to reach that today,' Endryk said. 'If tomorrow.' He frowned.

'What's the matter?' Rhavvan asked.

'Oh, nothing,' Endryk replied with a shrug. 'It's just a sour-looking thing. Grey, dead. Quite different to all the other peaks around here. It reminds me of something but I can't think what.'

They set off at a leisurely pace. At Endryk's suggestion they moved down for a while on to the lusher valley floor where they were able to replenish their supplies. Apart from a great many grasses and plant leaves and roots, they also brought down several plump birds, Thyrn actually killing one with his sling, albeit not the one he was aiming at. The others confined themselves to their bows, the Wardens in particular vying strongly with one another for the position of best archer, a competition that Endryk emphatically refused to adjudicate on except in so far as their clamour scattered their prey.

The strange events of the previous day behind them and their immediate destination agreed upon, their mood was good, though, just as the watery sky occasionally darkened and threatened rain, the underlying grimness of their position was never far away from their thoughts.

'What if we run into more valleys that are like the last one?' Adren asked edgily. 'No vegetation, no animals – just rocks.'

Endryk was matter-of-fact. 'When we're in places like this, we gather what we can, store it as well as we can, and then we live on it for as long as we can. If we come on hard times, we ration ourselves, then we go short, then we go hungry. But throughout, we keep putting one foot in front of the other.

And we don't burden the present with an unknowable future.'

'I was only thinking ahead,' Adren protested indignantly.

'No, you weren't. You were beginning to mither, as my mother used to say.'

'Mither?'

'Fret, fuss, fume, bite your nails, for nothing.' This caused Hyrald and Rhavvan some amusement but Adren's eyes narrowed dangerously.

'If you're going to think ahead, then plan properly,' Endryk continued. 'Don't forget, this range isn't that wide, and a fit, determined person can last a long time without any food at all.' He turned, and seeing her expression, gave her a provocative look. 'And, of course, we've always got . . .' He patted his horse.

'Stop that!'

It was a command and a menacing finger that had deterred more than one Arvenshelm miscreant from continuing with his misdeeds. Catching the full force of it, Endryk laughed and held up his hands in insincere surrender.

When they stopped to eat, however, Thyrn was unusually sombre. After a few mouthfuls of his meal, he stood up and with an, 'Excuse me,' he took a sword from one of the horses, unsheathed it and began performing a basic cutting exercise that, following Endryk's teaching, Adren had shown him.

The others watched him in silence for some time, their anxiety growing in proportion to his intensity. Eventually, in response to a silent appeal from Nordath, Endryk went over to him. Thyrn turned to face him, the sword in a guard position.

'What's wrong?' Endryk asked.

Thyrn frowned, then said, 'My distance. If I want to cut you, I'm too close. If I want to lunge, I'm a little too far away.'

Amusement broke through Endryk's concerned expression, and, chuckling, he shook his head. 'That's not what I meant, but you're quite right – well observed.' He took a pace back

357

and said, 'Cut!' bouncing his hand off the centre of his forehead to indicate the target.

Thyrn craned forward a little, as if not understanding the instruction. Endryk repeated it. 'Cut, now. Quickly.'

'But—'

'Do it! Now!' Endryk clapped his hands loudly and stamped his foot with a movement that made him seem to be advancing. Thyrn's sword shot up and, his face screwed into an apologetic and fearful rictus, he stepped forward and swung the sword down alarmingly towards Endryk's head.

Without any apparent haste, Endryk stepped quietly to one side of the descending blade, looped an arm around Thyrn's shoulder and placed his other hand on the now lowered sword hilt. As Thyrn made to snatch the sword back, Endryk made a slight movement which arched Thyrn backwards and slipped the sword from his hand. The whole movement was so seemingly casual that it drew spontaneous approval from the bemused watchers.

With the same ease that he had disturbed Thyrn's balance, Endryk restored it and returned the sword to him.

'Not bad,' he said, leading him back towards the others. He looked at him seriously. 'I'll teach you what you need to know from now. But remember what we agreed. Don't keep anything to yourself. What's the matter? Why this sudden need to put sword practice before food?' He handed Thyrn his plate and motioned him to sit.

'I don't know,' Thyrn said, picking at his food. 'It's very strange. I hadn't really noticed it until we sat down but there's something about this call I can feel that is making me think that I'm walking towards a fight of some kind.' He looked at Endryk. 'Where would I get a feeling like that from? I've never been in a fight in my life.'

'I wouldn't hazard a guess,' Endryk replied. 'But there's a high risk that this entire venture will come to blows before it's finished, you know that. That's why we've been preparing ourselves.'

Thyrn rejected this suggestion unequivocally. 'No. That, I understood. This is different. It's as though a part of me I never knew about has suddenly appeared. Something that's just said, "No – no further", and has planted its feet in the ground in defiance. It's there whenever I think about last night. And when I sense this call inside me.'

Endryk looked to Nordath for guidance but received none. Thyrn abruptly seized his arm.

'Teach me how to fight,' he said desperately. 'Teach me what I need to know to be a warrior like you. Please.'

Endryk made a half-hearted effort to free his arm but to no avail. For the first time since they had met him, he seemed to be violently disturbed.

'I can't,' he said, finally freeing himself. 'Not just like that, in a few days. It takes years. Besides, I'm no warrior. I'd have probably been a saddler like my father if . . .' He faltered again. 'I'm just someone who's been taught how to fight should he need to. We all were. It was the way of my people – the tradition. We were taught fighting skills and many other things. Not to fight – we had no enemies, as we thought – but to be self-sufficient, independent, self-disciplined, yet still part of an ordered and peaceful society.'

'Odd way to go about things,' Adren remarked, almost sneering. 'Teaching people to fight to keep order on the streets.'

'You think so?' Endryk's manner was challenging. 'Well, until our trouble came, there was never rioting on the streets. No need for the Cry, still less the Death Cry. No half-witted government oblivious to those who trust it with their authority, and no need for Wardens to maintain order by a mixture of force and corruption.'

Adren went pale and anger drew her face tight in response to this unexpected passion. She was about to retort when

Hyrald laid a restraining hand on her arm. Endryk pressed on. He slapped a hand on his chest.

'The fact is that we're dangerous and wildly erratic creatures. All of us. More than any other animal you'll ever meet. And only if you find the violence within yourself and accept it will you stand any chance of controlling it. Deny it, ignore it, and one day, if circumstances let it loose, it'll control you instead of you it, and you'll be lost. Don't tell me you haven't seen that in others, or felt it in yourself, Warden.'

Hyrald's restraining hand tightened. 'We understand, Endryk,' he said quietly but earnestly. 'More so than ever, these past weeks. Just go gently.'

Endryk held his gaze for a moment, then his face softened and a look of regret passed over it. 'I'm sorry,' he said. 'It's just – I don't know. Perhaps I'm more frightened about what's happening than I'm prepared to admit.' He took Adren's hand briefly. She glowered at him. Then, rather self-consciously, he turned back to Thyrn. 'I apologize to you, too. It was a fair request. I don't know how I can help, but let's talk about it, if you still want to.'

'It's not a matter of wanting,' Thyrn said, apparently unaffected by what had just passed. 'It's a need.' He looked at the others then glanced at the distant peak he had designated as their destination. 'Can we move on?'

His request was accepted with some relief and a small flurry of activity helped to ease the tension pervading the group. The horses well rested, they decided to ride for a while.

'Tell me what you want, what you need, as clearly as you can,' Endryk said to Thyrn, when they were under way.

Thyrn's face darkened. 'I don't really know. All the things you've shown me have been great fun. I've enjoyed it, like a game – though I see the value of it,' he added hastily. 'And even though I can't envisage being able to stab someone, or shoot an arrow through them, I still feel easier in myself knowing it's an option I have. But this is different. This thing that I felt drawing Vashnar last night, seems to have woken something inside me. Thinking about fighting Vashnar, man to man, makes me tremble.' He gave Endryk a significant look. 'I know – you'd say to avoid a fight whenever possible. But, as I said before, this feeling inside me is reaching out to oppose this thing. It's telling me that running away *isn't* an option for me. I don't understand what it is or what it wants me to do.'

'And I'm no wiser than I was a few moments ago,' Endryk replied. 'Understanding other people is hard enough at the best of times. As for understanding the peculiar insights of a Caddoran – where would I start?'

Thyrn nodded and they rode on in silence.

'Are you sure this isn't just imagination – or a misinterpretation of what you're experiencing?' Endryk asked after a while.

'As sure as I can be.' Thyrn looked distressed. 'I've been thinking hard about what's happened the last two days. What occurred between me and Vashnar was strange enough, but perhaps understandable in some way. Maybe my extreme sensitivity and Vashnar's part Caddoran nature came together – brought our minds too close.' He pointed towards the distant mountain. 'But this is different. I can't help feeling that it was our coming together that woke this thing. Stirred something into life that was long dead.' He blew out a noisy breath. 'I've no words to tell you how awful it is, or how Vashnar's darker nature is being drawn to it.'

Endryk looked at him sharply. 'You can't take responsibility for the actions of another. Whatever Vashnar does is his to account for.'

Thyrn stopped him. 'But I'm responsible for the circumstances that led him to these actions.'

'No, no, no. Absolutely not.' Endryk looked around for help. 'Tell him, Nordath, Hyrald. He can't—'

361

But Thyrn addressed them all, cutting across him. 'You're all older and cleverer than me at this kind of thing. Maybe I am responsible, maybe I'm not. But the fact is, I *feel* responsible and I've learned enough from you since all this started to know that I can't walk away from it; I have to face it. I'm the only one who can.' He looked round at them all. 'What I want is your help – your advice.' He turned to Endryk. 'You've faced things that nearly drove you mad. Tell me what it's like. Tell me what I have to do to win.'

Chapter 24

Thyrn's plea was greeted by a difficult silence. The effect on Endryk was almost palpable and Nordath and the Wardens watched him uncomfortably, torn between the raw pain in Thyrn's voice and the brutality of what he was asking.

Eventually, Endryk reined his horse to a halt. For a moment he looked as if he were about to turn around and ride away.

'I don't know what to tell you,' he said. 'I can teach you how to survive out here, how to fight, perhaps how to be like you think I am, if that's what you want. But that won't make you either a survivor or a fighter. That comes from somewhere else in the end. I can't take you back to what I went through, even if I wanted to – which I don't.'

'I need your help,' Thyrn said simply.

'I don't think I've any more to offer than I already have,' Endryk replied.

Reluctantly, Hyrald intervened. 'You're the only person who has.'

Endryk straightened up and looked along the valley. The others followed his gaze. As they did so, a solitary shaft of sunlight made its way through the clouds to fall on the lake. It gave it a brilliance and vividness that made all else around them seem unreal.

'If you're asking yourself why you came with us, I think this might be one of your answers,' Adren said, quietly bringing her horse alongside him.

The clouds moved to extinguish the shaft of light, turning the sun back into a pallid disc and restoring the valley.

Endryk looked at her enigmatically, then gave a prosaic sniff and clicked his horse forward. He made a final faint attempt to avoid the burden that Thyrn was asking him to carry.

'I was surrounded by trusted friends . . .'

'So am I.'

'I had skills born out of years of training . . .'

'So have I – where I must fight.'

Endryk yielded. He gave Thyrn a look which Hyrald recognized. It was that of a Commander about to lie to an eager novice who has just volunteered for a dangerous task – a task he might well succeed in if unclouded by the greater wisdom of his superior. The look was full of confidence and trust, immediately behind which lay agonizing doubts and prayers to whatever forces its giver believed shaped the lives of men. As for the lies, they were necessary if those very doubts were not going to infect their recipient and bring about the doom they feared.

'I can't make you into a weapons master overnight. The essence of almost everything you need to know in that regard, I've already shown you. What you know, you know better than you think and it will work for you when you need it.' He began to speak more confidently. 'I've told you before, not to be afraid of being afraid. It's your greatest protection – the inner knowledge of your deepest self and that of generations long gone. When I think back to fighting in the line, much of it is vague, with only occasional, terrible images left now. But though the details have gone from me, I do remember that everything was vivid and simple.' He became pensive. 'There was only the moment and its single solitary task – infinitely clear and focused, each fraction of time the totality of everything I'd ever been. Yet too, there was a deep awareness of everything else that was happening around me.'

Endryk gave a fatalistic shrug. 'I did what I did because I was there . . . and because I could. True, we'd sought the battle, but we hadn't sought the war, and now there was no choice. No acceptable choice. To yield would mean not only my death, but would bring others down with me. An endless wave of crumbling destruction would ripple out from me, spreading through my immediate companions and thence across the battlefield and far beyond – right down into the heart of my homeland and everything I loved and valued.'

He shook his head reflectively and drew the others into his conversation. 'And if that had happened, you'd all be far wiser about the lands to the north of here than you are now, believe me. Far wiser. And your present problems would be as nothing.' He fell silent. Then he turned back to Thyrn. 'It was as though, like you, something had awakened in me. All of us have resources we can't begin to imagine – you touched on part of that last night. Be grateful for it. Be glad it's there. And know that it'll come to your aid when you need it.'

He was silent for a while, his eyes fixed on the distant peak. 'If this enemy you're set on facing is a Caddoran thing, I can't begin to tell you how to deal with it. Besides, you don't need my help. But I do know that winning and losing will be for the most part in your mind. It will hinge on how much you value yourself.' He leaned over and gripped Thyrn's arm powerfully. 'And you *must* value yourself! Value yourself as we value you. I consider myself better for having met you. Maybe, like me and my former comrades you'll have to fight just because of where you find yourself. I can't imagine you'll have sought a conflict or done anything to warrant an attack against you, but if such a thing happens, remember that, above all, you have the right to be, and no mercy is due to anyone who'd deny you that. *No mercy.* Not until they offer you no further threat. Do you understand what I'm telling you?'

'I think so,' Thyrn said. He kept his eyes on Endryk's face, searching. 'But what if circumstances are such that I do start the conflict?'

Endryk released him and met his gaze clearly. 'If that is necessary, then it's necessary. And nothing I've just said is changed. But don't burden yourself with such a prospect. I know enough about you to believe you'll do no foolish thing, still less an evil one. I've no doubts about that whatsoever. Whatever you do it will only be to prevent a greater harm, Thyrn. You can trust your judgement.' He turned away. 'That's all the help I can give you.'

Vellain was nibbling at her thumbnail. Not actually biting it, just clattering her teeth off the edge of it. It was something she had not done since she was a child but she caught herself doing it several times as the coach and its escort clattered south from Degelvak. Finding herself victim of this childhood habit added a frisson of vicious anger to the deep concern which was racking her and she smacked her clenched fist against the coach's lavish upholstery.

Vashnar had been ablaze with frantic, driving energy when he awoke.

'I've been blind, Vellain,' he told her afterwards. 'Blind. All these years. Confining my ambitions. Restricting myself. Hedging myself in.'

It had taken her some time to quieten him down sufficiently to get him to divulge the source of this revelation. It had come as a shock.

'Was it a dream?' she had suggested hesitantly, despite anticipating his well-known response.

'I don't dream. Never have.'

He had faced her. 'Trust me. As you always have. What happened was just as real as my encounters with Thyrn. More so, perhaps.'

'I do, I do,' she forced herself to say enthusiastically. 'But it's such a strange tale. A hooded figure – a grey hall – voices – different worlds.'

'I felt the power, Vellain! Just as I felt it in Nesdiryn when I met Hagen. Only much more so. It was tangible this time; it struck me – held me.' He brought his ring close to his face. 'Hagen gave me this, do you remember? He looked at me – through me – I've never met anyone like him. He said I was one of them. Now I understand what he meant. And what a true gift this thing is.'

Before she could question him, he was pacing the bedroom. His moving bulk and its attendant, storming shadows ploughed through the soft lamplight, filling the room, like a manifestation of the very power he was talking about.

'Destiny, Vellain. That's what it is. It's not something I'd have given a moment's credence to before, but I can see it now. Why me? I've asked. Why should Thyrn reach into me, to disturb all our carefully laid plans with his grotesque talent? But just as people are drawn to a crowd, just as money is drawn to money as Darransen's always saying, just as rivers are drawn to the sea, so the same law works at many different levels. The reason's unknowable, but the reality's beyond debate; it just needs to be seen and seized. I couldn't have avoided this if I'd wished to. Destiny has moved these things to me inexorably – Hagen, the ring, Thyrn, Hyrald and the others, Aghrid's failure – all conjoined to bring me to this awakening. This revelation of the power that lies within the borders of Arvenstaat and is there for my taking so that these selfsame borders can be swept aside.'

Her own mood swinging between tearful doubt and breath-catching exhilaration at her husband's passion, Vellain had not been able to speak. Vashnar stopped pacing.

'It's there. Faint and distant, but as clear as someone talking to me.' He sat on the bed beside her, his great arm encircling her. 'No, I'm not going mad. I'm just seeing a pattern in events that I can't explain to you. But it's inside me.' He placed his hand on his chest. 'I must follow the call that they've left me. I must find this place. It's in the mountains.' He stood up and began pacing again. 'Thyrn will be drawn there, too. They told me this, but I can feel it anyway. Just as part of him has been lingering within me, so I can feel it being drawn by the same lure. And when he arrives, I'll be waiting, and . . .' He drew his finger across his throat.

Then he had charged into a flurry of planning and organizing. It had taken Vellain's every effort to prevent him from rousing their host immediately and announcing his new intentions then and there, in the middle of the night.

She had prevailed, in the end pinioning him with a fervent embrace. 'You might be bursting with energy, but everyone else in this place – including most of the Tervaidin – is either exhausted or drunk or both. They'll certainly not be fit for anything. If all this has been such a time coming, it'll be there in the morning, won't it? And there'll be more if you've rested for a while – you know that. You know your best plans come to you silently when you're asleep.' She tightened the embrace and lowered her voice. 'Besides, if you're dashing off into the mountains and dispatching me to attend to affairs at home, it'll be some time before we're . . . together again, won't it?'

Neither of them had slept well, though, and their parting had been clumsy and awkward, something that, like the nail biting, added anger to her doubts. For doubts she had had in the colder light of morning and the mundane routines of waking and breakfasting. After they had eaten, Vashnar had curtly dismissed all the servants and, with only marginal politeness, three other guests. 'The moment has come,' he told his startled host. 'Prepare your men. They must be ready to act as soon as you receive my final command, which will be within a few days.'

The man's knees had seemed to be troubling him as he

stood up, pushing his chair back noisily, but Vashnar's firm hand on his shoulder had steadied him. 'You know what to do. I have complete faith in you.'

The man had saluted and almost shouted, 'To the New Order.'

Vellain did not share all Vashnar's faith in these provincial followers and this performance only served to heighten her concern. It was her doubts about them that had marred their parting. They had stopped at a crossroads some way outside Degelvak.

'You're absolutely certain of all this?' she had whispered to him as he was about to step out of the coach.

'Yes, of course,' Vashnar replied, tapping his foot anxiously. 'I can see now that everything we've done has just been a preparation for greater things. This *is* the moment. We mustn't delay. If we miss it, it may be gone for ever.'

She had not been able to keep her doubts from her face. 'But some of your supporters,' she gesticulated vaguely back towards Degelvak, 'leave a lot to be desired.'

Vashnar's foot-tapping moved to his hand, resting on the handle of the coach door. 'I have their measure – all of them. They're trusted and capable. Don't speak like this is front of anyone else.'

'You know I—'

But he was through the door before she could finish her protest, and their parting consisted of a cursory nod on Vashnar's part followed by a sharp order to the coachman to move on quickly. Vellain had to steady herself as the coach jolted forward, but she kept her eyes on her husband as he strode away, signalling to Aghrid for his horse. He did not look back. This small neglect cut through her and a tangle of anger rose up inside her briefly. In its wake came a dark, visceral fear. She quelled both to some degree with excuses involving his preoccupation with urgent needs – having to plan quickly –

move quickly. But the fear in particular would not wholly leave her. There was also an odd, even incongruous, sense of disappointment. Such a parting should have been more heroic.

She looked at the sealed orders which Vashnar had prepared and which he had told her to deliver on her journey back to Arvenshelm. He was so confident that he could deal with Thyrn, acquire this strange power that had been offered him, and be back in Arvenshelm in time to take the reins that he had told her to gather for him. But though still powered by the force of her husband's sudden resolution, the haste with which events were moving kept her doubts swirling. She chose not to dwell too much on the hooded figure he claimed to have encountered. In that, she would have to trust him absolutely. But if he was late, what then? All could well be lost without his presence to sway any waverers. Yet if she delayed and he arrived ready to sweep to power, that could be even worse.

It took her a long time and more blows to the unoffending upholstery before she calmed sufficiently to think clearly about what was happening and what she must do.

It was a time of risk, that was all. And the coming of such a time had been seen as inevitable from the beginning, even though its precise nature could not be foreseen. And too, Vashnar was more used to risks than she was. His judgement in matters of immediate action could be trusted, she knew. As for discovering that he was a man of destiny, *she* had always known that.

She immersed herself in the details of the tasks he had asked her to perform, resolved now. She had all his authority. There would be no faltering on her part and she would ensure that there would be none by any of his supporters.

As Vellain's coach and escort galloped south, like the skittering pebbles that would unleash an avalanche, Vashnar was leading his Tervaidin west towards the mountains, his every sense attuned to the call that was luring him on.

Chapter 25

Conglomerations of people – towns, cities, countries – are strange. Minute by minute, hour by hour, day by day, thousands live their lives in a continual flurry of endlessly interweaving and varying activities, yet the whole changes little. The ceaseless bustle of ordinary people living ordinary lives somehow conjures into being a dynamic equilibrium which, once established, is seemingly immune to the countless inner changes that comprise it. Within this shifting stability grows the perception that cause and effect are related in extent as well as by their very nature: a small cause yields a small effect, a large cause, a large effect. Yet, like many apparently obvious perceptions, this is flawed. There are times when a body which has indeed demonstrated a small effect to a small cause many times without injury will, for no immediately discernible reason, suddenly respond catastrophically – a hillside crashes down into the valley, a warming coastal current drifts away, nourishing annual rains fall elsewhere, a crop-destroying chill comes prematurely – a society disintegrates.

As in most long-settled communities it was taken for granted by the Arvens that what had been, would always be, and that this truth was in some way independent of their actions as individuals. The Moot, with its rambling statutes and eccentric procedures, could be safely dismissed as a frothy irrelevance, and the Warding could be accepted as a broadly worthwhile institution despite the corruption of the Gilding and the fact

371

that many of its officers routinely administered their own forms of summary justice. But any society that scorns the leaders it chooses and fails to watch those who watch over it, nurses flaws that are deep and dangerous.

For the Arvens, these flaws now began to appear.

The proclaiming of the Death Cry, the appearance of the Tervaidin, and Vashnar's sudden departure from the city, had set in train a gathering hailstorm of stinging, anxious rumours. Once, these might have faded, melted into nothingness by the touch of common sense and goodwill, but now, tap tap tapping like a fore-echo of Vashnar's intended hammer-blow, they added the final splitting shock to the long over-strained sub-strata that sustained Arvens' society. As ever, the first to yield was the subtle fettering that restrains the darker natures of individuals and which allows them to live together in comparative peace. Wardens began to report an unexpected increase in violent assaults. Then they began to fret over them.

Bewildered. 'It makes no sense.'

Blind. 'One of those things. It'll pass.'

Shrewd. 'It's been getting worse for years, now it's getting out of hand.'

Inept. 'The Moot should give us more power.'

Plaintive. 'Vashnar should be here, not gadding off on a holiday.'

The patent inadequacy of their own trite debate added to the growing sense of unease.

And once Vellain had passed on Vashnar's order to begin his move against the Moot, unusual activities were noted and no amount of security could stop further rumours scudding wildly over the unrest, agitating it further.

Groups of people began to gather uncertainly.

By some strange osmosis, the general unease had even managed to spread into the Moot.

There was uproar. Striker Bowlott was furious, stamping his feet and pummelling the cushions which padded the arms of Marab's Throne. In his official position, standing slightly to one side and behind the Throne, Krim was holding himself more stiffly than ever in an attempt to stop the twitch that was struggling to take command of his left cheek. He was failing and his facial contortions were attracting the attention of some of the nearby Senators, who used the general din to cover their own considerable amusement. That Krim was aware of this unwanted ridicule did little to ease his predicament, but his dominant concern was for his charges. The blanching touch of the sun was wreaking relentless havoc in the Repository. Now they were being trampled underfoot and clawed at by Bowlott. Krim found his gaze being drawn inexorably towards the Blue Cushion underneath the Throne.

The cause of the uproar and Bowlott's frenzy was a new Senator – not a Moot General member, but an Outer Moot Senator no less. His name was Draferth and, unusually for the Outer Moot, he was a staunch and raucous member of the Strivers Faction. But then everything about Draferth was unusual, Bowlott had reflected more than once since he had arrived to take up his seat. Not the least of Bowlott's complaints about him – and Welt's and Bryk's, his ostensible leader – was that he seemed to be completely oblivious to the nuances of the Moot's intricate proceedings. For one thing, he possessed an almost overwhelming obsession with the views of his electors – a trait which was well-known to be highly undesirable in a Senator. How could a man preserve any sense of objectivity in handling matters of social consequence if he kept listening to the people who would be affected by it?

The very manner of his gaining his position was a measure of his unsuitability. His predecessor had vacated his seat in circumstances which had united the Moot in their efforts to garnish his name with honour and praise. The unexpected and noisy arrival of his wife at a house of interesting repute which he was visiting 'on Moot business', had coincided with his attempt to test an emergency exit from a first-floor window. Unfortunately, in the confusion between fulfilling his Moot duties and greeting his dutiful and concerned spouse, he stepped through the wrong window and fell into a manure cart. Subsequently there was some debate as to whether his death was due to the fall or his lying face downward in the ordure for a prolonged period, but either way there was enough uncertainty, in the local Wardens' view, to exonerate the short-sighted farmhand who eventually unloaded him with the aid of a pitchfork.

The seat had been held by the Keepers for as long as anyone could be bothered to remember and Draferth had been offered the position as the Strivers' representative in the Little Acclamation that followed, solely in the hope that he would be humiliated by the Keepers' representative – a man of towering patrician dignity whose contemptuous disregard for the views of others would make him an ideal Senator. In this, however, they had underestimated Draferth's wilful nature and, in a quite unprecedented manner, he had actually sought out the favours of his would-be electors. Consequently, attendance at the Little Acclamation had been unusually high, no less than one in fifteen of those eligible making themselves heard, and Draferth had been swept to victory on a tide of indifference.

All bad enough in itself, Bowlott and the Inner Moot members had agreed, but the Moot was a stern and ancient institution. Its elaborate proceedings and rituals were ideally suited to crushing independence and rational thought in newcomers.

And indeed Draferth had suffered some harrowing humiliations within days of arriving at the Moot. So much so that he had eventually retreated into a surly silence. Bowlott had warmed to him a little at this; it was the Moot's protective embrace – all part of the young man's maturing.

Now however, Draferth was on his feet and causing real trouble.

'Down! Down!' Bowlott was screeching, trying to make himself heard above every other Senator shouting the same. In the end, he stood up and raised his staff to strike the floor. In his haste he neglected to step down from his footstool and he staggered as he drove the staff vigorously down towards a floor which was some distance below where he expected it to be. Krim's twitch spread to both cheeks at this reckless treatment of his handiwork.

It was Bowlott's near tumble that brought a silence to the Moot Hall – part of it a shocked hush, part of it smothered laughter.

Bowlott levelled the staff at Draferth. 'Senator, I ordered you Down, did I not?'

Barking tones of agreement came from the Hall generally, and from Welt and Bryk particularly.

'I will not yield, Striker,' Draferth shouted. 'Nor need I. I have the right to be heard.' He touched the red kerchief wrapped untidily around his head.

Bowlott's hands began to emulate Krim's face as they opened and closed about the staff in frustration. It did not help that a few isolated voices were also being raised in agreement with this protestation. Welt and Bryk and their immediate underlings swivelled in their seats in an attempt to search out the guilty parties, but to no avail. Glowering, Bowlott sat down again, unable to prevent himself emitting a petulant snort.

The damned upstart was right! Normally, speakers in the Moot were chosen by Bowlott who, unless he had some scheme of his own afoot, usually worked from a list supplied to him by the faction leaders. Technically, however, anyone wearing Akharim's Kerchief was entitled to talk on any subject for as long as they wished – Krim flinched openly as Bowlott ground his foot into the stool. It was Welt's fault, for sure. It was not possible to set aside this peculiar practice, it was too well defined in the Treaties, but it was a long-established, if unstated agreement that Welt, as the leader of the Keepers, the Moot's dominant faction, would look to the 'safe-keeping' of Akharim's Kerchief – 'for the general well-being and smooth managing of the Moot'.

Now, somehow, Draferth – of all people – had the thing! There was no saying what the day's business was going to degenerate into; Draferth was young enough to stand there for hours and he was capable of saying anything! Still, Bowlott began to muse darkly, when the wretched man had finished his antics, he would ensure that he suffered for it. And for a long time. And that oaf, Welt, too, for letting this happen. The prospect made him feel a little easier. Something useful could probably be salvaged from this if he kept his wits about him. Tentative plans began to form. Firstly he would have to find out exactly what had happened – it was obviously an action 'liable to bring the Moot into disrepute'. Then he would have to decide what to do about it. Once that was done, he could set up an Official Inquiry to produce this decision as an 'independent' conclusion. All quite routine, really. In the meantime he had to get through whatever it was that Draferth was going to rant about. It was not an edifying prospect. He began picking irritably at the cushion under his right hand. As the stubby nails began to snag at his precious stitching, Krim gave up all attempt at restraining his twitching face.

'Continue,' Bowlott snapped churlishly.

'Thank you, Most Worthy Striker,' Draferth said with cold insincerity.

'Get on with it,' several Senators called out at once.

Resting his head on his hand, Bowlott casually covered his mouth to prevent any sign of amusement showing. However the man had won the opportunity to speak without restraint, let him see if anyone would be prepared to listen. And let him find out how difficult it would be even to speak once the Striker eased his stern grip on the proceedings.

'Worthy and most worthy Senators,' Draferth began.

The sound of sheep penetrated the momentary lull that followed. More than a few Senators took considerable pride in the accuracy of the animal noises which they could offer to the Moot's debate, some even seeking private tuition. It provoked the inevitable jeering laughter, but there were also some angry voices raised. Bowlott frowned and his eyes flicked rapidly from side to side in search of the culprits. In the course of this he scowled at Welt and Bryk. What were these two playing at? First the Kerchief fell into the wrong hands, now it seemed that Draferth had actually got allies in the Hall. Bowlott's mouth tightened.

Draferth, obviously unsettled by the opposition he was meeting, but grimly determined to speak, turned towards the offender. 'We'll see who'll be the shorn and who the shearer when this matter is over,' he said, to a chorus of catcalls and further farmyard impressions.

He turned a look of unconcealed scorn on Bowlott.

'Most Worthy Striker, I shall say what I have to say. If the Worthy Senators choose not to listen then the consequences will be on their heads.' His voice was unexpectedly powerful and the Hall fell silent. Bowlott made no acknowledgement and Draferth continued. 'I sought Acclamation to this place because for as long as I can remember, I have revered the principles which its existence enshrines.' He leaned forward. 'And because, for as long as I can remember, it has relentlessly turned its face away from these principles.' An ominous murmuring began, but he ploughed through it. 'So much so that the Moot has become a by-word for folly and irrelevance, and the very word "Senator" is used as an expression of the utmost contempt.' He pointed angrily towards the main entrance. 'Out there, tens of thousands of ordinary people – the people whose taxes and tithes pay our stipends and who trust us with their authority – are looking to us for leadership. Morlider threaten our shores, the loss of trade and commerce with Nesdiryn has destroyed the livelihoods of hundreds of . . .'

His voice disappeared under the mounting clamour. Bowlott watched him impassively, making no attempt to end the din. His voice broke through briefly. 'A dark unease is stalking the highways of our land, we ignore it at . . .' but the words were lost again and, after a moment, he stopped speaking. Slowly the cacophony of shouting and abuse faded away. As it did so, Draferth looked down at the sheaf of papers in his hand. Then he bared his teeth in a snarl of determination. 'Very well, Worthy Senators. I had hoped, against my wiser judgement, I concede, that perhaps once – just once – this gathering of the people's representatives would set aside its childish antics and listen to a measured account of the dangerous events that are unfolding beyond the sheltered folly of this Hall.'

Someone blew a raspberry. Draferth closed his eyes and took a deep breath. 'However, I see all too clearly that this was not to be. So I will go directly to the heart of my intention. I hereby move that Senior Warden Commander Vashnar be indicted for abuse of power, for seeking to instigate the murders of citizens of goodwill in proclaiming the Death Cry, and for instituting the formation of—'

Where before there had been uproar, now there was pandemonium. Virtually every Senator was standing, shouting and waving, demanding the right to speak. Even the hardier ones were waking. Bowlott himself was about to jump to his feet but he remembered his previous misfooting and hesitated. The pause gave him time to note the mood of the gathering. It was beyond anything he could hope to control and it would only serve to undermine his own authority if he stood up now and struck his staff for quiet. He would maintain a dignified silence, though it was not easy. Akharim's Kerchief gave privileges to the wearer, but this was madness. Had the man no semblance of a sense of proportion? He must be raving mad! He looked closely at Draferth. The man seemed almost relieved by what he had done. Bowlott's eyes narrowed. Lacing through the noise he could again hear angry voices shouting that Draferth be allowed to continue. He cursed himself. Draferth was definitely not alone. It *was* a conspiracy, and he'd caught not even a breath of it! His anger redoubled. He'd roast Welt and Bryk for this in due course. How could they have been so inept as to let such a thing come to pass? With an effort he dismissed his future vengeance and turned to what this conspiracy might be in aid of. It defied him. Surely Draferth was not looking for a position in the Inner Moot? And who would back him in such an attempt?

Foundering against Draferth's continuing indifference, the noise was beginning to subside. Picking his moment carefully, and equally carefully stepping off his footstool, Bowlott stood up and struck his staff for silence. It came almost immediately and all eyes were suddenly turned to him, anxious and intrigued to know what he was going to do to this preposterous newcomer. He did not get a chance to speak however, for Draferth seized the silence and continued as though nothing had happened.

'. . . instituting the formation of an illegal organization, namely the Tervaidin, contrary to the practices of peace in this land, and the laws vested by the people in the Moot and the Warding.'

As if spent by its outburst, the Moot could only greet this conclusion with collective shuffling and frantic muffled whispering. Everyone was awake now.

'I am *standing*, Senator,' Bowlott boomed indignantly.

Draferth turned to him and bowed with an unexpected grace. 'I am indebted to your skill in quietening the Hall so that I might be heard, Most Worthy Striker.'

'I am *standing*, Senator,' Bowlott repeated, even more portentously.

Draferth affected enlightenment and bowed again, almost servilely. 'Forgive me, Most Worthy Striker. I apologize wholeheartedly for my indiscretion in speaking while you were unseated. I am still not as familiar as I would like to become with the etiquette of the Moot. I thank you for your patience and forbearance – and your guidance.'

Despite the strongly caustic inflection in Draferth's voice, Bowlott was left with little else to do but return the bow and sit down again. Not speaking when the Striker stood *was* a matter of etiquette, not procedure as defined in the Treatise. Bowlott's sense of conspiracy and intentions of vengeance grew further. Nevertheless, the onus was now with him. Draferth's motion having been voiced could not be withdrawn. Uncharacteristically, he floundered, his search for the correct procedures for dealing with such a matter being grievously disturbed by visions of what he intended to do to Welt and Bryk when this was all done with. As if sensing this pending menace, the two faction leaders were sitting stiffly upright, chins withdrawn and brows furrowed, in the traditional pose of any politician whose only resource is to look sober, dignified and fully in command of events in the presence of a reality which is totally beyond him.

'You have first face evidence to substantiate this accusation?' Bowlott finally managed, wincing inwardly at the sound of the hoarseness in his voice.

'I have, Most Worthy Striker,' Draferth replied, holding out the sheaf of papers and indicating others bound in bundles at his feet. 'These are sworn representations from several reputable citizens concerning the activities of Commander Vashnar.'

Suddenly, relief washed over Bowlott. The Moot, as ever, had righted itself. In provoking Draferth to voice his motion prematurely, it had ensured that he would have to yield the Kerchief. Bowlott relaxed back into Krim's sustaining cushions. He would be able to deal with this very quickly, after all.

'Will you outline these for us, so that your motion can be considered and a vote held?'

'That will not be necessary, Most Worthy Striker,' Draferth said, not without a hint of triumph in his voice. 'There are the names of one hundred and seventy-two electors on this petition of claim, and those of thirteen Most Worthy Outer Senators. Conjoined with my right of speaking this is sufficient for my motion to be accepted without vote and a formal Inquiry to be instituted.'

Bowlott froze. Lumbering out of his vast knowledge of the minutiae of the Treatise came the realization that this was true.

'I have the supporting references for this,' Draferth said, wilfully misconstruing the silence.

'I need no guidance on the Treatise, Senator,' Bowlott croaked viciously. He felt the rows of staring eyes closing in on him like so many draining, parching suns. For a moment he seriously considered feigning collapse to avoid what he knew he must do next. Sadly, however, that would not affect the outcome of Draferth's actions. It would only serve to add strength to those who were conspiring against him.

Draferth cleared his throat apologetically. 'I have ancillary motions for acceptance, Most Worthy Striker,' he said.

Bowlott gave him a curt nod.

'I further move that the Death Cry be rescinded and the Tervaidin disbanded, pending the outcome of a formal Moot Inquiry.'

There was now complete silence in the Hall.

With an effort, Bowlott stood up. 'Under the authority vested in me by the Treatise on the Procedures for the Proper Ordering of the Moot, I declare the motions of the Worthy Senator accepted. Proceedings tomorrow will be confined to determining the constitution of the formal Inquiry which will look into the substantive content of the motions.' He took hold of the hourglass which stood by the Throne and laid it on its side. Then he struck the floor with his staff. It was not easy, for he was leaning on it heavily. Krim's cough barked through the crowd as he moved forward to escort him from the Hall. His eyes flared as they took in the damage wrought to his handiwork as a result of Draferth's eccentric intervention. It was too much – he would have to speak to Bowlott immediately! Two Tervaidin officers, who had been watching from one of the lower balconies, left quickly. Some spectators on the balcony above them left also.

Once Bowlott had gone, pandemonium broke out again as Senators rushed variously to leave the Hall, remonstrate with Draferth, and generally regale anyone nearby with what they had all just witnessed.

Draferth, flushed but hesitantly triumphant, was amongst the last to leave the Hall. As he went through the main door, a Tervaidin officer stepped forward to bar his way. At the same time, two Tervaidin Troopers moved to stand either side of him.

Chapter 26

For a while, as Hyrald and the others moved along the valley, the peak that Thyrn had indicated as his goal disappeared from view behind a ridge. The sun kept breaking through the clouds fitfully, promising a warm and pleasant journey, but constantly failed to fulfil it. Its uncertainty seemed to pervade the group.

Gradually the valley turned and the mountain slowly came into sight again. Even to the Arvens, unfamiliar with mountains, it looked odd. Hyrald spoke the common thought.

'It looks out of place,' he said. 'Almost as though it's just been dropped there, blocking the valley.'

'Or pushed up from underground,' Nordath added.

Endryk just looked at it unhappily.

'What's the matter?' Adren asked him bluntly.

He shrugged. 'I don't know. It still reminds me of something but it won't come to mind.'

'Bad or good?' Adren pressed.

'Not good,' Endryk replied, urging his horse forward.

As they rode on, Endryk gradually dropped back behind Thyrn so that he could watch him.

'Can you still feel this . . . call?' he asked him after a while.

Thyrn nodded. He massaged his stomach nervously. 'Clearer than ever. It's drawing Vashnar here, I'm sure.'

'Perhaps that's no bad thing,' Hyrald said with an air of grim resignation. 'On the whole I think I'd rather face Vashnar out here, now, than in Arvenshelm in two or three months' time or worse.'

Rhavvan was less sanguine. '*If* he's coming, he won't be coming alone, that's for sure,' he said. Endryk signalled that they should dismount and walk.

'This has always been a journey into unknown regions, in every sense of the word,' he said, patting his horse's neck. 'One without a destination. Now, if Thyrn's instincts are telling him true, the destination might be coming to us.' He looked round at his companions. 'I think you'd better decide how you're going to greet your former Commander if you do meet him. And you'd better decide what you're going to do if he's got the likes of Aghrid with him.'

His remarks were greeted with a silence that lasted for some time.

'I suppose you're right,' Hyrald said eventually. 'But where will *you* stand in all this?'

'By you,' Endryk replied without hesitation. 'As listener – or arbitrator, if I can. But I'll fight with you if you have to and fly with you if you need to. The only thing I won't do is surrender.'

'We're already in your debt far more than we can repay.'

'How can friends be in debt? Besides, you've no measure of how much I owe you, starting my life for me again. In any case, I dearly want to know what's been going on here. I'd be loath to leave without some kind of an answer.' He looked at the mountain ahead of them. 'And that place is bothering me.'

'And if Vashnar's coming? If we meet him?' Rhavvan drew them back to Endryk's stark advice.

'I think Endryk just answered that,' Adren said. 'We'll fight if we have to, and fly if we need to, but we'll start by keeping him at arm's length and talking and listening.'

Rhavvan pursed his lips. 'Bow's length, I think,' he said sternly.

'Could you put an arrow into Vashnar?' Endryk's question was stark.

Rhavvan met his gaze. 'If he picks a fight and we can't avoid it, yes.' He was unequivocal. 'Ever since he sent Aghrid and those Tervaidin after us. And I'd ride into Arvenshelm with his body across my horse and take my chance with my own kind.'

Endryk's expression was unreadable. 'And you?' he asked Adren.

Hyrald spoke before she could answer. 'We might not know what's going on, but we're all wiser than we were by years,' he said. 'We grasp the reality of our position. We'll do what we have to, to survive.'

Endryk's expression remained impassive as he studied each of them in turn. 'Yes, I think you would,' he said sadly. 'I apologize. I just didn't want to risk leaving the question unasked.'

As Endryk had foretold, it was not until the next day that they came to the mountain. The impression that it did not belong there grew as they drew nearer. It had the look of something completely lifeless, and while vegetation and trees grew quite a way up the valley sides, the mountain ran right down to the valley floor like a grey scar, quite devoid of any hint of green.

Endryk curled up his nose and looked at Thyrn who pointed straight ahead.

'I think not,' Endryk disagreed, staring up at the looming peak, ominous against the overcast sky. 'Let's go up on to that shoulder and see what's on the other side.' Thyrn raising no objection they began the ascent.

The climb was no steeper or more rugged than any of the others they had encountered, but the horses became peculiarly troublesome, whinnying and pawing the dull rock. Nals, too, was quieter. Tail drooping, he hung back with the group instead of trotting well ahead as he usually did.

When they reached the shoulder, it was to see a valley of jumbled red-grey rocks stretching south ahead of them. It was unlike anything they had seen before. As with the mountain itself, there was no sign of vegetation. Endryk grimaced and let out a soft sigh of recognition.

'There was a place I came across years ago that was like this – the Thlosgaral. A bad place.' He shivered. The response disturbed his listeners.

'What was the matter with it?' Adren asked anxiously.

'It was bleak, desolate, devoid of anything living – anything you and I would consider living. Yet there was an aura about it. I can't explain it properly. People worked in it, mining crystals of some kind, I think, to sell in a city nearby. Men, women, children. Desperate, dirty, aching work. I spent one day and one night there and then took the advice someone had given me: I got out and went round it. If it didn't kill me, bandits might well, they told me. I didn't believe them until I found out that the whole place moved.'

'*Moved?*' Hyrald exclaimed.

'Moved,' Endryk repeated. 'As I said, I didn't believe it, of course. Rocks don't move – at least not on their own. It was obviously some local foolishness just to account for the place being dangerous. I could cope with rocky terrain – hadn't I been born to it? It wasn't as if it was mountainous. But after one day of travelling through it I was a little less confident. The deadness of the place seemed to seep into my bones. And when I woke the following day, my surroundings had changed. Not much, but they were definitely different – I take note of where I am out of habit. And I'd seen some of the people who worked there by then. They were all listless, with dead eyes – as though the place was draining them. It was enough. Instinct set aside any reason and I left – quickly.' He shook himself to dispel the memory, then looked at Thyrn. 'Is this where you want to be?'

Thyrn's mouth twitched as though he were having difficulty

opening it. 'The call's strong,' he said, looking along the valley.

'If this place is dangerous . . .' Hyrald began.

'It is,' Thyrn said, cutting across him. He clutched Endryk's arm, partly for support, partly out of fear.

'It's not as bad as the Thlosgaral,' Endryk said quickly, trying to undo the impression he had given. 'That wasn't an enclosed valley like this. It was a great swathe cut across the land – much bigger – took me several days just to go around the end of it.'

But Thyrn was shaking his head. 'It's a dangerous place,' he said softly.

There was a note in his voice that prevented the others from questioning him. Very gently, Endryk said, 'We don't have to go into it, Thyrn. We can find another way westward. Carry on as we were.'

Thyrn was opening and closing his hands like an uncertain child. Nordath took a step towards him but Thyrn stopped him. 'My judgement,' he said, echoing what Endryk had said when they had agreed to follow the strange call he was hearing.

'And no one will reproach you if you change your mind,' Endryk said.

'No one, but me,' Thyrn replied unhappily. 'This call is to Vashnar. I'm an accidental eavesdropper – possibly. But it's a bad thing, I can tell that. I don't want to follow it – stars above, I don't want to follow it. But something inside's telling me that if I walk away from it, it will follow me, for ever. Terrible things will happen – things that will involve other than me.'

'You're thinking of the images you saw when all this started?' Nordath asked.

Thyrn frowned and shook his head. 'Worse,' he said. 'But nothing as clear as that – just shifting impressions.'

Endryk looked at the others, judging their mood. 'It is *your* decision. None of us can hear what you're hearing. All we can do is be here as your friends.'

Thyrn turned to Hyrald. 'You meant what you said yesterday

– you'd rather meet Vashnar here, now, than later?'

'Yes.'

'And if Aghrid and his men are with him?'

'I'll have even less hesitation in putting an arrow in Aghrid,' Rhavvan intervened.

'One step at a time, Thyrn,' Hyrald said, more circumspectly. 'At least we know what we *might* be running into.'

Thyrn lowered his head, then straightened up, took a deep breath and let it out in noisy gasps.

'Which way?' Endryk pressed gently.

Thyrn pointed south along the valley.

They moved off.

The going proved to be more difficult than it had appeared from the shoulder of the mountain. The disorder of the rocks existed at every level, from pebbles to man-sized boulders to rocks the size of houses and bigger. All were strewn about and tumbled together in a manner so wildly random that Adren's question of Endryk was inevitable.

'What's caused this?'

Endryk, however, could only admit his ignorance. 'I know a lot about how mountains are made,' he said. 'And I've seen some strange shapes and patterns caused just by weathering and glaciers. But this . . .' He shook his head. 'I've no idea. Even the rock itself is like nothing I've ever seen before. And this kind of disorder is almost frenzied, for want of a better word.'

Not that they had much time for debate, as the unremitting unevenness of the terrain meant that every footstep had to be taken with care and the horses needed constant help and coaxing. Occasionally, there were tantalizing hints of pathways which they were able to walk along comfortably for a while, but all of them petered out into the prevailing confusion. And time and time again, violent dips and clefts cut across their way, forcing them to search from side to side to find a way past, though these were not as disconcerting as the deepening and narrowing canyons which they found themselves being drawn into and from which the only escape was retreat.

It was exhausting work and it did not help that the sky was growing darker and the air stiller.

'Storm coming,' Hyrald said as they came to a halt on top of a small, comparatively level outcrop.

'The sooner it breaks, the better,' Adren said, wiping her forehead. 'This place is awful. I feel as if I'm suffocating.' Her face creased with dismay as she looked around. 'And look, we've hardly come any distance.' She pointed back to the mountain, still dominating the skyline.

'It's further than you think,' Endryk said, though not very convincingly.

'Hush!' It was Rhavvan. As he held up his hand for silence they became aware of a low, distant rumble. Slowly it rose in pitch until it became a nerve-jangling screech. Then it stopped abruptly. As if in reply, other sounds reached them, some short, some long and drawn out, some like hurt animals, others like cracking timbers. Then the rock they were standing on shuddered. It was not a great movement but it startled the already disturbed horses. By the time they had been controlled the valley was silent again.

'What in the name of pity was that?' Rhavvan gasped, wide-eyed.

Endryk was no less disturbed. 'It must be the same as the Thlosgaral — it moves.' He looked anxiously at Thyrn. 'I don't want to be here any longer than I have to be,' he said. 'Is this still the way forward?'

Thyrn was leaning against his horse for support.

'Are you all right?' Adren asked, taking his arm.

Thyrn nodded weakly and extended his arm. 'Everything's becoming confused,' he said, lifting his hand to his eyes.

Nordath intervened, urgently easing Adren to one side and

taking hold of Thyrn's face so that he could look into it. 'Even I can feel the confusion, Thyrn, strange images intruding into me. But there's something else, isn't there? Pattern. Shape.' There was no response. He released his nephew's face and shook him. 'Stay in this place, Caddoran. Stay with these mountains and Arvenstaat and your friends. Centre yourself. And stand apart. Speak to us or we can't help you.'

Thyrn's eyes opened wide, though with an effort that made it seem as if he was having to remember how to do it. 'The place is near,' he said. 'Fragmenting. Like reflections in a shattered mirror – but all different. A coming together that shouldn't be. Things meeting that shouldn't meet. Drawn here somehow.'

He looked round at the others and though his gaze was still fearful and wild it was clear and focused. 'Something dreadful's happened here,' he said.

'What? When?' Hyrald asked.

Thyrn's hands brushed the questions aside. He was obviously having difficulty in speaking. 'I don't know. But we're near the very centre of it. I must go on. On into the eye of it all.'

'You don't have to . . .' Endryk began.

But Thyrn was not listening; he turned and began walking away. The others followed him, Endryk hissing out the unneeded command. 'Watch him. See he doesn't harm himself. And don't get separated. Not in this place.'

It was not easy. Once or twice Thyrn let go of his horse and made to walk ahead on his own, but Nordath seized the reins and thrust them back into his hands, forcing him to stop until he had taken a firm grip of them again. Nevertheless Thyrn's urge to move on unhindered grew and they soon became a fraught and straggling line as Nordath found it increasingly difficult to control him. Eventually, having let the reins slip again, Thyrn pulled himself free from Nordath's grip and strode off.

'Get after him!' Endryk shouted to Rhavvan. 'Hold him until we're all together again.'

They had come to a fairly steep slope. Thyrn was stepping slowly but resolutely from rock to rock, Rhavvan closing with him, but it was obviously going to be difficult to walk the horses up it.

Rhavvan caught up with Thyrn just as they reached the crest of the slope. The others were far behind.

Ahead of the two men, the ground fell away into a shallow circular dip. Unlike the rest of the valley, it was smooth and undisturbed.

At the centre of it stood a group of mounted men.

And Vashnar.

Chapter 27

Draferth looked up at the large and intimidating figure of the Tervaidin officer standing in his way. The two flanking him were no smaller. Draferth smiled agreeably and made to step around the officer as though the obstruction had been accidental. The officer moved to bar his way.

Draferth's smile vanished. 'Excuse me, Officer,' he said pleasantly.

'There are crowds gathering outside, Senator,' the officer said. 'And their mood is uncertain. Given the controversial nature of your remarks in the debate, I think it would be wise if you came with us so that we can . . . ensure your safety.'

He held up a hand to prevent a further attempt by Draferth to move past him. Draferth stepped back. 'Let me pass,' he said, his manner colder now. 'You're exceeding your authority.'

The officer's eyes narrowed and his jawline stiffened. 'It is *you* who are exceeding your authority, Senator.' He could not avoid grinding distaste into this last word. 'Arvenstaat is governed jointly by the Moot and the Warding. You cannot—'

It was a mistake. Draferth was no subtle Moot politician but he *was* a politician and a debater. In offering an argument the Tervaidin had abandoned his most effective weapon – his physical presence and the authority accorded to his uniform, in so far as it still resembled that of a Warden. Draferth did not allow him to finish.

'Arvenstaat is governed by the Arvens, Officer,' he snapped

back, using the powerful speaking voice that had carried his Acclamation. 'We hold authority only by virtue of their trust, and it's they who are now calling both of us to task.' Draferth slapped the bag of documents he was carrying. 'And may I remind you that it's their will that your . . . little group . . . is disbanded with immediate effect, pending a full debate in Moot.'

For a moment it looked as though the officer was going to strike him, and while he did not give ground, Draferth flinched. The officer, however, simply nodded thoughtfully. 'Well, that's as may be,' he said with the weary dismissiveness of one used to dealing with troublesome individuals. 'But I've got reason to believe that you're unwell, Senator. That you've perhaps been undertaking more work than you can properly cope with and that this has obviously undermined your reasoning faculties. Why else would you have stolen the Red Kerchief and spoken as you did? That being the case, we've an obligation to—'

Draferth's anger burst out. 'What! Stand aside now, or—'

The officer straightened up and moved closer to him. 'Or what?'

'Or we'll make you stand aside.'

The Tervaidin turned sharply to find himself facing about a dozen of the spectators who had left the Moot Hall at the same time as he had. They blocked the corridor and others were still joining them. Draferth looked openly relieved, but the officer recovered quickly. 'Members of the public aren't allowed here,' he said sternly. 'Now move along – clear the way.'

The man who had spoken was as large as the officer, but when he spoke, his easy tone was markedly at odds with the menace he exuded. 'We're sorry if we're in the wrong place. We're here to see our Senator. We'll go now that we've found him,' he said, bowing conspicuously to Draferth as he finished.

394

The Senator used the change in circumstances to move quickly past the Tervaidin and the new arrivals closed about him protectively. Without further comment they began walking away, the former leaders now acting as a rearguard.

The three Tervaidin, grim-faced, followed them at a discreet distance.

Vashnar froze as the figure of Thyrn appeared in the distance. Relief and a dark anger welled up inside him simultaneously. Soon all obstruction to his ambitions would be gone. As he had followed the luring inner call that the hooded figure had left for him, it had grown stronger and at the same time he had felt his physical perceptions changing. Increasingly he began to feel that he was moving in several different places at once and that everything he could see and hear existed in forms beyond those which were immediately obvious.

At first this strangeness had been only slight, and Vashnar had attributed it to a combination of fatigue and exhilaration as he and his men had galloped across the countryside towards the mountains. As it had grown however, he had overcome an initial concern to find himself experiencing a sense of reassurance, of inevitability; the width and depth of the vision he was gaining were merely facets of the power that had been promised to him.

Now it was vividly shown to be so. For the Thyrn he saw now was not the young and awkward Caddoran that Aghrid and the others saw, but the source of a force which spanned across his every heightened sense and which defied him. Yet it was weak and uncertain, just as Thyrn had always been in front of him. But how could it be otherwise? In this place, nothing could hope to stand against him. For this was where the call had been drawing him. Here he could feel the source of the power that the hooded figure had shown him – the power that was to be his – the power that opened vistas which dwarfed into insignificance his previous petty ambitions.

Here was its heart, its focus. It pervaded everything – emanated from everywhere.

Everywhere except for this scar across it that centred about Thyrn.

But that was easily dealt with.

Slapping the hilt of his sword he turned to his men and shouted, 'Kill him! Kill them all!'

Aghrid snarled in anticipation and, drawing his sword, spurred his horse forward. The others followed him.

Then they were motionless. No part of them moved, nor their horses. Tossing manes, foaming mouths were caught as in a picture.

Vashnar's mouth opened in a silent cry. He released his sword and hesitantly reached out to touch the nearest rider. His hand moved through the seemingly solid figure as though it were not there. He snatched it back in terror, splaying it wide and staring at it wide-eyed as if expecting to find it suddenly missing. Then he gripped it with his other hand and massaged them both desperately. They were solid, warm and real. His ring glittered in the dull light.

And, though his men were still all about him, silent and unmoving, he was at the centre of the myriad clashing realities he had witnessed when he had encountered the hooded figure.

'Why are you not yet here?'

The figure was in front of him.

Vashnar was in no mood to be interrogated. 'I *am* here. You brought me here. What's happening?'

'Then he is here. The one who opposes you. Why have you not destroyed him?'

'Release me and I will,' Vashnar roared.

'I do not bind you,' the figure replied. His arms opened to

encompass the whirling chaos about them. 'Yours is the key. Destroy him now!'

Vashnar was suddenly beside himself with frustration and fury. 'Key! What key? I understand nothing of this.' He leaned forward and peered into the darkness of the deep hood. 'I am trapped here in this . . . half place . . . neither real nor unreal. I can do nothing.' He drew his sword and levelled it at the figure. 'Why have you brought me here? Why do you not use this vaunted power of yours to destroy Thyrn yourself?'

The figure did not move, but Vashnar felt its malevolent stare piercing him. It hissed – a sound like the wind across a bitter icy plain. 'Do not challenge me, Vashnar. Your key and what you are opens these Ways – but it is my will that brings together the power that remains from the unmaking of the Old World – my will and only my will. As it was then, so it is now, I will be for ever. Time does not exist for me. Yet, in time, another will come in your stead. *But you have only now.* Falter and you are lost.'

For an instant Vashnar quailed before the force of the personality he could feel before him. But something was flawed. The faintest hint of desperation? It steadied him.

'Do not challenge me either, shade. Whatever you are and wherever you come from, I feel your greed, your lust to be, your need for me. I ask you again, why do you not destroy Thyrn yourself?'

'Because sight of me is denied to him, Vashnar, while sight of him is not denied to me.'

Vashnar felt the tumult about him fade and the hooded figure slip into the same motionless unreality as his riders. The voice was Thyrn's. It filled Vashnar's mind. Knowing everything, denouncing everything.

'What have you done, you madman? What have you unleashed? Can you not see the horror of it?'

Vashnar had a fleeting vision of his men. They were below

him and charging towards him with painful slowness. At the same time he touched Thyrn's thoughts. All was weakness and doubt. Whatever restraint Thyrn had on the hooded figure, he neither understood nor knew how to use: he was a mere infant loose in the armoury – armed but helpless.

All was solid about him again. Aghrid and his men were charging forward, screaming and shouting. Vashnar drove his spurs into his horse.

Rhavvan swore as Vashnar's barked order reached him and the riders began surging towards him. 'Ye gods, there must be twenty of them.' He turned to flee, only to find Thyrn clinging to his arm, almost collapsing.

'Stand, Rhavvan!' the youth implored him. 'In the name of pity, stand with me. I've seen his mind – seen what he's going to do. There's a power – an evil – in this place which no one will be able to oppose if it possesses him.' He shook Rhavvan violently. 'It doesn't matter what happens to me. It doesn't matter what happens to any of us, but you must destroy him, for everyone's sake.'

Rhavvan looked at him, then at the advancing riders, then, with a cry of alarm he shook himself free and set off running down the slope they had just climbed.

Thyrn slithered to the ground. 'No!' he shouted frantically after him. But to no avail. Rhavvan kept on running. Thyrn's voice cracked into a whimper.

The image returned to him of that final brief contact with Vashnar. That searing touch of the appalling power that might become his, and the will behind it, gorged with all that was savage and unrestrained in the human spirit. He felt it arcing back to the destruction of another world, another time, a destruction that had trapped it here, ravening, but bound.

Every part of him cried out in denial. He did not know how he had spoken to Vashnar, or from whence his words came. Still less did he know what touch inside him had released

Vashnar back into this world. But it had had to be. Touched by his guiding spirit, Vashnar was protected. He could only be dealt with here, now.

On all fours now, tears of desperation clouded Thyrn's vision. He had become a solitary, fragile pivot in events far beyond his understanding.

Always there are choices, came the thought. But all he could choose now was the manner of his dying. Flight would not protect him, and it would yield the field to an enemy more terrible than any he could possibly have imagined.

His towering friend had deserted him, but *he* must stand.

His hand tightened blindly about a stone and he stood up unsteadily and turned to face the advancing riders. As he slipped the stone into his sling he found himself almost overcome by a feeling of forgiveness for Rhavvan's abandoning him. It mingled with a surging gratitude for everything that had happened to him during the past weeks. He wiped his sleeve across his eyes and tried to focus on his attackers. He was shaking uncontrollably but a residue of Endryk's teaching flickered sufficiently to sustain him. He knew that he must use the racking desire of his body to flee to save himself long enough to kill Vashnar. He gave no thought to how that was to be done for he knew too, that somehow he would use the dark resources which Vashnar's very persecution had led him to discover in himself.

At the sight of their quarry, the fatigue of their frantic dash across country and through the mountains had fallen away from the Tervaidin. Now Rhavvan's flight urged them on even more and their cheering became jeering as Thyrn launched an ineffective stone at them.

But as they reached the bottom of the slope, the solitary figure above them was suddenly six, as Thyrn's companions, drawn by Rhavvan's desperate urging, joined him, dark, ominous and immovable against the lowering sky.

Five arrows were released. Three men and one horse fell, bringing down two other riders. The charge faltered.

A bow was thrust into Thyrn's hand and arrows pushed into his belt.

'Take your time and pick your mark,' Endryk's voice said, cold and frightening.

Three more volleys of arrows ended the momentum of the charge completely but Vashnar maintained a demented pace and together with Aghrid and one other reached the ridge without injury. A savage kick sent Nordath reeling and, in pushing Thyrn to one side, Endryk too was sent tumbling down the slope by a sidelong blow from Vashnar's turning horse. As he slithered to a halt, he collided with one of the unhorsed Tervaidin. Recovering, the man swung his sword high to finish his downed victim, but Endryk's foot shot out and struck him squarely in the groin. Rolling over to avoid the falling man's sword, he snatched it up and hurled it at another of the Tervaidin charging towards him. The hilt struck him in the face and sent him staggering down the slope.

At the ridge, Rhavvan's staff had unhorsed both Aghrid and the remaining rider, and together with Adren and Hyrald he was attacking with a combination of hurled rocks and brutal swordwork those Tervaidin who had survived the arrows and were struggling up the slope to fight on foot.

For a while it was bitter and desperate work, but the guidance and instruction that Endryk had given the three Wardens combined with their deep and righteous anger at the events that had brought them here to make them formidable, and their opponents eventually retreated.

As the last of them turned and fled, Adren leaned forward on to her sword to catch her breath. Aghrid, however, though unhorsed, had merely been winded. Seeing Adren defenceless and with her back to him, he stood up slowly and lifted his sword to strike her. Hyrald saw the pending attack but was too far away to intervene. His hand was reaching out in instinctive warning and he could feel a cry forming in his throat even as Adren's head flicked slightly. Then she was stepping sideways, her sword held like a dagger and thrust backwards, the palm of her free hand pressed over its hilt. The blade went straight through Aghrid, lifting him off his feet. With another turn, she wrenched her sword free as Aghrid fell to the ground. His face a mask of hatred, disbelief and pain, Aghrid made a final cut at Adren even as he landed, but she avoided it with an almost casual step then finished him with a single savage blow.

The few Tervaidin lingering hesitantly on the slope, retreated further.

As she looked up, it was to see Vashnar attacking Thyrn. The young Caddoran had dropped his bow and was flailing his sword in a vain attempt to protect himself. The three Wardens began running at the same time but it seemed they could not reach him in time to prevent Vashnar pressing home his brutal onslaught.

Then, Nals was in front of Vashnar's horse, hackles raised, teeth bared, and Nordath, his head bleeding, was clinging on to Vashnar's leg, trying to unseat him. After a vain attempt to shake him off, Vashnar abandoned his attack on Thyrn to strike down this new assailant. Thyrn, seeing the danger to his uncle, lashed out at Vashnar but missed and struck his horse a glancing blow. Already frightened by Nals, the horse reared, dislodging Nordath and knocking Thyrn over. As he landed, the impact bounced the sword from his hand. Vashnar swung down from his horse and moved to finish on foot the task he had failed to do on horseback.

Scrabbling backwards over the rocky ground, Thyrn seized a rock and hurled it at him. It struck Vashnar on the chest without effect.

Vashnar's eyes were blazing, but terrifying Thyrn as much as his immediate physical danger was the fragmenting confusion

401

that swirled in Vashnar's wake – the shards of countless colliding realities. And illuminating all, the bloody light of the power that hung about this place – a power that he knew Vashnar would take into realms beyond imagining – a power that was the very essence of those who had destroyed an entire world with their ignorance and consuming hatred. The scale and horror of this vision threatened to unman Thyrn totally, but even as he felt his last control and resistance slipping away, something deep within him reached out and touched the hurt that was focused about Vashnar – denying it, healing it.

'No!' A chorus of screaming voices crackled around Vashnar's cry, and Thyrn's strange and tenuous touch was dashed aside.

But where there had been fear there was now anger. As Vashnar strode towards him, Thyrn's hand closed about a fist-sized rock and with a single sweeping movement, powered by that inner knowledge which as a child had bounced a precious, bright red ball to and fro, he hurled it at Vashnar's head, a great cry surging in its wake. Vashnar flinched, lifting an arm to protect himself.

The rock struck his hand.

It shattered his ring.

It seemed to Thyrn that suddenly he was alone on the mountain and that a deep silence and stillness pervaded the whole world. Then he was aware that the rent into this world which Vashnar had opened was gone, save for a trembling residue that shimmered about him. All was whole again. And the silence was not silence, but a noise loud beyond any hearing – the screaming of the ancient evil that some quality in Vashnar, or the ring, or both, had given form.

It was a scream of withering fury, but it was impotent now, and as Thyrn slowly stood up it faded to become nothing more than a dying, all-too-human cry from Vashnar's gaping mouth.

Vashnar's sword slipped from his hand and he sank to his

knees. Adren was the first to reach him. Breathlessly she kicked the sword away from him, then, her blade across his throat, she drew back his slumped head.

Vashnar offered no resistance. He was humming softly and tunelessly and his eyes were empty.

It started to rain.

Chapter 28

The next few days were dominated mainly by the practicalities of travelling through the mountains. The Tervaidin, already reluctant to attempt another assault on their intended victims after the resistance and resolution they had met, yielded completely on seeing the death of Aghrid and the sudden descent of their leader into idiocy. The dead were buried and the wounded tended. Concerned about travelling with prisoners, Endryk laid down a strict ordering of their travelling, but the Tervaidin showed little inclination to revert to their former ways. Nevertheless, he made them walk and carry on stretchers those who could not.

Nordath was offered a litter which he brusquely refused, taking an uncharacteristic pride in his bandaged head. A sharp eye, however, would have noted him surreptitiously rubbing his bruised back and ribs when he woke each morning.

There was no debate held about their destination.

'Time to go home,' Hyrald said as he and Rhavvan raised the broken Vashnar to his feet. Adren wiped the rain from his face and then from her own. Nordath and Thyrn embraced one another silently.

As they left the mountain they met four travellers heading north, three men and a woman. They would have passed with a mere exchange of courtesies, but the woman looked at the weary Tervaidin with some concern and then sternly announced that she was a healer and asked if she could help.

'You're not Arvens,' Hyrald said when she had examined the wounded and satisfied herself that they were being reasonably tended.

'We're from Gyronlandt in the south,' said one of the men, her husband.

The Wardens exchanged significant looks. 'I didn't think the southern mountains were passable,' Hyrald said. 'It must have been a difficult journey.'

'We're used to mountains,' said one of the other men quietly.

Endryk, who had been staring at the two men intently, started, then said something softly to them which the others did not catch. A subdued but intense conversation followed in a language that was not Arvens.

'These men are my countrymen,' Endryk told them apologetically when it was finished. 'I think we've a great deal to talk about. May they accompany us?'

Hyrald looked at the new arrivals. The two men in particular sat their horses with the same easy manner that Endryk always showed. 'I know nothing about your country, sirs, but we owe Endryk our lives, and if you honour such things, then honour is due to him. You're more than welcome to travel with us, if you wish, but there may be danger at the end of our journey.'

The older of the two men smiled, and extended his hand as he introduced himself. 'Tell us on the way,' he said.

Their entry into Arvenshelm was almost unremarked. Vashnar had swayed many of the upper ranks of the Warding to his plans but Draferth's actions had caused great confusion and alarm amongst them, and without Vashnar's unifying and force-ful presence they floundered, reducing his grand design very quickly to an undignified mêlée of mutual blame-shifting – a trait they were well-practised in. Lesser supporters discreetly faded into the background.

A great many impromptu street meetings had occurred,

several of which had broken up in disorder and violence, but the most critical point had come with an attempt by Tervaidin officers to arrest Draferth. Two of his supporters were killed before a group of Wardens finally intervened and arrested the leading Tervaidin. It gave Hyrald considerable satisfaction that they were his men.

One other casualty was Striker Bowlott. He was attacked by a frenzied Krim with the Blue Cushion. Though unhurt, he was so disturbed by this culmination of the sudden rush of reality into the Moot Palace that he hastily retired, citing a desire to write his memoirs and a dissertation on the Treatise. Krim subsequently pleaded extenuating circumstances due to the acute distress caused by Bowlott's curt refusal to order Ector to repair his curtains, and also, unexpectedly shrewdly, immunity by virtue of the definition of his office. After a brief period of rest – and the fitting of new curtains to the windows of the Cushion Repository – he was reinstated.

The Moot rapidly reverted to its old ways by holding a great and solemn debate to discuss how it should learn from what had happened and not simply revert to its old ways.

Hyrald was made Senior Commander of the Warding. He still walked the streets however, as did all the new District Commanders that he appointed.

Vashnar was given to the care of his wife who nursed him tenderly.

Nordath offered Endryk and the four travellers the hospitality of his house, and together with Hyrald and the others they spent several agreeable days wandering about Arvenshelm and discussing the trials and tribulations of their respective travels. It seemed that dark events had not been confined only to Arvenstaat.

Only Thyrn seemed to be ill at ease. He talked a great deal to Nordath.

'There's a skill – a gift – inside me, that I don't understand. It's something important – something that I need to learn about.'

He also talked a great deal to Endryk's countrymen.

Then came the time for parting. They all rode to the edge of the city. It was early morning, hazy with the promise of a fine day.

'Thank you for everything,' Endryk said. 'It's been an honour to ride with you.' He embraced his former companions in turn, Adren with unexpected and returned fervour, which caused raised eyebrows and cautiously amused looks from Hyrald and Rhavvan.

Following much heart-searching, Thyrn had decided to go with them. It was a decision that upset Nordath more than he chose to say, but he offered no word of reproach. Endryk's companions had spoken to him also before agreeing to Thyrn's request to accompany them.

'There are scholars and learned men at home who can help him, bring him to the knowledge he needs. And too, they need to know what's happened here; they need to know about that place in the mountains.'

Nevertheless Nordath could not fully trust himself to speak as he clasped Thyrn's hand in both of his.

'I'll be back,' Thyrn promised as he mounted his horse. He looked at the Wardens significantly and Adren placed her arm around Nordath's shoulder in a silent promise of continued companionship.

The three Wardens and Nordath stood motionless for a long time watching the departing riders, Nals trotting beside them.

Then they were gone, lost in the bright morning mist.